THE PURPLE-BELLIED PARROT

BEING AN ACCOUNT OF HIS LIFE, TIMES,
ADVENTURES AND MISADVENTURES, INTRODUCING
SUNDRY CHARACTERS ENCOUNTERED, BOTH
NEFARIOUS AND UPROARIOUS

WILLIAM FAGUS

For Sonia

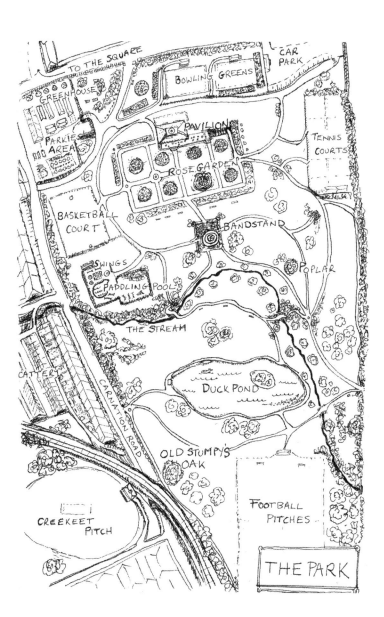

Most folks can do most things if they've a mind. You just have to fight the Badhbh between your ears and the dangle-jawed bum-scratchers.

— SAR'NT LOFTY N. TROGGERS

PREFACE

EDITOR'S NOTE: The author has seen fit to include footnotes. The editor has had neither the time nor the desire to read them all, and in his professional opinion they detract from the main text. Aside from the manifold errors contained therein, the footnotes are erratic in quality and inconsistent in style, and the editor was inclined to expunge the entirety. The author, however, vehemently insisted that they remain, and, indeed, threatened to *'throw a wobbler'* if they were removed. It may be allowed that they do possess a certain novelty value, but the editor disavows all responsibility for their inclusion, and under no circumstances should statements be accepted as factual without further corroborative research.[1]

Prof Donald Anas, PhD (Cantab), Hon.FRSA, FSA, FRICS, FWC, MUFC, IISPC

PROLOGUE

THE MERCHANDISE

Darkness, din, motion, stink. That is all he knows. Not that he has ever had any choice. Darkness, din, motion, stink are all he remembers. But there must have been something before. Surely.

Now it is happening again.

The door creaks open. Human voices. One is the cheese-breath man. His clothes smell like old wee.

He is lifted up and slid into something. A bag? He is swung about. Yes. The door creaks shut. For a moment he senses outside. Another door opens and, din. Humans shouting. Human music thudding. Bottles clinking. Through a gap in the box, yellow light slices in and he glimpses movement. The cheese-breath man speaks again, answered by the new voice. A door slams; the light disappears and he senses outside again and, cold.

The traffic monster roars and yelps.

The new man huffs as he walks. As his feet hit the ground they make a heavy 'tonk' like he has metal feet. The new man swings him about and he bashes into the side of the skin-cage. The cold air finds him and he shivers.

The tonks stop. Keys are rattled. He knows the noise of keys.

'Bip-bip.'

Another door opens, but this makes a 'shoosh' noise. He is bumped about but his landing is soft, and he recognises the stink of a car. The door slams, the engine thrums and music thuds. Motion. The car keeps stopping and he is joggled about. When it stops he hears, 'Oh come on, for pity's sake,' and other words. But when the car moves he feels sick, like he always does.

The car stops.

Silence.

The new man speaks. 'Yeah, I got him. Yeah, the one I saw last week. Nah, knocked him down like I said I would. Yeah, desperate to get rid. Told you he was a pratt.' His voice is like the whine of a mosquito.

Tonk-tonk-tonk-tonk. They are climbing steps. Stillness. Two 'kerr-lonks', a 'beep', and his tummy hits the bottom of the skincage. He crouches to join it, shivers, and sings his little song to himself.

I

THE FLAT

THE POWER OF THE HUUUT

He liked the new perch and the seed and the cuttle fish. He couldn't remember ever stretching his wings like this. But then he had never sat on a perch like this. It had a bowl at each end, one with water, one with sunflower seeds. Below was a short perch he might clamber down to if he felt like it. This held the cuttle fish wedged onto the end, and below that was a big shiny tray. He didn't know what that was for, but he noticed that his poo landed on it.

From the perch he could look around the room and watch the window of moving colours which slept only at night. He could look out of the clear window and into the tree with the dangly balls and the fat-fingered leaves that waved in the breeze. The Purple-Bellied Parrot hadn't seen so much light for a long time.

A pink-faced man also lived there, and it turned out that he was the one with the mosquito voice. At night, and every day when he went out, he shut the Purple-Bellied Parrot in the cage.

The new cage he hated. But then he hated all cages. It was much bigger than the skin-cage though — he even had room to open his wings. But if he flapped they clattered the bars and his feathers tumbled. The bars gleamed, and the floor was like sand but tore like paper. The cage contained a bowl of seed and wedged between the bars another cuttle fish. A pipe on the end of an upside-down bottle of water held a drip that, even if he slurped till his purple belly got all tubby and tight, never disappeared. The cage was much better than any of the tiny boxes he'd lived in. But any cage conjured scrambled memories of being taken in the hot green land far away he never knew the name of.

Each evening the pink-faced man poured red water out of a green bottle into a clear glass and toddled up close, so close that the Purple-Bellied Parrot saw the tiny red veins in his nose and the tiny hairs sprouting at the end of the nose and the gristly hairs growing out of the nostrils. It looked like he had a spider living up there. The pink-faced man would put on an strange voice, much deeper than the usual mosquito — a bit like a small dog the Purple-Bellied Parrot had once heard — and he'd repeat words.

'Hello! ... Hello! ... Hello!' Or, 'Hello Polly! ... Hello Polly! ... Hello Polly!'

The Purple-Bellied Parrot would cock his head and listen — it was only polite — but he made no sound. He watched, fascinated, the pudgy lips working up and down in the middle of all that pink flesh. Why was the pink-faced man saying these words, and what could they mean?

Sometimes the pink-faced man would say other words, words like, 'B***ocks... B***ocks ... B***ocks,' or worse words. He'd stroll away chuckling and pour himself more of the red water. Sometimes he would say, 'Who's a pretty boy then,' and 'Pieces of eight ... Pieces of eight!' and 'Shiver me timbers.'

The long hours shut in the cage were dreary. But the Purple-Bellied Parrot had the window of moving colours, the precious light, the fat-fingered tree and the cuttle fish, and, for the first time he could remember, he felt safe. So it wasn't too bad. And at least it wasn't smelly, like most places he had lived in. He also spent long hours studying the upside-down bottle of water, trying to work out why the water didn't pour out all over the floor. He clambered around the cage and inspected it from all angles, but it was no good. It was bamboozling.

One morning, the pink-faced man did something different. Munching his breakfast, he put his face up to the cage. His mouth gaped as he chewed and the Purple-Bellied Parrot saw the milky cereal churning around and around. The pink-faced man watched him for a bit, gulped down the cereal and muttered something in the mosquito voice. Before the Purple-Bellied Parrot knew what was happening, he had opened the cage door, grabbed him and put him on the perch. Shoving his arm down a coat sleeve, he rushed towards the door, paused and wagged a finger, 'Now you, behave.'

He stared at the Purple-Bellied Parrot a moment scratching his chin, and slammed the door behind him.

The Purple-Bellied Parrot would remember this first day alone on the perch for a long time. First, he sat for ages and just looked around, head cocked, at the bare room with its lumpy furniture and black boxes. He looked around some more. Something was wrong. It took him a bit of time to work out what it was, but then he twigged. His view of the world had always been through straight metal lines. A wave of panic surged through him and he wobbled about and had to cling tight to the perch. He'd never been alone and surrounded by so much space. He found himself gazing back at his cage and the cuttle fish, trembling.

Don't be so stupid, he scolded himself. You've wanted this for so long and now look at you. He shook his feathers, took lots of deep breaths and soon felt better.

Now he was outside, there was something he ought to be doing, but he couldn't think what. So he watched the window of moving colours for a bit. He soon got bored of that, so he gazed out of the window at the tree.

The tree was nearly bare after the winter but a few crinkled leaves still dangled, and their outline reminded the Purple-Bellied Parrot of the pink-faced man's stubby hands. The tree was old and lumpy and full of holes, and when he looked hard he saw small brown birds flitting about. The birds were inspecting the holes. One went into a hole with a feather. It was in there a long time and when it came out the feather was gone. After a bit of this the brown birds lined-up together on a branch and began to shout all at the same time. The Purple-Bellied Parrot heard the cheepings even through the glass. A fight broke out and one bird leapt onto another and pecked it repeatedly on the head, the others shouting encouragement. But then the fight stopped and they both settled down like nothing had happened and batted one of the dangly balls between each other.

The more the Purple-Bellied Parrot gazed at the tree and watched the brown birds, the more he thought their doings connected with the thing he ought to be doing. He imagined himself among the twigs and leaves clambering about the branches and inspecting holes like they were, but he had no clue how he arrived there. His wings might have something to do with it, and he looked at them for a long time. He decided he ought to flap them to see what happened.

He gave them a shake. He spread one wing, and then the other. He flapped one wing, but that felt really strange, and he overbalanced and nearly fell off the perch. So he thought for a bit, and flapped both.

A foggy memory stirred. He tried hard to clear the fog so as to see the memory, but it was like trying to reach a tiny seed in the angle of a cage that was too small for him to bend down in. It was a memory from before the cheese-breath man, from before the cage in the shed next to the big house with the shouty men and the thuddy music that never stopped till deep in the night and the cage so small he wore it like a skin. A memory even before the stinking black din and the room that never stilled. The stinking black din that was the beginning of his life. But he looked back at his wings and was suddenly certain that, once, he knew how to do this. So he flapped again, harder.

'HhuUUUUUUUUUUUUUUTTT.'

Now, this felt right. Old green feathers worked loose and spiralled down to the carpet. The Purple-Bellied Parrot stopped flapping and cocked his head and watched a bright green piece of him drift down. It twisted in a draught and its iridescence caught the light. He took a deep breath and flapped again.

Something was wrong though. He was flapping hard and getting out of puff, but he was sure something else ought to be happening. So he got his breath back and had a good preen. He attended to every single feather on his body; those impossible to get at with his beak — like those on his crown — he tackled with a claw or two. It took ages, but when he had everything zipped back together and smart, he took a deep breath, gritted his beak, and concentrated with all his might.

HhuUUUUUUUUUUUUUUUTTTTTAAAAAaaaahhhhhh.'

Preening had worked. As he flapped he felt his body become lighter. He felt it lifting off the perch. This is it! This is what is supposed to happen!

He flapped harder and harder, but no matter how hard he flapped he wasn't getting any higher. Now what was wrong? He looked down and saw his claws clamped around the perch. Perhaps that might be it.

Heart in beak, he uncurled his claws, one by one. His body became even lighter. He was nearly — flying! Flying! That was it!

The last claw on the last foot — but he just couldn't let go. The room around him was now moving in a way he'd not seen before: the floor was appearing above his head and disappearing again. Flapping hard with one claw attached, he was performing a loop-the-loop around the perch, and all the spinning was beginning to make him feel sick.

He unclipped the last claw.

'WhhoooHHHAAAY!'

He catapulted up, clonked his head on the ceiling and crashed to the floor. Now his head felt like a feather and his body like a big stone, and he thought he saw tiny birds flying around his head and heard tiny bells ringing. Best to lie there for a bit.

When he came to, he folded up his wings and looked up at the perch. Ooooh, it looked a long way back. He had crashed next to the leg of a wooden chair, so he clambered up it and onto the chair's back. The perch was closer now.

'HHHUUUUUUuuuuttt.' He leapt and flapped, chin up, beak pointing to the ceiling. The perch was a small target, and if he missed he doubted he'd have the strength to try again. It was a clumsy landing and, tail feathers akimbo, he overbalanced and nearly fell off the other side.

He'd made it, though his heart thumped and his newly preened feathers were rumpled. And his heart thumped not just from terror and effort, but from the pride that welled up into his breast. He had flown.

After a long breather, he decided to fly to the moving colours to see what they were all about. Again, there was a lot of flapping and not much forward progress, and when he landed on the shiny ledge he skidded along, claws scrabbling. When he settled he was so excited he couldn't help but have a poo.

He walked along the ledge and peered over and watched the colours and realised that the moving shapes were humans. He wondered why they were upside-down. The humans were sitting in chairs talking, but just as the Purple-Bellied Parrot was getting bored the colours flashed and changed, and now upside-down animals and birds and trees and a river replaced the humans. He watched on and became so engrossed that he didn't notice the tiny eyes that watched through the window. Now he heard big voices.

———

Feathers all plumped up, the spuggies had been packed scapular to scapular on a bouncing twig, nudging each other.[1]

'Blimey. Call yourself a bloomin bird?'

'Worst flappage ever!'

'You're an embarr-arse-ment to h'ornithflapology that's what you are!'

'He even flaps his big feet — like thems is going to keep him aloft.'

'Coo, and what was that landing! Like a duck on a frozen pond … I arsk you!'

'Wouldn't last two minutes out here.'

'He'd be chomped up by some moggie and no mistake.'

'Must be that big hooter of his weighing him down.'

'You're telling me. Never seen such a big un.'

'Oi mate! What kind of bird are you then?'

Two spuggies nudged each other, 'Alfie said "embarr-*arse*-ment" he did.' They guffawed.

The window was open a crack and the Purple-Bellied Parrot heard everything. He'd never had anything to do with other birds, and he was bewildered what to do or say. He thought for a bit and decided the best plan was to tuck his head under his wing and pretend to go to sleep, but keep one eye open. Perhaps they'd get bored and go away.

The Purple-Bellied Parrot didn't know spuggies.

'Wakey wake-HAAAYYY!'

'Cooo-EEEEEE!'

'Oi! Oi, you! Big Nose!' Alfie yelled. 'You with the purple belly. Don't give up! Remember Robert the Goose![2] You're a bird aintcha — although lawd knows what kind! Fly you lemon!'

spuggie, paler than the rest, leapt off the branch and yelled, 'Like this!'

'Yeah. Goo on. You show him Chalkie.'

Chalkie whizzed about between the branches shouting 'Look at me!' He spotted a dozy bluebottle and tried to catch it but, despite a long pursuit dodging about between the twigs, it escaped. The Purple-Bellied Parrot, who had sneaked a peek, saw his empty beak snap shut. The rest of the spuggies leapt up and down guffawing.

'Bout shattered his perishin beak he did!'

Chalkie returned to his twig, looking cheepish.

But they still wouldn't leave the Purple-Bellied Parrot alone, and the insults became louder, and more and more they featured the word 'arse.' The Purple-Bellied Parrot felt his crown feathers prickle. Why on earth was he a lemon? He took his head from under his wing and gave his feathers a good shake. He stretched his wings. He'd show them.

The movement was noted.

'Ooh, hello. He's got his gander up now he has. Look out!' The spuggies quietened to watch.

Following his shake-stretch, one of his green feathers had come out and was floating towards the floor. That's it. He'd swoop down, catch it in what he was now discovering was his 'big hooter', and soar back up to his perch. While he was at it, he may as well take a turn around the room to show off his prize. He saw himself as he wheeled past the spuggies feather in beak, cocking them a snook — whatever that was — he must have heard it from a human somewhere. He would execute the routine precisely: flap, swoop, grab, soar, snook, perch.

He leapt off the ledge.

Well, the flapping part went okay because he'd been practicing that bit, but the swooping part, not so good. And it's probably best if eyes are hidden from the soaring and snookering part, or at best peeping through clenched feathers.

The Purple-Bellied Parrot fell off his perch, flapped hard and made a lunge for the feather as he fell past. He did manage to grab the feather just before it hit the floor, and for a moment he even managed to fly in a straight line, but then he was so excited he'd caught the feather that he forgot to carry on flapping.

WHAMPFF!

He slid along the polished floor, ploughing a little mound of dust, until his slide was halted by the skirting board.

The crash sent the spuggies into hysterics. They were so excited they had to leap up and fly about a bit to calm down, and when they landed they still couldn't settle and bounced about in the branches debating the event, all talking at once. Then the insults flew.

'If you wanted to sweep the floor mate, there's a brush over there!'

'Just breath in a bit and that big hooter of yours will hoover up the dust in a jiffy!'

'Nice one Roy.'

'Nor bad yerself Gert,' and Roy and Gert slapped primaries.

But after a bit the spuggies noticed the Purple-Bellied Parrot remained still. They fell silent. Well, silent for spuggies.

'Oh gawd, now you've gone and done it … Praps he's hurt isself.'

'I told you not to pick on him like that — you nitwit.'

'Tut-tut … I reckons he's only a young un anall.'

'Come on young un. Get up. You can do it!'

Three of the spuggies leapt onto the window sill for a better view and to shout more encouragement, tapping on the glass with their beaks. Chalkie called: 'Come on mate. Up you get. Flap your wings!'

The crash had knocked the wind out of the Purple-Bellied Parrot, and he lay sprawled gulping in big beak-fulls of air. After a bit, when he got his puff back, he struggled to his feet and looked about — but everywhere had gone foggy. He thought he heard tapping on glass and cheeping. He looked up to the light and through the haze made out small brown balls bouncing around on the window sill. He sat, swaying. What was all the commotion about now?

The fog cleared and he had a good think. He decided he'd better fly back to his perch. He didn't know why, but he sensed that the pink-faced man would be angry with him — and he knew all about humans' anger. He flapped.

'Hhuttppnnnnnnnnnnnnnnnnnaahh.'

Nothing happened. He tried again. No upwards motion. He couldn't take off because every time he flapped, his wings hit the floor. His legs just weren't long enough to leave enough space for flappage. He tried again — but it was no use — and it was beginning to hurt. So he gave up and sat just there.

The three spuggies peered down.

'Nah what's wrong with im?'

'Come on mate. Get up.'

'Fly! Fly like the bird you are, you big-girl's blouse!'

'Why don't he fly?'

'He's not jumping. He's got to jump up as he flaps. Ruddy Nora! He ain't even got the gumption to do that.'

'Crikey chaps, can't you see?' said Chalkie. 'He never learned. I reckon nobody's never showed him.'

The Purple-Bellied Parrot tried once more, but it was useless. So the spuggies flew back into the tree and did their favourite thing: they had a conflab.[3] After a good few moments Chalkie flew back to the sill, with half a dozen more in tow. Alfie shoved him aside.

'Oi! Oi, Big Nose! Listen. If you ain't got the strength like what we has to jump up and fly off, why don't you climb up to something higher. Then you can just fall off. But this time, don't forget to flap you bloomin lemon.'

Why hadn't he thought of that. After all, he'd climbed up a chair leg earlier to get closer to the perch. The nearest thing for the Purple-Bellied Parrot to climb was another chair, the square one the pink-faced man sat in every night in front of the moving colours. It was a long way off though, and the Purple-Bellied Parrot would have to walk. But what was wrong with that? It had never before occurred to the Purple-Bellied Parrot that he might walk. He'd done a fair bit of sidling in his time — but he'd never walked anywhere in his life. Worth a try.

So he walked over to the chair and, using his beak and claws like hooks, he clambered up onto the flat bit. When he got there he looked back and saw he'd pulled out a few threads and tufts on the way up, so he leaned over and tidied them up as best he could. The flat bit smelled like sweaty human bottoms so he climbed higher to get away from the pong, aiming for the bit where the pink-faced man rested his greasy head. As he climbed he realised he was enjoying it. He sensed that he'd done this before, that once — it must have been before the stinking black din — climbing had been a big thing in his life. He reached the top, and sidled away from the greasy bit. Now it was a short flappy hop back to the perch. Easy.

Again, he had been concentrating so much he hadn't heard the uproar outside. But this time they weren't jeering. They were cheering.

2

BELLY UP

The instant the lock turned and the light snapped on, the Purple-Bellied Parrot knew that the pink-faced man was angry. He slammed the front door, threw his keys onto the table and went straight to the box where he kept the red water. But tonight he took out a different bottle, a brown bottle that held brown water the colour of human wee. He slammed that door too. The Purple-Bellied Parrot fluttered into the safety of his cage.

The pink-faced man sat for a long time in front of the window of moving colours. He stared into it, silent, like he'd forgotten the Purple-Bellied Parrot existed. The Purple-Bellied Parrot noticed his bottom lip stuck out more than usual, and that his single eyebrow, rather than being straight, was shaped like a seagull in flight. Finally, he sighed, looked over towards the cage and heaved himself up. His shoes clicked on the floor and he looked wobbly on his feet. When he opened his mouth he smelt funny, a bit like the shed where the Purple-Bellied Parrot had lived with the man whose breath smelt like old cheese and whose clothes smelt like mouldy sunflower seeds and old wee — the shed where he'd lived in the skin-cage.

The pink-faced man stared at the Purple-Bellied Parrot a long time. The Purple-Bellied Parrot retreated further into his cage, scrunching on the floor and squeezing up against the bars.

'Well? Are *you* gonna talk to me tonight? Are YOU? Let's see.' He put his face even closer to the bars. 'B***ocks … B***ocks … B***ocks.' He said worse words. His face twisted; both lips now puckered out and the vee of the flying seagull deepened. The bars now pressed into his nose. 'Say iiiIIIT! SAY it!' he hissed.

The Purple-Bellied Parrot cowered away from the pong, and as he cowered the pink-faced man lashed out with the flat of his hand. The cage swung violently, squeaking on its hook. The Purple-Bellied Parrot closed his eyes and clung on.

When it came to rest the pink-faced man grunted, 'Pah. Thought not.' He turned and trudged back towards the window of moving colours. He froze. The glass of brown water smashed into tiny bits as it hit the floor.

'Whaaa…!'

He walked over to the TV and peered at the poo. The Purple-Bellied Parrot saw that it had dribbled down the screen and was now solid.

'Whaaa …!?

The pink-faced man ran his hands over the scratches on the ledge where the Purple-Bellied Parrot had crash-landed.

'Whaaa the…!'

He was over by the chair now, tugging at threads pulled out where the Purple-Bellied Parrot had clambered up.

'Whaaa the…!? What have you done to my chair you dope?'

He was picking at another solid poo on the headrest. This one had black bits in it. It must have been all the excitement. The Purple-Bellied Parrot hadn't even realised that one had sneaked out.

The pink-faced man was silent for a bit. Then he turned, and the Purple-Bellied Parrot noticed the pink-faced man was no longer the pink-faced man: he was the purple-faced man. He marched over to the cage and the Purple-Bellied Parrot thought he was about to clout it again. He raised his hand, but then held it there for an age. Then he reached forward and slammed the door. The cage again swung wildly, its imbalance worsened by the Purple-Bellied Parrot, squeezed in the angle of the gritty floor and steel bars.

The pink-faced man left early the next day. Before he went he made certain the cage door was firmly shut. He made certain the next day, and the day after that. Before he left on the third day, with the Purple-Bellied Parrot cowering, he put the cage in the corner of the room away from the window. He didn't pay too much attention to keeping the cage upright and water spilled out of the Purple-Bellied Parrot's drinker. His floor was soggy all day.

The Purple-Bellied Parrot now saw only the edge of the window of moving colours. It didn't matter anyway because the colours and the humans inside slept for most of the day and only woke in the evening at the pink-faced man's touch. And, he couldn't see the fat-fingered tree and the spuggies.

So the Purple-Bellied Parrot spent his days locked in his cage, just looking about or sleeping. If he was lucky, a spider might try to climb up the wall and he could watch it for a bit. Spiders better watch out here though, because the pink-faced man had a little machine. When it came alive it whined and he pointed it at the spiders and they disappeared. The Purple-Bellied Parrot wondered where they went.

Sometimes, especially if the window was open, he heard the spuggies nattering, and once he thought he heard Alfie call out, 'Oi! Oi, Big Nose! Big Nose! Where's you gone then?' and he remembered his adventures. At first he didn't care that he no longer saw the spuggies. All they mainly did was insult him. But as the days dragged by, a bit of banter would have spiced things up, and he did miss looking into the tree. On windy days he heard the branches as they slapped against the window and he thought about the spuggies hopping about, inspecting holes, clinging to a flailing twig, or whacking the dangly balls about.

One day the Purple-Bellied Parrot noticed that one of the purple belly feathers was sticking-out at a weird angle. So he pulled it out. That was better; much tidier like that. But then he noticed that, in pulling out that feather, another had come loose. So he pulled that one out too. That day, when he wasn't sleeping, he scrutinised his plumage for signs of imperfection, and any feather that did not come up to scratch, he whipped out. By the time the pink-faced man came back, a little pile of feathers lay on the cage floor.

That day, the pile-of-feathers day, the pink-faced man did not talk to the Purple-Bellied Parrot. He did not so much as glance at him. He just touched the window of colours into life, pushed food from a silver box between the lips of his tiny mouth and drank the brown liquid.

The next day, the pile of feathers grew taller. By evening the Purple-Bellied Parrot noticed a bald patch on his belly. He would soon become the Pink-Bellied Parrot if he didn't watch out, so he tried to comb over the remaining purple feathers to hide his pink belly. But he pulled a bit too hard and another purple feather came out. He patted them back into place and tried to zip them together, but they soon parted, and his pink pimply belly was exposed once more. He sat for a bit wondering what to do next. He let out a big yawn. Then the Purple-Bellied Parrot noticed a big green feather poking out from his thigh. Now that *was* untidy.

That night, after feeding, the pink-faced man strolled over to the Purple-Bellied Parrot.

'Whaa! Whaass 'appened?' The Purple-Bellied Parrot could see right to the back of the pink-faced man's throat where a wobbly thing wobbled.

The pink-faced man stalked around the cage, his eyes boring into the Purple-Bellied Parrot. The Purple-Bellied Parrot swivelled his head around till it would go no further, watching him.

'Right ...'

The pink-faced man stomped away and talked into the thin black box that always seemed to be in his hand. To the Purple-Bellied Parrot it was the usual prattle:

'Vinnie? Right, I want me money back ... What for? What FOR? You joking? That bird you sold me — that's what for.' His face was turning from pink to purple again. 'Why? WHY? He's going bald — that's why. It's like somebody's been and plucked him. I've got feathers all over my parquet.' He began to shout into the black box, and as his voice grew louder his purple face grew purpler. It was now darker than the Purple-Bellied Parrot's darkest belly feather.

The last words he yelled were: 'You'd better look out for me the next time I am in the Prince Albert, Vinnie,' and he threw the thin box onto the chair, where it bounced and its colours faded. He stood for a long time, hands on hips glaring at the Purple-Bellied Parrot, tutting. He sounded like a spuggie and looked a bit like the vase in the window — the one with two handles.

After a few moments, he stomped back to the cage, eyes burning below the seagull eyebrow, round pink face filling the Purple-Bellied Parrot's world. The pudgy lips parted and more words came out.

'God, you look pathetic. Cost me nine hundred quid you did. Nine hundred quid.' The second time he said 'nine hundred quid' very slowly, and between the 'hundred' and the 'quid' was a very bad word.

Now he was back in the chair, staring at the window of moving colours that he hadn't touched into life, soon to be up again and talking into the thin black box, pacing to and fro across the room. Now he was no longer angry. He was decided, intent. Like he had a plan.

'Yeah, Frickling Insurance? How do I make a claim on a pet? … It's a parrot … Right … So, just so I've got this right, I can claim for loss, theft — or death. Cheers mate.'

By the end of the week the Purple-Bellied Parrot was in a right old state. His glorious purple belly had gone, replaced by a thing resembling the skin of the plastic-wrapped dead chickens the pink-faced man sometimes brought home. His thighs, no longer trousered by glossy green feathers, too were bald and pimply. Somehow, in an amazing feat of dexterity, he had managed to yank feathers out from his neck, so that he now resembled a miniature vulture. Stripped of so much plumage you could see his true size, which was puny, and baldness also meant that he now spent much of the day huddled at the bottom of his cage, shivering.

He hadn't pulled any feathers from his wings though. Something in the back of his head told him that he had flown once, and he might need to again.

'Apparently, you're bored.'

The pink-faced man had come home cheerier that night.

'Been reading bout you on the internet. You're bored you are … Yes you are … Yes you are … You are … You're a bored little thing aren't you.' He poked his finger into the cage and tried to tickle the Purple-Bellied Parrot under the chin, but the Purple-

Bellied Parrot shrank away. 'I've got some prezzies for you …Yes I have … I have … haven't I.'

He held up a gaily coloured plastic bag and rummaged. He extracted an assortment of objects and dangled them before the Purple-Bellied Parrot, who eyed him warily. The objects were: a mirror, two tiny bells linked together, a ball with a bell inside it, a short length of blue rope, and a miniature roll of toilet paper in a miniature toilet-paper holder.

'These'll sort you. We've got to get you all better again if I'm going to sell you. Yes we have … Yes we have … We have … Haven't we … Yes … yeayz … Daddy has got to get his money back hasn't he … Yes he has … Yes he has. He has — hasn't he. Yeayz.'

The pink-faced man hung the toys up around the cage and then looked around the flat.

'Seems like I've also got to put you where you can look outside and watch the world go by.'

He carried the cage and the Purple-Bellied Parrot over to the window. The Purple-Bellied Parrot's heart soared as he realised he'd be able to see the fat-fingered tree and the spuggies. The pink-faced man stood back and scratched his chin.

'Nah … Nah. That'll never do,' and he carried the cage back. The Purple-Bellied Parrot's heart sank. 'Hmmm …' the pink-faced man had stopped scratching his chin and was now scratching his head. His face lit up. 'I know,' and he disappeared.

Since the pooing incident, the perch had been shut in a cupboard. Now the pink-faced man returned and put it by the window, by the tree and the spuggies.

'There! I'm even going to leave the telly on for you as well. You'll be an antiques expert in a fortnight.' He turned away, chuckling. Over his shoulder he called, 'Anyway, you'll need it. It's going to get a bit noisy outside. '

Although there was barely any room left in the cage — what with all the toys cluttering the place up — the Purple-Bellied

Parrot hopped up and down. He discovered a sudden urge to hang upside-down, but he would have banged his head on the floor. Tomorrow he could watch the window of colours — the telly — and look out at the fat-fingered tree again. And, though the prospect was a bit scary, the spuggies might be there. Most of all, he was overjoyed because he would have another crack at that flying lark.

That evening, even though the telly was on, the Purple-Bellied Parrot couldn't stop gazing at the perch by the window. He was so excited he forgot to pull out any more feathers.

Later he dreamed kaleidoscope dreams. He was flying. He flew higher and higher until he rose above every other living thing and he could look down on the world and everything in it. He saw, not the damp city streets the he had glimpsed through the window, but, lit by dazzling sunlight, an undulating emerald forest. Half-remembered creatures flitted about among its branches. The Purple-Bellied Parrot soared even higher, lifted by a warm breeze under his wings. He closed his wings a little and, feathers riffling, dived towards the emerald. The leaves tickled his purple belly and he opened his wings and soared high again. Then, as is the way with dreams, he was deep in the foliage of the fat-fingered tree, batting the dangly balls about with his big 'hooter.' Perched on a branch, sandwiched between his new friends the spuggies, he was listening to their chatter and enjoying the warmth of their bodies.

Grey light seeped in from the window and leaves twirled in the unheard breeze. The Purple-Bellied Parrot heard the squeak of his cage door and through one eye saw pudgy fingers reaching in.

Soon the fingers opened and he was stepping gingerly onto his perch. Through the window, the Purple-Bellied Parrot noticed a sparrow perched on the very end of the slenderest of branches. The branch was whirly-gigging in the breeze, but the sparrow nonchalantly clung on enjoying the ride, watching him. It was the pale one they called Chalkie.

The Purple-Bellied Parrot heard a tinkle behind him. The pink-faced man had bought him another toy. It was a shiny silver snake. But the Purple-Bellied Parrot wouldn't have time to play with any silver snake — he was going to spend his day flying about and watching the spuggies. Now the pink-faced man was putting the snake's mouth around the Purple-Bellied Parrot's leg. The Purple-Bellied Parrot felt its jaws tighten. Perhaps the game was to free himself. He tested it. It felt strong and unyielding — much as he imagined a real snake's jaws would feel. Then the Purple-Bellied Parrot cocked his head and watched as the pink-faced man tied the tail of the snake to the perch.

'There. Won't be having no more accidents now will we … Will we … Will we … Nooo.' He gave a final twist to the snake's tail. 'You've got your telly. You can look out the window. So, I don't want to see no pile of feathers on the floor when I get back — got it?' His stubby finger poked the Purple-Bellied Parrot in the breast.

After the pink-faced man had gone, the Purple-Bellied Parrot pried at the snake's jaw. His beak could crack the toughest nuts and seeds no trouble — but the clasp refused to budge. He spent a long time working away at the metal, but all that picking and prying chafed his leg, and soon blood oozed.

Chalkie, who had continued to watch from the twirling branch, hopped onto the windowsill.

'Oi, mate! Mate! Where's you bin? And, crikey! What's

happened to all your feathers?' He flitted away. 'Oi! Spuggies! Old
Big Nose is back — and he ain't looking too perky.' Soon a gang
of spuggies had congregated on the nearest branch and were
peering in through the window.

'Ooh no … tut tut … don't look too chirpy do he.'

'Gawd … he's gawn bald!'

'Ere, mate! Wass happened to your paloomidge?'

'Scrawny lil thing ain't he.'

'Looks oven-ready don't he,' said Gert.

The Purple-Bellied Parrot had no clue why, but the spuggies
enjoyed Gert's joke, and they all leapt up and flew about a bit,
cackling, before bouncing back onto the branch and jostling each
other for a good view. They noticed the chain.

'Ooh, now then, now then. What do we have here,'
said Alfie.

'Ere mate, wass that round your leg?'

'Ooohh, Now, do I *not* like the look of that. What do you
reckon to that Vi?'

'Got a chain raarnd is leg he has Roy,' said Vi.[1]

'Somebody's only bin and gone and done and put a chain
round is leg ain't they!'

'Poor little twite.'

The Purple-Bellied Parrot shrugged his scapulars. He couldn't
think of anything to say, so he went back to gnawing at the
snake's mouth.

The spuggies began to argue about the best way to get it off.
'Now, what *he* wants to do is …' and they were off, chirping and
cheeping, expositing and expounding, all yattering simultane-
ously. Soon, it got rather heated and a few pecks were thrown.
More spuggies arrived and joined the mêlée. The racket was
deafening — even through the glass. They seemed to forget all
about the Purple-Bellied Parrot, until a female, who had been
perched apart well clear of any beakicuffs, said, 'Ere, mate, ave
you tried the other end?'

Sudden silence. Then Alfie said, 'Yeah, good idea Flo. Was about to say the same meeself. Goo on my son. Try the other end.'

The snake's tail coiled round and around the perch and ended in a knot. The Purple-Bellied Parrot began to work at the knot. But it was solid. As he gnawed, he overbalanced and nearly fell off the perch, and only some vigorous flapping saved him. This gave him an idea. He flapped his wings again. He was glad he'd kept those feathers — perhaps he could *fly* himself free. If he flapped hard enough, perhaps the snake will snap. He took a deep breath.

'Hhuutpnnnnnnnnnnnnaahhh!'

He felt himself lifting off, but also the tug of the snake.

HhutnnnnnnnnnnneeEEEAAARRRGGGHH!'

He flapped and flapped with all his strength, but the snake held firm. Then he was falling forward, and he did a loop-the-loop around the perch — banging his head on the stand on his way round. But now he was out of puff and had to flop back onto the perch, gasping. The spuggies tutted again.

'No, no, no, no, no, no, no, no, NO. This'll never do,' and they went back to arguing. All at once they quietened down, and shuffled uneasily along the branch.

You tell im Alfie,' said Vi.

'Nah, you tell im Betty,' said Alfie.

'I ain't tellin im. Sid can tell im,' said Betty.

'Oh no I ain't. Chalkie, you can tell im,' said Sid.

Chalkie was shoved off the branch. He dropped out of view for a moment, but then fluttered up onto the windowsill.

'Ahem, erm … Well, we've, erm, had a conflab … and it's like this you see. As we see it, there is only one way out of your predickybirdament.' He glanced back at the others who were tutting and firing icy glares at him. Chalkie stammered on. 'Yeah, well … Ahem … It's like this you see …'

'Gerron with it!'

'Yeah, well … erm, as I was saying, we've had a good lower-mandible-wag[2] you see, put our noggins together, and erm, the upshot is …' He looked back for support, but none came. 'Well, it's like this, erm … You've got to bite your foot off mate.'

The Purple-Bellied Parrot expected them to all leap off the perch and go for a good fly about to celebrate the joke. But they were serious. For once they were silent, and they just shuffled around the branch looking at their toes. Chalkie spoke again.

'I mean, crikey mate, you don't need two feet anyway. Look at all them pigeons flying about. Some of them ain't got no feet at all to rub together, and they do aright, dotting about on them stumps.'

'It'll be easy with that big beak of yours,' Betty piped up. 'One quick snip and you'll be free. One of our lot did it once and he's as spry as a spotted flycatcher.'

'You could come out ere and have some fun with us — look your window's open,' said Alfie. At this the spuggies cheeped loudly and bounced about on the branch.

'Yeah, come on, we'll show you the sights. We can go to the park and tease the berts,' said Chalkie.[3] 'You should see old Reg and them berts. Dab hand he is. He's got more of their feathers lining his nest than they has. Show him Reg.'

Reg disappeared for a moment and returned holding aloft a glossy blue and white feather. The Purple-Bellied Parrot noticed that Reg was missing a few feathers himself from his crown.

He looked up at the open window. He wasn't sure he could squeeze through, but he was tempted. Outside, the spuggies, the tree, all seemed so close, and one thing was for sure: being with the spuggies wouldn't be boring like being with the pink-faced man. But it seemed a bit extreme. Bite off his own foot? He looked down at it and twiddled its toes. He'd always been rather attached to it. How would he scratch his ear? No. Anyway, the snake will probably get tired soon and give up.

But then, with one loud 'eek' and not so much as a 'cheerio,' the spuggies were gone and the fat-fingered tree was deserted.

The branches shook violently, and it wasn't because of the wind or a huge bird landing. It was like a giant had grabbed hold of the trunk and was trying to shake the spuggies loose. Then the giant was climbing up. An orange head appeared, with bulging red ears like they'd been bashed and were all swollen up. The ears were connected by a band passing over the creature's head, and the Purple-Bellied Parrot thought the band might be holding them on. The head had a face, but it was featureless. An orange body soon followed, but this was not featureless. Its sticking-out arms and legs told the Purple-Bellied Parrot it was human.

The man looped a rope around one of the boughs and let the free end drop.

'Right!'

He heaved on the rope. He heaved and heaved until a thing came into view. The Purple-Bellied Parrot knew the thing, but could not call it by name or describe its purpose. It was a thing that stirred again the fog of memory, and it conjured one emotion: terror. The man now had the thing in his hands and was tinkering with it. One end it was fat and orange like his head, the other thin, flat and metallic. From the circumference of the flat end stuck out hooked teeth. The man adjusted his red ears. He pulled at something at the fat end, a string. He jerked at it hard, again and again.

The Purple-Bellied Parrot heard, 'Thrummmmm … Thrummmmm … Thrummmm-mmm-mmm-mm-m,' and 'Bugger.'

The man twisted something on the fat end, and jerked the string again. The Purple-Bellied Parrot wished he was back on the floor of his cage, as the exploding roar obliterated *Bargain Hunt* and knocked him off his perch.

'BRAAAAAAARPPP BRA-BRAP BRAP-BRAP BRAARRRPP BRAARPP BRA-BRAP BRAP-BRAP BRAP-BRAP BRAARRRPP

BRAARPP BRA-BRAP BRRRA BRA-BRA BRR-BRR-BRR-BRR-BRRR BRRR.'

As he dangled, fluttering, from the silver snake, the Purple-Bellied Parrot knew that sound, and terror surged through his heart.

'bbbbrrrrRRRRRRAAAAAWER-AAAWER-AAAWER-AAAWER-AAAWER.'

Upside-down, the Purple-Bellied Parrot watched with one eye. A severed branch creaked and fell, and its stump sprayed yellow liquid onto the window.

'BBRRRRRRRRRAAAAAWER-AAAWER-AAAWER-AAAWER-AAAWER.'

Apart from a gentle 'put-put-put,' the sound ceased. A fat limb and its branches and its twigs and leaves and its nests and its caterpillars and bees and wasps and flies and beetles swayed in the breeze. The orange man climbed higher and kicked down onto to the limb again and again. It groaned, and fell, its branches clattering into the window, leaves sliding down the panes. Insects, suddenly smears. Silence, and then a crash.

'BBRRRRRRRRRAAAAAWER-AAAWER-AAAWER-AAAWER-AAAWER.'

It was a sound from before the stinking black din. It was the sound that ended his should-be life. The sound that brought his home crashing down, the sound which parted him from brothers, sisters and mum and dad.

'BBRRRRRRRRRAAAAAWER-AAAWER-AAAWER-AAAWER-AAAWER.'

Soon the Purple-Bellied Parrot could see no fat-fingered leaves. The tangle of branches and wizened leaves and spring buds and dangly balls and spuggies was gone, replaced by grey sky. He fluttered and flailed, trying to get back on his perch — desperate to see if they were leaving anywhere for the spuggies to live. But it was no use. Flying upside-down was just too hard, so he gave up. The snake was relentless. Wings drooping, he dangled by one leg, gasping.

———————

The Purple Bellied Parrot heard the key turn in the lock and watched as the pink-faced man came in and walked across the ceiling towards the window, where he gasped and clapped his hands.

'Well hoo-ray. They've finally got round to doing it. Bout time too, ruddy council. Sick of phoning the buggers.' He walked to the far end of the window and stood on his toes and peered out over the roof tops. 'Wow, amazing. I can even make out the top of the shopping mall.' He stood for some moments searching the new cityscape and then grinned. 'This'll put a few grand on the place.'

He saw the Purple-Bellied Parrot.

'Oh my God! Look at the state of you! What's happened?'

The Purple-Bellied Parrot turned his head away as the pink-faced man lifted him back onto the perch.

'There, you'll feel better now. Look at that view. You'll enjoy that now won't you. You wheeeeel … Won't you … Yeee-eayz … [etc.]. Ooh, your poor foot. It must be all hurty.'

The Purple-Bellied Parrot nearly fell off the perch again, he felt so weak and lop-sided, and his foot throbbed and he had to stand on the other one. He stood wobbling for a good bit before he got his balance back. He leaned over and took a drink of water, which made him feel a bit better; then he plucked up the courage and peeked out of the window. Spread before him, where once fat-fingered leaves and spuggies had danced, was the city. Pierced by yellow streetlights, drizzle smeared the pane and mingled with the sap, and the sticky mixture rolled down the glass in big blobs. The Purple-Bellied Parrot turned away and pulled at one of his green feathers, and watched with one eye as it lilted and settled on the parquet.

By the end of the week he was almost bald. He spent the days with his back to the window, and when he wasn't tidying his feathers he tried to sleep, his head under what was left of his wing.

But sleep was impossible. The man with the orange ears and the bbBRRRAAAaaw-bbBRRRAAAaaww had seen to that. He had blown away the fog, and memories from before the stinking black din had thundered into in his head, all sunlit and stark. Being flung from the nest, the whumph as he thudded onto the dust, the heat of the sun on his back, the beak-full of dust. The shrieking yellow beast, its giant squeaky feet that never moved and never left the ground but somehow coming ever closer, carrying his home, closer still, until he was certain he must be crushed, hoping to be crushed. The orange-eared man's hand looming over him, until it touched him. And then the tiny cage where he couldn't stand up; the clamour of the market — so many humans — when he'd never seen a single one before. The time of the roaring black and the stink and the room that never stilled, a world he still could not comprehend.

The pink-faced man now spent ages in the chair, staring at the Purple-Bellied Parrot and scratching his chin, only occasionally distracted by the telly or the black flat box like a mini telly. Sometimes he would cup his hands over his face so that the Purple-Bellied Parrot could only see his eyes and his shiny scalp and bristly hair. Sometimes he would clasp his hands and point his fingers to the sky and tap them together. But the eyes would still be there, watching him. Sometimes, the stare would be a glare, and the chin scratching intensified.

The constant staring and the sound of fingernails on whiskers frightened the Purple-Bellied Parrot. After the fat-fingered tree went, he had concluded that the pink-faced man was a bringer of bad things, and that another bad thing was bound to happen. It was just a case of when. He pushed his head further under his wing and spent hours that way. He felt safer when he could see nothing.

One evening, while he sat and stared and scratched, the pink-faced man drank more of the brown liquid than usual. Then he huffed loudly, got up and approached the cage.

'Well, you won't talk. You poo everywhere if I let you. You're nearly as bald as a coot. What use are you? There's nothing else for it. You've left me no choice.' He jabbed a finger, 'This is all your fault.' He took out his flat box and the colours came to life. 'Hello, Frickling Insurance? I'd like to report the loss of a rather expensive parrot. What? No, it was my stupid cleaner. Silly woman left the window open.'

The pink-faced man extinguished the colours and went into the kitchen. The Purple-Bellied Parrot heard him rummaging through a draw, the clatter of spoons and forks, and knives. The pink-faced man said, 'That'll do,' and there was a thud as something heavy was placed on the worktop, a 'shump' as the drawer slammed shut.

The pink-faced man swung open the cage door and grabbed the Purple-Bellied Parrot from where he cowered. He jabbed him with the point of a finger. 'You've had everything you needed, but you just won't behave.'

In the kitchen, a ragged old tea towel was laid out on the worktop, and beside it a piece of wood, long, cylindrical and smooth. The lid of the flip-top bin was open. The pink-faced man wrapped the Purple-Bellied Parrot in the tea towel, and placed him on the worktop. The tea towel was thin and gauzy and, silhouetted against the strip light, the Purple-Bellied Parrot watched the cylinder of wood rise above him.

'This is your fault,' the pink-faced man said again, breathing hard, and the Purple-Bellied Parrot concluded he was probably right, and tried to sing his little song.

The arm and the wood hovered there for an age.

Then they slowly fell. A clunk, as the pink-faced man replaced the rolling pin.

'It's no good,' he said. 'Can't do it.'

He stood looking out the window to where the tree had been and took a long drink from the bottle of brown water. He pushed the window open into the night. The din of the traffic poured in. He marched over to where the Purple-Bellied Parrot sat shivering on the perch. He grabbed him with both hands and yanked — yanked hard — until he realised the Purple-Bellied Parrot was chained. He cursed and strode off and returned with a metal thing with toothy jaws. With a 'tink,' the jaws bit through the chain and it rattled away. He carried the Purple-Bellied Parrot to the open window. The cold air made his bumpy skin bumpier. Circles and squares of white and red and yellow lights were everywhere, some moving; some blinking.

He held the Purple-Bellied Parrot out into the orange night. With a 'Hhuutt' he threw the Purple-Bellied Parrot away.

II

THE CITY

3

SPUGNACITY

The Purple-Bellied Parrot watched the rectangle of light fly away. Cold air buffeted his body. Grey walls and glass windows hurtled past. The hard pavement rushed up. He was in big trouble. It was then, for the very first time, that he spoke.

'Boll-oooooooOOOCKs!'

He had kept most of his wing and tail feathers, thank goodness. This is it, he thought. The emerald forest and all its creatures flashed before him. He saw himself soaring above it with the hot sun on his back. He decided then, at that moment, he would go back.

He was falling back-first, feet-up — so if he flapped he would merely accelerate his fall. So the first thing he had to do was to right himself. The wind whistled through the remains of his feathers. He spoke again.

'You can do theez. The sparrows say you are a bird. Now is the time. Fly you Beeg Nose!'

He flipped himself over — which went better than he expected — then opened his wings. He closed his eyes so he couldn't see the ground as it rushed up and imagined himself soaring towards the sun. He flapped, hard.

'HHUUUUUUUUUUUUTTTTT.'

WHAMMPFFF!

He belly-flopped into a polystyrene carton. The carton had a golden M on it and contained a greasy mush of human food. It lay in a patch of spindly grass on a pile of mashed-up fat-fingered tree. So the landing had been soft, but it still knocked the puff out of him, and he lay there for a good bit, chest pumping.

With a 'shlock,' he pulled his head from the food and looked about. On one side, a busy pavement; on the other, the crawling traffic monster. The Purple-Bellied Parrot turned away from the dazzling white lights and the wheels and the smoke and watched legs and feet rush past.

The legs and feet were indifferent to his presence, indifferent until a pair of smaller legs and feet came trotting towards him. They stopped, and a tiny hand stretched towards him.

'Mummy, look!'

'Not now Toby. Mummy's late for her nails,' said a female human with another small flat box clasped to her ear.

'But mummy, look!'

'What? Oh my God … It's one of those horrible pigeons. Toby, stay away. It's got something wrong with it. Eeaargh. Toby! Come here at once.'

The tiny hand pulled away, and the small feet were dragged off along the pavement. But despite his predicament — being thrown out of a window into the cold city, being unable to fly and landing on an old cheeseburger, being bald — the Purple-Bellied Parrot discovered that the thing that most irked him at that moment was being called a 'pigeon.'

He shook his head. He must get out of this fix. Right. He can't fly away, and he can't resort to his usual tactic in hopeless situations: bury his head under his wing. Soon, he'll be discovered — and then what? More humans? More cages? He though hard, but soon his thoughts were waylaid by a more immediate danger.

Scuttlings. Scuttlings coming from under a nearby bench. He

saw a flicker of movement and heard more scuttlings. Through
the spindly grass, he couldn't see what produced the scuttlings,
and he'd never experienced scuttlings before, but he thought it
best to assume that something unseen that scuttled should be
suspected at least of mischievous motives.

He stared hard into the darkness under the bench. More scut-
tles. More flickers. For a moment, the flickers resolved into a
pointy nose and whiskers. The nose and whiskers twitched
constantly — and the Purple-Bellied Parrot noted that they were
twitching in his direction. More human legs and feet approached,
and the nose and whiskers retreated into the darkness. When the
legs and feet had gone, the twitching nose and whiskers emerged
once more, to be followed by a pair of tiny black eyes, glassy but
impenetrable eyes. The creature raised its nose and whiskers and
waved them, still twitching, in the direction of the Purple-Bellied
Parrot. It was like it was trying to make some final calculations:
location, speed, angle of attack, time required for completion of
attack. Apparently satisfied, the creature fully emerged.

The nose, glassy eyes and whiskers were attached to a great
fat body. This assemblage darted towards the Purple-Bellied
Parrot, dragging, he noted, an incongruously long tail behind it.
The Purple-Bellied Parrot shrank back as pointy teeth matching
the pointy nose grabbed the carton and began to drag it towards
the shadows. But then more human legs and feet appeared, and,
with a squeak, it released its grip and shot back to its lair, string
tail waving.

The Purple-Bellied Parrot was now struggling desperately to
unglue himself from the cheeseburger. He had felt the twitchy
whiskers brush against his face and hadn't liked it. Now he was
convinced that the twitchy thing was going to eat him — and he
wasn't even going to need much plucking. He tore at the carton
with his big beak; he felt cold grease soak his bottom. Swivelling
his head, he watched with despair as another lull in the legs and
feet approached. Nose and whiskers appeared again. Now they'd

stopped twitching — which the Purple-Bellied Parrot took for a bad sign. Bollocks. He was nearly free.

Oh well, it hadn't been a great life and, what with all the horrible things still to come, it was probably best if it ended now. He was just sad he'd never go back to the emerald forest. He settled back in the carton. He even nibbled a bit of cheese and wondered why the humans ate such horrible stuff. The lull was upon him. The dark eyes zeroed in. He saw the rat tense his body, and then explode from the shadows. The Purple-Bellied Parrot closed his eyes and tried hard not to think about the pointy teeth.

THWACK!

He was airborne — still stuck to the carton — but airborne, sailing high above the traffic monster, the legs and feet, the twitchy nose and the pointy teeth. He opened one eye and saw far below boys in big shoes. One had his leg raised and was roaring:

'Yeeeeeeaaay! The crowd goes wild. Ramphard does it again. Right in the top corner. Keeper, pick that one out.'[1] The boy was running around in a big circle, arms outstretched like aeroplane wings.

The Purple-Bellied Parrot had seen a human do a kick like that on the telly. Now it had saved him, and for a moment he relaxed in his cardboard armchair and enjoyed the ride. But soon he realised that the boy had put side spin on the carton, and the spinning was making him feel sick. Then he was losing height. Luckily, his trajectory was taking him towards a clump of bushes away from the pavement. A Balotelli miskick could easily have sent him spiralling into the roaring traffic. The bushes hurtled towards him. The carton clipped the top of a fence post and spun around. The Purple-Bellied Parrot shot out, tumbling into the greenery. Caroming through the twigs and branches, bouncing off all the knobby bits, he scrabbled for a hold, until at last his claws locked onto something branchy. They held.

The Purple-Bellied Parrot spent a long night hunkered down in the middle of the privet. How he wished he had some feathers to fluff out. What an idiot he had been to pull them all out. When the traffic quietened, white dots began to drift down from the sky. They landed on his pimply skin and on the end of his beak. They were cold and at first crunchy, but then, astonishingly, they turned into water.

Luckily, the privets were next to a takeaway and poking out of the wall was a metal vent which hummed and pumped out hot air. The air smelled like old fish cakes, but he snuggled up as close as he dared and was able to doze. The fish-cake air made the Purple-Bellied Parrot dizzy, but without it he surely would have frozen to death.

Dawn was the colour of the cloth the pink-faced man wiped his toilet with and was just as damp, so the Purple-Bellied Parrot stayed close to the heat of the vent. The night had seemed endless. One side of his body — the side next to the vent — was always roasting; the other side always freezing, so he had spent much of the night turning around and around like he was on a spit. It was only when the sky began to brighten that it dawned on him to sit on top of the vent, and he spent a blissful hour baking his bum. The heat surged up his body like mercury rising in a thermometer and he had nodded off into a heavy sleep. Now, he was hungry.

He pecked at the leaves nearby, but they were bitter and he coughed them out. After checking as best he could for rats, he clambered down to the ground and poked around in the litter. But there was nothing. A nightshift of crawly scuttly things had probably got there before him. The Purple-Bellied Parrot shivered. He looked around and wondered what had happened to that cheeseburger.

As the day brightened the trickle of legs and feet trudging past his bush turned into a torrent. The Purple-Bellied Parrot was picking through the litter when he noticed something whirling in the corner of his eye. He looked up to see something big and yellow sailing towards him, and was about jump for cover when he realised it was not some many-legged monster swooping down to smother him. The banana skin wrapped itself around the branches above and the Purple-Bellied Parrot clambered up to inspect.

Yes! The banana-skin chucker had left the nibbly nub-end in the bottom, like humans always do, and so the Purple-Bellied Parrot scoffed the nibbly nub-end in a trice. But it only made him feel more hungry and, away from the vent and with his present plumage predickybirdyment, his beak was soon chattering.

He climbed back up to the vent and peered through the tangle of twigs and leaves at the legs and feet. Where there was one flying banana … And sure enough, eventually sundry items sailed towards him.[2] Most, like the flying carton that had carried him there, were inedible, but he found a few scrummy morsels amongst the fag ends and plastic cups. A wine gum — nice, but took some getting through; half a bun with half a sausage in it — the bun didn't taste of anything, but it filled him up. The sausage didn't taste of anything either, but he enjoyed the fat and the salt. A piece of nutty chocolate tumbled to his feet. MMMmmmm — despite the human teeth marks. He even nibbled a fag end, there were so many of them, but it tasted like the pink-faced man had smelled — EEeaaarrrgh.

Back at the vent, he had a good think. He might never move from this spot. He could spend the rest of his life here, flitting from vent to morsel, in a permanent state of glowing full belliedness. What else did he need? It would be a much better life than he'd had so far. Then two things happened.

Something bright and white sailed towards him — like a mini cloud. It plopped into the debris below and glistened enticingly. He clambered down to investigate. He'd never seen anything like the white thing before, and something about its texture nagged him — but it did smell sweet. He walked around it a couple of times, head cocked, thought, and decided to risk a bite.

Instantly, the white thing was trying to eat *him*. The Purple-Bellied Parrot tried to open his beak, but the white was wrapping itself around it, binding his jaws tight. The more he tried to chew the tighter its grip became, until in the end his beak was clamped shut. So he scratched at it with his claw, but the thing seized his foot and soon trussed that in sticky tendrils. He thought about using his other foot to scrape away the monster, but that wouldn't leave him anything to stand on. So he stood on one leg with the other leg stuck to his beak, panic rising in his breast.

He decided to put his head under his wing. That usually calmed him down. Luckily, he realised just in time that that would have been awful. The beast would then have him trussed-up by three important body parts. Think.

He realised that the white monster only attacked *him* if he attacked *it*, so he decided the best thing was to ignore it. Sure enough, the monster let him alone. But it still held him by leg and beak — a beak he couldn't even open now. How would he ever eat the flying morsels? Hunched over, the Purple-Bellied Parrot hopped disconsolately back up to his steely perch for a warm. Then the second thing happened.

No hum.

The Purple-Bellied Parrot pressed his body desperately against the vent, but only cold metal struck through to his bones. He inspected it from all angles, tapped it hard with his beak, but no fish-cake air flowed out to warm him. Soon he was shivering so much, the twig he was sitting on was bouncing up and down. The twig squeaked as it scraped against the vent. It was a loud, piercing squeak — a squeak that would carry a long way.

He thought about trying to sing his little song, but remembered he couldn't open his beak. So the Purple-Bellied Parrot stood on his one leg and looked about him and shivered, and

wished he could just tuck his head under his wing and dream of
the emerald forest. He sobbed.

Scuttling.

Silence.

Scuttling.

The Purple-Bellied Parrot heard the sounds and saw flickers
of movement, but couldn't focus on their source — and his brief
stay in the city had taught him that scuttling noises should
provoke the response: 'Uh-oh.' Now, scuttling was coming from
multiple directions. Scuttling came from above and below, from
left and right and behind and in front. The Purple-Bellied Parrot
peered into the foliage, and discerned dirty-brown shapes flitting
about, coming ever closer. The rat had gone to fetch his pointy-
toothed, glassy-eyed mates. Frank Ramphard couldn't save him
this time.

They were upon him.

'Tut-tut. Now then, now then, now then, now THEN. What
dooo we have here? Hey, spuggies! Come look at this. Well, if it
ain't old Bignose isself.' Alfie was the first to arrive.

The spuggies mobbed round him, cheeping and tutting,
inspecting his gummy body. They poked and prodded all his
nooks and crannies — a process the Purple-Bellied Parrot found
not a little disconcerting. Then they all talked at once.

'Look at the state of im.'

'Ooh, he ain't grown any more palloomidge has he?'

'Ahhh, look at his little pink belly. Ain't it cute.'

'Ticky-ticky-ticky.'

'Freezing though ain't he — look at the shivers on him.'

'Look at all them goose-bumps.'

'And look what he's got wrapped round his mush.'

'Oi, Bignose! How did you manage to get all that chewing
gum round your mush?'

'Got it all over his cheeses anall.'[3]

'Helps him concentrate don't it.'

'Concentrate?'

'Yeah, look at ol' wassisname, Alec, Fergie's son.'

'What's ol' Bignose got to concentrate on?'

The Purple-Bellied Parrot tried to answer these questions, but he couldn't open his beak on account of the white monster. So he went, 'Mmum-mmm-mm-mm-mmmumm ... mmirm mirrmm,' and 'm-m-m-mmmir-mmir-mumm.'

'Whassee sayin?'

'Summat about his mum.'

'Didn't know he had a mum.'

'Was it your mum, was it? What done this to you?'

'Poor little twite.'

'Rotten mum.'

'Must have been naughty.'

'Rotten mum.'

Chalkie shouldered into the gang. 'Come on then chaps and chapesses. Stop messing about. Let's get this stuff off of him.'

Then they were jumping all over him, and the Purple-Bellied Parrot felt them poking their beaks into even more nooks and crannies. Their method was to snip a tiny piece off, and then shake their heads vigorously to dislodge it. Snip – shake, snip – shake.

'Oi watch out! That lot landed on me!'

'Well don't stand so bloomin close then!'

Ada sat on top of his head and worked away at his beak; others dangled from twigs and cleaned his feet. For once they worked mainly in silence — apart from the odd complaint, shout for help and reminisce.

'Oi, help me with this bit will you Reg. Getting tangled up a bit 'ere meeself.'

'Bloomin stuff ain't it Flo.'

'Ere, remember when old Charlie got his foot stuck in a gobbit and that moggie come along and chomped him?' Flo said.

They all stopped working for a moment to remember Charlie.

Charlie could cheep with the best of them; he was no slouch in a scrap, and could spot a discarded chip a mile away.

'Poor old Charlie.'

'It was 'paw' old Charlie though werntit,' said Alfie. 'Get it? *Paw* old Charlie? … Cos moggies got them paws don't they. 'Paw old Charlie.'

One or two of the younger spuggies chuckled, but the others groaned.

'We only found his beak didn't we, and one of his lil feet.'

'Yeah, one of his lil feet,' Vi said wistfully, 'just sitting there on the floor like he was coming back for it.'

'Yeah, moggies they don't like them bits do they.'

A conflab followed about which bits of a spuggie a moggie will, and will not, chomp. The Purple-Bellied Parrot squeaked, and they went back to work.

'Ooh, proper talker ain't he. Bet we won't get a word in edge-wise once he starts, will we Doris,' said Gert.

At last, the spuggies' snippy-snippy-shake-shake was complete, and a pile of gummy clippings lay below. The Purple-Bellied Parrot shook himself, ruffled the few feathers he had left and worked his mandibles up and down a bit. He thought he ought to make a little thank-you speech.

He 'ahemed,' paused, 'ahemed' again and began. 'I wheesh to thank you, you the spuggies, for what you do for me. I theenk you save my …'

'Ooh — ark at im. Don't he talk funny.'

'Ere, where's he from then?'

'Ain't from round here, and no mistake.'

'Praps he's from the same place as them flash-harry green fellas we see flying about.'

'Never stop squawkin.'

'Never shut up do they.'

'Squawk-squawk-squawk-squawk all day long.'

'Enough to drive a birdy round the bend.'

'Hope he's not like that.'

'Ere, mate, where's you from then?'

'Yeah, where's your gaff?'

'Your manor?'

'Your abode?'

'Su casa?'

'Who's she when she's at home?'

'Your home?'

'Yeah, where's that then?'

The Purple-Bellied Parrot sat for a moment and thought, but it was hopeless. 'I do not remember,' he said crestfallen, 'I really doan. All I remember is that everywhere is very, very green, and it is hot and the sun, it dazzles, and you smell salt in the air and that …'

'Definitely not from round ere then!'

'Decidedly not.'

'Indubitably not.'

'You what?'

'Nah, nuttin bright green around here mate, and we only get about two hot days a year,' said Reg.

'Which is when we go down to the river for a paddle …'

'Ooh yeah, love a good paddle me.'

'And the only h'aromas you gets here is from the takeaways and the smoke from the lorries and the red buses,' said Roy.

'And Alfie's trumps.'

'Oh yeah, Alfie's trumps. Strip your plumage off they can.'

They all guffawed.

'But I must find out,' the Purple-Bellied Parrot tried to continue. 'I have to go back. I cannot stay here. It is bad for me here.'

'Well, good luck with that one Bignose. The first thing you got to do is find out where 'back home' is,' said Betty.

'Not easy.'

'Noo, not easy.'

'Not easy at all.'

'About as easy as sneakin' a battered sausage out from underneath a maggie's claw.'

''Ooh — saveloy?'

'Not half!'

'Mustard or ketchup?'

'Shut up you lot,' yelled Chalkie. 'This ain't getting us nowhere.' He turned to the Purple-Bellied Parrot. 'Mate, Betty's right. If you don't know where home is, how you gonna get there?'

The Purple-Bellied Parrot struggled to come up with an answer. It was like his brain was shutting down. In the excitement of the rescue the he had forgotten he was cold, and now he realised he was shivering again, and his beak was clacking more than ever. The spuggies noticed.

''Ave to grow isself a few more feathers anall if he's going to fly home.'

'Gawd. Walking disaster ain't he.'

'Looks like he's gone ten rounds with a gang of maggies.'

'I should cocoa.'

'Apart from moggies and maggies, the shivers is a spuggies worst enemy.'

'Spect it's the same for him, especially as he hails from warmer climes,' said Chalkie.

'Moggies, Maggies *and* spugghawks,' corrected Alfie.[4]

'Yeah, spugghawks — got to have eyes in the back of your head!'

'Air rifles,' added Reg.

'Woss "climes" then?'

'And woss hail got to do with it?'

But before the spuggies could get stuck into another conflab, the Purple-Bellied Parrot keeled over and fell backwards, landing in the crook of a branch.

'Oh Gawd — he's gawn.'

'That'll be the cold.'

'Oh yeah? And there was me thinking it were the heat. Come on.'

The spuggies crowded round the Purple-Bellied Parrot. One pressed an ear to his breast and listened for a heartbeat; another peeled back an eyelid and peered inside; another shouted 'Coo-eee' into his ear; while a fourth held a downy feather to his nostrils and looked for signs of breathing.

'Yep. He' ain't croaked. It's faint, but his lil heart is still chugging away.'

The spuggies heaved the Purple-Bellied Parrot back onto his feet and all squashed up against him to try and get some warmth into him. After a few moments the Purple-Bellied Parrot revived and coughed and gazed about. He coughed again.

'I wheesh to thank you spuggies again for h'all you do for me. I theenk you again save my …'

'Oh Gawd — he's speechifyin' again.'

'Yes … yes. Blah-blah-blah-blah-blah. That's enough of that rubbish,' said Gert. 'Listen. Somehow, we got to get you sorted'

The spuggies squeezed in even tighter to the Purple-Bellied Parrot and began a conflab.

'We got to get him warmed up, but we can't hang about here all day.'

'Might be a moggie about.'

'And I for one is getting peckish.'

'I know, what if he jumps up and down to get isself warm?'

'What — and he does that all day does he?' said Gert.

'Think!'

'Think!'

'Think!'

'I am thinkin!'

'I know! We'll stand him on top of a chimeney pot — be warm as toast up there.'

'And leave him a sitting duck for all the passing maggies and spugghawks? Why don't you give him a lil dinner bell to ring anall?' said Vera.

'Think!'

'Think!'

'Think!'

Then Chalkie cried, 'Got it!' and with a cheep he was gone.

He came back a few moments later, a huge fluffy red thing flopping about in his beak. It was playing havoc with his aerodynamics, and when he landed on the edge of the bush he was fagged out.

'Give us hand you lazy sausages!' he gasped.

The spuggies hauled the fluffy red thing into the safety of the bush.

'Well?' said Alfie.

'Well what? It's a sock,' said Chalkie.

'I can see it's a bloomin sock. You've been raiding them washin lines again. But how does that help us out of our present predickybirdament?'

'He wears it don't he. We put it on him.'

'We put it on him? And then what? He just sits there all day does he, wrapped head to toe in a sock?'

'Look like a big fat sausage he will,' said Betty.

Chalkie slapped his forehead with his primaries. 'Watch,' he sighed.

He dragged the sock over to a puzzled Purple-Bellied Parrot. 'Give us hand then!'

Ada and Flo twigged what was happening and helped him lift the sock over the Purple-Bellied Parrot's head. They pulled down hard until it reached his legs. The sock bulged tight over his head and beak.

'His hooter looks even bigger like that don't it!'

'Now then ladies and gents,' said Chalkie. 'Feast your mincey pies on this!'[5]

Whistling as he worked, Chalkie snipped a hole into the top

of the sock. Once the hole was complete, he said, 'Righto. Pull!' and the three of them pulled down again. The Purple-Bellied Parrot's head popped out, and soon they had the sock all the way down to his toes.

'But ...' said Alfie.

'Crikey, enough buts. Just watch!'

Chalkie nodded to Flo and they snipped two long holes into the sides of the sock. Then he whispered into the ear of the Purple-Bellied Parrot. It was a struggle, and Flo and Ada had to tug hard, but the Purple-Bellied Parrot soon had one wing shoved through. The other soon followed, and the Purple-Bellied Parrot stood in his woolly tank top and flapped his wings. It was so warm, his beak instantly stopped clacking. He was about to say thank you again — but then thought better of it.

'Voila!' said Chalkie.

'You what?!' they all chorused.

'It's your French lingo,' said Chalkie.

'But ...' said Alfie.

'But? But what? Gawd, what's wrong now?'

'Erm ... Well ... ahem ... The colour? Spose red was all what was h'available.'

'Why?'

'Well, if you want him to stand out like a sore bum to every hungry moggie, maggie and spugghawk in the vic-hinity — then there's nothing bloomin wrong with it. I mean, I'm sure a bird with a green head and a huge hooter poking out of it wearing a red tank top — whom, I may add can barely flap his delicious little body off the ground — won't attract any h'unwanted h'attention at all. While we're at it, why don't we shove a ruddy great olive in his cakehole and sprinkle some salt and pepper on im?' Alfie was puffing his breast out now. If he'd had lapels, he'd have been tucking his alulae behind them.[6] 'Do me a bloomin favour. He'll be pooed-out on some bin's titfer before you can say Cock Robinson.'[7]

Alfie let his oration hang there for a moment. Some spuggies cheeped agreement.

Chalkie remained unruffled. 'Well done Alfie. Well done chaps and chapesses. Glad you spotted that,' and with a 'cheep' he was off again.

4

PARK LIFE

The Purple-Bellied Parrot didn't like the brown sock as much as the red one. The red one had reminded him of his lost purple belly, but he knew why the spuggies had changed his socks. The brown one kept him just as warm, but it camouflaged him too and, in his state of feeble escape flappage, he needed that. To make certain he remained warm and safe from hunters, that night — after 'grubbifying' most of the day — the spuggies returned to the privet to roost, and bookended him between their fluffed-out bodies.[1] The Purple-Bellied Parrot's heart soared. The chorus of tiny beating hearts meant everything was alright. The only snag was that the spuggies chattered and quarrelled till late and woke early, when it all began again. They also trumped incessantly.

They only spent the one more night in the privet by the hot vent. Though the spuggies were sorely tempted by the heat — 'Like Majawca,' said Alfie — they said the bush was too low and exposed to stay. Some prowling moggie would find them sooner or later — not to mention the rats. The takeaway was near the park, so at dusk the following night they moved deep into it.

The Purple-Bellied Parrot struggled to keep up. He flew from tree to tree, half flapping half gliding, and to keep the flights short he always clambered through to the branch that was nearest the next tree. The spuggies got more and more impatient.

'Ooh, Ol' Bignose is slow ain't he.'

'Needs a bomb under him.'

'An embar-arse-ment to birdkind, that's what he is.'

'Flies about as well as a bin.'

'Come on mate. Hurry up. The tawnies'll be out soon,' called Chalkie.

It was dark by the time they made it to their favourite roost, high in a spikey hawthorn.

'Bloomin Ada,' moaned Alfie. 'Barely got time for a conflab.'

———

Chalkie told him that they hung about in the park most of the time. Always grub opportunities at the pavilion café where a bit of cake was guaranteed; plenty of dustbaths; no shortage of anywhere to go for a drink and a bath — what with the blocked gutters on the greenhouses, the duck pond, the fountain and the paddling pool; plenty of opportunities for a bit of mischief with the parkies; and no end of nooks to snooze in or hide from the maggies and the moggies. And there were more grub opportunities in the square outside the park.

One day Chalkie asked, 'Fancy dining on pan-fried potatoes and spit-roasted essence of lamb enrobed in a coulis of pois vertes served on a bed of pavement accompanied by a mixed fruit pressé?'

The Purple-Bellied Parrot said he didn't know what he meant, so instead they went down to the square, to Spiro's Chippy on the far corner, and had kebab, chips and mushy peas washed down by Tizer. If the spuggies fancied a Chinese — they loved moo shoo pork — they went down to the Dragon's Garden on the opposite corner and rummaged about in the skip at the back. But they never dined at the Bombay Blue — way too hot.

When it came to finding grub, the Purple-Bellied Parrot was pretty hopeless at first. For as long as he could remember food had just been put in front of him by bins. So he just followed the spuggies about and did what they did. If they ate something — he ate it. Leftover kebabs drenched in chilli sauce took some getting used to, but he liked chips, and became especially fond of Swiss roll. He had to wait until the spuggies weren't looking, but sometimes he'd sneak across to the greengrocers and nab something juicy from one of the boxes piled on the pavement.

The Purple-Bellied Parrot was curious about a couple of things. First, the spuggies seemed to drink their own bath water, but he thought it impolite to ask Chalkie about that. The second thing he did ask about.

'Chalkie, do you ever eat food that does not come from the bins?'

'How do you mean?' said Chalkie, wiping a bit of pizza off his beak onto a twig.

'Oh, I doan know. Theengs like seeds, nuts, leaves, berries, grubs and insects?'

'You what! Crikey, no mate. Don't eat any of that muck.'

The park was not without danger, but the spuggies knew all the tricks of the local hunters and were excellent lookouts. One or two spuggies would take turns to keep watch, and at the first sign of any danger a shriller variation on 'CHEEP!' alerted the others and they then had a conflab about what to do.

'Tawnies. You got to watch out for tawnies at night,' Chalkie told the Purple-Bellied Parrot as they were settling in for some 'shut eye.'[2] 'Tawnies either swallow a spuggie whole in one gulp, or carry it off half-croaked to feed to their chicks — bit by bit.'

The Purple-Bellied Parrot thought about this and couldn't decide which he would prefer. In the end he looked down at Chalkie and then at himself and thought that he must be too big to swallow whole, so they would tear him up into little bits anyway.

One night a tawny came.

They had been putting up with his 'bloomin hootings and screechings' all night. Alfie had no sooner called out, 'Pass me his sock so I can shove it in his cakehole,' and he was there, a football of shadow in their tree, featureless apart from two black eyes reflecting the moonlight. No one had heard it arrive, not even a rustle.

Spuggie for tawny is 'CheeOP!'

'CHEEOP-CHEEOP   CHEEP-CHEEP   CHEEOP-CHEEP CHEEP-CHEEOP CHEEOP!'

The spuggies all leapt up, and in an instant were mobbing, dive-bombing, pecking, head-butting, nipping, wing-slapping and scratching the tawny. Ada even pooed on it. She must have had one ready to go. The Purple-Bellied Parrot watched, head cocked. Chalkie had told him that one spuggie was no match, but a whole gang of spugnacious spuggies might fight off a tawny before it got one of them. But this tawny seemed unperturbed by all the nipping and slapping and scratching. It swivelled its head and blinked, waiting for its opportunity. It opened its wings and leapt forward.

'Betty!'

Her 'cheeeeeEEEEEEEP!' was deafening.

The tawny's wing clouted the Purple-Bellied Parrot as it made its escape — Betty hooked by one talon, flailing the air.

Later he couldn't remember making the decision, but now the Purple-Bellied Parrot leapt forward. He grabbed the wing, and bit down hard. Something went crunch.

'ScreeeeeEEEEEEEECH'

Betty fell away and the Purple-Bellied Parrot let go. The

tawny exploded out of the tree and into the night, Roy and Dot giving chase. Vera even grabbed a leg and held on, but soon they realised none of the others were joining in, and they turned back.

No more sleep that night. The spuggies celebrated victory with a big conflab where they recounted their heroic deeds at great length and including every detail. Betty held up a feather she'd somehow nicked from the tawny's tail, waved it about a bit, and presented it to 'Old Bignose.' Chalkie hopped over and whispered in his ear: 'Take it. You did good tonight,' and all the spuggies cheered.

And the Purple-Bellied Parrot felt something that night he'd never felt before and that he couldn't name. It was like his heart was growing bigger and bigger and was about to burst out from his breast; like he was flying about high in the sky looking down on everything, and yet here he was still perched on this branch. Quietly, so the spuggies couldn't hear, he sang his little song, and on his belly where the purple feathers used to be, he felt a prickle.

The Purple-Bellied Parrot now kept close to the spuggies during the day, and they kept close to him. Since biting the tawny, he, 'Ol Bignose', had become an 'honorary spuggie.' That's what the presentation of the tawny's feather had meant, Chalkie told him.

The Purple-Bellied Parrot was surprised at how organised the spuggies' day was.[3] After waking up and a quick stretch and a long conflab, they set off to find 'brekkie grub.' This was easy — as long as you got there early enough. Outside any local takeaway the pavement was adorned with the 'chuckaways' of the previous night's 'noshers,' but you had to be quick before the bins with the brushes and bins arrived.

After brekkie it was time for a bath. If it had rained, any puddle would do, as long as somebody kept an eye out for moggies and maggies. But now they had to find deeper puddles to accommodate the Purple-Bellied Parrot. If it was dry they went over to the fountain — which was brilliant if it was working — or to the paddling pool which had a sloping end. If any parkies were about, though, they chased the spuggies away.

An alternative if it was dry — rare at this time of year — was a dust bath. The spuggies preferred a dust bath to a water bath, 'because you don't have to hang about half the bloomin morning with you paloomidge looking like a wet lettuce,' explained Flo. At first the Purple-Bellied Parrot thought having a bath in dirt was crazy, but then he caught some of the spuggies' ticks and mites and soon learned to treasure a good dust bath, even with the tank top on. They spent the rest of the mornings just flitting about, keeping an eye out for the odd 'bit o' grub,' but they weren't really hungry, just bouncing around having fun.

Always the spuggies were on the lookout for a bit of mischief. They would visit a nearby garden and snip the heads off freshly budding flowers and watch them, head cocked, tumble to the ground. They looked for pots freshly filled with compost and dug up the seeds. If washing was pegged out, they sat on the line and pooed on it — that was Ada's favourite. They particularly loved to torment the parkies. By their shed was a birdfeeder, and they would hop on and pull out all the boring seeds and drop them on the ground to sprout. If the parkies had just washed the van, they sat in the gutter and turfed out bits of moss onto it, or flew over and pooed on the windscreen. The bowling green was always worth checking out. If the parkies had scattered seed over the bare patches, they'd leap down and eat it — no matter they didn't like seed very much.

Their favourite mischief was 'counting coo.' Walters were the victims — the big fat ones who got fed by big fat bins sat on benches by the bandstand. They'd wait in the bushes, and when the walters were bent over feeding they'd dart out and make a grab for a tail feather. If they got one, the walter would always turn round and go 'Coo.' The spuggie who got the most coos was the winner and got 'first dibs' on any grub they found. The spug-gies stuffed the walter feathers in their nests, but Chalkie explained that now their tree was gone, they didn't know what they were going to do with them.

The spuggies thought the walters were stupid because they relied so much on bins chucking them food and so deserved everything they got. The Purple-Bellied Parrot considered this a bit rich seeing as they had just dined on half a pasty they found outside Spiro's Chippy. 'Walters' was spuggie for pigeons, 'named so after a film star from yore,' Chalkie explained solemnly. The Purple-Bellied Parrot was none the wiser for this piece of infor-mation. Chalkie also told him that they called the green-headed ducks that dabbled about in the pond 'berts,' but the reasons for this had been lost in the midges of time.

Come the afternoon, it was time for a snooze — after a good conflab about the morning's events of course — and they'd flock to one of their favourite thorny bushes to doze. Then it was time for tea — perhaps a cream tea — pinched from the posh tearoom in the pavilion. Again, you had to be quick before the poodle-haired ladies, alerted by the rattling teaspoons and the clinking crockery, came out to shoo you off. It was at the tearoom that a couple of bins spotted the Purple-Bellied Parrot.

'Ere, Sheila come look at this. What … What kind of bird is that?' The bin's gaze followed him as he fled with the spuggies. Sheila shaded her eyes.

'Lawks Ern, I ain't no Phil Loddy, but scraggy lil thing ain't he.'[4]

'Stone me,' said Ern. 'Looks like he's wearing a woolly jumper.'

They went to roost when it got dark. But they always checked to see what was on telly first. The bins at Me-and-Er, across from the park, never drew their curtains, and a wooden fence stood at just the right height in front of their window. At dusk the spug-gies lined up to see what was on.

'Hope its animals.'

'Hope its footie.'

If it was neither, they usually went straight to bed.

They didn't understand football, for which the Purple-Bellied Parrot was relieved because he wouldn't have to offer an opinion, but they liked to watch the ball bouncing about and the bins running after it and all the colours. If anything, they thought the point of the game was to see how many times the bins could kick the ball into a crowd of other bins watching in a big rectangle. The bins got most excited when the ball got kicked into the crowd at the ends of the big rectangle. A couple of traps with nets were set there though, and if the ball got stuck in one they all gave up and picked the ball up and took it back to the middle of the rectangle where they started all over again. The spuggies shouted things like 'offside' and 'man on' and 'he's no good in the hole,' things they'd heard the bins shout at the pitches in the park on a Sunday morning.

Football was runner-up to nature programmes though. All those birdies and beasties they never imagined could exist, crashing oceans and massive mountains; and no buildings, buses or bins. Some of them moggies were big though. Watching nature programmes, kipping and hiding were the only times the spuggies were ever quiet.

The tank-top was now gone. Frayed edges and gaping holes had signalled its demise some days before, and Chalkie had offered to find him another. But the Purple-Bellied Parrot didn't need it any longer. New plumage had been poking through a while now and, as the spuggies stirred that baking early spring morning, he was glad it was gone. Happy feathers were now growing all over his body, and the Purple-Bellied Parrot looked down at the glossy new purple belly and preened it with pride.

The knitwear had fallen off the day before after getting

caught on a branch and unravelling during a helter-skelter flight from a spugghawk. It was a serendipitous unravelling because the spugghawk got caught up in it and had to stop and untangle herself. When they had all got their breaths back, Alfie looked him up and down and said, 'Well, get you and your new duds, all lardy-dah.' Later he asked Chalkie what 'duds' and 'lardy-dah' meant.

Soon after taking off for brekkie grub that spring morning, they spotted the carrier bag. The carrier bag was not blowing about in the wind or hanging in a tree or floating in the duck pond. It was sitting by a bench near the bandstand, stuffed full of goodies. An empty cider bottle lay at its side.

'Some bin's forgotten it after boozing himself silly,' said Gert.

They dropped down to inspect the bag — all except Stan who hopped off to see if there were any dregs left in the cider bottle. Some fox had been along and ripped the bag open, but it was still packed with stuff. They saw why: everything was in stiff cardboard packets or tins. The spuggies pecked and tugged but it was no use; the packaging defeated the punches and prisings of even their bills. The tins they ignored.

The tins. An idea was hatching in the Purple-Bellied Parrot's mind. It was something he had seen the pink-faced man do countless times before pushing food into his face. He was about to blurt it out when:

'CHeeeAP!'

Only a subtle difference — just a small hard 'a' going up at the end that no bin would ever notice — but the Purple-Bellied Parrot knew it to be spuggie alarm for one of their deadliest enemies. The spuggies shot into a hawthorn and, although he was a bit tipsy by then, even Stan made it. But the Purple-Bellied Parrot had been concentrating so much on his brilliant new idea, he was slow to react.

Too slow.

'Clack … Clack … Clack-clack.' The maggies were upon him.

In a panic he sprang up to fly away but the maggies were faster and battered him back down with their brawny wings. He tried again and they battered him down again. He tried again. This time he climbed away. Incredibly, he was escaping. He heard the spuggies urging him on from the hawthorn. He saw Chalkie and Vi part the twigs to allow him into the thorns. He was nearly there and he folded his wings to slip through the gap.

WHHACKK!

He was spinning, whirly-gigging through the air in a cloud of his own new feathers, clobbered by the big maggie who had been waiting in the tree above for just such an escape.

Crruump.

He hit the ground, and before he could move he was pinned to the earth by the needle claws of the big maggie. Above a huge shiny black beak, two shiny black eyes bored into him. Only two points of white light told him that they were eyes and that they were alive. The Purple-Bellied Parrot tried to look away, but found he was mesmerized, gripped as much by the two points of light as by the tightening claws. Beaks, unseen, prodded and poked and tugged and nibbled.

'CLAACK! Steady now chaps. Plenty for all. I just want to see …,' the big maggie took her foot off the Purple-Bellied Parrot and began to turn him over, '… just what kind of a specimen we have here. Now, please … Please don't struggle or it will only be the worse for you.' The Purple-Bellied Parrot stopped struggling. 'That's better, thank you so very much.'

One of the poking maggies said, 'What is it ma'am? What do we have?'

Big Maggie ignored it. The two points of light were roving all over the Purple-Bellied Parrot's body. The Purple-Bellied Parrot wished he had his tank top back on.

'Well, my.' Big Maggie was gazing down at the purple belly. 'What an exotic little creature you are.' She bent and tugged out a new purple feather and held it up to the light. She dropped it and watched, entranced, as it drifted down capturing and releasing the sun.

'Well, thank you so much. Splendid. Terrruuly splendid. I've not seen anything quite like this since that divine creature we caught that time. Now, what was it? Araminta, Piers, Harriet, Ptolemy?' Big Maggie looked to her cronies for a prompt, but they shuffled their feet, glancing at each other. 'Escaped from an aviary he had. Barely a mouthful in the end.' The white dots searched the sky for inspiration before returning to settle on the Purple-Bellied Parrot. 'But he had feathers like jewels — much like yours, my pretty one.' Distractedly, Big Maggie dispatched a hapless tick that had just emerged from her plumage. 'No matter. I can't *wait* to see how they look adorning my nest. I do hope you taste as good as you look.'

Big Maggie raised her beak for the final strike. It glistened in the sun, and began its descent.

'Do you like pineapple?'

Doi-oi-oi-oinnng.

The beak juddered to a halt a gnat's gonads breadth from the Purple-Bellied Parrot's eye.

'WhhaaaAAATT!?'

'Do you like PINEAPPLE?' Chalkie had shot out from the bush and was now clinging to Big Maggie's head shouting into her ear. With a flick of her head, Chalkie was airborne, and before he could take wing, Big Maggie thwacked him like a Dandy Murray forehand into the care of the other maggies.[5] For a bit they played beaky-uppy with him, and managed twenty-three before Chalkie flopped into the dust. Even in his terrorised state, the Purple-Bellied Parrot had to admit that was impressive.

Big Maggie strutted over and stood over Chalkie, tail flicking in irritation.

'You talk of pineapples, little brown *jobbie,*' she spat. 'Please, do go on.'

Chalkie leaned up. 'Well, everybody knows pineapple's your

favourite — right? You'll go miles for a decent chunk or two. Am I wrong?'

Big Maggie glanced around at her cronies. All were nodding eagerly, slobber flying off the ends of their beaks.

'Well, I own that we are somewhat partial to the luscious yellow flesh of that sweet, sweet cabbage of the tropics.' She sprayed flecks of slobber over Chalkie's face. 'What of it?' she snapped.

'Well crikey, *he* can get it for you.' Chalkie nodded towards the Purple-Bellied Parrot.

'Keep talking, *jobbie*.'

'Erm, better if we show you me old China. May I?'

Chalkie struggled to his feet, dusted himself off and hopped over to the carrier bag. He tore the plastic apart.

'There.'

'Yes, yes. I see. I see. I see a *tin* of pineapple. And, if I am not mistaken, pineapple chunks no less. But, as you are aware my dear *jobbie*, the tin can has long been the nemesis of the mighty magpie. The best maggie brains have applied themselves to the problem, but alas in vain. It has baffled intellects the magnitude of which your tiny mind cannot conceive.[6] So, *jobbie...*' The 'job' of 'jobbie' was accentuated by a prod from Big Maggie's beak, '... unless in the next ten seconds you solve this, erm, can-undrum, I'll be picking my teeth with your spindly metatarsals.[7] One ...'

Chalkie flew over to the Purple-Bellied Parrot and landed on his head. He whispered. 'Okay, time to save your life and mine. Use the force.'

'Two ...'

'What?' the Purple-Bellied Parrot said.

'Use the force. Use the force of that great big hooter you got. Look at the size of it. Use it!' Chalkie nodded towards the can.

'Three ...'

But the Purple-Bellied Parrot was ahead of him. It was the

very idea that had been hatching in his own brain moments before.

Chalkie looked up at Big Maggie and said, 'May we?'

Big Maggie released her claws.

The Purple-Bellied Parrot stalked over to the can. He circled the can once, eyeing it like it was his greatest enemy. He stopped, huffed, squatted, stood tall, and took a deep breath.

'Four …'

He grabbed the can and dragged it, 'Five …,' to a flat spot on the ground.

'Six …'

He fixed his lower mandible under the rim of the can.

'Seven …'

He placed his upper mandible on the top of the can, inside the rim.

'Eight …'

He squeezed, with all his might, Chalkie hopping about yelling encouragement, 'Come on my son. Squeeze that big hooter together. Heave! Squeezit … Squeeze iiiiIIIT!'

'Nine …'

'HhuutrrrrrrrrnARGH.'

Just as the Purple-Bellied Parrot thought the tip of his beak was going to break off, a hiss, and the metal gave.[8] Sweetness poured out onto his tongue.

Big Maggie stopped counting. She strutted over and peered down.

'May I?'

Elbowing the Purple-Bellied Parrot out of the way, she inspected the clear liquid oozing from the puncture. She tasted it, turned very slowly to her cronies, paused for effect, and nodded. Araminta, Piers, Harriet and Ptolemy whooped.

'Well, my polychromed Polly, I think you've earned yourself and your little dun friend here a reprieve.[9] Please, do continue.'

The Purple-Bellied Parrot again fixed his beak on the rim of the can and began to scissor his way around. Puncturing it had been the hard part, and in no time he was halfway. He levered the lid up a bit, and saw the luscious yellow chunks, sloshing about in the syrup. The maggies could wait no longer and crowded round. Big Maggie shoved the Purple-Bellied Parrot aside. She pushed her beak in and prised up the lid. Soon, they were all guzzling.

Forgotten now, the Purple-Bellied Parrot and Chalkie sidled away. Drowned out by the slurpings, Chalkie was grumbling. 'She called me "little brown jobbie" she did.' He turned and yelled 'Faecal sack!' and they both dived for the safety of the hawthorn.[10]

'With the power vested in me,' Alfie was saying, I hereby dub you "Ooterus Maximus." May Gawd bless it and all who sail in it.'

'It's just summat he's heard off of the telly,' said Vi.

'What power?' said Stan.

He' ain't wearin' a vest,' said Flo.

But Alfie wasn't listening. He had taken the ceremonial twiglet from its matchbox and was now solemnly tapping it on the Purple-Bellied Parrot's scapulars and 'barnet.'[11] He paused and snipped a bit off the twiglet. He gave it to the Purple-Bellied Parrot and handed the remainder back to Gert who put it back in the matchbox with great ceremony. Alfie motioned for the Purple Bellied Parrot to eat the twiglet. The Purple-Bellied Parrot munched on it for a bit and then stuffed it in his cheeks. Later, when they weren't looking, he spat it out.

Spring stayed warm. Some of the spuggies got so plump feasting on Maggie leftovers that they had trouble taking off and had to go on a diet. No cake, chips or kebabs for a week, and they had to fly once round the park before they were allowed any brekkie grub.

These lazy, full-bellied days the spuggies passed conflabing, mischieving or snoozing. With the maggies no longer a menace, it was just the moggies and the spugghawks you had to 'keep em peeled' for. But, despite them living 'high on the bog' the Purple-Bellied Parrot sensed a change in the spuggies. They still joshed and scrapped and conflabed, but their hearts seemed not to be in it. He decided they were sad, and he asked Chalkie why.

'Crikey, haven't you noticed what time of year it is? Haven't you seen all them birds flying about with them bits of twig and feathers in their cakeholes? Not heard the sound of faint tweetings? No?' The Purple-Bellied Parrot stared at him vacantly. 'No, course you haven't noticed. How could you, being an orphan and living in them little boxes all that time.' He opened his wings. 'Follow me.'

They flew out of the park, and the Purple-Bellied Parrot felt his heart race as he glanced behind and saw the trees getting smaller. Ahead were low grey buildings and monster traffic and bins, bins everywhere and no trees. They flew for a long time, and the Purple-Bellied Parrot kept glancing back to be sure he could still see the park and so be able to find his way back should anything happen to Chalkie.

They arrived at a low grey building much like the others. Crows were loafing about on the roof, and the Purple-Bellied Parrot thought they might come after a weirdo like him, but then he saw they had a dead walter to dismember. On a concrete yard beyond the grey building stood one-armed yellow monsters. On the ends of the arms were bucket-like hands with big claws. He knew these monsters.

The Purple-Bellied Parrot cried out, 'Chalkie, pleeze, we need to go back to the park … Chalkie, pleeze! We go back now, pleeze.'

'It's okay, we're here,' Chalkie called over his shoulder.

They flew on past the yellow monsters to an area which, from above, looked at first like a patch of ragged low bushes. But big fallen trunks lay at the side of the ragged bushes, and no spring green fringed their branches. Here it was still winter.

'Down there,' called Chalkie.

They landed on one of the trunks. It had been cut into three lengths. The Purple-Bellied Parrot peered over the end of one and saw rings like a cut onion, although many, many more. Yellow sap still bled out, congealing into blobs. Most of the branches were gone, but from the few that remained, fat-fingered leaves flapped in the breeze. The Purple-Bellied Parrot glanced around and realised that the surrounding bushes were not bushes at all, but chopped-off treetops

Chalkie was quiet for a bit, and then said, 'This was our home — where you used to watch us hopping about and playing with them balls?' He hopped further along the trunk. 'This was our tree, where we lived, where we conflabed, where we rowed and scrapped and made up, where we fought-off moggies and maggies and tawnies, where we kipped and canoodled, and where we nested and raised our spuglings.' Chalkie hopped lower onto a dead branch. 'Look, look down here.'

The Purple-Bellied Parrot hopped down and peered at a point where the trunk met the stump of a limb. A hole, and stuffed into it — made from lawn clippings, bits of old string, twigs, strips of newspaper, spiders' webs, bin hair, lolly sticks and feathers — was a nest, all packed so tightly it was spilling out.

'Born in there, I was,' said Chalkie, nodding down, 'me and my brothers and sisters there anall. All fledged. Most of them still alive and peckin'. See them walter feathers?' Two huge white-striped feathers were sticking out. 'I nabbed them myself with my own chirper. My first coo.'

Chalkie hopped down beneath the trunk and peered up. 'Look there,' he sighed to himself. 'Gert and Stan's old nest. And there, Ron and Ethel's. Eight littlies they fledged last year.'

He hopped back up and looked about and was quiet again. The Purple-Bellied Parrot said nothing. Chalkie looked about at the plastic buildings and the broken trees. 'Now what we spost to do?' he said. 'All the holes in the park are taken. And there ain't no holes in houses no more — half-plastic they all are now. Ruddy bins.'

He leapt away and landed deep in the jumbled branches. The Purple-Bellied Parrot stared hard after him but soon lost him in the tangle. At last he heard, 'Oi! Come over 'ere!'

Relieved, the Purple-Bellied Parrot flew towards the voice and found Chalkie deep in the brash. He was sitting on a twig next to a pair of testicle seed pods; they were wizened and hard as stones.

'Fancy a game?'

But they only batted them once, and they fell off.

5

BRAZIL

Now that the Purple-Bellied Parrot was Ooterus Maximus and an 'onerable spuggie', he was invited to all the big conflabs. He was always invited to speak, and even though he could never think of anything to say, the spuggies all waited patiently for a split second before aheming and resuming the cacophony. He adored the spuggies, and he was happy and safe for the first time in his life, but deep down behind his purple belly something gnawed away. Sometimes he thought a mouse had moved in there. The mouse nagged him that the spuggies were not his kind and this was not his land. He had no clue where it might be, but he longed for the emerald forest, and for the hot sun and the scent of the sea, and maybe other birds with big hooters and purple bellies. He shivered at the prospect of another winter.

'I will go home,' he announced to himself one day as he watched a grey squall shroud the grey city and soak its streets. But where was home?

He asked the spuggies and even the maggies if they had seen a bird like him before, but they all said no. Araminta said that he should think himself lucky and 'not get ideas above his station.'

He asked some graces who roosted in the next tree, but they all shrugged, apart from one who pointed to a bunch perched by themselves further along the branch.[1] She said they might know because they were from across the sea somewhere, somewhere towards the rising sun. But they were just as clueless, and they had strange voices and made jokes that even the spuggies wouldn't find funny.

'Perhaps you are falling into a tin of green paint when you are a chick, yah?' suggested one, nudging his friends.

One evening while the sky turned the colour of oranges, he sidled up to a blackbird as he chortled out his song. The Purple-Bellied Parrot had always thought it a happy song, but the blackbird eyed him angrily at being interrupted and opened his wings to shoo him away. The Purple-Bellied Parrot waited until he'd finished singing and clapped his beak.

'I weesh I could sing in such a beautiful way,' he said.

The blackbird mellowed, a bit. 'I know what you want. I seen you going about pestering folk. But a piece of advice chum, you are asking the wrong birds.' He ruffled his feathers. 'Most of the birds around here have never travelled more than a spit from this park. You want to be asking some of them fellas what have just turned up.' He nodded up to the sky where black dots bucked and dived and caromed.

The Purple-Bellied Parrot had seen these newcomers whizzing through the skies, and the next day he asked the spuggies what they were and where they came from. They told him they were screamers, swallies and marties.[2]

'Bloomin' flash Harrys,' grumbled Alfie.

'Johnny-come-latelys,' muttered Vi.

But as for where they came from, they mostly shrugged and said they just turned up when the days got longer than the nights.

'There's some as say they live under ponds in the winter and only come out when the weather warms up.' Flo told him.

The Purple-Bellied Parrot thought that unlikely, so he went to ask Chalkie. He found him by the swings watching ants lugging grub back to their nest.

'Fascinating creatures,' Chalkie said. 'Their organization is amazing. We could learn a bit from them.' He swept a few up into his beak. 'Crikey, not-half tasty too.'

Anyway, all Chalkie had to offer on the newcomers was that they came from somewhere 'far away', before he pondered for a bit and pointed to the midday sun. 'Probably from that direction, "south" the bins call it, because that's where they always seem to fly in from. Come autumn they go back that way. Praps cos' it's warmer there. Hmm, now there's an idea.'

The Purple-Bellied Parrot wasn't sure about 'south', but 'far away' sounded promising. It was unlikely the emerald forest and the sea could be anywhere nearby.

On calm evenings, the Purple-Bellied Parrot watched the screamers chase each other, black-moon wings beating the air furiously, before spiralling higher and higher until lost from sight. He tried to follow the movement of their wings — he might learn something — but all he saw was a blur. It all seemed rather exhausting, but at least no moggies or tawnies up there.

He noticed them one day across the square, clinging to a wall at the top of a block of flats. They must be looking for somewhere to nest. He flew over and alighted on the edge of the roof and looked over, the wind buffeting him. He'd never been this high before and as he looked down he felt queasy. The screamers clung there, eyes constantly darting about, and when they did touch on him, they looked straight through him. But he never had a chance to ask his question. The screamers stayed hooked to the bricks only for a moment before they plunged away. One of them shrieked, 'Must fly. Must fly. Must fly,' as it hurtled off in pursuit. He'd never seen wings move so fast; each wing even appeared to be flapping independently. Such strange creatures — they might be from another world.

The next day he parked himself in a tree overlooking the

bowling green and watched the marties.[3] Their white bums flashed in the sun as they went about their business, catching flies or stuffing their mouths with gobbets of mud gathered from the trampled bit near the duck pond. They stuffed the gobbets of mud under the eaves of the pavilion roof.

It dawned on the Purple-Bellied Parrot that not everybody was born in a tree like he and Chalkie had been. And, watching the marties pack the mud under the roof, he remembered something he'd seen when he was outside the park with Chalkie, something he hadn't understood: netting hanging from the tops of bin houses, even bits of rope, hose and old bicycle tyre. Now, as the marties zoomed in under the eaves, he realised what they were for.

He decided the best time to talk to the marties would be at sunset. This was when they gathered on a wire stretching between the pavilion and a big pole, for what he guessed was their version of the conflab.

As he flew towards the wire, he remembered his nervous encounter with the screamers. The marties' way of flying was less frenzied; they took frequent glides, instead of constantly beating the air like it was their enemy. And, rather than shrieking, they chirruped gently to each other. These were going to be friendly birds.

The Purple-Bellied Parrot thought an indirect approach best, so he landed some distance along the wire, and then gingerly sidled over, making sure to take a deep interest in everything but the marties. New acquaintances usually found his appearance weird, if not downright hilarious, so the Purple-Bellied Parrot was ready for anything. But as he 'accidentally' nudged into their bunch, the marties carried on chirruping to each other. He wondered if they had even noticed him.

Finally, one of them turned and said, 'Alraht?'

The Purple-Bellied Parrot thought about this question for a moment and decided the best thing to do was to say 'Alright' back to him. The martie appeared satisfied with this and turned back to resume chatting with his pals. Relieved, the Purple-Bellied Parrot pondered how to get himself into the conflab. He didn't want to upset them like he'd done the blackbird.

Two other marties alighted and began to chatter. One, a female, turned and said, 'Alraht?'

'Alright, thank you.'

She looked at him for a bit, and then said, 'How was the trip?'

'Treep? What treep?'

The martie glanced at her mate. He was now holding his head high to catch the last rays of the sun.

'Well, you're clearly not from these parts. The trip — *the* trip, from down sahth?' She jerked her head in the direction of the midday sun.

The Purple-Bellied Parrot gazed at the two marties, beak slack, head cocked. The female scrutinised him from below a brow the colour of the sky on a full moon, her black eyes sparkling like they had tiny stars inside.

'Hmm, looking at you, you've not come as far as us. You're from the jungle somewhere, somewhere near the middle ... above the brown river somewhere.[4] Am I raht?'

The Purple-Bellied Parrot weighed up the question for a moment and groaned, 'I do not know. Maybe. I am trying to find out.'

'Hold on a mo,' she said. 'Of course. You guys don't make the trip do you. Year-rahnd jamboree for you down there in that jungle. As much fruit and nuts as you can stuff down your gizzard.'

'Whah don't we eat fruit n' nuts Millie?' said the sunbathing martie, still with his eyed closed. Make life a sight easier.'

Millie was bending to inspect the purple belly. After a moment she cried, 'I know what this guy is Steve — he's an escapee!'

'Yeah, raht Millie, anything you say babe.' Steve had begun to nod off.

'What did they do kid, take you as a chick?' Millie said. 'I bit you really don't know where you come from do you.'

'No. All I remember is the sea and the green forest, green the colour of me, and there were the yellow monsters then everything cold and dark and loud and stinky. I had a cage like a skin, and then there was the metal room that never stopped moving and then there was the man that smelled like old wee.' The words tumbled out like seed when the spuggies de-clogged a feeder. But then Millie was gone, a flick of the wings and of the tail, forked like a fish's.

Steve jerked awake and watched her go. 'Spotted a flah dude,' he explained. 'No martie can let a juicy flah go past. Against our nature so it is. Forgit your fancy-pants swallies swanking about with their 'Ooh look at me' red bibs and them long streamers. Look at us!' He stepped back so that the Purple-Bellied Parrot could take in the composition. 'Sleek, compact, agile, not one surplus barbule of plumage — we're the orca of the skies.' He snapped his beak a few times right in the Purple-Bellied Parrot's face, and then jerked his head high and chittered.

A blur of feathers and Millie was back, her beak crammed with a mush of insects, most still squirming. She presented them to Steve. The Purple-Bellied Parrot thought Steve would take just a few, but he chomped the lot. Millie continued the conversation like there'd been no interruption.

'We've seen your kahnd in the markets as we've flown over. In those tiny cages stacked one on top of the other. Bit that's what happened to you.'

'Yes, yes, I theenk so too.' He hardly dared ask the question. 'So … you know my home? Yes?'

'Might be,' said Millie.

The Purple-Bellied Parrot's heart soared. He felt a sudden urge to hang upside from the wire and swing about, but resisted it — he didn't want them to think he was crazy or anything —so he contented himself with a bit of head bobbing. 'So where is my land … my home?' he said when he'd calmed down

'Will, we're Efricans — Sahth Efricans,' Steve said. 'You fellas tend to come from the middle bit. We flah over your bit every year. We sometimes stop there to grab a bit of grub and a kip; great big fat rivers there are. Lots of flahs. Loooots of flahs. Yeah, that's where you'll be from dude.'

'So, I am from this place … this Efrica.' The Purple-Bellied Parrot gazed in the direction of the midday sun. 'Then that is where I must go, to my home.'

Millie was furrowing her brow. 'Now hold your pinions there fella, before you flah off on some wild bug chase. Steve's not always the most reliable when it comes to facts. He tends to have his mind on, erm, higher things. Isn't that right Steve?'

Steve, who had gone back to soaking up the sun, said, 'Aww, only two summers and already you know me so well babe.'

Millie reached over and preened him under the chin. Steve groaned, 'Oohhh yeeaaahh babe, right there,' and stretched his neck so tight he almost overbalanced and fell.

They stayed like this a good bit and, horrified, the Purple-Bellied Parrot thought for an awful moment they might start mating. The spuggies did that all the time and didn't care who was watching and even appreciated shouts of encouragement and offers of advice. But Millie stopped preening and, because he'd been pressing onto her so hard, Steve lurched forwards and nearly fell off the wire.

'That was real good babe,' he sighed, and pecked her on the cheek.

Millie turned back to the Purple-Bellied Parrot. 'Now I'm not sayin' you is, and I'm not sayin' you isn't from Efricah. Might be you're from some place I never heard of. But this is the seventh spring I've made this trip and storms, headwinds, big supplies of grub, mean I've hung around the land of the fat rivers a good few days. But in all my time there, I've never seen a bird quaht like you.' She glanced down. 'It's that. It's that purple belly. I'd remember it for sure.'

The Purple-Bellied Parrot looked down and contemplated his purple belly.

'And, the voice too. You don't talk like any Efrican I've ever met.'

The Purple-Bellied Parrot looked towards the south and thought for a good bit. Then he said very slowly, 'Thees Efricah, does it have many beeg trees the colour of my feathers?'

'Yis,' said Millie. Steve was now fast asleep.

'Is the sun very hot?'

'Yis.'

'When you were there, could you smell the salt of the sea?'

'Yis.'

'Is it possible we might have been there, but that you just didn't see us? Perhaps we are shy.'

'Yis ... yis, it's possible.'

'Then, I theenk this, thees Efricah, is my home.'

Millie sighed. 'It could be. I'm not saying it isn't. You just need to be sure. It's many days travel — even if the wind is in the raht direction. You have to fly over ocean where you can't stop to rest unless you are a duck — which you most certainly aren't — and desert you can't cross unless you are a camel — ditto. When you reach the forest there's a million mouths just waiting to chomp you. You think your maggies and moggies are bad here? Wait till you meet the noras and the crownies and the lions!'[5]

But the Purple-Bellied Parrot had stopped listening. 'Yes, I must go home. I must go home to,' he paused to test out his new word, 'Efricah.' Then he said it again more slowly: 'Ehhfreecaahh.' It sounded like a deep breath held long when you were hiding from a moggie, held till you couldn't hold it any longer, until you were about to gasp and then you knew you were safe and you could let it out: 'Eh-free-cahhh.' It sounded a good place to live.

Chalkie found him the next morning doing loop-the-loops in the middle of a hazel. As he twirled around he was singing, 'Yippee! I am from Efricah … I am from Efricah … I am from Efricah! Yippee!' He released one foot and twirled around on just one, and then swopped round. He spotted Chalkie and stopped twirling.

'Chalkie! Chalkie! I am from Efricah!'

'So I hear,' said Chalkie. Where were you last night?

'It is in the direction of the midday sun!'

'I believe so.' The spuggies knew a bit about Africa from watching telly outside Me-and-Er. 'Probably a long way you know. And what about all that water?'

'I do not care about water. I am going home.'

Later, when they met for the evening conflab, the spuggies told him all about the sea.

Chalkie said that he had seen the sea once. As a young spuggletto he had woken up one spring morning and decided he would go and see what happened to the fat river. He followed it right to the end. It got fatter and fatter until he looked around and all the land was behind him, and all was water with big boats floating about on it and georges flying about.[6] But the water wasn't like the water in the river or the duck pond. It was moving constantly, up and down, up and down, like it was alive — like it was breathing. The wind was not that strong, but when it gusted the sea threw itself up into little peaks, and Chalkie wondered what those peaks must be like during a storm.

Reg chirped in and said he knew a spuggie from Cheepside called Archie who'd also seen the sea. But that was all he had to offer on the subject, and Gert told him off for wasting everybody's time. But as they had all seen the sea on the telly — they were all experts.

So the spuggies told the Purple-Bellied Parrot that it is like a hungry grey monster that you can never creep past because it never sleeps, and it is so big you can peer out on the clearest day and never see the end of it. You'd fly and you'd fly as it heaved beneath you, waiting to swallow you up, its patience limitless. Surely there must be land soon, and you fly on, wondering if you should turn back — until you know it is too late. You don't have the strength to go back, and now all you can do is go on, and on. You search the horizon, but you see only more sea, heaving, waiting. You panic and, though your wings already scream out for rest and your lungs are about to burst, you flap harder, till your wings give their last beat and you tumble, feathers riffling, down towards the hungry grey monster, to land with a 'plop' nobody hears.

The spuggies loved scaring the pants off folks.

A day much like any other: conflab, grub, dust bath, conflab. Late morning, Vi had spotted a hoodie bin dropping half a burger next to the goalposts, and now the spuggies and the Purple-Bellied Parrot were gorging themselves.

The spuggie sentry, Stan, was distracted. Instead of keeping 'em peeled for moggies and spugghawks, ready with the approved call of 'CheeeiIP,' he was watching them all scoffing, salivating and thinking about his turn. 'Oi! Save some for me!' he yelled, hopping about.

Wings closed, the spugghawk exploded out of a gap in the privets.

'CheeeIP!' Stan yelled, too late.

They rose as one and scattered, and the hawk, confused by all the flapping bodies and whirling feathers, hesitated, as if spoilt for choice. She reached out a bald leg and flicked out a talon to pluck Flo away, but missed. In a trice she had wheeled around — like the handbrake turns the hoodie bins did outside the park — and was attacking again. In the blurring feathers and spiralling dust, her yellow eye caught a contrast of green and purple.

The Purple-Bellied Parrot squawked when he saw the spug-ghawk in pursuit. This was not supposed to happen. Spugghawks don't bother pursuing — Chalkie had told him. If they don't get you first go they go and sit in a tree for a bit. Ambush is their tactic. One minute you are having a nice dust bath; the next: WHAM! An explosion of browny-grey feathers and its croakage time for one of you or one of your chums. Old Cecil it was last time, dangling from the talons going 'cheep.' But perhaps the Purple-Bellied Parrot had seemed slower and clumsier than those little brown jobbies. Perhaps he'd just seemed bigger and juicier.

The Purple-Bellied Parrot glanced behind and saw the yellow eyes getting bigger. Dense foliage, dense foliage. 'Dive into dense foliage,' that's what the spuggies had drilled into him, pronouncing 'foliage,' 'foli*arge*.' But now there was no dense foliarge. His panic had propelled him into the streets of brick and glass and concrete.

'Anyway, you can't outfly spugghawk,' the spuggies had said. 'Like a Ferrari on wings.'

So that was it. He didn't know what a Ferrari was but he knew he was a gonner. He waited for the stab of the talon. 'Then they nip you on the back of the neck for the "coo de grace".' And just when he was about to go home.

The Purple-Bellied Parrot flew as fast as he could and weaved about. Still the hawk hadn't struck. Perhaps she was getting on a bit. Perhaps she was toying with him.

He swooped down and weaved about among the bins.

'Ooh!'

'Oi!'

'Hey!'

'Whhoooaah!'

'Well I never!'

He saw a grinning kiddie bin come out of a shop holding an ice cream, and heard him wail as it plopped onto the ground. A car pulled up at a junction, the windows open, a beat blasting out. He closed his wings and dived through, 'What the!'

The spugghawk followed.

A bin wheeling out a barrowload of oranges. The bin diving out of the way and the oranges tumbling onto the floor and rolling into the street. The bin falling backwards into a stack of cardboard boxes which too fell into the street. Cars screeching to a halt, horns blaring, driver bins yelling. As he climbed away from the mayhem, the Purple-Bellied Parrot glanced back and saw wheelbarrow bin climb to his feet and shake his fist — and *her* yellow eyes.

It was like she was tied to him by a very short piece of string.

He glanced in a shop window. He was beating the air like a screamer. She was cruising; she even took the odd glide. He saw her flick out a talon. He saw her inspect it and, as though she'd spotted a speck of dirt, polish it on her plumage and then hold it up to the light to admire its gleam.

They reached a street corner and, like she'd grown bored of the chase, she closed in for the kill. The Purple-Bellied Parrot saw an old telephone wire dangling from the wall of Napolina Pizza. She unfurled her talons and reached forward. The Purple-Bellied Parrot stretched out a foot and made a grab for the wire. The talons snapped shut.

Her only trophy was a single green feather, and when she spread her tail to wheel around and give chase, incredibly, the green and purple thing had vanished.

The Purple-Bellied Parrot had grabbed the wire and hand-brake-turned around the corner, but he'd forgotten to let go. The last thing he saw was green, a green the like of which he had never seen before — except on himself: luxuriant, dense, safe. Foli*arge*.

'WHAAMMMPFFF.'

The green was all hard. For an instant he thought how unfair it all was, but then he began to slide down, like the hard bits in spuggie poo on a clean window. But the green wasn't concrete-hard, and though he was dazed and the puff had been clobbered out of him, he told himself to cling to the green because it would make him safe.[7] With a 'Huuuuuttttt', he dug in his claws — only a barbule's breadth — but it was enough.[8]

And the bins below, dreaming of tropical holidays, gazing up at the rainforest with its monkeys and macaws and jaguars and porcupines and tapirs and toucans and green parrots, never saw that the paper forest contained the real thing, scrunched and trembling against its foliage, tail resting on the top of a huge red B, part of the slogan which implored:

Visit Brazil!

The Purple-Bellied Parrot clung on to the hard forest. It took a few minutes for his head to clear. Then he risked a look behind. Walters, a few graces, walters, a maggie, more walters — but no spugghawk! He relaxed his claws and instantly slid down. So he re-fixed them and pondered what to do.

He sensed he was being watched. In a panic, he glanced behind, but no living thing was taking the remotest interest in him. He leaned away from the hard forest. Two eyes were peering out. They were eyes like his. The eyes sandwiched a big hooter like his, and both were connected to a body of green plumage — like his green plumage. It was like looking in the mirror, the one the pink-faced man had put in the cage to stop him pulling his feathers out.

The Purple-Bellied Parrot cocked his head; he bobbed his head, he circled his head, but the head didn't mimic him like it had in the pink-faced man's flat. He pecked at it. It was hard, not like him, and — seeing as it didn't wince or peck back — he had a chew. Part of the head peeled away leaving a white spot; but the peeling felt nothing like his feathers. More like the paper from a tin of pineapple chunks. The Purple-Bellied Parrot thought about all the creatures that lived inside the telly and concluded this bird must be something like them.

He glanced around again to check all was safe, and then leapt away from the hoarding. He flew about a bit, scrutinizing the bird but not a bird and the forest but not a forest. He sensed the hot sun, and the salt of the sea. The bin symbols: 'Visit Brazil'. They must be the key. One of these symbols was familiar — but from where, and what did it mean?

He flew back to the park and sat at the top of a tall poplar near the bandstand.

He thought hard. The symbol was connected with his early days in the flat, when the pink-faced man was still friendly. Sometimes he'd bring over a small packet and dangle it in front of the Purple-Bellied Parrot.

'Here you are, a little taste of home.'

He'd rip open the packet and take out nuts. Mottled brown and white, they all were crunchy and oily — and the Purple-Bellied Parrot loved them. And always he'd say, 'A little taste of home for you … Isn't it … Yeeess … It is, isn't it … Yeeess … A taste of home.'

Now he remembered. On the packet was the same symbol: 'Brazil.' Somehow Brazil was connected with home.

Brazil must have something to do with Efricah.

'Do you know anybody who can read bin seembols?' He'd clattered into the spuggies' privet by the tennis courts, all puffed out, and they nearly fell off their perches when he shot into their midst mid-conflab like a shanked ball.

They had thought he was a gonner, 'Spugghawk poo for sure by now,' Alfie said.

'Probably spat out that big hooter though. Looked proper indigestibable did that,' said Vi. She caught Chalkie's eyes boring into her, and looked down.

Before answering his question Chalkie wanted to know all about his escape. So he told them about the pandemonium in the street and the handbrake turn and the hard forest and the paper bird, and at the end Chalkie said, 'Crikey!'

'Ahh, that sounds like your h'advertising does that,' Reg piped up. 'Lucky bit of camarflooarge was that.'

'Anyway,' said Alfie, landing beside him, 'you're just in time. We was just about to have a little wakey-wakey for you.'[9]

'Yeays, but — the seembols.'

'All in good time, all in good time my green and purple hooter transporter. We was all rather upset at your demise, and so Flo here wrote you a little h'omelette.'

Flo nudged him hard and whispered into his ear.

'Ahem, ah … it seems it's an 'omilee. Well, whatever it is, here it is.'

Flo stepped forward, patted down a tuft of dun plumage that had sprung up, tucked a wing tip under her breast feathers and cheeped:

> Oh green parrot of the green green woods so fairest fair
> Gone from us you are to a spugghawk's lair
> To be chomped and guzzled by chicks hawkish
> And no danger of them gettin, like, mawkish.

Flo turned cheepishly, ''Ad a bit of trouble with that bit I did.'

'Doesn't scan,' said Gert.

'Clumsy arse-sonance,' said Sid.

'Diabolical metre,' said Roy.

'Gerron with it!' yelled Vi.

> *Oh fain! Of your like never more will we see the ilk*
> *Notwithstanding having no one to open our milk*
> *Oh espy! To a forest in Jove's sky our hero goes*
> *Forever and h'eternity remembered as 'Old Big Nose.'*
> *Hark ...*

'Yes, yes, alright, alright, very moving I'm sure,' Alfie interrupted. 'I'm getting hungry for one of them vole-ev-ants, so let's get down to business. Now then, these bloomin symbols. What are you rabbiting on about?'

'I memorized them. Look.'

The Purple-Bellied Parrot leapt off his twig and dropped down to a patch of dust. He scratched out the letters with his beak, 'Visit Brazil!'

'Anybody know what thees means?'

The spuggies looked at one another and began to cheep very loudly all at the same time. A full-scale conflab was in danger of developing.

'Quiet Quiet QuiET! For once, could we please have a bit of bloomin shush.' Alfie nodded down to the Purple-Bellied Parrot, 'Get back up here before some moggie gets you. I couldn't abide another one of them bloomin h'omelettes.'

Meanwhile, Chalkie had been studying the symbols. Now he piped up. 'They are words — bin words. There is only one spuggie who can read bin words, and we all know who that is.' He glanced around the gang. 'Anybody feel like going to fetch him?'

6

OLD STUMPY

The Purple-Bellied Parrot knew Old Stumpy was something of spuggie legend. Known as 'Umpee' to his closest chums, he was the oldest and wisest spuggie in their gang. He was called 'Old Stumpy' because he was old and he only had one foot. The Purple-Bellied Parrot admired the common sense in the name. Old Stumpy was so old he remembered the days before the plastic houses when there were still holes for the spuggies to nest. He was so old he remembered a time before kebabs were invented.

Old Stumpy lived in the top of an old oak on the edge of the park near the railway line. He spent his days hunched on his favourite twig, feathers all fluffed out, watching the goings-on, idly aiming poos at passing bins. It was the perfect spot for him. One side of his twig looked out over the field beyond the railway cutting where the bins played 'creekeet'. The other side looked into a street named after a dianthus flower.[1] Spuggletti were tasked with ensuring he had a steady supply of grub all day, but this was no plum job.[2] Old Stumpy was famously a grumpy sod. Either he'd tell them to 'Bugger off' (after taking the food of course — he especially liked bits of Battenburg), or he'd grumble about the young spuggies and their crazy plumage-dos or the crash in the quality of kebabs or he'd tell endless stories about his heroics in the maggie wars, all delivered in an indignant monotone. Nobody liked Old Stumpy. But he could read bin words.

Old Stumpy didn't like lots of visitors bending his perch and interrupting his creekeet, so Gert volunteered Reg to go and fetch him.

'This might take a good bit of time,' Chalkie said. 'Old Stumpy hates being shifted off his twig.' So the Purple-Bellied Parrot asked him how Old Stumpy had ended up in the park. Chalkie warned him that the story was very long and it was hard to work out which bits were true.

Old Stumpy came from Yorkshire. One of his oft-repeated sayings was, 'I'm Yorkshire, I am!' He often said it at the end of heated conflabs before stomping off, like that was the end of the matter and further discussion was pointless. Yorkshire was one of the few things that the spuggies could be certain of about Old Stumpy.

How he had ended up in the city though, well, Old Stumpy was always fly. Sometimes he told them that, in search of fame and fortune, he'd flown all the way down, non-stop. Other times he told them that he'd hitched a lift, clinging to the tailfin of a passing jumbo, feathers a-ruffling, feet a-flappin. Chalkie, though, believed he'd got the real story.

He'd found Old Stumpy one evening wobbling about on his twig singing to himself. He appeared to be happy, and this was very odd. He even invited Chalkie to share his twig. Below was an upended can of beer — a brown puddle spilling out onto the tarmac. He asked Chalkie if he'd like to hear the real story of how he ended up in 'this poo-hole.'

Old Stumpy didn't wait for a reply.

One day, 'up north' on his local patch, Young Stumpy noticed a van pulled over in the lay-by. The driver was munching a sandwich and dipping into a bag of crisps. Young Stumpy noticed that she'd put a crisp in first and then take a bite of the sandwich, without biting the crisp, and then munch them both together. This is the kind of detail that Old Stumpy liked to put into his stories. Anyway, it was a hot day and the driver wanted the breeze to blow through, so she had opened the back doors and wound all the windows down. Young Stumpy followed each crisp on its journey from packet to cakehole. Slobber dripped from his beak. He watched, longing to see a stray crumb ping out of the window. None did, and he saw her screw the packet up and jam it in the angle between the dashboard and windscreen. Heartbroken, his gaze drifted along the side of the van. There, in bold letters, he noticed something just as tantalizing:

Beauchamp's Bulk Bird Seed
Suppliers to pigeon fancier's, budgerigars and canary breeders [3]

Young Stumpy couldn't read — that would be bonkers — but by this time he had learned to link certain of these human symbols to the possession of a full belly. Two of these symbols he recognised: 'Bird' and 'Seed.' Whenever he had come across these two squiggles before, decent grub had always been got — got without grubbing about in dirt.

Young Stumpy flew over to inspect.

He scented the seed before he landed, and sure enough, there, just inside the back door, a split sack was spilling its golden scrumptiousness. He couldn't help but let out a loud cheep. The driver jerked round. She surveyed her load for a moment, and shrugged and went back to her Curly-Wurly.

'Must be silent. Shilentahh … shilent as a fart at the queen's funeral,' Young Stumpy whispered to himself.

He lost count of how many silent trips he made, his beak and crop so stuffed that he could hardly take off.[4] He took it all away to a hidey-hole in a warty hawthorn to stash as a winter cache. 'What luck!' he congratulated himself. 'At this reet I won't have to go out fer't whole winter and grub about in all that perishin' cold.'

Young Stumpy did not return to his gang to tell them about the grub he had plundered. 'Just one more load and then I'll goo and tell em,' he excused himself, after tightly packing each batch. And then his cache was full — no room not even for one tiny oatletie. He arranged a curtain of moss to cover his cache; he kicked twigs and bits of bark onto it, and, as the final touch, he hovered over it and pooed. He stood back and said, 'Aye, that's reet champion.'

An idea struck him. 'I know, I'll goo back t't van and stuff me face so much — I won't have t'eat for another week!' and he gorged and guzzled and chomped so much that he keeled over and fell flat on his back, and it took some kicking and fluttering to right himself.

Movement from the front of the van. Time to scoot.

He sprang his legs and flapped. But no gap appeared between his feet and the metal floor.

He was so stuffed, he couldn't take off.

What to do? He considered sicking-up some of the seed. What a waste. Walk back to the hawthorn? Don't be silly. He peered towards the darker recesses of the van, at the escarpment of sacks, and began to climb.[5] He had to flutter and clamber and slither, but finally, gasping, he reached the summit. He took a deep breath, looked out to the square of sunshine and green framed by the van doors, and jumped.

He was flapping as usual, but it was like he had turned into a tortoise or something. He plummeted. He wasn't going to make it. Then a breeze rattled through the doors and lifted him. He dived for the sunshine and green.

'Creeeeaak.'

The square of sunshine and green rapidly narrowed.

'ClUu-Uu-Uu-Uunnngggg!'

Darkness. Young Stumpy couldn't stop and flew right into the door. It marked him for life.

He woke up to the click and creak of the door opening again. As the driver began unloading, he dragged himself into a gap between the sacks. Young Stumpy peered out: no warty hawthorn or green or sunshine. Brick, concrete and cars — endless cars — and big red buses. Grey rain beat on a grey pavement. Din, constant din. And above all the din, in the distance somewhere, a big bell clonged.

'Bugger.'

***

Chalkie nudged the Purple-Bellied Parrot. 'Here he comes.'

The Purple-Bellied Parrot found he was holding his breath. He'd never met Old Stumpy, but had heard tell of his awesome grumpiness and clobbering put-downs, so he was determined to keep on his good side. He heard him before he saw him.

'Ouch ... ooh me leg. What the ra-hoody hell ... just when I'd put me feet up. Dragged down ere through all this ruddy foliage just when I'm settling down to watch me ... ouch ... ooh ... bugger.'

Chalkie whispered, 'Only cheap when you're chopen too, don't look him in the eye, and for Gawd's sake don't stare. You'll soon know what not to stare at. Oh, and he talks funny — just ignore it.'

The leaves rustled and parted and, at first, the Purple-Bellied Parrot thought Reg was dragging in a discarded tennis ball that had rolled through the mud and had a twig stuck in it. It was certainly no use to the thwackers and tonkers because it was all saggy and mostly bald with a just few tufty bits sticking up. He blinked and saw the most wizened-up spuggie he had ever seen. As well as the absence of plumage, the warty nub of his missing foot dangled as he croffled along, and he had the weirdest beak. It was almost non-existent, as if all the years of grubbing about for food had worn it down to a knobby stump. But there was something even more strange about the beak. The bottom mandible was longer than the top mandible, and it was turned upwards — like the hook of a spugghawk's beak, but in reverse. It looked like he'd been whacked in the face by a moggie, or perhaps had a door slammed in his face and was enormously grumpy about it.

The Purple-Bellied Parrot found his gaze was anchored to the beak. Chalkie gave him a dig in the ribs, but he was spellbound. Something else, though, wrenched his gaze away. As Old Stumpy got nearer, the Purple-Bellied Parrot saw that he only possessed one eye. But it was a lively eye; it was the most alive part of him, and it was constantly on the move, darting hither and thither looking, the Purple-Bellied Parrot thought, for weakness. Finally it settled on the Purple-Bellied Parrot.

'What! What the rahuddy hell … What in buggeration do we 'ave here,' he said, followed by, 'Just look at t'hooter on that!' His beak emitted a grating noise; it sounded like a maggie scraping out the last bits from a pineapple tin. It was Old Stumpy's laugh.

'Now, now Umpee,' said Gert. 'Be polite, he just wants to ask you a quick question, and then you can get back to watching Carnation Street.'[6]

'Ewd up, ewd up.'

Old Stumpy hopped over to the Purple-Bellied Parrot and inspected him from head to toe, his vital eye roving over all his nooks and crannies. When he'd finished, he hopped back a couple of steps.

'Foreign bugger I'll be bound,' and he turned away, chuntering, 'Cummin over 'ere and taking all our cobs.'

As he turned, a rare feather dropped from his body. But it didn't see-saw to the ground or get wafted by the breeze like a normal feather. It dropped, ricocheting off a twig, to land on the ground with a 'crump' and vanish in a puff of dust.

'Crikey, he's dropping to bits,' Chalkie whispered.

'Now then, Umpee. No need for racialism,' said Gert. 'We just want to ask you what these two words mean and you can be on your way.'

'What's in it for me?' Old Stumpy chupped.

Gert sighed and nodded to Sid and Betty. 'Bring it out then chaps.'

The two spuggies reached into the foliage and dragged out a chunk of yellow cake. Battenburg, with plenty of marzipan and jam — Old Stumpy's favourite. It was grubby and a bit nibbly round the edges, but he wouldn't mind that.

'All you can eat of this.'

'Now you are talkin. Gis a nibble. I have to test the merchandise before I commit me'sen.'

'Okay, chaps, just a crumblet,' said Gert.

Betty snipped off a bit, more than a crumblet, more like a smidgeon really, but she was expert with her snippage — it held the scrummy trinity of cake and marzipan and jam.[7] She shuffled along the twig past the other spuggies, 'Scuse I ... pardon I,' and deposited it with exaggerated — some might say sarcastic — ceremony which involved a cavalier flourish of the primaries, at the feet of Old Stumpy. He sniffed it twice, and then it was so quick the Purple-Bellied Parrot almost missed it. In an instant he had hooked it on his bottom mandible, flicked up in the air and down his gaping chirper.

Old Stumpy coughed. He coughed again and tried to speak but only a squeak came out. Because it had no feathers on it you could see his face and it was going all red, and his one eye looked like it was going to pop out. He retched. Somebody shouted, 'Quick! Give him the heinz-lick manoeuvre!' Chalkie reached over and gave him an enormous clout on the mantle. Old Stumpy coughed once more, was silent, and then gulped. The Purple-Bellied Parrot watched the lump of Battenburg travel down his neck, and when it disappeared he heard a faint 'splosh.'

Old Stumpy shook himself, made the sound 'Brooooagghh,' paused, and said, 'Nice bit of Battenburg was that. A mite dry, but a nice bit 'o keeirk nonetheless.' He preened a feather — which promptly fell out. He said, 'Bugger.' He trumped, and then said, 'Now then, weir are them words?'

They all dropped down to a low twig and surveyed the symbols the Purple-Bellied Parrot had scratched. The Purple-Bellied Parrot bobbed up and down. Old Stumpy remained silent.

'Well? Can you tell me what theese mean?'

'By eck, toks reet funny duntee,' said Old Stumpy.

His eye surveyed the inscriptions. He stayed silent for a long time. He started retching again and for a moment looked like he was going to vomit the Battenburg onto the words. Then he was quiet again.

Someone shouted, 'Gerron-with-it.' It sounded like Alfie.

Gert stepped forward. 'Stop wastin time Umpee. You're just building up the suspense so we offer you more Battenburg. That ain't going to happen. Now, are you able to tell us what these words mean or not.'

Old Stumpy's eye searched the writing once more. 'Well …' He paused again; he noted a dishevelled feather on his breast and preened it. It fell out. He turned back to the scratches in the dust. 'Well, I'm not saying I is, and I'm not saying I isn't.' Now he was talking like an old-timer in a western.[8]

Gert nodded to Sid and Betty. 'Right, down the grid with it.'

The two spuggies flew off to a nearby storm drain and dangled the Battenburg above the abyss.

'Ewd up. Ewd up. Ewd UP! Ruddy hell … always in a ruddy rush the younger generation.' He turned to Gert. 'Now then, I get all that chunko?'

'Every last crumbletini.'

'Well, I only know one word. It's a place. It says ... It says Brazil. Brazil is a place — where the nuts come from. I've et many a fine Brazil nut me'sen. Grand they are.' He turned to Sid and Betty. 'Now, take that keeirk back to my twig pronto.' His one eye winked at Betty. 'And if you want to hang about a bit when you get there, there's many a fine tune played on an old fiddle.' It winked again. Betty shuddered. 'Reet, I'm off.'

'Now you hold on a mo,' said Gert, and she asked the question the Purple-Bellied Parrot was desperate to ask but was so excited he hadn't worked it out yet, 'Where is this Brazil?'

'Buggered if I know. But reckon it's somewhere warm to grow them nuts. They don't grow on trees round here you know. And, if it's somewhere warm, I'm tellin you, it's somewhere south, because believe you me, the further up north you get the colder it gets. And it'll be somewhere nice. Not like this poo-hole where you have to fly about arse first t'keep t't crap out your eyes. I'm telling you. I'm Yorkshire you know.'

With that he trumped and clambered back into the foliage and, apart from ever fainter 'Bugger's, was gone.

7

DOGHOUSE AND DOLDRUMS

S o, Brazil was his home. Brazil was south. Brazil was nice. Was Brazil in Efricah? Didn't matter. Both were south. Head south and he would find out. South, must go south. But now? Alone?

At dusk the Purple-Bellied Parrot flew off to see Millie and Steve. They had built a nest now, in the corners of the old pavilion round the corner from the café.

'Alraht dude?' Steve said as he settled beside him. He couldn't see Millie.

'Alright thank you', said the Purple-Bellied Parrot.

They sat together on the gutter above the nest, silent for a moment. Then the Purple-Bellied Parrot said, 'Is Millie around?'

'She is. But I have to tell you dude, you're in the doghouse.'

The Purple-Bellied Parrot gazed around the park for a moment. Then he said, 'Where is thees doghouse, and why am I in it? I do not like dogs.'

'The doghouse, *the* doghouse dude.' Steve searched the sky. 'It means you're persona non grata.'[1]

The Purple-Bellied Parrot looked at him, head cocked.

'It means … you are in disfavour.' Steve sighed like he'd just done a big poo. He looked hard at the Purple-Bellied Parrot. 'You've done something bad dude.'

The Purple-Bellied Parrot's jaw dropped open. Steve went off to catch flies, and meanwhile the Purple-Bellied Parrot racked his brain. What could he have done? When Steve returned he said, 'Pleeze tell me what I did.'

'I'll let her tell you.'

Steve chirruped, and an answering chirrup came from the nest. 'She's incubating,' Steve said. The Purple-Bellied Parrot peered over and saw Millie's head poking out of the entrance.

'Ahh, it's him. Tell him I don't want to talk to him.'

'She doesn't want to talk to you dude,' said Steve.

'And get him away from here. They've probably followed him.'

'You need to leave dude.'

'But, what did I do?' said the Purple-Bellied Parrot.

A flash of blue and white and Millie was out of the nest and beside him.

'What did you do? What did you do? Are you kidding me? You are with *thim*.' She searched the park and the sky above frantically. 'Get away from here, now.'

'But who is *them*?' the Purple-Bellied Parrot sobbed.

'Don't act like you don't know. *Thim* — the spuggies. They are probably watching us right now. Waiting for their chance.'

The Purple-Bellied Parrot had nothing left to say. He sobbed a bit more.

Steve nestled up close to him. 'Sorry dude, time to go.'

'Okay,' he said, 'I go now. I do not know what I did, but I am very sorry.' He opened his wings.

'Wait,' Millie said. 'Tell me you don't know about the spuggies.' She was glancing nervously around.

'The spuggies? Pleeze. I do not know what you are talking about.'

Millie stared at him a long time. She looked at Steve and nodded towards the nest. Steve said, 'Oh yeah. Right babe,' and dived in to incubate. She looked back at the Purple-Bellied Parrot.

'You really don't know do you,' she said.

'Know what?' he croaked.

So Millie told him. Told him about the how the marties come every year, they fly all this way and build their nests. Spend days ferrying gobbets of mud about. Sometimes they have to fly miles to find it. And what happens? What do *they* do? No sooner have they finished than the spuggies come along, the big beefy loud-mouthed spuggies, and turf them out. It had happened the last couple of years, so they thought they'd try the park this year. And then then he comes along — all butter wouldn't melt. And guess who he's chummy with.

The Purple-Bellied Parrot thought hard for a moment and said, 'I understand. I go now. But I come back soon.' And he raced away.

He found the spuggies easily; they were engaged in their pre-kip conflab, and the din carried a long way. He took Chalkie to one side and told him what Millie had said.

'I have heard of that,' said Chalkie, 'but it ain't nothing that our gang would do. You know our lot — they're too lily-livered.' He turned to the rest of the gang. 'Oi you lot! What do you reckon to this? Goo on. Tell them.'

The Purple-Bellied Parrot repeated the story, and they all expressed deep shock, apart from, he noticed, the two biggest and oldest spuggies, Stan and Gert, who shuffled about and looked at their toes.

Alfie said that he had never heard of such a thing, and suggested that they, 'take a spuggie oath to make sure that it don't happen to them two marties Old Bignose is pals with.' The custom was to swear on the life of the most recently croaked of the gang. Alfie hopped up to a higher twig.

'Spuggies, repeat after me.'

'After me,' they chorused

'You bloomin well do that every time and it's wearing thin. Nah then, ahem, after me ... I do solemnly swear ...' The spuggies repeated the oath. 'On behalf of the plaintiff residing in this ere park ... the Onerable Spuggie what is known as ... Old Bignose ... Ooterus Maximus ... Schnozzmeister General ... upon the life of our most recently croaked Charlie ... h'erstwhile maggie fighter and moggie tormenter h'extraordinaire ... mile-away chip spotter incomparabile ... what is nah pushin up the daisies ... that heretoforthwith we the spuggies of the park ... shall henceforth renounce and repudiate the einous h'activity ... of turfin them marties out their nests ... Specifically speakin, them marties with the names of ...' He whispered to the Purple-Bellied Parrot, 'Whass the names of them bloomin marties again?' The spuggies repeated that too. '... Minnie and Beefy ... and that they shall heretoforthwith be left in peace ... to bring up their sprogs ... while we the spuggies of the hereto-aforementioned park ... reside in the park, erm, what I just mentioned ... Amen.'

'Amen.'

The Purple-Bellied Parrot bobbed his head. 'I must go back and tell Millie and Steve that they are safe,' he cried.

Vi chuckled, 'Alfie said "anus activity".'

Before the Purple-Bellied Parrot rushed off, Chalkie told him that he needn't worry, the spuggies had found a couple of holes in an ash tree that has recently croaked near Old Stumpy, although he was pretty sure Old Stumpy wasn't the culprit. Vera and Madge had laid, and the rest of them were going to muck-in to bring the littlies up.

It wasn't the spuggies they should have been worrying about. The next day, while Steve was out hunting, a bin opened an upstairs window and started poking at their nest with a broom handle.

'Teach you to ruddy-well mess on my windows,' he said.

Millie and Steve had built it well. The mud had set like concrete, and it wouldn't budge. While he poked, a shrieking Millie buzzed past his head, and twice she managed to slap him with her wing. After a bit the bin gave up and closed the window, and Millie went back to incubate the eggs. But soon she heard a clanging outside and looked out to see a ladder, and the bin climbing up. He was holding a hammer.

She did her best, but the bin slapped her away, and soon the nest lay on the ground in bits. Mixed in with the shards she saw the yellow yoke of her eggs.

Something odd then happened. Three other bins arrived, two young females and a male. They shouted at hammer bin and pointed at the broken nest. A huge row broke out with lots of arm waving and soon other bins came to watch, and some joined in. A grey-haired female tried to whack hammer bin with an umbrella.

The next day the Purple-Bellied Parrot watched Millie and Steve plastering gobbets of mud in the eaves again — this time well away from the windows. He wished he could help, but knew that his beak was the wrong shape.

***

'Brazil! Did you say Brazil?'

A gloomy dusk, he and Millie sat on the ridge tiles. Steve was below, incubating the new eggs. The Purple-Bellied Parrot had thought it best to wait a couple of days until they were settled in their new nest before he asked them.

'Yeays, Brazeel. I was told that it is south. Is Brazeel in Efricah?'

'Who told you?'

The Purple-Bellied Parrot said that a friend had told him.

'Spuggie was it? Bit it was a spuggie. Trouble with spuggies is they only know half the story.' She took a deep breath. 'So,

Brazil eh? Hmm. Well, it is south, but I'm pretty sure it's not in Efricah.'

'What!'

'Yep. I've heard talk of it. An albatross I know spoke of it once. I wasn't paying much attention, but I remember he talked like it was far away. And he'd know. What those wanderers don't know about the sahth you could write on the back of a fairy wasp.[2] They can flah this land from top to bottom in one day.'

'Far away? Is it across a beeg ocean?' the Purple-Bellied Parrot choked out. Spuggies' tales of ocean ploppages flashed through his mind, and he felt like he'd been thumped in the belly by Big Maggie.

'Don't know. When we flah sahth and we hit Africa, there's a big ocean that stretches away to the sunset. But I don't know how big it is. No martie or swallow I know has flown across it, or if they have, they sure haven't come back.'

The Purple-Bellied Parrot's head thudded onto his breast.

'There is land beyond that ocean,' Millie continued. 'The albatrosses talk of a great land, way bigger than this, a land of fire and smoke, of vast savannah they call another name and endless green forests and steamy rivers, a land of strange creatures. Perhaps you are one of those strange creatures.'

'So Brazeel is there, across thees great ocean?'

'Could be. But there are other lands in the sahth. For all I know, Brazil could be just beyond the savannah where we winter. Could be where the sun rahses. Only the albatrosses have seen all the lands. You would need to ask them.'

'But how?'

Millie looked up to the sky as though scanning for flies. A big bluebottle droned by, but she ignored it. Steve popped his head out of the nest and said, 'It's okay, babe. Go ahead.'

Millie sighed, 'That albatross I spoke of, you fly sahth with us and you'll meet him. He lives on the edge of the great desert.'

The Purple-Bellied Parrot was silent as his mind churned. It took a moment to dawn on him that Millie was inviting him to fly south with her and Steve. He wanted to jump up and down and fly around the park and find a smooth branch and swing around it. He was so excited, all that came out of his beak was, 'Millie, what is an albatross?' [3]

The Purple-Bellied Parrot soon realised that he would have to wait out the rest of the summer until Millie and Steve left. For the time it takes for a spuggie to eat a crumblet he thought about setting off alone. But how would he find the way? Let alone find the albatross. And there might be sea, and he sure couldn't cross that alone.

He still did his chores for the gang, opening packets and tins, snipping off twigs for them to shore up their nests, standing sentry. He still joined the spuggies in their daily bouts of mischief. But even as he watched the spuggies playing his favourite game at the pavilion tearoom: pinching the currants out of the teacakes and rattling the teaspoons for derring-do, his mind drifted away to settle on the great journey ahead.

He began to spend long hours alone, high in the branches of the poplar. After the spugghawk chase it had become his thinking tree. He would look out over the city and dream of Brazeel and the emerald jungle and the new animals he would discover. Perhaps he had brothers and sisters there.

Like a thorn caught in the bum plumage, something was prickling about that last talk with Millie. They were so busy though. He sat watching them one day from a beech across from the pavilion. From dawn to dusk they darted in and out of the new nest with mouthfuls of flies for their littlies. A quick word, never mind a big chat about albatrosses, was out of the question.

One day it rained cats and dogs. 'Rain in the woods wets you twice' is a spuggie saying, and they were all duly lined up under the eaves of the greenhouse looking grumpy. Millie too had sheltered, and was perched under the angle of the pavilion roof on a spout.

'Alraht?'

'Alright, thank you.'

Steve poked his head out of the nest. 'Alraht dude?'

'Alright thank you Steve.' He heard tiny tweetings and bobbed his head. 'How are the littlies?'

'Doin' good, but no flahs today.'

'Too wit,' Millie grumbled. She looked up and searched the sky. 'Stop soon though.'

The Purpled-Bellied Parrot looked up, but all he saw were flat grey clouds with water leaking out of them.

'She's a whizz with the weather,' said Steve. 'It's like magic so it is. You watch dude, sun'll be out soon.'

'So, what do you know kid?' said Millie.

The question stumped the Purple-Bellied Parrot. He considered he didn't know very much at all, apart from what Chalkie and the spuggies had taught him and the bit he'd learned from Millie. So he ignored it.

'May I ask you both something?' he said. 'It is about our journey to the south and the albatross.'

'Fire away,' said Millie.

'The albatross, the one that will tell me about Brazeel. You tell me he is the great wanderer of the oceans in the south. Then how can I meet him? Will he not be out wandering the oceans? But you also say that he lives on the edge of the great desert. I am confused.'

'He don't do too much wandering nowadays, does he Millie?' said Steve.

'They are good questions, and if I tell you the answers, you must promise not to tell him that I told you — he is very embarrassed about it.'

'I promise.'

'Okay, there's a few things you need to understand.' Millie took a deep breath. 'First off, the bins would say that he's not in the sahth — that he's in the north.'

'I see.' The Purple-Bellied Parrot did not see.

'He has been in the north many summers now, from only his sixth summer, so only a little older than you are now. One day, at the beginning of that summer, he was wandering the great southern ocean.'

'They cannot hilp themselves. It's what they do,' Steve said. 'They are the screamers of the ocean — except they hate flapping. You should see their wings dude. They are as long as from here to the ground.'

The Purple-Bellied Parrot looked down. Steve must be exaggerating. No bird could have wings that long.

'They glide and soar,' Steve said. 'They master every draught to keep themselves aloft, the tiniest wafts that you and I wouldn't even notice. Nobody knows how they do it.'

'Well anyway,' Millie continued, darting Steve an irritated glance, 'on that day he drifted too far north. He's cagey about whah or how; he was still a littlie really. From what I can work out, he got caught in a terrible storm, like no one could remember. The wind raged from the sahth for days, and it blew him over the fat belly of the earth and into the north. Now he cannot get back.'

The Purple-Bellied Parrot was silent as he absorbed this. Then he asked, 'Why not? If he is such a good flier?'

'It's what Steve was saying earlier. Albatrosses glide, they don't flap. They need the wind to lift those great wings, and then they can go in any direction they like. Now, at the belly of the earth, the doldrums reign. No wind ruffles the ocean of the doldrums. Flat calm. And not like that day we just had when the flahing ants came out.'

'Mmmm,' said Steve. 'Flahing ants.'

'It goes on for days and days. You just have to flap your way through it, and for an albatross to flap — well, he's not built for it. He's puffed out in a jiffy.'

'A screamer could do it,' said Steve, 'but they're not interested. No flahs out in the great ocean, and screamers hate fish.'

'Can he not paddle his way across the dum-dums?' The Purple-Bellied Parrot remembered the duck-pond berts and their webbed feet.

'Doldrums. Ahh, you are so innocent. You know nothing about the ocean, and yet you want to conquer it.' Millie preened a dishevelled feather on the Purple-Bellied Parrot's neck. 'No. The doldrums is not some river or lake. It is vast, yet you never know how vast. Its margins, they are always shifting. You never know when the wind will blow again.'

The Purple-Bellied Parrot mulled on the mysterious dum-dums for a moment, and then his mind shifted back to the albatross. 'So he lives on the edge of a great desert. It seems a strange place for such a bird to live.'

Millie hunched down on the spout and ruffled out her feathers. Her toes disappeared. 'He spent many years in the far north, in the islands of this land. He said the islands there reminded him of those in the southern ocean. Every year he would build his nest. It was a wonderful thing. Any mate would be honoured to bear her young there. He adorned it with strands of seaweed, shells of all shapes and colours, bits of fisherman's netting. Albatrosses don't normally do that. Then he would flah to the highest cliff, to the highest rock, and cry out for a mate. He cried out all summer long. No mate came. Many summers he cried out like that. He flew further north, across the cold sea to an island where rivers are made of ice and rock boils out of the ground like red water. He built his nest. He cried out. But for all those summers he never felt the touch of a mate's bill grooming his crown. So one autumn he kicked his nest into the sea far below and set off towards the midday sun. Now he sits on a rock and watches the wind blow the sand into the ocean.'

'So, he will sit there, what, until he croaks?' asked the Purple-Bellied Parrot.

'He wants to go home dude,' said Steve. 'Oh yeah, real bad. But he's too scared to try.'

The Purple-Bellied Parrot hadn't noticed the rain had stopped. The sun broke through the clouds and Millie shot away to hunt.

———

The Purple-Bellied Parrot began to spend nights alone high in the poplar. It was not only the endless late-night and early-morning conflabs that were wearisome. It was the constant pong. The spuggies trumped a lot — they called it bottom burpage.

Praarrp! 'Ahem … scuse I.'

Prreeehp! 'Oooh hark at me. Better out than in.'

Phusst! 'Phooar, who did that!'

'Im as smelt it dealt it.'

Like a bin's fine wine or Cuban cigar, trumping was one of the joys of life to be savoured. They took it very seriously, even instituting a colour-coding system to identify their trumps.

'Prrraaaaaaaarrrrp', long and plappy, lots of noise but little pong: Yellow. The sign of a rank amateur. 'Pprrep,' short but cloyingly dense, almost heavier than air, pungent enough to strip your barbules at twenty paces: Purple. 'Phusst' — almost silent, lighter than air, stealthy, worming into every cranny: Magnolia. Purple was the gold standard to which every spuggie aspired.

The spuggies debated the subject of trumping at length. They discussed subtleties of sonics and nuances of aroma, and suggested refinements to their colour-coding system. On still summer nights no waftage carried the trumpage away, and they all sat huddled together, enjoying the fug of their own bottom burpage, giving scores.

The Purple-Bellied Parrot would sit apart with his head

tucked under his wing. But the constant noise and pong kept him awake. On a couple of nights he had almost keeled over through lack of oxygen. So it was a good excuse when, after a particularly purple night, he said he wanted to spend the occasional night alone.

'It is a long way to Brazeel. I must have my sleep so I can stay strong for the long journey.' The spuggies all nodded solemnly.

The occasional night spent in the poplar became most nights. He wanted to be alone so he could dream undisturbed of Brazeel and his new life there. It would be so warm, so much sunshine, so many nuts and juicy fruits, so many parrots just like him, with glossy green plumage and purple bellies. There he would bloom, his purple belly growing bigger and ever more splendid. His splendid belly would attract the most beautiful mate and they would build a nest far away from the bins and have many littlies together.

One evening he was considering his purple belly — it was a favourite occupation — when he noticed something was different. It was like he'd eaten a george egg or something. His belly was all round and was resting on the branch between his feet. That never used to happen. He was getting tubby. All the tinned grub and chips and kebabs and Swiss roll must be mounting up. He wasn't dashing about with the spuggies like he used to, and when he did, he got out of puff.

A stifling afternoon, and the Purple-Bellied Parrot was gazing at the thunder clouds cauliflowering on the horizon, the south horizon, thinking about Millie and Steve. He hadn't spoken to them for ages. He hoped they hadn't forgotten him and their promise to take him south. Brazeel seemed further away than ever. He'd sat alone high in his poplar all day, a day when industry and mischief had surrounded him. He sighed and looked down and surveyed his plumage; he pulled out a feather and watched it drift on the breeze, south.

A dun blur shot past and snatched up the feather. A rustle of foliage and Chalkie was beside him, green feather in chirper.

'I think you dropped something,' he said. 'Now if you don't want it, I'll give it to Madge to shove in her nest. She's a bit short of the warm stuff.' But rather than taking it away, Chalkie poked the feather back into the Purple-Bellied Parrot's plumage.

'Now we can't have you starting this palaver again can we,' Chalkie scolded. 'Need all of these you do for your big trip. Can't have you looking like Old Stumpy.'

When he had finished poking, the feather — now in the wrong place and tatty — stuck out at an angle. 'There,' he said, stepping back to survey his handiwork. 'Right as ninepence.'

The Purple-Bellied Parrot looked down at the feather. He couldn't remember pulling it out.

'Now,' said Chalkie, 'we need to get you busy. Can't have you down in the doldrums before you're down in the doldrums now can we. For a start, you can help Vera and Madge with feeding their chicks. That'll keep you fit.' He stepped back and surveyed the Purple-Bellied Parrot. He frowned. 'Tut-tut. You're letting yourself go. Now then, it's an awful long way to Brazil you know. There's all that sea, and them marties don't exactly hang about. What you need is a training reggie-ment. So-called because Reggie's the spug who's sorts them out. He's got a mate.'

The Purple-Bellied Parrot couldn't twig training regiments so he simply asked, 'Chalkie, how far is south?'

'How far? How far is south?' Chalkie slapped his primaries against his crown. 'Crikey — you haven't got the brains you was born with. South isn't a destination, it's a direction. You keep going in a direction until you get where you want to be. Then you stop — that's your destination. You, though, will probably need to go in more than one direction, because nobody seems overly certain where this Brazil of yours is located.'

'What if I lose my way?'

'How you goin' to do that? You'll be setting off with Millie and Steve — not that Steve seems much use — and later you'll find that big ruddy albatross. I seen them on the telly.'

The Purple-Bellied Parrot looked doubtful. 'But what if I cannot keep up?'

'That's why Reg is organising the reggie-ment.' Chalkie sighed. 'Listen, you're a bird. You *know* which way south is — the knowledge was in you when you was all mush inside the shell. Innate innit.' Chalkie regarded the puzzled parrot a moment and then said. 'Close your eyes and turn around.'

'What?'

'Close your eyes and keep turning around until you've forgotten which way you was facing.'

Soon the Purple-Bellied Parrot was giddy.

'Now, keep your eyes closed and imagine which way you would fly if you wanted to head south away from Blighty, and imagine.[4] Don't think. There's a difference. Imagine. And when you feel ready, just take off.'

The Purple-Bellied Parrot kept his eyes closed but didn't know quite how to imagine a direction. First he imagined the midday sun, and then the sun rising and falling over land and a big sea. He imagined the emerald jungle where he was born. He imagined tall grass twirling in the breeze. He imagined desert and a surf-edged coast and ocean with a big albatross wandering about over it. He imagined he was ready. He took off.

'That's my boy,' yelled Chalkie after him, 'Goo-on my son. You can open your eyes now. Open your eyes! Oh crikey …'

The Purple-Bellied Parrot's foot caught a telephone wire. He spun round twice and was flung away vertically, before dropping — legs akimbo — onto the wire.

'Oooof,' the Purple-Bellied Parrot groaned.

'Oooof,' Chalkie groaned.

The Purple-Bellied Parrot bounced up off the wire, high into the air. For a moment he looked like he would miss it on the way down, but then a breeze caught him.

'Oooof,' the Purple-Bellied Parrot groaned.

'Oooof,' Chalkie groaned.

The Purple-Bellied Parrot lay crumpled, spraddling the wire.

Chalkie had watched behind parted primaries. 'That'll smart in the morning,' he muttered. He leapt up and in a second was beside him on the wire.

'Just put your head between your legs mate. Take deep breaths … Deeeep breaths. That's it. Don't worry about your nuts — I'll go and fetch them.' He chuckled, and instantly regretted the joke.[5] When the Purple-Bellied Parrot had his puff back and the pain had dwindled a bit, Chalkie said, 'See, I told you you could do it.'

'Did I fly south?' the Purple-Bellied Parrot croaked.

'Well … yes. Yes you did. Due south like a penguin with a gob-full of fish for his littlies.'

The Purple-Bellied Parrot would have bobbed his head, but then remembered his sore bits.

'Now, just you remember that. If you get lost, imagine. Don't think. Imagine and follow your imagination. It'll just happen.'

Chalkie turned away. 'Pitiful,' he muttered. 'He's never going to make it. North like a plover in spring he was. He'll be on the tundra in a jiffy with the bloomin ptarmigans, shivering his nuts off — if he's got any left.'

8

SAR'NT LOFTY TROGGERS

The Purple-Bellied Parrot spent the night alone high in the poplar cradled in a sprig of fresh poplar leaves, rocked by a warm breeze. Despite such luxury, he struggled to sleep. The pain between his legs still nagged, and he was consumed by thoughts about Brazil. He knew which way was south. Perhaps he should go on his own. Eventually the breeze on the soft leaves worked its magic and rocked him to sleep. As he drifted off, he thought that, after all the excitement of today, he'd have a lie-in tomorrow. It was going to be a nice day, and he'd let the sun slowly rouse him — not some spuggie trumping or a pre-dawn conflab.

'PRRAARPPP!!'

It was still dark, and the Purple-Bellied Parrot thought he must have dreamt the yellow trump or be back in the privet with the spuggies. That would have been odd though. A trump while everybody else was asleep was a wasted trump. Spuggies seldom trumped in the pre-dawn darkness. They would start a conflab though. He sighed with relief as he dozily realised that he was snug in his soft bed in the poplar. He fluffed out his feathers for more snoozing and successfully rekindled his dream.

He was having a leisurely bath in a forest pool, lying back, flipping warm water over his purple belly. Droplets, remnants of an earlier shower, fell from the canopy and plipped into the pool, splashing his face. His mate, whose name he'd decided was Flo, had just bought him a luscious sweet red berry she called a passion fruit. He'd polished off the pulp and was crunching up the seeds. Sunlight filtered in through the leaves, making his belly glow, and he admired its glossy plumpness. Flo came over and nibbled his ear; he made a funny chuckling noise. She twirled one of his belly feathers around and around and around.

'TAD-DA-LA-DA-DAT-DAT-TAAR!'

It was the loudest noise he'd ever dreamt. He looked round the forest to see where it had come from. It must be some huge bird with a beak even bigger than his. Or some bin car had invaded the forest and was blasting its horn. He saw nothing so he shrugged and turned back to munch his passion fruit and continue canoodling, but it had disappeared. As had Flo.

'TAD-DA-LA-DA-DAT-DAT-TAAR!'

The Purple-Bellied Parrot opened one eye a crack. Apart from a talon moon and a bright star shining where the sun should be, it was pitch black.

'TAD-DA-LA-DA-DAT-DAT-TAAR!'

'I can go on like this all day boy,' an unfamiliar voice clanged into his ear. It sounded like somebody shaking a biscuit tin with a half a brick in it.

The Purple-Bellied Parrot levered opened both eyes.

He made out two shapes silhouetted against the setting moon, one much, much smaller than the other. He recognised the tubby form of the bigger silhouette, Reg. The small one resembled the thick end of a golf club the bins might use on the footie pitches sometimes. The golf club opened his beak.

'TAD-DA-LA-DA-DAT ....'

'Yes, yes alright ... that'll do. Don't want to wake the whole bloomin neighbourhood do we,' said Reg. He had his wings clamped over his ears. He bent forward, pulled up an eyelid, peered into the Purple-Bellied Parrot's eye, and let it flap down again. 'Yep, done the trick. Back in the land of the livin he is.'

The Purple-Bellied Parrot fluffed his feathers up into a ball. 'What is happening? What is the time? Who is thees tiny person?'

'What is happening, is what is known in the h'army as revelry.[1] The time is wakey-wakey time. This tiny person with the perpendicular tail is Lofty — Sar'nt Lofty Troggers to you.[2] Sar'nt Troggers is going to lick you, my son, into shape.'

The Purple-Bellied Parrot closed one eye and used the other one to look down on the tiny person. It was a wren; a twig was tucked under his wing, the function of which the Purple-Bellied Parrot could not imagine. The wren looked very angry.[3]

'I doan want to be licked by thees tiny bird. Let me sleep.' He turned his back on the pair, re-plumped his plumage and closed his eye.

Reg slapped his forehead. 'Oh no. You shouldn't have said that.'

The Purple-Bellied Parrot felt something land on his head. It was so light he could hardly feel it — but it was definitely there. Then he felt something hard beating his head and he heard: "TAD-DA-LA-DA-DAT-DAT-TAAR!' right in his lughole.

Sar'nt Lofty Troggers stopped beating the Purple-Bellied Parrot's head with the twig and leapt down and clung onto his breast. He could feel his tiny claws digging in. His beak was a poppy-seed-breadth away from the Purple-Bellied Parrot's beak. The Purple-Bellied Parrot's ear was still ringing but he heard:

'Now you listen 'ere you spoiled, prissy, poncey, Polly.'

The Purple-Bellied Parrot felt globules of spit spraying his face and noticed that Sar'nt Troggers had terribly smelly breath.

'I ain't got up at three-o-clock in the morning for you to go all big-hen's-blouse on me.' He leapt away and started fluttering around his head, 'Oooh don't wake me up — I need me beauty sleep. If I don't get me beauty sleep I might trip over a butterfly and drop me POSEY! STAND TO ATTENTION!'

The Purple-Bellied Parrot had no idea what Sar'nt Troggers was talking about, but the terror imparted by the tin-can voice was like a bucket of water with ice cubes in it. Suddenly he was the awakest he'd ever been in his life. He leapt up and stood as tall as he could, which he hoped was 'Attention.'

Sar'nt Troggers landed back onto his breast and was in his face again. 'Do you want to make this trip to Brazil? Do you? Well — DO YOU?'

'Yeays,' the Purple-Bellied Parrot winced.

'Well gimme twenty.'

'Twenty?'

'GIMME TWENTY!'

'Twenty what?'

'Twenty girlie sneezes into your tiny silk hankie with the daisies on it. SQUATS!!! Whadya think?'

Sar'nt Troggers leapt off to demonstrate. He extended his wings and bent and extended his legs: Hup ... hup ... hup. 'Now your turn Schnozzmeister General.'

The Purple-Bellied Parrot began, his belly bouncing up and down, Sar'nt Troggers counting them off, but after ten he was puffing, fifteen wheezing, and at eighteen he gave up, gasping.

Sar'nt Troggers regarded him, scratched his chin and shook his head. 'Pitiful,' he said. 'Truly pitiful.' He hopped over to Reg for a conflab.

They talked rapidly, and all the Purple-Bellied Parrot could pick up were phrases like, 'Worse than I thought ... Never going to make it ... Needs his arse kicking ...'. 'Big hen's blouse' came up again as well. All the time they were glancing back at the Purple-Bellied Parrot with crumpled brows. After a bit Reg hopped back to the Purple-Bellied Parrot.

'He's a bit rough around the barbules but he's a good bloke deep down. Worked marvels for us he did in the Maggie Wars.

He's pint-sized, but don't underestimate him. Just don't give him any lip and you'll be pukka.' Reg clapped him on the mantle and called over, 'He's all yours Lofty', and hopped away.

'Pleeze doan leave me with …' but Reg had gone back to bed.

Sar'nt Troggers hopped around and inspected the Purple-Bellied Parrot from top to bottom and from back to front. The Purple-Bellied Parrot racked his brains trying to remember what 'lip' was so he wouldn't give him any and everything would be pukka. Sar'nt Troggers finished his inspection.

'Look at you. You're soft. What are you?'

The Purple-Bellied Parrot looked down at Sar'nt Troggers with his beak open.

'You sorry-arsed simpleton,' the Sar'nt growled.

He prodded the Purple-Bellied Parrot in the tummy with his stick, 'You're soft. Soft like all the puddings and pies and pastries you eat.' He prodded him on each 'p'. He scrutinised the Purple-Bellied Parrot's beak. 'Open your cakehole.' He hopped up and peered inside. 'Hmm, don't look like you eat worms. We're gonna put you on a strict diet of fruit, nuts and seed. No more cake and kebabs. Henceforth your body is a temple. When I'm done with you'll be able to fly to Brazil and back ten times carrying a suitcase full of half-enders between your chops. Now, follow me.'

'Okay.'

Sar'nt Troggers turned. He seemed even angrier. 'When I give you an order or demand confirmation of a statement you will say "Sir, yes Sir" or "Sir, no Sir." Is that clear?

'Er, yeays.'

Sar'nt Troggers waited, tapping his stick on his flanks.

'I mean … erm … Sir, yes. Yes Sir.'

Sar'nt Troggers led the Purple-Bellied Parrot to the stream that divided the park. Two footbridges crossed it and it was lined with birchs that formed an avenue. Grey light was leaking into the horizon as they landed in the tallest. Sar'nt Troggers scissored off a long twig.

'Now, listen up. I will fly upstream to that bridge. I will drop this twig into the water. The twig will float downstream. When the twig contacts the water you will hear this sound.' Sar'nt Troggers opened his beak and emitted a deafening 'Phheeep'. 'On hearing that sound you fly to the top of that birch.' He pointed across the stream to a birch with a bare crown. 'You will see a tall bare branch. You will fly around that branch. You will proceed to fly back and forth between the birchs. You will fly as fast as you can. You will continue to fly until this twig reaches that bridge.' He pointed downstream to the other bridge. When this twig reaches the bridge you will hear this sound: "Phheeep". On hearing that sound you will stop.' Sar'nt Troggers thought for a moment and then added, 'You will not stop in mid-air and plummet to the ground. You will proceed to the nearest birch. Questions?'

'No Sir, Sir no.'

'Close enough.'

Sar'nt Troggers flew to the bridge, checked that the Purple-Bellied Parrot was watching and dropped the twig.

'Phheeep!'

The Purple-Bellied Parrot set off. He flew as fast as he could. He found he desperately did not want to do anything that might displease Sar'nt Troggers. By the third circuit he was already gasping and decided to slow the pace a bit. He tried to spot the twig in the water but it was still too gloomy to see. After a bit he lost count of how many circuits and was just praying for the Phheep. His lungs were boiling though, and in the end he collapsed onto the tall bare branch without the Phheeep and waited.

'Phheeep!'

The Purple-Bellied Parrot watched the tiny golf-club end flutter towards him. He nearly had his breath back by then, but he decided to pant anyway.

'You'll have to get up very early in the morning to fool me

son,' Sar'nt Troggers chirped as he landed. The Purple-Bellied Parrot thought he had got up early in the morning — very early indeed.

'Did you hear this sound: "Pheeep"' Sar'nt Troggers yelled.

'No, sir No.'

'Then why in God's green earth did you stop?'

'Sir, my lungs, they felt like someone had set fire to them ... Sir.'

'Pitiful. Truly pitiful,' Sar'nt Troggers began. 'That's eight circuits. I do eighteen circuits in that time. Hear that son? Eighteen! And I must be five times your age and a quarter of your size. How old am I?'

'Quarter of your age, Sir ... Sir.' The Purple-Bellied Parrot knew there was something wrong with his reply but couldn't figure out what.

'How many can I do?'

'Sir, eighteen Sir?'

'You asking me or telling me?'

'Sir ... Sir?'

Sar'nt Troggers groaned, hopped to the top of the bare branch, looked at the sky for a moment, and then hopped back down.

'Listen up. You are going to show me how good you can be. How many are you *going* to do son?'

'Sir, how do you mean Sir?' He was finally getting the hang of this. Begin with 'sir,' end with 'sir,' begin with 'sir,' end with 'sir' — that's all there was to it.

'I'm gonna train you so you can outfly and out-dodge them noras on the coast. 'I'm gonna train you so you can fly all day and all night in a dusty headwind in desert heat without a drink of water to wet your chirper carrying one of them marties on your back and singing *Jerusalem*. I'm gonna train you so you can fly across the ocean de-primaried. You're gonna be fitter than a butcher's dog on a detox. What you gonna be?'

'Sir, fitter than a butcher's dog on beeswax Sir.'

Sar'nt Troggers hopped up and landed on top of the Purple-Bellied Parrot's head. He bent over and peered into his eyes. The Purple-Bellied Parrot's vision was filled with the wren's upside-down face. 'Now, give me a target son. What's it going to be?' he growled.

The Purple-Bellied Parrot remembered how he'd struggled and tried to imagine what would be a reasonable number of circuits.

'Er ... Sir, twelve Sir?'

Sar'nt Troggers leapt from his head and fluttered around him.

'Twelve? TWEEELLVE! You yankin' my chain boy? Listen to me. You hate me. You despise me. So what d'ya want to do?'

The Purple-Bellied Parrot racked his brain but was stumped. Sar'nt Troggers was now flitting about like a moth who had drunk spilt cider. The Purple-Bellied Parrot kept looking around for the source of the voice, but always he had gone.

'You want to BEAT me. You want to show me you're ...' and he whacked the Purple-Bellied Parrot on the rump with his twig, '... the better bird. You want to rub my nose in it. Make me eat dirt. So (whack) what's it gonna (whack) be (whack). How (whack) many?' (whack).

The Purple-Bellied Parrot thought that he certainly did not want to make Sar'nt Troggers eat dirt. He thought that it would be horrible. Then he focussed his mind on the question. How many? It didn't hurt much, but he wished Sar'nt Troggers would stop whacking him with that twig. Now, how many?

'Er ... Sir, nineteen Sir?' the Purple-Bellied Parrot ventured.

'You askin' me or tellin' me?'

'Sir ... Sir, twenty Sir.' He didn't know how many twenty was, but he liked the sound of it, and he was relieved when Sar'nt Troggers seemed satisfied but unimpressed.

'Well alright. We start tomorrow, zero five-hundred hours.'

On the first day Sar'nt Troggers told him to fly around the park once without stopping. He said that before he set off for Brazil he must be able to do this ten times. The Purple-Bellied Parrot thought this unfair for a bird like him who was clearly designed for short grub flights between trees.

After his efforts between the birches, the Purple-Bellied Parrot set off from the poplar at a leisurely pace. Below, bin joggers and big-bottomed old females on bicycles overtook him. But after only a quarter of the circuit he was puffed out. He looked for a shortcut, and he soon worked out that he could chop off the corner of the park where the football pitches were. Sar'nt Troggers would never know. But as soon as he deviated off course, Sar'nt Troggers landed on his head and chirped into his ear.

'You *will* stick to the prescribed course. You *will* not deviate without prior permission from Sar'nt Troggers. Is that clear?'

'Sir, yes Sir.'

'Carry on.'

With a little nudging from Sar'nt Troggers, the Purple-Bellied Parrot found his way back to the perimeter of the park. Sar'nt Troggers disappeared into the foliage, but the Purple-Bellied Parrot felt his eyes still watching.

Three-quarters of the way round his pecs were screaming and he was out on his wings. His flight became wobbly; he battered into branches; once he dropped so low he scraped his feet on the floor and made a yapper jump. Sar'nt Troggers appeared at his side — he must have followed him all the way round. Sar'nt Lofty Troggers was not out of breath.

'Keep going son. You can do it. Imagine that green forest with all that tasty fruit and them crunchy nuts and those pretty purple-bellied ladies. Come on now.' The Purple-Bellied Parrot expected a whack from the twig, but none came.

Rather than land gracefully at the top and nonchalantly folding his wings, the Purple-Bellied Parrot clattered into the bottom of the poplar head-first. He just managed to grab the bottom branch with one foot and dangle upside-down — but he'd made it. Sar'nt Troggers landed beside him and wafted a beech leaf in his face.

'Well done son. You did good. You'll be doing ten of those before you head off to Brazil. Take five and we'll crunch some conkers.'

'Sir ... yes Sir', he panted. It was only three words, and he didn't really understand why, but Sar'nt Troggers saying 'You did good' made his heart soar.

When he'd recovered and had a drink (Sar'nt Troggers needed neither), they flew over to a nook in a hawthorn. Two gnarly old conkers were waiting. Sar'nt Troggers had got the woodpecker to drill holes in them and he'd threaded-through some twine he'd found somewhere. He hooked one conker over each set of his primaries.

'On the count of three you will carry out the following exercise.'

Sar'nt Troggers squatted down, straightened and then opened his wings and slowly raised the conkers. 'Hup!' He did this ten times.

'Questions.'

'Sir, no Sir.'

The Purple-Bellied Parrot managed three.

'Pitiful. Now, upside-down crunches. Observe.'

Sar'nt Troggers hooked his feet round a suitable twig, let himself fall, put his wings behind his head and curled his body up and down, kissing his feet on each completed curl, 'Mwa ... Mwa ... Mwa ...'. He did twenty of these before unhooking his feet, performing a somersault and barking, 'Questions.'

'Sir, no sir.'

He liked hanging upside-down, so this should be easy.

'Hutnnnnn ... Hutnnnnn.' He was astonished to find that nothing happened. He looked up at his belly which, rather than being in its usual position down around his toes, was now lodged against his chin. Perhaps that had something to do with it. He flung his wings forward and tried again, but still only managed half way.

Sar'nt Troggers's twig came out and whacked the Purple-Bellied Parrot on the bum. 'Again,' he yelled.

This time, despite even more vigorous wing flinging, he barely budged. Sar'nt Troggers pressed his beak up the Purple-Bellied Parrot's beak and peered into an eye. This was not going to be good.

'What is your major malfunction bumnuts?'[4]

'Sir?'

'I'll tell you. You can't do it, can you boy,' Sar'nt Troggers shrieked. 'And you know why you can't do it? Because of this.' Sar'nt Troggers whacked the Purple-Bellied Parrot on the belly. The Purple-Bellied Parrot felt the flab ripple. 'You're a tub of lard boy, that's why. What are you?'

'Sir, a tub of lard Sir.'

'And why are you a tub of lard boy?'

The Purple-Bellied Parrot thought for a moment. 'Sir, because I am full of Swiss roll and kebabs Sir.'

'Correct. And henceforth you will no longer be full of Swiss roll and kebabs boy.'

'Sir, yes Sir ... I mean, no Sir.'

'And why will you no longer be full of Swiss roll and kebabs?'

This was harder. 'Er ... Sir, because my body is now a tent pole Sir?'

Sar'nt Troggers spun around and sighed.

'You asking me or telling me?' he groaned.

'Er ... Sir, telling you Sir.'

'Dismissed.'

The next day the Purple-Bellied Parrot again managed eight of the birch circuits, but because he was 'knackered', as the spuggies say, from yesterday, he didn't think this was too bad. He was chuffed because he managed to delay his landing to coincide with the 'Pheeep.' Sar'nt Troggers said nothing, and merely stood watching him, tapping the twig against his leg.

Sar'nt Troggers then led him to a tennis court and they both sat on the tarmac. He closed his eyes and muttered something. He fixed a circle of bright red cloth around his head, paused, and then opened his eyes, raising his face to the sky. He opened his beak and bellowed out his song, finishing with the usual 'rat-at-tat', but adding a 'pheep.' The Purple-Bellied Parrot resisted the urge to put his pinions in his ears, but thought the volume was most inconsiderate for this time of day when everybody else was still in bed. Sar'nt Troggers leapt up and flew once around the court in a rhythmic undulating flight. He landed a few paces in front of the Purple-Bellied Parrot, took a deep breath and turned to face him. Something was wriggling under his wing.

'This is a sacred moment Son.' He spoke softly, solemnly. 'You are about to face the ultimate test. This test will determine if you are bird enough to take on the challenge of the south. Successful completion of this test will endow you with the ability to escape any predator on God's green earth. You will conquer this test. Failure to conquer this challenge will result in the withdrawal of permission to fly south. Questions.'

The Purple-Bellied Parrot wanted to ask 'Sir, what permission Sir?' but in the end settled for, 'Sir, no Sir.'

'Son, I'm gonna make you eat thunder and trump lightning — or is it the other way round. I forget.[5] Anyway ...' He rummaged under his wing and drew out a piece of shiny cloth the same colour as his bandana. The cloth was wrapped around something. The something moved. He held the cloth high in the direction of the dawn for a moment, and then slowly lowered it and began to unwrap it. Inside was a beetle. It was about the size of a tadlet and the shape of a sunflower seed.

'This here is a click beetle, *Alfous emorroidis*.[6] The click beetle is the quickest thing on six legs on these green islands. Now listen up. I will place the click beetle on this tarmac. I will step back. There will be no "PHEEEP!"' He held the square of the red fabric high. 'I will release this cloth. The instant this cloth contacts the ground — not one second before — you will proceed to catch the click beetle. To accomplish this mission you may use any part of your body you so desire. Questions.'

'Sir, no Sir.'

'Then we begin. Good luck Son.'

Sar'nt Troggers bowed and placed the beetle on the tarmac. He held it for a moment with his toe to ensure it was still, and swept his wings back and retreated, still bowed. He raised himself up, held the shiny red cloth aloft, and paused.

The Purple-Bellied Parrot looked at the beetle. How difficult could this be? Catch beetle. Eat beetle. Fly south. Adios Sar'nt Troggers.

Sar'nt Troggers released the shiny red cloth.

The Purple-Bellied Parrot waited until it had fluttered to the ground, and began his approach.

The beetle remained motionless, apart from one feeler waving about shaped like the edge of a nettle leaf. And, what was more, the beetle was on its back! The Purple-Bellied Parrot bobbed his head. This was too easy. He'd better pounce before the wind blew it away.

The Purple-Bellied Parrot got closer and closer until he was a spuggie-length away. Then he was a spuggie-beak away. The Purple-Bellied Parrot noted that the click beetle appeared unperturbed by his presence. He slowly opened his beak to pick it up.

His beak snapped shut with an empty 'tock.' The beetle had vanished. It must have vanished between opening his beak and closing his beak. How? He didn't see it go, just heard a 'click' and it was gone. It must be some kind of Sar'nt Lofty Troggers prank. He glanced back and saw Sar'nt Troggers, wings folded, smirking.

The Purple-Bellied Parrot blinked and looked about. The beetle was scurrying away like the clappers towards a patch of grass at the edge of the court. He ran after it, but the beetle zig-zagged and dodged until he was almost in the grass. The beetle stopped. It turned and waved its antennae at the Purple-Bellied Parrot. The antennae formed a V. The Purple-Bellied Parrot too stopped, wary of another trick. They faced-off for a moment, and then, taking a circumbendibus, the Purple-Bellied Parrot sidled towards the beetle nonchalantly.[7] He looked about as though admiring the scenery; he stopped to preen; he tossed aside a fag packet some bin had chucked. Then he leapt, like Tankona, both feet flying.[8] He landed on nothing but tarmac.

Sar'nt Troggers snorted. 'Not as easy as it looks, eh boy?'

The Purple-Bellied Parrot whirled around to see the beetle now scuttling off to the other side of the court. He galloped after him. The beetle again stopped. It lifted its bum as high as it would go and squirted a tiny jet of poo in the Purple-Bellied Parrot's direction. Enough is enough. The Purple-Bellied Parrot hatched a crafty plan. This time he'd fluff out his feathers and spread his wings and flop on top of it and smother it.

The Purple-Bellied Parrot executed the plan perfectly. He had it! But the beetle started running about in his plumage. The tick-ling became unbearable, so he leapt up and flapped high, shaking his feathers vigorously. He reached as high as the tennis-court fence before he finally dislodged it, and he watched it drop hard onto the tarmac.

He'll never have survived that.

He swooped down and landed, placed a foot on the beetle and held the pose a moment for Sar'nt Troggers to see. He bent for the 'coo de grace.'

'Click.' The beetle was gone.

This went on for quite a bit. Sar'nt Troggers paced back and forth watching the chase, muttering constantly. The longer it went on, the harder he slapped his flanks with the twig. Finally, he removed his bandana.

PHHEEEP! 'You will cease chasing that beetle and you will facilitate his departure from this location.'

The Purple-Bellied Parrot looked around, dazed and exhausted. At that moment he didn't know the location of the click beetle. As it turned out, it was behind him, beetling off through the fence into a patch of dandelions.

Sar'nt Troggers beckoned him over. 'As anticipated, you have failed in this task. Failure is part of life. You will learn from this failure. You will not give up. What will you not do?'

'Sir, not give up Sir.'

'You will repeat this task weekly until you catch the click and consign him to me in a fully secured condition. Upon my receipt of the click you will receive a certificate of capture and have my endorsement to fly to Brazil. Questions.'

'Sir, no Sir,' the Purple-Bellied Parrot gasped.

'Dismissed.'

But he did have one question he didn't dare ask: how had Sar'nt Lofty Troggers caught the click beetle in the first place?

So this became the weekly regiment of late summer. Strength and Stamina one day; Speed and Agility the next, with Sundays off.[9] And though he got fed up of the early mornings and the diet of fruit and nuts, the Purple-Bellied Parrot could feel his belly getting smaller and his body getting fitter. He wondered if under his purple belly plumage he was developing a six peck.

One day, he discovered he had done ten birch circuits. He'd lost count as he returned for the final time and flopped into the tree, but on the bridge Sar'nt Troggers was flitting about in glee and rat-at-tatting.

'Not bad Son. Not bad. Go on like this and we'll soon lick you into shape.'

Soon he'd gone one-and-a-half times around the park, and it was head-bobbage unbounded when he did his first upside-down crunch. He immediately flew off to demonstrate his new skill to Chalkie and Reg, who watched him and exchanged glances.

Being both knackering and boring, the long flights around the park were the hardest. Sar'nt Troggers followed him round, flitting through the foliage shouting insults and encouragement. He even composed a poem to help him round.

'You will repeat each line after me.'

'Sir, yes Sir.'

> *I'm not in this for the thrill*
> I'm not in thees for the trill
> *I'm homeward bound back to Brazil*
> I'm homeward bound back to Brazeel (etc.)
>
> *If I die in the tomcat zone*
> *Parcel me up and send me home*
>
> *Ain't no nora on me gonna feast*
> *Cos I'm much stronger than a wildebeest*
>
> *I'll punch them noras into the briny blue*
> *Cos I'm one of Sar'nt Lofty Troggers crew*
>
> *If I die in the stormy gales*
> *Feed my bones to the spermy whales*
>
> *I won't need to land on no ships*
> *Now I don't eat no kebabs and chips*

I can overtake now all them joggers
Thanks to the work of Sar'nt Lofty Troggers

Tweet off
Tweet off
Tweet off, one two,
One two, three four

Sar'nt Troggers never let up. He missed not one day of training. One morning it was chucking it down and blowing a gale.
The spuggies were using sycamore leaves as umbrellas but were
still soaked. The Purple-Bellied Parrot thought Sar'nt Troggers
might spare him, but he turned up sodden with a heavy-duty
elastic band and a Brazil nut. It was Strength and Stamina
morning and Sar'nt Troggers was in a worse mood than usual.

'Get your arse moving boy. Today I'm handing out lollipops
and arse-kickings, and I'm all out of lollipops,' he said.

He led him off to a spot below a fallen log where no moggies
went. The Purple-Bellied Parrot dared not imagine what purpose
Sar'nt Troggers had dreamed up for the elastic band and the nut.
But by now he was sure they'd be connected with some devilish
exercise. His beak watered as he eyed the Brazil nut. If he ate it,
that would be the end of the exercise.

Sar'nt Troggers worked silently. One end of the elastic band
he tied to the trunk of the tree; the other end he tied around the
Purple-Bellied Parrot. He marched four spuggie-lengths away
then held out the nut.

'At this sound, PHHEEEP! you will take this nut from my
chirper.'

'Sir, yes Sir.'

'PHHEEEP!'

The Purple-Bellied Parrot took off in glee, but no matter how
hard he flapped he couldn't get any nearer to the nut. Sar'nt
Troggers held the nut a bit closer. The Purple-Bellied Parrot tried

a bit harder. He could smell its oil; he lunged and almost got it, but still he couldn't clamp his beak around it. Did Sar'nt Troggers jerk it away? He was so close now that Sar'nt Troggers began to bash the end of his beak with it.

'Come on you soggy-arsed piece of hedgehog cack. Take it! Take it! What's wrong with you!'

The Purple-Bellied Parrot concluded that his lack of progress had something to do with the elastic band. So he turned, snipped through it, and had the nut in his squawker before even the great Sar'nt Lofty Troggers knew what was happening.

'Ahem … Nice use of initiative there Son. Excellent beakwork. Excellent beakwork. I had, of course, hoped you would use exactly that tactic to get out of your predickybirdament. The Golden Rule of survival son: "Use the tools you have at your disposal." That beak of yours is one heck of a tool.'

The day came when he did the twenty birch circuits. When he finished he flew around Sar'nt Troggers's head yelling repeatedly, 'See, I did it Sir. You said I couldn't but I did *Sir*. I beat you. I … beat … you! *Sir*.'

He even concluded with the spuggie phrase, 'Get it up yah!' He had no idea what 'Get it up yah!' meant, and later he wondered what on earth had come over him. Sar'nt Troggers didn't get upset though — he seemed to enjoy it.

That same week he flew six times around the park. And, he did ten belly crunches. Ten! As many as Sar'nt Troggers. But he still aimed to beat him.

Then he caught the click beetle.

He remembered Sar'nt Troggers's words 'use the tools at your disposal,' and, as he was never going to be quick enough to catch it, he had devised a cunning plan. First, he marched towards the beetle, a steely glint in his eye. He paused, and then feigned an attack. He watched it smugly click into the air, land and flick the V antennae at him.

Now, he'd noted during their previous encounter that the click beetle invariably sprang to the right. He marched towards it again. 'Click.' He watched it sail into the air. Watched it begin to drop.

With his beak, he whacked it into the dandelions. It was like a Dandy Murray drive-volley. Whistling, he sauntered over to where it had landed, bent and said, 'Not so clever now, are you, Mees-ter Cleecky.' He picked up the stunned beetle and played keepy-uppy with it on the top of his beak for a moment and then carried it over to Sar'nt Troggers. He deposited it at his feet and then backed away, bowing, wings spread.

But Sar'nt Troggers was no longer interested in the click beetle, and as it staggered off he ignored it. He took off his red bandana and spoke calmly.

'Son, you're nearly ready. What are you?'

'Sir, nearly ready Sir.'

'What new ability do you possess?'

The Purple-Bellied Parrot thought for a moment, and then he remembered. 'Er … Sir, eat thunder and trump lightning Sir.'

Sar'nt Troggers held the bandana aloft and flew onto the Purple-Bellied Parrot's shoulder. He placed the bandana around his head.

'Well done Son. There is just one challenge left.'

The Purple-Bellied Parrot detected the glee ringing through his voice.

'How far is Brazeel?' the Purple-Bellied Parrot asked Millie one early autumn day. He had completed ten circuits of the park, and while he was overjoyed, he wondered whether it was enough.

'You know I don't know. You'll just have to keep going till you find it.'

'What if I am not strong enough? What if I must cross a big ocean and I become knackered and fall in?'

'Look at you now. Look how fit you are. That wren is not everyone's cup of tea but he's worked some magic on you.'

She flew off to catch a bluebottle and popped it into the littlie's mouth that had come to join them on the spout. 'Now scoot Number 2,' she said. 'Time you started catching these for yourself.' Number 2 just opened her massive yellow gape, squeaked and shivered her wings.

Millie turned back to the Purple-Bellied Parrot. 'And the autumn trip isn't like the spring trip. Spring is a race. You have to get to your breeding spot before some other flapper gets it. Unlikely you'd keep up with us, even now,' she said, surveying his new body.

The Purple-Bellied Parrot heaved a sigh as another fear welled up. 'But what if I lose my way?'

'You'll stick close to us. Autumn, we take it easy. Only flah in the good weather; plenty of nice warm evenings snoozing in a rock-a-bye reed bed. If we find a spot with plenty of grub we hang around, feed up for a few days. Nah, you'll keep up. You're pretty fit now — not up to martie standards — but you'll do. And you'll get fitter as you go along. Later we'll find the albatross, and he'll point you the way to Brazil.'

Steve buzzed past, almost clouting him on the earhole, 'Let's race dude!'

9

YEE-HAW!

Sar'nt Lofty Troggers's final challenge was the toughest yet.
He'd brought 'kit' with him: an assortment of elastic
bands, a packet of chilli powder, a flattened matchbox, a length of
twine and two of last year's conkers — big ones. The Purple-
Bellied Parrot watched, head cocked, as he punched two holes in
the matchbox and threaded the twine through. The conkers too
had had holes bored into them, and through these Sar'nt Troggers fed the elastic bands. The conkers were hard as pebbles and
as big as george eggs.

'Been pickling in moggie wee all winter,' Sar'nt Troggers
explained. 'Then come spring I sneaked into the greenhouse and
wedged them by the stove to bake. I got the woodpecker to bore
the holes when they were fresh off the tree.'

He motioned for the Purple-Bellied Parrot to come closer and
to spread out his wings. He looped one elastic band and conker
over each wing and told the Purple-Bellied Parrot to close them
again. The conkers still ponged of moggie wee.

'How does that feel Son?' he chirped.

'Sir, like I've got two hard conkers strapped to my back Sir.'

'Good, that's how it should feel.' He looped the twine over the

Purple-Bellied Parrot's neck, and then tugged at the connection between the twine and the matchbox. He muttered, 'Hmm, that's alright,' and dragged the chilli powder on to the matchbox behind him. He squatted and dug in his claws.

'Now listen up. I've taught you the essentials, just enough to get you through this feather-brained trip, no more. But you will meet tribulations the like of which your tiny mind has never dreamed. So this is what this mission is all about. To get ready for them unknown unknowns. You ready for this boy?'

'Sir, yes Sir.'

'Well alright then. On my command you will fly. You will obey every order I give you. If I tell you to turn to the right you will turn to the right. I tell you to turn to the left you will turn to the left. I tell you to dive you will dive. I tell you to shove that great hooter up a moggie's arse and whistle *Jerusalem,* you will insert said proboscis into said anal cavity and chirp said sublime air. Questions.'

Sar'nt Troggers had lost him with that last bit, but the Purple-Bellied Parrot said, 'Sir, yes Sir.'

'You will make two circuits of the park. Fly.'

The Purple-Bellied Parrot leapt off the branch, but immediately plunged, the weight of the conkers and Sar'nt Troggers clinging to the matchbox behind dragging him down. But he managed to convert the plunge into a controlled dive, and bottomed out and then soared upwards. He glanced around and noticed spuggies flitting through the branches and marties whirling low overhead, like they all knew something he didn't.

'Goo-on my son!' chirped Chalkie.

After completing the two circuits, Sar'nt Troggers issued his first order. On the basketball court below one of the hoops had been twisted around so that it was now vertical instead of horizontal. Sar'nt Troggers told him to dive down and fly through it, and by Jiminy he had better still be attached after or he'd 'have his arse for breakfast.'

The Purple-Bellied Parrot got the gist and swooped down. Folding his wings a little at the crucial moment, he and Sar'nt Troggers and the matchbox sailed through. Piece of cake.

'That was just the warm-up Boy,' Sar'nt Troggers yelled.

Sar'nt Troggers told him to climb and then pointed to two rows of low sheds just beyond the park railings. A long alley divided the rows, and each shed had its own perimeter fence. The Purple-Bellied Parrot recognised Pussycat Purr-fection, the local moggery. Sar'nt Troggers told him to dive down, assume level flight and fly along the alley.

As he dived, the wind rushing through his feathers, Sar'nt Troggers sang his piercing song, ending each phrase with the deafening, 'Rat-at-tat-tat.' The Purple-Bellied Parrot approached low, like a spugghawk would, and at the last moment swung over the perimeter fence and into the alley. At first, the startled moggies just goggled, dangle-jawed. Then, in a cacophony of caterwauling, they hurled themselves at their fences, all unsheathed claws and glistening teeth. Paws reached through the wire, swatting and grabbing. Behind, Sar'nt Troggers, sailing along on his matchbox, was tommy-gunning out his song and making obscene gestures with his pinions and waving his bum in the air. He stopped singing and sliced through the end of the chilli packet. The red dust erupted out. Then they were at the end of the alley, and the Purple-Bellied Parrot rollercoastered over the fence and climbed. Below, chilli was billowing over the compound and Sar'nt Troggers was whooping. 'Yee-haw! 'Yee-haw! Look at em cough and sneeze!'

They swung back into the park and Sar'nt Troggers told him to weave through the branches and undergrowth. He'd tied tiny pieces of cord to twigs – some red, some blue. The Purple-Bellied Parrot was told to keep the blue ones on his left and the red ones on his right. As he slalomed, the Purple-Bellied Parrot recognised where this course was leading him — straight to a couple of maggie nests.

'Stay cool Son,' yelled Sar'nt Troggers from behind. 'I'm just going to dangle myself from this here matchbox. I want you to shave that maggie nest with your toes. I'll do the rest.'

The maggie nest sped towards them, Araminta and Piers clacking. The Purple-Bellied Parrot glanced back to see Sar'nt Troggers hanging upside-down off the end of the matchbox. 'Steady Son, Steady. Maintain your present course.' A tufty-shouldered chick saw them coming. It gawped, bottom beak flapping, and hunkered down, tight. As he zoomed past the Purple-Bellied Parrot felt a tug, and looked behind to see a burst of maggie-chick feathers and Sar'nt Troggers hoicking himself back up onto the matchbox. He was clinging onto something metallic and sparkly.

'That was some mighty nice flying Son,' Sar'nt Troggers yelled when they were clear. He leapt off the matchbox and clambered along the Purple-Bellied Parrot's back until he was crouched on his nape. The Purple-Bellied Parrot saw the sparkly thing dangling in front of his eyes. 'Don't mean nothing to me, but the maggies are like the bins — they go nuts for this stuff.' It was a fat yellow circle with a twinkling stone stuck in the top. 'Take a left Son.'

'Sir, yes Sir.'

They swung past the tennis courts and towards the sheds and the greenhouses. As she did every morning, the female parkie was pouring seeds and nuts into the birdfeeders.

'Come in low ... not too fast,' Sar'nt Troggers called, and clambered back to the matchbox. As they passed the feeders he dropped the ring. It hit the gardener on the top of the head and bounced onto the ground.

As they glided away they heard, 'Oh my ... Oh my! My ring! But how?' She looked up and around, arms spread, turning circles, but all she saw was a green and purple blur towing a flattened matchbox with the end of a golf club on top.

'Alright, take five,' ordered Sar'nt Troggers. 'We'll just cruise around in the open for a bit while I get my bearings.'

No sooner had he said the word 'bearings,' than a spugghawk burst out of the foliage, yellow eyes boring into them.

'Initiate evasive manoeuvres,' Sar'nt Troggers said, a little too calmly thought the Purple-Bellied Parrot. The instant before the spugghawk struck, the Purple-Bellied Parrot dived, and the spugghawk whizzed overhead, swiping a talon. The Purple-Bellied Parrot felt it rip through a tail feather. He bottomed-out and swooped into the bushes, the spugghawk in pursuit. He twisted and bucked and weaved like he'd never done before. This was the spugghawk's domain, yet glancing behind the Purple-Bellied Parrot saw that he was out-flying him. What a difference Sar'nt Lofty Troggers had made! Astonishingly, the spugghawk then swerved away and settled on a branch and watched them go. He'd out-flown a spugghawk!

'That's some nice agility there Son. See what happens when you listen to Sar'nt Lofty Troggers? A month ago you'd have been flopped over his plucking post getting an unrequested short back and sides by now.'[1]

They rocketed out of the undergrowth, coming out just by the football pitches. Sar'nt Troggers told him to climb and make a right towards the duck pond.

'You pull this one off son,' he yelled, 'you'll go down in the annals of spuggiedom till kingdom come. You'll be the cock o' the park.'

At the far end of the duck pond was a large hopper where the parkies kept the duck food. At the foot of the hopper, almost lapped by the water, was a glass inspection panel. After all, you don't want to feed those berts mouldy food. Sar'nt Troggers leapt from the matchbox and onto the Purple-Bellied Parrot's back. Tapping on his head, Sar'nt Troggers told him to come in low over the opposite end of the pond.

They swerved round a cyclist, flicked the bum of a big female bin bending to smell the bizzie lizzies, and ruffled the hair of a boy bin chucking out bread to the berts. As they reached the railings that stopped the bins falling in the water, Sar'nt Troggers told him to dip even lower. The Purple-Bellied Parrot felt his toe flick the head of a bert.

Sar'nt Troggers was now peering over the top of the Purple-Bellied Parrot's head, 'Left a bit ... right a bit.' He had lifted a couple of the Purple-Bellied Parrot' nape feathers, and was using them like reins. They rounded the island and the hopper came into view. 'Straighten up ... that's it ... Steady ... Steady.' Sar'nt Troggers snipped one of the elastic bands and a conker rolled away and splashed into the water. The Purple-Bellied Parrot glanced down, and what he saw dumbfounded him. Rather than sink, the conker bounced along the top of the water going like the clappers — straight towards the glass panel. But then the conker lost momentum. Its final bounce was a 'plop', and with a bump it washed against the foot of the hopper.

'Bank! Bank! Climb! Climb! Climb!' Sar'nt Troggers was bellowing, pulling on the reins. The spuggies, watching in the bushes, covered their eyes. The Purple-Bellied Parrot flapped hard, and they just missed smashing into the top of the hopper by a barbule's breadth.

Sar'nt Troggers bellowed again into the Purple-Bellied Parrot's ear, struggling to make himself heard above the wind noise and the sound of flapping. 'Our approach was too slow and too high son, and we need to release the conker a smidgeon later. Go round for another sortie.'

The Purple-Bellied Parrot climbed and banked and went into a steeper dive, this time aiming to level-out well out over the water so he could keep his dive speed. The one conker made him lop-sided, and he had to compensate, but his speed was incredible — he barely had to flap. This must be what a peregrine feels like when stooping towards some dozy walter.[2]

His feet grazed the water as he levelled, and then he was on course. Sar'nt Troggers didn't even have to shout a tweak or pull on the reins. The boy-bin chucking bread at the ducks aimed a few rounds at them, and he had to take evasive action, but he was soon back on course again, zeroing in on the hopper now rushing towards them.

Sar'nt Troggers yelled 'As soon as you feel the conker go, climb, climb, climb. Give it everything you've got son, or the maggies will be garnishing their supper with your gizzard.'

The hopper reared up before them like a skyscraper. He's leaving it too late, thought the Purple-Bellied Parrot. He felt the conker drop.

He didn't hang about to see where it landed, but flapped and banked and climbed with all the power he could muster, the hopper getting bigger and bigger until it was all he could see. Sar'nt Troggers was yanking on the reins and yelling, 'Climb! Climb! Climb!' He wished he'd shut up.

'HUUUUUUUUUTTTT.' Below, he heard 'crunch' and 'tinkle.'

He clipped the hopper with his belly, purple feathers exploding, Sar'nt Troggers pulling hard now on his nape, and then they were clear and away and soaring, Sar'nt Troggers roaring again, 'Yee-haw! Yee haw!'

'Look down there boy. Look down there,' he roared. 'Yee-haw! See what you did? What a shot! Look at all that grub just spilling out.' The spuggies had already flocked down and were stuffing themselves. 'Their great-grandlittlies will be telling the tale of this derring-doo-doo to their grandlittlies. Let's head on home son.'

'Sir, yes Sir.'[3]

They landed on a large branch halfway up his poplar. Sar'nt Troggers patted him on the back, unhooked the matchbox, and then stepped back. He stood silently for a moment and then saluted him. 'Son, you've made me proud today.' He rummaged about in his plumage, and took out a tiny strip of gold foil shaped like a tennis racquet. Taking a blackthorn spine, he pinned it to the Purple-Bellied Parrot's breast. He saluted again. As he dropped his wing, he coughed and turned away.

'Well done son,' he croaked.

Then the poplar was alive with spuggies. They could hardly fly, they were so stuffed. They could still talk though, and they cheeped and chirped endlessly about the deeds of 'Ol Bignose and 'Wren Hur', as Alfie called Sar'nt Troggers, about the bouncing conker, reliving the moment when the conker struck the glass and the grub came gushing out. They took turns to clap them on the back. 'Spugnacious ... truly spugnacious,' chirped Gert and Ada — and there could be no higher accolade. Then they went back for more grub, before the maggies, the berts and the walters got it.

The Purple-Bellied Parrot and Sar'nt Troggers were left alone.

'My work here is done,' Sar'nt Troggers said. 'It's up to you now son. There'll be tough times to come, but in the opinion of this old warrior, you're mission ready. What are you boy?'

'Sir, mission ready Sir,' the Purple-Bellied Parrot said. He felt like he had a malteser stuck in his throat.

'One final thing,' Sar'nt Troggers said. 'This is a great endeavour you're embarking on. Your most mortal enemy is not the ocean or the noras or the dangle-jawed bum scratchers or some moggie the size of which you have never dreamed. It is the Badhbh between your ears. Remember that.'[4]

They stood in silence or a moment.

'Well alright,' Sar'nt Troggers said at last. 'Carry on, and good luck ... son.'

He saluted him again, and with a flick of the wings and a final 'Rat-at-tat-tat' Sar'nt Lofty Troggers was gone.

That evening, the Purple-Bellied Parrot flew to the top of his poplar and danced and swung around and around a branch on one foot. He clapped his wings together and bobbed his head so much he nearly did himself a mischief. The year's spuglings joined him and hopped about and quivered their wings in joy.

Autumn barged in cool and squally. Many martie chicks struggled; some even died of the chill and fell to the ground to be chomped up by rats and maggies. Millie and Steve lost their second brood, and Millie told the Purple-Bellied Parrot they had to stay longer and try again.

No screamers now careered through the sky. One day they were here, the next gone. Strange birds passed through. Swallies and marties from the far north, a wheatear who told tales of polar bears.[5] One morning after a night of pounding rain, the park was full of willow warblers and chiffchaffs and other warblers no one knew the bin name for. They talked of glaciers and fiords — whatever they were. After fuelling themselves up on cold-stunned crawlies, they were up and away. The spuggies dismissed these travellers as 'dicky-birds', and barged them about whenever they got the chance.

Millie and Steve fought on to feed a new brood. They were no longer Steve's sleek orca of the skies. The clean lines of Millie's blue and white plumage faded as the feathers shredded from the constant toil. One morning the Purple-Bellied Parrot saw two new marties on the spout, all shimmering wings, tufty noggins and yellow gapes. The survivors of Millie's final brood had fledged. But still the marties made no sign to leave. Millie said that they needed time for their littlies to grow strong. Time was spiralling away like rain down a drain; the weather grew cooler by the day, and winds from the north-west chilled the Purple-Bellied Parrot's bones.

Chalkie sidled over one day. 'Crikey mate. You leaving or what? At this rate we'll have to knit you another tank top.'

The Purple-Bellied Parrot shivered at the idea of spending the winter in the park. For most of the last one he'd been in the pink-faced man's flat, and at least it was warm there.

Chalkie inspected the Purple-Bellied Parrot's plumage. 'I know you,' he said. 'And, what's going on here then?' he said, poking away in the vicinity of the Purple-Bellied Parrot's bum.

The Purple-Bellied Parrot looked round at the pimply bald spot. Again, he'd not even realised he was doing it.

He decided to go. It had dawned warm and bright and only a gentle breeze riffled the leaves. It was now or never. He couldn't wait for Millie and Steve forever. How hard could it be to find Efricah, a walloping great desert and a giant galumphing bird waiting on the edge of it. He knew which way was south. After all, Chalkie had told him he was a natural navigator.

He'd go and see the spuggies to say goodbye. Better look his best for such an occasion, so on the way he stopped for a bath. His favourite puddle was full of fresh rain, and it twinkled in the rare morning sunshine. He splashed about a bit, ruffling his feathers and letting the water soak in, and then flew up onto a sunny branch to dry off and have a preen.

As he zipped his feathers back together a bumble bee staggered out of a floppy pink rose. Her legs were like yellow pillows and she was tipsy from all the nectar she must have guzzled. She tottered on the edge of a petal, fell over, got up, walked around in a circle for a bit, paused, her sugar-puff body gasping for breath, and tried to fly away.

The Purple-Bellied Parrot was amazed she even managed to take off. The flight, though, was brief. She went sideways for a bit; she went sideways the other way; she flew around in ever tighter circles. Then she plummeted. Her plummeting was so accurate, the Purple-Bellied Parrot thought she must have been aiming. Perhaps she too fancied a bath. With a tiny 'plap' she belly-flopped bang in the middle of the puddle.

The puddle was around six maggie-lengths by four maggie-lengths. It would have been like him plopping in the middle of the duck pond. She had quite a swim ahead.

The Purple-Bellied Parrot cocked his head and watched. At first she just floated, spinning slowly, and the Purple-Bellied Parrot thought she might have croaked. She started to kick her legs. But all she managed was to go around in circles, and meanwhile her furry body and yellow bum and pillow legs were getting more and more soggy. She began to sink. She stopped kicking for a bit as though she had chucked in the towel. But just when he thought she'd popped her clogs, she started up again. This happened three more times, and then she really did yield, and she lay there sinking, the breeze spinning her slowly around.

The Purple-Bellied Parrot thought about the great rolling roiling endless waters ahead. He thought of floundering, soggy wings slapping the water. He thought how long it would take him to yield, to submit to the black sucking waters and sink down to unimaginable depths, getting darker and darker until the sun was blotted out forever. Then he thought about the park and the spuggies and the chips and kebabs and the Swiss roll and Chalkie. Even the maggies were not that bad, as long as he kept opening tins for them. Why not live here? The parakeets had done it, and they were doing alright. The biggest bit of water to fly over was the duck pond, and that was a piece of cake. Brazeel was probably full of monster moggies and super spugghawks and all kinds of beasties just waiting to chomp you. Millie had said Efricah was like that.

Best to stay put.

The Purple-Bellied Parrot left the bumble bee on a sunny twig to dry out and flew off to tell Chalkie the good news. Chalkie was bound to be pleased. He'd spend tonight with them all in the hawthorn. He found Chalkie having a dust bath with Alfie.

'What?' Chalkie roared, hopping up and down. 'Are you out of your ruddy mind? It's all you've been going on about since spring.'

Alfie chimed in, '"Ooh, I must go hoam …I must go back to my beeutiful Brazeel, with the green forest and the salty breeze. Nermy-nermy-nermy." You're like a bloomin stuck record mate.'

Chalkie went off for a fly about to calm down. When he landed he said, 'No. I won't have it. You are not banjaxing yourself right at the last minute. You my multi-coloured chum, are going home, like it or not.

Alfie huffed and said, 'I'm gonna call a bloomin Cahncil about this. Yeah, a Grand Cahncil. That'll sort him.'[6]

They flew off with the Purple-Bellied Parrot in pursuit. As they flew, the Purple-Bellied Parrot put his case, but all his arguments came to nothing. The Purple-Bellied Parrot thought his point about the parakeets was a good one, but Chalkie even pooh-poohed that. They landed on a branch and he beckoned for the Purple-Bellied Parrot to join them.

'Think for a moment,' Chalkie said. 'How many of them parakeets are there?'

'Erm …'

'Ruddy hundreds, that's how many. How many of you is there?'

'Erm … H'wan?'

'Exacterly. You need more than one post to make a fence. You'll never have a mate. You'll never have any littlies. Have you thought about that? Well, have you?' Chalkie pecked him in the breast on every 'you.'

'Yeays. But I will be okay. Please, what is thees post? And I have you and the spuggies. I will not be lonely. And, who will open your tins for you?'

'Crikey, we managed fine before you turned up and we'll manage fine when you've 'opped it.' Chalkie hopped around him, silent for a bit.

Alfie, who had been watching the Purple-Bellied Parrot closely, finally spoke. 'You've bottled it aintcha … You have, aintcha. And after all that work ol' Loft put in with you.' He looked him up and down, disdain written all over his face. 'You stay around here my friend, beginning of winter you'll be a bald as one of them coots over there. And we ain't knitting you no more of them woolly jumpers. No. It's an h'extra h'ordinary meeting of the Cahncil for you chummie.'

10

OSTRICHISM

They cancelled the late-afternoon mischief to dine early and held the Cahncil that evening in the dense oak by the football pitches. The Cahncil was about him, so the Purple-Bellied Parrot was excluded, but he watched the proceedings from high in the branches, trying to make out the tweets.

The Cahncil was held on a fat flat branch by the trunk, Gert presiding. She held an acorn with a twig shoved into it like a handle; this she kept banging on the trunk like a big hammer. The Cahncil was raucous, but every time she banged the spuggies fell silent. By dusk they got peckish, so they concluded proceedings with a show of primaries. Chalkie was dispatched to fetch the Purple-Bellied Parrot to hear the verdict.

Grand Cahncillor Gert called, 'Order ... Order', and began to render judgement. The Purple-Bellied Parrot, though worried about the verdict, couldn't help wondering why she had a piece of cotton wool stuck to her crown.

'Ahem ... It is the decision of this Grand Cahncil regarding the fate of the avian known as Ol Bignose, otherwise known as, Ooterus Maximus, Schnozzmeister General, that we the spuggies of this 'ere park hold the aforementioned avian in great affection.'

All the spuggies chirped their agreement, except Alfie who shouted 'Objection!' He turned to Vi and whispered, 'I always wanted to do that.'

Gert banged the acorn. 'Order … Order! I will have silence in the Grand Cahncil.'

The spuggies nudged each other grumpily. When they were all silent, Gert resumed.

'We, the spuggies of the park, have come to admire said avian for his deeds. Indeed he has become a great friend of the spuggie.' The spuggies murmured agreement. 'Silence!' bellowed Gert and stared at them all tawny-eyed. 'But the time has come for the avian to leave this gang and make his own way. The avian will not leave of his own vole-ition, so, it is the decision of this Cahncil that we, the spuggies of the park, shall leave him.'

Silence.

'Silence!' yelled Gert, and then muttered 'Oh', and looked cheepish. 'I must emphasize, however,' she continued, 'this verdict is for the avian's own good and will cause us much pain, but under the present circumstances we, the spuggies of the park, feel it necessary to impose this sentence.' She turned away a moment and blew her beak on a leaf, before resuming, 'The sentence will take effect immediately. The avian is duly ostrichised.' She adjusted the cotton wool on her head and croaked, 'This Grand Cahncil is now closed.'

Without looking at the Purple-Bellied Parrot, the spuggies silently melted into the foliage. Chalkie sidled over.

'Sorry mate. It's for your own good.' He slapped the Purple-Bellied Parrot on the back. 'You'll be fine,' he said, and then, 'I won't forget you.' He spoke like he had a crumbo stuck in his throat. Gert shot him a demolishing glare. He turned to go, but then paused and without looking back croaked, 'Send us a post-card from Brazil will you.'

Back in the poplar, the Purple-Bellied Parrot's beak lay on his breast. They can't all just leave me, he thought. How? Where will they all go? The park is their home. He decided that when it went dark he would go to their roost and nonchalantly nuzzle his way into the plumped-up bodies like he used to. But when he landed in the hawthorn they were not there, and there was no tell-tale scent of purple trumps. Where could they be? The Purple-Bellied Parrot returned to his poplar. He'd find them in the morning and everything would be alright. It was probably one of their jokes.

He woke before the first glimmer of dawn, dozily aware that something bad had happened. At first he thought he'd had a bad dream, and then it all came back. He had a good shake and a bit of a preen, and determined to set off to find them. He was about to take off when he noticed a takeaway box wedged in a fork in the trunk. It was crammed with goodies: big juicy sultanas, an apple, half a peach — all only slightly nibbled; a couple of crop-fulls of sunflower seeds, some dried pineapple, prunes, curly cashews, peanuts and — wonderfully — Brazil nuts. There must have been a big spill outside the health-food shop. They'd even managed to find his favourite: a couple of the Brazil nuts coated in chocolate. The whole hamper was crowned with half a kebab and a dozen chips and a half-ender of Swiss roll. It must have taken them ages to lug it all up there — and he'd slept right through it. There was enough grub to keep the whole gang of spuggies going for a week.

He must find them. They'd be out after brekkie grub now and could be anywhere. He'd wait till the sun was halfway up the sky and catch them at a dust bath.

By midday, he'd checked all their favourite dust baths, the goalmouths on the football pitches, the rose beds by the café, under the holly bushes by the duck pond, but they were nowhere to be found. He asked a song thrush sat high in a holly. Yes it was strange, she said, she'd hardly seen a spuggie all morning.

By now they'd be having a snooze somewhere. Surely they'd

be at the café later for some mischief. But the café too was spug-gieless. The crumbs remained unchomped, the teaspoons unrat-tled, the table clothes un-pooed on. Where were they all?

He asked a couple of graces. Yes they'd seen a few of the little blighters this morning round by the café, but as to their current whereabouts they were clueless. Crestfallen, he returned to his poplar and fluffed out his feathers and spent the evening crouched by his box of goodies. But he had no appetite.

Next morning, just as he was about to set off to search, Millie arrived.

'What's all this I hear?' she demanded.

'What do you mean?' replied the Purple-Bellied Parrot, all innocent.

'You know very well what I mean.'

'I have changed my mind — I can change my mind, can't I?'

Millie looked about, as if searching for the right words in the trees and sky and clouds. Finally she said, 'Well, I'm not going to argue with you. If the weather is raht we leave in two days. You do what you want. But I'm telling you, if you don't come you are making one big mistake.' She hesitated as if she was about to say more, but simply said 'Pah,' and flew off.

The Purple-Bellied Parrot was flummoxed. Why was everyone taking this so badly?

For two days the Purple-Bellied Parrot saw neither beak nor claw of a spuggie. Occasionally he thought he saw a bum disap-pearing into a bush, or thought he heard a couple of cheeps emanating from some foliarge, but the spuggies were never to be found in their usual haunts. The Purple-Bellied Parrot spent most of his day hunched glumly in his poplar, picking at the hamper and wondering why on earth the leaves were turning brown and crinkly.

The weather turned even cooler, and the Purple-Bellied Parrot even found himself thinking about the vent in the take-away. The swallies had long gone. The marties were skittish, dancing about on the wires, taking whirling flights to hoover up what scanty flies remained. In the evening Steve came calling.

'Last chance dude,' he said tartly. The Purple-Bellied Parrot had not heard him speak like that before. 'We leave in the morning. Make your mind up.'

'Thank you Steve, but I theenk I will stay.'

'Whah? Don't you get it? Wise up. Your spuggies are not coming back. Trust them — and Millie. Come on. Come with us.'

The Purple-Bellied Parrot said nothing, he just shuffled his feet a bit and thought about the big ocean.

'Okay,' he said. 'Your funeral dude,' and he flew off.

That night the Purple-Bellied Parrot dreamed of Sar'nt Lofty Troggers. Sar'nt Troggers was hovering above his head, yelling and whacking him with his little stick. The Purple-Bellied Parrot could not hear what he was yelling, but he thought the dream might mean something.

The morning — the morning the marties were to leave — dawned grey and breezy. Amidst tumbling leaves, the Purple-Bellied Parrot watched as Millie and Steve gathered their brood on the telephone wire. The two marties flew around a bit, as though making sure all five were there, the littlies all jumping about excitedly. Then Millie chirruped twice, and in one movement they were up and off. The Purple-Bellied Parrot stared after them. They became dots and then disappeared towards the southern horizon — and Efricah.

He sat, numb, like he'd been clobbered by a big spugghawk. Apart from a few graces and the odd walter flying about, the skies were empty. He wondered how he'd got himself into this predickybirdament — it was all that bee's fault. If it wasn't for her, he'd be on his way to Efricah and Brazeel by now. He thought about whether to go and look for the spuggies, but he knew it would be hopeless. They'd have spuggletti lookouts, and the spuggies were expert dodgers. So he sat and felt sorry for himself, and contented himself thinking that he could always go to Efricah and Brazeel next year. Millie and Steve would be back, wouldn't they? To flee from his thoughts, he dozed off.

The sun was halfway up the sky. Through half-closed eyes he saw a flash of blue and white, and something landed on the branch beside him. It was Millie, breathless.

'If you change your mind,' she gasped, 'flah towards that big pointy thing over there.' She nodded towards a TV transmitter on the horizon. 'Flah towards the midday sun until you escape the city. It'll take a while, but keep going. You will flah across a big bin road below. You cannot mistake it because none of the cars will be moving. Then you are beyond the city. You will see a little river. Follow it. Follow it until you scent the sea. Then look for a lake surrounded by reeds. You can't miss it,' she said doubt-fully. 'We call it the Lake of Flahs. We stop there for a big feed-up before the first of the big waters. Three or four days max, and if the weather looks like turning we go earlier.' She pecked him hard on the breast. 'Hey, listen to me. We won't wait.'

The next day the Purple-Bellied Parrot had another visitor. A flash of white epaulettes and Big Maggie thundered into the poplar.

'My dear old thing, well hello there.' She did her prance and strutted towards the Purple-Bellied Parrot, who tracked her with one eye. 'My sources tell me your little brown jobbies have deserted you.'

The Purple-Bellied Parrot opened his beak to respond but Big Maggie clacked, 'Bap-bap-bap-bap-bap-bap-bap-baa.' She pinched his beak together with her beak, and then said, 'Big Maggie talking. Ooterus Maximus listening.' Her glinting eye noted a centipede wriggling along the branch. She shifted a toe and pinned it in place and, while it squirmed, continued the conversation.

'I have a business proposition for you my dear. Come work for me. There were never any prospects with the jobbies, and now you must surely see that they were never to be trusted. I can offer you an excellent package. A cardboard box stuck in a tree, you could live in it. Very snug,' she cackled.

The Purple-Bellied Parrot waited until he was sure Big Maggie had stopped talking and asked, 'H'what would I be doing?'

'Why, what you are good at dear boy, opening things. Nothing you're not used to of course, tins, packets, bags, that sort of thing. As you know, we have always admired your uncanny ability to open pineapple tins. Oh, and would you be so kind as to open wide?' She tapped the Purple-Bellied Parrot's beak with her own. The Purple-Bellied Parrot obliged, and Big Maggie peered inside.

'Ahh, all good, good, good — no cracks or bits missing. You may close it now. Forgive me. Always best to inspect the goods I always find. We may also require that big beak of yours, perhaps … erm … for other purposes, as and when required.'

'H'what other purposes?'

'Well, sometimes, how can I put this my dear, things need to be cut off … things. Things that have been … misbehaving. But you needn't worry your bright green head about that.'

'But, h'what would I …?'

'Get out of it? Get out of it? Oh dear. Oh dear, oh dear, oh dear. I hope you are not going to talk about anything so sordid as payment are you? So depressing. Why surely, being part of the great Maggie enterprise is payment enough — for one such as you.' Big Maggie leaned forward and preened one of the Purple-Bellied Parrot's neck feathers with surprising tenderness. The Purple-Bellied Parrot shuddered.

'But if you really want to know what you'll, ahem, "get *out* of it," I'll merely say one word: pro-tection. Protection dear boy. Without our, erm, maggienanimous protection, who knows what kind of terrible mishap might befall a poor friendless orphan like yourself. Do I make myself plain — birdie?' Big Maggie took a pace back, and saw the centipede squirming under her toe. She regarded it curiously, as if for the first time, before turning back to the Purple-Bellied Parrot.

'You will, of course, have to forget all that nonsense about going to — remind me again, where was it? Ahh yes, Brazil. Brrrraaahzil. Well, if such a place really does exist, you can put all those silly notions out of your head.' Big Maggie placed her black eye close to the Purple-Bellied Parrot's eye, as if peering inside his head. 'But you never really had the guts did you my dear old thing — did you.' Her dagger bill poked him in the breast. He looked at his toes.

'So that's settled then. My people will talk to your people ... Oh silly me. You don't have any people do you.' On the 'p' of 'people' she spat into the Purple-Bellied Parrot's eye. 'So bring your things over, I'll introduce you to the chaps and chapesses, get you settled in and we can, erm, take it from there. Make it the day after tomorrow.'

She released the centipede which instantly dashed towards the nearest hole. As its bum was disappearing inside, Big Maggie pulled it out and chomped it.

No spuggies, no Sar'nt Lofty Troggers, no Chalkie, now the maggies trying to bully him again. He certainly didn't like the sound of the 'things' that needed to be cut off 'things,' and tried to shut his mind as to what that might mean.

Life was getting pretty dismal. But then there was all that water out there just waiting for him to plop into. He wanted to tame the Badhbh between his ears like Sar'nt Troggers had said, but the big ocean was in there too, sloshing about, wild and swallowing everything. Another day went past; then he had a brainwave. He knew where he could find at least one spuggie.

He flew over the duck pond and into the top of the old oak. He was easy to find. He was on the topmost branch, sat under the only sprout of foliage that grew on his bare twig. In a shallow depression below were a few smidglets of Battenburg. If there was cake, the spuggies were definitely about somewhere. Old Stumpy was pecking at the Battenburg indifferently, taking more interest in the field just beyond the railway. He glanced at the Purple-Bellied Parrot as he landed, and turned away.

'Excuse me,' the Purple-Bellied Parrot began, 'but could you tell me where ...'

'Ewd up, ewd up, ewd up. I'm watchin t'creekeet,' he interrupted. 'Just look at that big'un runnin in.' Long moments of silence followed as Old Stumpy peered into a field of bins all dressed in white. Occasionally he shouted 'Shaaaarrt!' or 'Howzaaart!' but the Purple-Bellied Parrot had no clue why. This was hopeless, so the Purple-Bellied Parrot opened his wings to leave.

Old Stumpy ruffled his few feathers. 'Aye, they tewd me you were still 'ere. Can't say I'm surprised. Want a bit of spuggie steel in your backbone, that's what you want. Wouldn't let a bit of water put us off — I'm telling you. Look.' He held up his stump. 'See that foot?' The Purple-Bellied Parrot stared. 'No you don't see it you half-soaked bugger, cos I bit that off me'sen with me own chirper. Got it stuck in some barbed wire and this big george was coming down to chomp me.' He waved the stump about. 'Took guts did that — what you anner got. But I'm Yorkshire I am.'

The Purple-Bellied Parrot gazed at the stump and wondered whether to believe him. He shuddered at the thought of biting his own foot off and shrank from imagining any circumstances where it might be required. Another bout of silence followed. He opened his wings again to leave. No information as to spuggie whereabouts was forthcoming, and anyway he hadn't come here to be insulted. He was about to fly when Old Stumpy erupted once more into speech.

'By eck! Now have a look at that. There's summat for you — summat you could learn from.' He was staring into the scrubby grass on the edge of the creekeet field. The Purple-Bellied Parrot followed his gaze.

It looked like somebody had torn up a sheaf of multi-coloured paper into tiny bits and thrown the fragments to the breeze. Hundreds of jewel-like scraps were now drifting, no, fluttering, across the field. The Purple-Bellied Parrot stared hard, and then he realised that the scraps were butterflies.

'Painted Ladies t' bins call 'em — ruddy idiots — 'cos half of them is chaps. Must be on migration.' Old Stumpy gazed on. 'Them tiny fellas fly all the way t' a big water called t' Mediterranean, over land — and over t' sea. Them tiny fellas, over all that water. Makes you think ...' And for the first time ever, Old Stumpy turned and looked at the Purple-Bellied Parrot squarely in the eye, '... Don't it.'

III

SOUTH

11

CHICKOVA CHICKOVA

A set of slim cables angling into the ground anchored the TV mast. In the morning glare they were almost invisible, and the Purple-Bellied Parrot nearly clobbered into one. That would have been a really bad start: the sun barely above the horizon, sprawled on the ground with a broken wing, flopping about until some fox strolled by with the tummy rumbles.

Beyond the mast, the houses and roads and cars stretched endlessly to the horizon. He flew on without stopping — the last thing he wanted to do was deal with any bins. Sar'nt Lofty Troggers's strength flowed through his muscles and soon he was above the road Millie had spoken of. She was right. It was full of cars, and none of them were moving and the Purple-Bellied Parrot wondered how they had all got there. The river was harder to spot, and he had to cruise about and search. He looked for a fat river like the one in the city, but the only one he could find was more like a stream. It twinkled as it stretched out towards the sun, winding through stubbled fields before disappearing into woods. This must be it.

It was a doddle to follow and, with the sun on his crown and the breeze on his wing, he was cruising along effortlessly. He was even enjoying himself.

'I can do thees,' he said. 'I can do thees.'

At noon he dropped down to a sandy bank for a drink. Bony 'ploppy-bottied mooers,' as the spuggies called them, stared through him, jaws churning, stumpy tails vainly swishing at the flies chomping on their ploppy botties. He searched the sky for marties and swallies, but only spotted a couple of lone birds as they darted by hurdling the mooers. Even though the day was warm with insects aplenty, they did not pause to feed so late in the season. He found a bramble and gorged on the bubbly black berries.

The river, losing its tributaries on the rising ground, narrowed and quickened. It wriggled through fields and woods, through villages and a town choked with cars. By late afternoon the Purple-Bellied Parrot sensed a change. The breeze freshened, and on it the Purple-Bellied Parrot tasted a salty tang. He peered towards the horizon beneath flat-bottomed clouds with tops shaped like the hairdos of the females who wiped the tables and chased the spuggies at the pavilion. The land seemed to end, and beyond he made out a line of silver. The silver line undulated and shimmered. In his belly, the Purple-Bellied Parrot felt the black-berries undulate.

So transfixed was he by the silver line, he almost overshot the reed-fringed lake. He banked round and slowly descended, looking for a safe nook to spy out the Lake of Flahs. As he drifted down, he looked out for marties. A few skimmed the lake, and more were spiralled high in the dunnock-egg sky. He would see Millie and Steve soon and they would be so amazed and happy. Surely they will have waited for him.

He fluttered into a spindly alder. It had just enough foliage for cover, but not too much that he couldn't look out and survey the goings on. Strange grey birds with twiggy legs and skewer beaks and shaggy plumage stalked the shore. One speared a frog, flipped it and swallowed it in one gulp.

There were scarcely any, but he inspected each martie as it hurtled by, longing to call out. Once he thought he saw Steve and yelled out his name, but the martie just shot him a baffled glance before swerving to snap up a fly. All were strangers, and they were so intent in feeding they did not notice the green and purple oddball peering out from the leaves.

When he gave up, the sun was sandwiched between the flat-bottomed clouds and low hills, glowing copper like a new penny a maggie might stow away. He didn't feel hungry, but he thought he should fuel up on something. He shuffled out of the alder and found crab apples and a few filberts the squirrels had missed, but the apples were sour and hard as stones and the nuts were mouldy, so he looked about for something else. A yellow plastic bag dangled from a hazel bush. The type of bag a bin might put his sandwiches in. Probably had some leftovers in they'd chucked away. Might be something tasty. He flew over to inspect. The bag was opaque and he couldn't see inside, but it looked promising. From the shape it looked like it might be half a banana. He just hoped it wasn't a sausage. He reached forward to snip it open.

The sun's embers were wobbling crimson on the horizon by the time he had finished thrashing his beak around in the lake. It had never been so clean. While he'd slooshed and thrashed, he'd wondered how they managed it. I mean, how did they get it in there? Had dogs allowed themselves to be so well-trained that the bins only had to hold open the bag, call, 'Here boy,' for the hound to then back up and deposit his doings? Or was there some kind of between-the-knees neck clampage involved. Whatever the case, he couldn't imagine any circumstances in which a bin would pick *it* up — of all things — and put it in a plastic bag. And then what? Hang it in a tree? He knew bins were pretty bad but … No, can't be. Some freak wind must have blown it there.

He shuddered as a final wave of nausea swept through his body and then forced his brain to think about more urgent problems. Where to roost. He chose a low hawthorn and after squeezing in though the thorns he fluffed out his feathers and thought hard about a second problem. Where were Millie and Steve and the littlies? They were not here. And, looking around him, very few of the creatures that gave the lake its name buzzed about. They must have moved on to a place with better grub. But where? The Purple-Bellied Parrot wished marties could write and he could read, like Old Stumpy. They could have left a note.

The sky suddenly darkened — the crimson light blotted out. The air was full of sound, a sound like a gale snapping though a million pairs of pants pegged out on a giant washing line. In an instant, light was revealed again as the pants hurried on. The Purple-Bellied Parrot climbed up to a bare branch.

He caught the tail end of them, a mass of thousands of graces as they rose and swirled as one, veering and plunging. As they receded they transformed into a cloud of dark, indefinable shapes, for the shapes to then flame as they twisted in the up-slanted rays. Sometimes they thinned out into a skinny undulating trail. Then they were a globe of dense smoke. But always they were the one creature.

The Purple-Bellied Parrot saw the creature bank around for another pass. It closed, morphing yet again, and swept over him. The noise deafened. He couldn't resist it. He leapt up to join them.

'What is going on?' he called out to no one in particular — the mass pitching and switching directions. A couple of graces smacked into him and yelled, 'Watch where you're going you twerp.'

A young grace dropped in next to him. 'Keep your eye on the bloke in front. Just do exactly what he does!' He could barely make himself heard above the din.

The Purple-Bellied Parrot did just that, and he didn't bump into any more graces. The writhing creature absorbed him into its body. He glanced at the young grace who was still beside him before locking his eyes back onto the one in front.

'Why are you doing thees?' he yelled.

The grace in front had just swooped up into a steep climb. The Purple-Bellied Parrot replicated the move.

'Search me! It's just something we do. Dunno who invented it. But I tell you what …,' he nodded to a group of green-clad bins below who were peering up through elongated eyes they gripped in their fists, '… blows their minds man.[1] They just can't get enough of it. Call it a "murderation" or somink. And all we are doing is flying about a bit before bedtime.'

An older grace nudged into them. 'There's some bins as say we do it to avoid the spugghawks and the pidgyhawks. Pahh,' he snorted. 'They know nowt. Nothing rings the dinner gong like a million graces flying about. The preds just dive in, reach out and grab themselves some supper.[2] You just hope you are not the one. Chances are you won't be, but if you really want to avoid the preds, hunker down in them reeds and keep shtum. No, we just does it for a lark.'

The creature swept up high, arced and pitched downwards, nosediving into the reeds. Dissolved now into individual graces, they settled on the stalks and began to chatter. The Purple-Bellied Parrot landed with a crash — he'd never landed on a reed before — and it bent over and he got a right old bum-wetting.

The young grace called over, 'Did you like that? Alright weren't it, flying about in a big mob like that?' The Purple-Bellied Parrot bobbed his head. Yes, it had been very much alright.

Thinking he would be safe in a big crowd of birds, the Purple-Bellied Parrot decided to spend the night in the reeds with the graces. But they were fidgety and chatty, and liked to stab out their beaks if you shifted too close. So as the moon rose and the

Purple-Bellied Parrot saw the silhouette of his hawthorn, he returned and settled into a hidden nook. He closed one eye. The other quickly followed.

He awoke to the sound of clicking. At first he suspected the arrival of a myriad of click beetles sent to torment him, and he searched the foliage, ready to fight them off. But he soon sensed the clicking was coming from elsewhere, and through a gap in the leaves he spied bins, a big crowd of them, all with those elongated eyes clasped to their faces, or even longer clicking eyes fastened to the ends of sticks. At first he thought the eyes were looking at him, but he soon realised they were directed a little way off, towards the next bush along. The bins were murmuring excitedly and pointing.

'Can you see him?'

'Not at the moment. Showing well half an hour or so ago though.'

A dirt track, crammed with parked cars, led down to the lake. Dust billowed as new arrivals scrunched to a halt, their occupants tumbling out to extract themselves and their portable eyes, before rushing off to join the mob.

'Where is it?'

'Reckoned to be in that hawthorn over there.'

'Have you seen it?'

'No.'

'Have you seen it?'

'No.'

'Have you seen it?'

'No.'

'Has anybody seen it?'

'That chap in green with the mutton chops reckons he seen it twenty minutes ago.'[3]

'Is he sure?'

'Reckons so.'

'A first for the British List isn't it?'

'Reckon so.'

'Nah you numpties. Been seen on Fair Isle loads.'

'Adult or juvenile?'

'Adult.'

'THERE IT IS!'

A sudden hush. All the bins on their tiptoes.

'Where?'

Pointing, a hum of excitement, shoving and jutting elbows, aggravation.

'Oi! Watch where you are shoving that tripod.'

'Ssshhh!'

'In theee … left hawthorn, at … 10 o'clock.'

All the big eyes shifted as one, like the murderation.

'Where is it? Ahh.'

'Ooh … are you sure? Looks like a dunnock to me.'

'Isn't that a dunnock?'

'It's a ruddy dunnock!'

'Calm down everyone. It's a ruddy dunnock.'

'A ruddy dunnock! Wow! That's a new tick for me.'

In murderation, a groan, and '10 o'clock' melted into the crowd.

Absorbed in the spectacle, the Purple-Bellied Parrot suddenly felt something pointy sticking in his back.

'Do not move muscle,' the pointy thing said. 'Now, turn a-round … veer-ry slowly.'

The Purple-Bellied Parrot seriously doubted if he could turn around without moving a muscle, but nevertheless he turned very slowly to see a tiny bird the colour of the used teabags they chucked out at the park café. The teabag was almost as small as Sar'nt Lofty Troggers, although not as tubby. It looked a bit like the willow warbler the Purple-Bellied Parrot had met on his last day in the park called Phyllis.

The teabag spoke again, 'My apologies. I het to do that. Sudden movements, espicially from something as ...,' it looked him up and down, '... conspicuous as you, and they vill notice, and they vill turn their big eyes and they vill vetch me, and more vill come to vetch me, and more still, and it vill go on all day, with the cameras clicking with the "oohs" and the "aahs". They drive me insane. Can you imagine vot is like not to be able to take poop without hundred eyes on you?'

The Purple-Bellied Parrot thought hard about that for a moment and had to admit that he couldn't. 'H'why do they want to watch you?' he asked.

'Because, a-peerantly, I am "booted warbler" and they are tweeters and I am veery rare in your country, and this makes me veery eenteresting to tweeters. No matter that I am, as they say, "rather dull in appearance." No matter there are millions of me in my country.'[4]

The Purple-Bellied Parrot looked down at the warbler's feet. He expected to see at least some galoshes, but it just looked like its toes were a bit dirty.[5] He said, 'Where is your country?'

'You vill not have heard of it. It is far, far to east, place the humans call Russia. My name is Chickova Chickova. Vot is your name?'

The Purple-Bellied Parrot had never been asked this question before and was stumped for a moment. He didn't want to say 'Ol Bignose' or 'Ooterus Maximus,' but the first thing that came into his head was Betty. So that is what he said. 'Why are you here?' he asked, 'Did you get lost in the dum-dums?'

'The what?' Chickova looked at him like he was crazy. 'No, I should be far in east by now, beyond great river Ganges. But I had to flee. A bad cat was after me, somebody I offended, a beeeg cat called Raz Pootin, called so because he was veery fastidious and would only poo in tin. His real name is John. But I got caught up in beeg storm and I was swirling around and around for days, and then clouds part and I see lake below. Then tweeters arrive, just one or two at first — now look at them.'

Most of the bins were still peering into the other hawthorn, but a few had lost interest, and were pointing their eyes elsewhere — towards them.

'Down!' hissed Chickova, raising her crest a little, 'Squeeze up against trunk. They see you, their eyes vill pop out and then they vill shout into their leettle boxes and there vill come thousands more.'

The Purple-Bellied Parrot squeezed in tighter. 'H'why doan you just fly away?' he said.

'Caught up in thet storm, I not eat for many days. I lose much weight and am feathers and bone, so I stay to feed. Soon, when I am strong again, like buffalo, I vill leave. Tomorrow maybe. And you vill come too. I hev been expecting you.'

The Purple-Bellied Parrot's beak fell open.

'If I say the word "Brazil", that vill mean something to you — no?'

'No, I mean, not no, yeays!' cried the Purple-Bellied Parrot. 'Yeays! You know where Brazeel is?'

'No,' Chickova said. 'I hev not, how you say, the foggiest. Do *you* know where is India?'

The Purple-Bellied Parrot opened his beak to respond, but Chickova was talking again. 'But I know who Millie is, and she lee-eft message for you. Now, vot she say? I make note on loose leaf somewhere.'

Chickova hopped up a couple of branches higher, the Purple-Bellied Parrot following. A dead leaf was pinned to the bark by a thorn. Marks were scratched on it, indecipherable to the Purple-Bellied Parrot. Chickova muttered as she traced the marks with her beak.

'Ahh yeeas,' she said. 'It says, "Could not vait. Not enough flies. Follow stream till you see line of poplars pointing to hill shape of sleeping pig. Beyond pig, is beeg pebbly field and sea. Follow coast to rising sun until earth turns white and you find stone man sitting in three-petaled flower. We vill vait, but not long." '

Chickova ate the leaf. 'You can never be too careful,' she rasped.

───────

'Has anyone *actually* seen this booted?'

As the day wore on the bins got disgruntled, and the crowd dissolved into little groups who trudged off to explore the remoter corners of the lake, humping their big eyes with them. Chickova and the Purple-Bellied Parrot took their chance for some grub. When the bins were all looking away at a suspected 'buff-breasted', Chickova darted out towards the near shore and landed in a low willow where she spent the day snaffling gnats.

'I meet you beck here at sunset,' she said as she left. 'Don't do anything stupid.'

The Purple-Bellied Parrot found a wild apple tree with a load of windfalls at the bottom, but he had trouble getting them down — they were so tart.

When Chickova flopped into the hawthorn at sunset, bits of fly were stuck around her beak and she looked a good bit tubbier.

'Tomorrow we go,' she said, and tucked her head under her wing.

The Purple-Bellied Parrot had fancied a chat.

───────

A big star in the east still cast a shadow when they awoke to the sound of monsters crashing through the undergrowth. Below, bins were clodhopping about, twigs snapping, mud sucking, pausing to peer up into the branches with their big eyes. On the dusty track, a green crowd was already forming.

'Enough of this nonsense,' said Chickova. 'We hev breakfast on road. I am so sick of these guys. Before we go, you do one thing for me — no?'

The ball of the sun lay on the horizon when the Purple-Bellied Parrot flew onto the hawthorn's topmost branch. The branch was leafless, exposed. He checked where the bins were and squawked loudly, flapped ostentatiously, and preened nonchalantly. The green mass shrieked and surged towards him.

'What the ....!'

'What the dickens!'

Silence as they peered goggle-mouthed, some rubbing their eyes with their fists before they stared again.

'Erm ... anyone have an I.D. on this?'

'Some kind of parrot?'

'Er, durr.'

The Purple-Bellied Parrot stretched his wings took a short flight to the topmost branch of a nearby willow, similarly bare. The mob went 'Ooowooaaah!' The elongated eyes locked on. Pages were flicked, phones thumbed, heads scratched.

'Make way, coming through, mind your backs.'

A blonde-haired man in a white suit was striding through the crowd. The crowd parted before him as if shifted by an invisible force. The Purple-Bellied Parrot saw that the man's eyes seemed to point in different directions — which he thought must be an advantage for a bin. A lump of shiny yellow metal dangled from one ear and a silver cross hung from his neck — just the sort of gear the maggies would make a grab for. He must be plagued by them.

The rest of the bins stood back and regarded the white-suited man with awe. He must be very special. The white-suited man stopped and glanced towards the Purple-Bellied Parrot. He yawned, blew a speck of dust from his spare eyes, and pressed them to his divergent ones. He snorted and lowered them.

'Purple-Bellied Parrot. *Triclaria malachitacea*. Western Brazil, but clearly an escapee. Tut-tut.' He turned to the crowd who held their gazes low. 'Now where is this so-called booted. I haven't got one this year.'

But while the bins had been distracted by the exotic in the willow, Chickova had flown.

'Mission accomplished, no?' asked Chickova.

They'd met up as planned in a pylon halfway to sleeping-pig hill.

'No, yes,' replied the Purple-Bellied Parrot. 'And there's more,' he said, all excited. 'I know what I am!'

'Vot do you mean?'

'I know what I am, just like you know you're a booted warbler.'

Chickova looked down his beak at him. 'So vot are you?'

'Well, I always knew I was a parrot — the spuggies told me that. But it turns out I am a Purple-Bellied Parrot.' The words tumbled out like the duck food from the hopper.

Chickova looked down at the Purple-Bellied Parrot's belly. 'Hmm, you are a parrot and you have a purple belly. Must have taken some kind of genius to theenk that one up.' She launched herself to snap up a passing mozzie before continuing.

'Listen comrade,' she said, 'Don't let them tell you who you are. It doesn't matter vot humans say. They call me booted warbler because my toes are ever so slightly darker than my legs.' She held up a foot and twiddled her toes. 'Phahh! None of my friends call me that. The humans want to put everyone into leettle boxes. Then they can order you about, just like that bad cat Pootin wanted to.' Chickova squinted up at the sky and felt the breeze. 'Now. We go — no?'

'No! Yes!' replied the Purple-Bellied Parrot.

They followed the stream until they came to the line of poplars and headed towards sleeping-pig hill. Chickova flew in silence, staring resolutely ahead. The spuggies would have discussed the weather, past, present and future, potential grub stops, moaned about all the cars, insulted a few walters and picked a fight with a crow by now. The Purple-Bellied Parrot may as well be flying alone. He thought he would try a spuggie-style joke to lighten the mood.

'So ... Ahem. So they, erm ... booted you out of Russia you say.'

Silence.

'Ahem ... so they *booted* you out of Russia then.'

Silence, Chickova staring ahead, beak jutting. Then, without altering the aspect of her head, she said. 'You make joke — no? You think you are funny — no? I tell you, that cat Raz Pootin is not a thing to joke of.'

Chickova drew a primary across her throat and went, 'SShhhlerrk.'

The world looked as if it was being illuminated from below as well as from above. The Purple-Bellied Parrot had been trying to ignore it for a while now, but since they had swept over sleeping-pig hill the silver strip on the horizon had been growing bigger and bigger. Bumpy and glittering, it was like a big crisp packet that had been turned inside-out, scrunched up then opened out again. Suddenly he was having flashbacks. The hole in the tree where the sun came in; the sun blocked out as his parents appeared with food, big beakfuls of mushed up fruit; shouldering a brother or sister out of the way to get first dibs. The roar of the chain-saw. But what should conjure these pictures now? Was he born near the sea?

All vegetation vanished and they were flying over a vast land of pebbles, like some monster had torn away all the turf to go off and make a giant bowling green. They flew over blocky bin buildings from which pylons and powerlines snaked back the way they'd come. They swung past a tall round house painted black with a greenhouse on top — and then they were upon it. Chickova nodded down and spoke, her first word for a very long time: 'Sea.'

They landed on a rusty tin can, way too big for the Purple-Bellied Parrot to open, and he watched the waves roll in. He searched the horizon and tried see their source, but couldn't. Countless waves were queuing up to replace those that had just dissolved on the shingle. He watched them swell and curl and topple, and couldn't fathom how all that might vanished instantly into the pebbles.

He peered out again, searching for something solid, somewhere he might land. Gulls rode the waves like it was a game, disappearing as though sucked below before bobbing up again. They circled lazily, indifferent to the heaving monster below. How could they? He'd dash across as quick as possible. Some big white birds were even diving head-first into the sea. A few big ships clung to the horizon. They seemed motionless. He'd look again, and they were gone. Had the sea swallowed them? Finally he had to look away: he'd seen no piece of solid land. His lower mandible hung slack and wobbled about in the breeze.

Chickova saw the panic written into his face.

'Of course,' she said, 'this is just peeddling bit of sea. This is just puddle that separates your tiny islands from great land that stretches to Ganges and beyond. But you are young and strong.'

She punched him in the ribs. The Purple-Bellied Parrot went 'Ooof.'

'You could fly across this in half morning. On clear day you can see other side. Is just a hop for strong bird like you. Did I tell you you have great physique? You work out, no?' She tried to punch him again but he dodged the blow. 'Come,' she said. 'We go.'

Chickova — so confident in him. How could she know that the biggest water he had ever flown across was the duck pond.

While Chickova went off to pick flies out of a stinking tangle of orange rope and green seaweed, the Purple-Bellied Parrot flew to the top of a telegraph pole and searched for marties.

'Vell?' Chickova asked when she joined him.

The Purple-Bellied Parrot shook his head.

They followed the coast in the direction of the morning sun, the Purple-Bellied Parrot staring ahead like Chickova, trying hard not to look at the sea. But he couldn't help it. It was true what Millie and the spuggies had said all along. It never slept. It was always awake and ready — the worst moggie of your night-mares — ready to pounce, play with you, and then drag you down.

The land rose, turned white and plunged into the sea. They saw a big round field cut short by the bins' machines, and three huge white petals. They dropped lower. Where the petals met, the stone man sat, gazing out to sea.

'Thees must be it,' said the Purple-Bellied Parrot.

'You think?' said Chickova.

They descended.

'I have seen this place many times. It is where they have their last feed before they fly over this spit of sea. I don't see them though.'

Lots of bins were milling about gawping at the stone man, so they flew on a little further. They spotted a shed. It looked a good place to perch for a breather and a look around, and they tumbled down to settle on the roof. The wind had now swung round to blow from a chilly north-east, and only a couple of tubby bins with tubby dogs braved the path hugging the cliff. The Purple-Bellied Parrot shivered. He scoured the sky and the horizon for marties and swallies. A few hurried by, but no one he recognised, and with a flick of their wings they were gone.

'It is veery late in season,' Chickova told him. 'You must understand. They did not want to be caught on wrong side of sea with weather failing. They must think of themselves first.'

A line of old telegraph poles marched past the shed, plodding east before turning north and disappearing into sea mist. Some, at precarious angles, seemed about to topple. Here and there, sagging, tattered remnants of wires still clung on. If the marties were to take a breather anywhere, that's where they'd be — swinging on those wires. The Purple-Bellied Parrot leapt from the roof, Chickova on his heels. As he turned into the breeze, a splash of cold rain stung his face.

The wood crumbled, blown away in the wind as they landed on top of the pole. The Purple-Bellied Parrot spied along the wire as it writhed in the breeze. He followed its curve as it fell and rose between the posts, and then again between the next two posts, and again, until the wire ended and the skewed posts staggered away untethered. A last length of wire hung, slapping against its post. But no matter how hard the Purple-Bellied Parrot peered, no tell-tale knots interrupted the flow of the line — knots which could suddenly untie and spin away to catch a fly.

They flew on to the pole where the loose wire slapped and flailed. They looked back, but the only scrap of life they saw was a wren. It leapt onto the wire, riding what was now a crazy snake, tommy-gunned out half a song, and disappeared back into a cranny beneath a fallen pole.

He was trying hard not to sob while Chickova was still there, and then he realised that she had been talking to him and was now tugging at his tail feathers.

'Listen comrade, I must go. This wind is going to turn again. I know it. I do not want to fight it across this sea.' She flitted in front of him. 'Look at me. I do not have your strength. I am built for forests, for fluttering between twigs catching gnats — not for battling storms.'

'Just a bit longer, pleeze, just to be sure,' begged the Purple-Bellied Parrot.

'No, I go. You come with me or you are on your own. No matter anyway, once we cross sea we separate. You go south, I go east, to Ganges.' She slapped him on the mantle. 'I am offski. Perhaps you stay, no?'

She leapt up, and as she rose into the glowering sky she said something else, but it was caught away by the wind. The Purple-Bellied Parrot watched after her until she disappeared.

He stayed atop the pole. Chickova was right — she always was. He needed Millie and Steve to show him the way to Efricah and to the albatross who knew where Brazeel was. Without them he may as well stay. The spuggies might even let him back into the gang if he got a chance to explain.

The Purple-Bellied Parrot lingered, hunched on the pole gazing south. Behind, the mist was blowing in, cold and grey, curling towards him. He shivered and fluffed out his feathers. He began to sing his little song to himself, but his head sagged onto his breast and he couldn't continue. Presently, he noticed that to the south, beyond the edge of the cliff, the rays of the low sun were saturating the haze and the air was golden, the colour of a Crunchie. The sea had disappeared.

A dot rose above the line of the cliff into the gold and then dropped away. He blinked and stared. There it was again. And again. He saw the dot was shaped like a fat cigar and had wings. A flash of a white. He leapt from the pole and landed a little way back from the cliff. He ran forward to the edge. A cloud of flies had taken shelter from the wind, and five, no six marties were chasing them. Was it them? They were flying about so fast, it was hard to tell.

A movement caught his eye. A martie perched on a rock below the mist, face up to the watery sun, catching the last few rays. It saw him.

'Glad you could make it dude.'

GUNS 'N AMMO

Millie was livid. 'Boy, do you know how to cut it fine. Another moment and we'd have been gone. Look at this weather! We need to leave — now. We might just make it before dark.' She calmed a little and preened a dishevelled green feather. 'We know some nice bushes where we can roost up.'

'How did you find us?' Steve said. 'Chickova?'

'Yes, but she left as soon as we got here.'

'Ahh, those crazy Russians.'

They followed the line of telegraph poles until they turned north, and then they continued east, the breeze cutting across their faces. The Purple-Bellied Parrot glanced over at the five chicks who were ahead of everyone. Millie had to keep calling them back.

'They are bold because they do not know what is ahead,' she said. 'It is a big adventure to them.' She looked hard at the Purple-Bellied Parrot. 'I know you are scared. When we get out over the water, just close your eyes and follow our chirrups.'

The ground disappeared. The green fell away into white, and then the white was lost in heaving grey. The Purple-Bellied Parrot looked down and gulped. He closed his eyes and listened out for the chirrups. The Badhbh between his ears tried to get him to open his eyes and look down, but he fought it off and thought about the chicks — chicks who just a few weeks ago were flopping about in the nest, all tufty-eared and blind. He forced himself to chant a Sar'nt Troggers-type rhyme he'd made up for this moment:

> *If them chicks can fly this sea*
> *Then so can I, Ol Bignose me*
> *They can*
> *I can*
> *They can*
> *I can*
> *I can, I can, one-two, three-four!*

Sar'nt Lofty Troggers would have hooted in derision, but his wingbeats took up its rhythm.

After a bit, he realised that he had flown quite a distance and nothing bad had happened, yet. The breeze was still across them, so they weren't fighting a headwind, and it was even giving them some lift. Most important of all, the sea had not reached up and dragged him down. He could feel the strength in his wings — strength infused into them by the Sar'nt. Now *he* wouldn't be afraid to open his peepers.

The Purple-Bellied Parrot opened one eye — and quickly closed it again. His glance had revealed the marties close ahead, but also georges circling beneath him, and far below a huge ship stacked with boxes rolling on the swell. He steeled himself, chanted his rhyme, and opened them again.

Millie glanced back and called, 'Look straight ahead! Believe in your strength!' She spun round and flew beside him for a moment. 'We'll be there in no time,' she called.

She swooped back to her chicks. Steve was now leading, with Millie flying behind chirruping encouragement. The Purple-

Bellied Parrot saw one of the chicks glance back, and he too looked behind. The final rays of sun slanted crimson across the white of the cliffs. Ahead, all he saw was grey sky, and a faint wavy line where the grey sea began.

Suddenly, Millie's chirrups were frantic. One of the chicks had veered around and turned back. Steve flew on oblivious. Millie wheeled around and around, caught between shepherding the rest of the chicks onwards and going back for the stray. The Purple-Bellied Parrot looked back. Already it was becoming a speck.

A twist of the wings and a flick of the secondaries, and he dived and turned — back towards the cliffs.

'I'll get him!' he called back.

His eyes focused on the speck. The Badhbh put on a voice like Sar'nt Lofty Troggers's: 'Now, you won't let me down — will you boy.'

The Purple-Bellied Parrot saw through the trickery and flew on.

The chick was confused and scared. He'd fly dead straight towards the cliffs for a bit, and then hesitate, looking about and flying in a circle. Then he'd resume course. The Purple-Bellied Parrot caught up while he was circling.

'Phew!' he called, 'You took some catching. What is your name?'

The chick tweeted that he was called Number 2.

'It's okay Number 2,' he said. 'You stick with me. I know you are scared. I am scared too. But we will do thees together. I promise.'

The Purple-Bellied Parrot flew beneath Number 2 and nudged him upwards and then around, away from the cliffs. The chick chirruped something he didn't understand, but soon they were back on course, flying towards the tiny group of marties they could just make out in the distance.

The Purple-Bellied Parrot kept close, and as they flew, he told

Number 2 a story about a tiny bird he once knew called Sar'nt Lofty Troggers, the story about the moggery for pampered moggies and the duck food and the bouncing conkers, and how he'd thought he could never do it — no chance — but had gone and done it anyway, and about one of the Sar'nt's favourite sayings: 'Most folks can do most things if they've a mind,' although he thought Number 2 didn't twig. But he kept talking anyway, because at least it was doing him good.

It took a while, even though the marties had slowed a little so they could catch up, and a couple of times the Purple-Bellied Parrot thought he'd lost them in the gloom. But soon Steve was buzzing by, calling out, 'I owe you dude.' Millie chirruped something he didn't hear, and flew on, chivvying her chicks. Between the grey of the sky and the grey of the sea a black line had appeared.

'Nearly there,' Steve called.

The Purple-Bellied Parrot still kept Number 2 close. He noticed that they were losing height, and the rest of the family were now quite a bit above. Number 2 was tiring and his wing-beats were slowing. Sometimes he'd close his wings completely to rest, relying on his momentum to stay aloft. But all the time they were getting lower.

Millie looked down anxiously.

'I will stay with him,' the Purple-Bellied Parrot called up.

Millie plunged down. 'Look ahead,' she said. The Purple-Bellied Parrot peered through the gloom towards the black line. 'Dead ahead,' she urged. 'See that?' The Purple-Bellied Parrot stared hard and saw that the black line was cut by a vertical line. 'Aim for that. We'll be there.' She climbed away.

They were still getting lower. Rather than simply a heaving grey mass he could make out white foam where the waves coiled over. He saw dark seabirds shaped like crosses skimming the waves. Some settled on the water. They must be waterproof like the berts. But he and Number 2 were not waterproof. He looked up and saw Millie and Steve and the littlies, getting further away.

He talked quietly to Number 2. He told him about his dreams of Brazeel and the emerald forest. But the chick, flapping mechanically, was now half-asleep with exhaustion. The Purple-Bellied Parrot stayed beside him, occasionally nudging him upwards — after all, he'd made a promise. But ever downwards they drifted. The Purple-Bellied Parrot thought it was rain that stung his face. But he tasted salt. The sea was coming to meet them. Number 2 fell onto his mantle, and he pushed him up again.

Ahead he saw their goal. It was an enormous flower. Three petals, like the one where the stone man had gazed out to sea, but this one had a stem and was upright.

Millie perched on one of the turbine's still blades. For an instant she thought about returning, but she knew that she too would plummet alone and exhausted into the sea. And anyway, it would soon be dark, and hopeless.

It was only natural. She'd made the crossing five times now, and never without losing at least one. As they'd left the white cliffs she'd wondered who it would be this time.

Beneath the black cloud a line of crimson clung on. She peered. The sea roared and the wind moaned as it funnelled around the turbine, and hissed as it sifted through the bushes below. No more birds arrived. They had been the last — others chirped astonishment as they had settled in the foliage. She fluffed out her feathers and sat lower on the cold steel. She chirruped Number 2's name. She watched the crimson line fade and then vanish.

She heard before she saw. Continuous chatter. It was a voice she knew well — but only one voice. He's talking himself home.

She strained her eyes. She saw a shape — but only one shape. She sighed and swallowed hard. It was only natural. This time it was Number 2. This is why she does not name them until they reach the savannah.

The struggling shape grew. She watched it labour in, recognising its tail and broad wings. The shape slumped onto the blade above, panting, and lay still. Millie opened her wings to fly over but then froze. Something odd happened. The shape divided into two shapes, one large; one small. The small shape shuffled along the blade, and Number 2 chirruped for his mum.

The Purple-Bellied Parrot told the tale the next day in the yellow dawn. He told them about the sea-spray on their faces, whipped up from the foamy crests. He told them how they had looked for something — anything — to land on, a boat, a piece of driftwood even. He told them how they had flown into a trough between two waves, the water louring above them, Number 2 almost flying head-first into a wall of sea. And then he told them how Number 2 had flapped his last, just as they were nearing the rocks, and had plummeted down, and how he had flown under him and caught him on his back, and how his foot had dipped the freezing water, Number 2's claws digging in his back, before he found the strength to carry them both away. He turned and showed them the bit where the claws had pulled his feathers out.

They stuck close to the big sea, keeping it on the wing of the setting sun. Apart from rivers, no big waters barred their way. They flew over endless patchwork fields of shades of brown and yellow, sprawling bin towns that all looked the same, countless cars sludging in and out of them. Food was plentiful. Berries, apples and hazel nuts for the Purple-Bellied Parrot, lots of flies for the marties. After a few days they saw a range of mountains rising above the haze, snowy tops twinkling in the sun. But the weather was so calm, Millie decided to stick close to the sea and skirt around.

'Some fly right over the top,' she said. 'They must be crazy.'

As the mountains ahead grew larger, the land below crumpled into low hills of small fields and forests of broccoli trees.

Lots of birds were in the air all going the same way, and now they were behind a bunch of three walters — at least that's what the Purple-Bellied Parrot thought they were until Millie put him straight.

'What the bins call turtle doves,' she chirped. 'You don't see many of them about these days.' She was silent for a moment as she watched them. She looked down and scrutinised the fields and forest edges. Finally she said, 'You know what? We ought to stay away from these fellas. Come on.' And with a call to the littlies to follow, she veered away.

The Purple-Bellied Parrot had been gazing at the turtle doves. They looked slow and clumsy, and he had been trying to overtake them, but now he grumpily realised they were a lot quicker than they looked. He heard Millie say to steer clear of them, and she sounded worried, but they hardly looked dangerous. Not hooky beaks or pointy talons. What were they going to do? Poo at you?

He was staring at the tail of the leading dove, puffing as he tried to catch up, when something happened that he could not explain. The dove exploded. One minute it was there — then a slapping-tearing noise — and it was a cloud of feathers. The Purple-Bellied Parrot was by then so close he flew through the plumage cloud. He swallowed a feather and felt something warm and sticky hit his forehead. He glanced back. A ragged body was plummeting.

The Purple-Bellied Parrot's mind whirled. What could it be? The only time he had seen anything similar was in the park when he'd seen a peregrine clobber a walter. But the glance around had revealed no beefy falcon. And anyway, the sky would have been full of alarm calls of fellow travellers.

As his mind worked — another slapping-tearing noise — and his wing exploded. He stayed aloft for a moment as his momentum carried him on, but then he was cartwheeling down amidst a cascade of green feathers. He flapped hard to try and right himself, but he discovered only one wing was working, and that just made things worse. He stopped flapping and closed his wings a little and tried to glide. That worked. He managed to get his downside down and his upside up and stop tumbling — but now the trees were rushing up to meet him.

He aimed for what looked like the softest foliage.

He slammed into the branches and crashed down, bumping into every hard bit, 'Ooh … Ow … Oof … Ouch … Ooh yer bugger', before he was stopped by a flat bit where a branch met the trunk. Some big bird had built a nest there so luckily he whumped onto a bed of twigs rather than whacked onto hard branch.

He was out cold for only a few moments, but when he woke he heard dogs. Dogs with dark, deep barks: 'Rrroff … Roff … Rrrroff.' Big, bitey, dogs. The 'Rrroffs' were coming closer.

He peered groggily down from his branch. Two floppy hounds came galumphing through the forest, ears a-flapping. They reached his tree and sank their noses into the leaf litter and rootled about, tails waving about like garden canes on a windy day with a spuggie on top. When they had searched through the leaves and found nothing, they looked gormlessly about, like they had been outfoxed and were waiting for somebody to tell them what to do next. One of them sniffed the air — the Purple-Bellied Parrot saw his nostrils glisten and twitch — and looked up.

The howls were deafening. Both of them went at it, and their slobbering jaws gaped so wide that the Purple-Bellied Parrot thought he might see all the way down to their bums and out the other end. Their eyes had locked onto him, or rather onto the point where he had been before he had squashed himself into a crevice. He heard crashing noises and saw two large shadows appearing and disappearing among the trunks. The two shadows got closer and turned into two fat bins. They were dressed in clothes the colour of the forest floor, all shadows and light and leaves and earth. They wore hats with sticky-out bits over their eyes like beaks, and carried metal tubes with lumps of wood stuck to the ends. From a silver ring attached to the belt of one of them, a beardy bin, the broken body of the dove dangled. The dove looked much smaller now, but the Purple-Bellied Parrot saw how the ruined plumage still gleamed in the sun.

The bins looked up to where the dogs' noses pointed. The Purple-Bellied Parrot scrunched himself tighter into his crevice. A no-beard bin cupped his hands and lit a cigarette and said something and they both laughed. Beardy-bin kicked through the leaves, searching. Ciggy-bin snapped at the dogs, who both fell instantly silent. He turned and struggled with his flies and peed into a bush, and then put it away and flapped his hands about, a black dribble down his thigh. They laughed some more. They looked up in the direction of the Purple-Bellied Parrot, exchanged a couple of comments and nodded. Beardy-bin raised his metal tube. The Purple-Bellied Parrot watched with one eye as Beardy-bin closed one eye and peered along it.

It spat fire.

'CRACK!' like the biggest branch snapping off the biggest oak.

The flat bit shattered and the nest vanished. The Purple-Bellied Parrot was sprayed by sap and shredded wood. The splintered limb swayed, clinging on by a few straining fibres, and then sagged and clattered into the branches below. The Purple-Bellied Parrot squashed himself in even tighter. His crevice had saved him, but he noticed, lodged in the bark by his head, a tiny metal ball. It smelled of smoke and he felt heat glowing from it. If they fired again, they would blast away his crevice and he too would be dangling from the silver ring.

They were laughing again, like the blasting of the branch was the funniest thing they had ever seen. But they did not fire again. They looked at the ground and at each other a bit and had another chat. Then they strode away to become lost in the trees. The dogs lingered, panting, slobber dangling, staring at the spot they knew the Purple-Bellied Parrot to be. A command echoed out, and they meekly trotted away. One turned, gave a final 'Rrrroff' and bounded away.

The Purple-Bellied Parrot heaved a big sigh. He waited to be sure they were really gone — it could be one of the sneaky bin tricks Sar'nt Lofty Troggers had told him about — and then eased himself out of his crevice. He climbed higher to a hidden spot and took stock.

He was dazed and bruised and bashed, but his body seemed to have survived the tumble through the trees okay. He could still walk and clamber. But what was going on with that wing? Originating somewhere near the tip, pain was whizzing along it. Gingerly he unfolded it. He saw the blood ooze and almost fainted but quickly looked away and let the wing fall and hang. He wobbled and said, 'I theenk I will be — how do the spuggies say it? Ah yes, pushing up the daisies soon.' He crumpled, crestfallen.

After a bit, he climbed up a few more branches so as to be in the sun. 'I may as well be warm when I croak,' he said. He sobbed a little and lifted his face to the sun. 'Now I never go to Brazeel and see my home,' he sighed. He sang his little song to himself and closed his eyes.

He must have nodded off, because when he opened his eyes and looked about and could see things, he knew he hadn't croaked. The spuggies had told him that once you croak that was it. Croakage was for keeps. So he took a deep breath, gritted his beak, and lifted his wing.

'OOOOh-ooooh-OOOH', he groaned as the pain shot along it. He poked at the bit where the blood was; the blood trickled — but not much of it. That made him feel a bit better, but the better didn't last. Something was embedded in the bloody bit that he didn't remember being there before, something hard and round. He moved a feather aside and whimpered as he pushed the wound apart. A metal ball like the one stuck in the bark glistened out at him.

He wobbled a bit and had to take a few deep breaths, so he rested a moment. He steeled himself and picked the debris from his plumage that the nest and the exploding branch had sprayed, and decided to climb to the top of the tree. Millie must have seen what happened and might be looking for him. He mustn't worry her. He clambered out onto a bouncy twig, and looked up.

A martie circled against the dazzling blue.

Millie heard the squawk, plunged into a dive and swept up to land beside him on the bouncy twig.

'You've been shot,' she said.

The Purple-Bellied Parrot was still dazed. 'What does that mean?'

'The bins, they tried to kill you with their guns. Guns — the sticks that spit fire and hot stones.'

'Yeas, they had some of those. But ...' he was baffled, 'but why do they want to croakif... kill me? Do they want to eat me?'

'Nahh. Lift your wing.' She inspected his wound. 'They do it for fun.'

The Purple-Bellied Parrot thought about this hard, trying to understand, but he couldn't. 'For fun?' he muttered. Then it clicked, 'Ahh, a bit like the maggies and moggies.' He winced as Millie poked at the metal ball.

'Now don't be such a fledgling,' she said, dropping his wing.

She seemed pleased. 'Well, better if it had gone straight through, but not as bad as it maht have been. Those guns shoot lots of little balls so they can still get you even when their aim is rubbish, so you're lucky only to get hit by one.'

The Purple-Bellied Parrot didn't feel very lucky.

'Hmm, now you've got two choices. You can leave it where it is. It might heal over okay and you'd have a nice souvenir of your trip to Brazil to carry around for the rest of your earthly and show off to your mates.' Millie tutted doubtfully. 'But you've a long trip ahead and it might go bad. My advice, go down to the beach and get it whipped out. You haven't lost too may feathers so you'll still be able to flah.' She nudged him in the ribs. 'Come on. Let's go.'

The Purple-Bellied Parrot tried a few trial flaps. The pain was bearable, but he knew he wouldn't have the same lift in that wing. Sure enough, as they rose above the trees he found he was flying all lop-sided and wobbling about, and to stay straight and level he had to flap less hard with the good wing — which was tricky. He also did a fair bit of gliding, so progress was slow. They struggled over a hill and saw the sea in the distance. He asked Millie why they needed to go to the beach.

'Cos there's guys down there who'll have that thing out in a jiffy. And they are not exactly short of antiseptic wash.'

They flew along a surf-pounded boulder-strewn shore until the coast curved and Millie spotted a muddy estuary. A big pointy rock stuck out of the mud so they landed on it and watched a flock of big-billed peeps dotting the mud.[1]

'Hold on while I go and have a word with that stint,' Millie said, and she darted over to a tiny peep with a ruddy head and a spangled back and a bill shorter than the rest. They spoke, Milllie nodding at the Purple-Bellied Parrot, the stint nodding solemnly. Soon they had both joined him on the pointy rock.

The stint yelled over to the other peeps, 'Which of you guys has the slenderest, niftiest bill? Slenderer than the Slender-Billed

Curlew's slimming champion, their slenderest mud poker, Slender Bill Slim. We need the kind of bill that can probe the cranniest of crevices and wheedle out the wee-est of winkles.'

The peeps glanced at them like they were crazy and went back to their pokings. The Purple-Bellied Parrot, regarding all these enormously long bills, was wondering how they ever managed to preen their backs and breasts and bums. Curiosity then got the better of the peeps, and in dribs and drabs they plodded over to inspect the green and purple oddity. Millie held out his wing for them to see.

A big peep with a breast the colour of red brick piped up, 'Hmm, fella's been shot-up ain't he.' [2] Yep, that'll happen in these parts.' He feinted as if to probe the injury, but at the last instant redirected his beak and snatched a purple feather.[3]

'Well, yee-hah, lookee here. Look what I got.' He held his trophy aloft. 'Purty ain't it.' He eyed the Purple-Bellied Parrot. 'Wonder if this purty thing can dance.' He started stabbing his beak into the mud right close to the Purple-Bellied Parrot's toes. He came so close that the Purple-Bellied Parrot had to hop about to avoid getting skewered. 'Yee-hah,' he bellowed, 'Dance purty birdy ... Dance!'

Millie leapt up. The Purple-Bellied Parrot wondered where she was going. She gained height, dived down and with clenched claws whacked the peep on the crown. The blow knocked him sideways and he splatted in the mud, legs flailing up in the air. The purple feather fell from his beak and tumbled away on the breeze.

'Now listen,' Millie bellowed. 'I haven't brought him along as some kind of exhibit for you to poke with your stupid beaks. He's been shot by the bins. He needs help. Now which of you mud chompers is going to give it.'

All this time, a big black and white peep with the longest and pinkest legs of the whole bunch had been observing the proceedings one-eyed from yonder. It turned and approached, methodically raising each foot and shaking the mud off before planting it down again. Though its movements were slow, the cranked legs gobbled up the distance. The Purple-Bellied Parrot thought that he could stand between those legs and not even come up to its belly. Why were they were so long? The must be awfully inconvenient when flying about — clattering into treetops and such all the time. And they were so thin, they looked like they might snap if he ate too much or got constipated.[4]

The legs arrived. The bird on top said, 'My name is Herman. If you would be so kind, let me examine the injury please.' Herman's head was of the purest white, which made his orange-rimmed eyes all the more intense.

Millie stretched out the wing. Silently, Herman inspected the wound.

'May I?' he said finally, and gently probed the wound with the tip of his beak. The Purple-Bellied Parrot squeaked and flinched. 'I'm so sorry,' Herman said, and then, 'Hmm, this shouldn't take but a moment. Now then, what we need is something solid.' He looked about. 'Ahah! If you'd be so kind, just pop yourself on that flat rock there and stretch your wing out. I'll be with you in a moment.' He strode over to a rock pool and sloshed his bill about in the briny for a good bit.

'Now that's better,' he said, shaking the drips off his bill. 'Now, could somebody irrigate the wound please.'

A brown short-legged jobbie of a peep leapt up and flew to the edge of the water. In a trice he had returned with a beak-full and was spraying it all over the wound. It stung.

'And we also need someone to hold him down and someone to hold the wing still. We don't want him to move it while I am in 'mid stab' now do we,' he chortled.

The Purple-Bellied Parrot was alarmed by the phrase 'hold him down' and the word 'stab,' but something about the manner of this bird with the stilt legs filled him with trust. A bird with a bent bill they called Curly then volunteered to sit on his body, and Millie squatted on the end of his wing.

'Oh yes. And perhaps something for him to bite on might be a good idea.'

The short-legged jobbie returned with a sun-bleached twig and Millie told the Purple-Bellied Parrot to open wide. She put the twig between his beak. 'Bite down on that.' The Purple-Bellied Parrot wondered what on earth the twig could be for.

Herman looked down at the Purple-Bellied Parrot. 'Now, you may feel a slight sting.'

The Purple-Bellied Parrot gulped.

'Attention please ladies and gentlemen,' Herman called. 'Are we all ready?' He peered once more at the wound, and drew back his head. The head and bill remained motionless.

The Purple-Bellied Parrot never saw it, only felt it, and he chomped down hard on the twig. In that instant he knew what it was for, but it snapped and his mandibles clanked together. Then all was black.

Wet woke him. He turned to see his wing lying in a puddle, Millie sloshing seawater over it. She saw him wake.

'You should have seen it. What a blur. One flick of his neck and out it came. Talk about precision.' She stopped sloshing. 'You're done. And here, you'd better decide what you want to do with this.' She presented him with the metal ball.

The Purple-Bellied Parrot held it for a moment in his beak, testing its hardness. It tasted like the bits of wrapper he always had to separate from chocolate and spit out. With a flick of his neck, he launched it out to sea.

Millie was quiet as they flew back, and the Purple-Bellied Parrot thought he had done something wrong. But at last she said, 'That was my fault. I should have warned you. But you were already worried about the sea, and I did not want to fill your head with dangers you might never meet. But I should have warned you about the hunters.'

The Purple-Bellied Parrot thought about this near-croak experience and then back to how he'd rescued Number 2. 'I am not scared of the sea anymore,' he said.

'Well you should be!' Millie snapped. 'You may have to cross a sea that makes the one we flew over look like a puddle of bee pee. It's not a sea — it's an ocean. Do you know what that is?'

'A big sea?' the Purple-Bellied Parrot ventured.

Millie ignored him. 'You must be scared, or the ocean will swallow you up. But master your fear, and don't let it stop you doing what you want to do. Number 2 told me what the old sergeant used to say to you — what was it?'

'Most folks can to most things if they've a mind.'

'Yes, not bad. Could be pithier. But think on that.'

The Purple-Bellied Parrot thought too about the Badhbh, and how it went oddly silent when the danger was most intense.

The little band flew on over the folded, forested land; over rivers that sped through canyons; over torrents that carved the land into shapes like moggies' paws. Millie took them higher to be out of reach of the guns.

The ground rose and they followed it, the roads below disappearing into burrows in the hillsides. They crested grey escarpments, and the land fell away and the forests petered out into fields of pink and green, bowling-green flat.

The Purple-Bellied Parrot watched the sea disappear as Millie chose a route that took them inland. Hills rose again and forests swirled around them leaving only the bare tops. Then the mountains were gone, and fat rivers sprawled across plains. The land turned to dull yellows and browns, green only where it fringed the rivers. It looked like all the grass had withered and died, and the Purple-Bellied Parrot felt the heat radiating up from it — so much hotter than the hottest summer day in the park. 'Thank you Sar'nt Troggers,' he whispered as he kept pace with the marties.

Few houses now. But everywhere the rooty lines of bin roads probed the wilderness. The yellows and browns, shimmering in the heat, seemed endless, and the Purple-Bellied Parrot found himself longing for the sea and its cool breezes.

Suddenly the land filled with water. Millie nodded down. 'The old ones say this lake was not here just a few summers ago. The bins made it.' She dropped down, the others following, and they spent a lazy afternoon drinking and bathing and preening in tree-shaded shallows. The trees looked like the oaks in the park, but these were all twisted and bent like they were trying to escape the sun.

They crossed a big river, the first that day, and then the bins were back with their houses and factories and neat fields and big holes in the ground. The land rose again and turned as green as a bert's head. They swept over a ridge and found another river. Millie seemed pleased and followed it, south. Birds of all kinds were now everywhere, funnelling down to a place they all knew, a place passed down from generation to generation.

The Purple-Bellied Parrot saw the horizon clearing and the light shining from below. Ahead, clouds of birds, more than he had ever seen — more even than in that flock of graces — hung in the air. The land swept up once more as though seizing one last chance to stop what lay ahead, and then it ended in the arc of a bay fringed with white sand, and the Purple-Bellied Parrot saw a blue finer than that of any kingfisher.

Millie nodded across the blue, towards a knobby land rising from the haze.

'Efricah!'

13

EFRICAH

They alighted on a stone tower bleached white by the sun and looked towards Efricah. The Purple-Bellied Parrot thought back to his first sea crossing, how from the white cliffs he could not see across to the other side, and how he'd landed exhausted in the bushes with Number 2. Efricah was there before them, and seemed only as far as a couple of times around the park with Sar'nt Troggers.

They dropped down to a pool for a drink and a bath, and then flew to the top of a low bush for a preen. Steve began to sunbathe. As the sun dried them they gazed at the countless birds surrounding them. Many were preds, and Millie knew some of the bin names and rattled them off.

That was an osprey, it eats fish. That one that looks like a cross between a pigeon and a buzzard, they call it a honey buzzard, but it eats bee-grubs. That one there cruising over the bushes is a harrier, he will pounce and eat you if he finds you. She looked up to the huge silhouettes circling high. That's an eagle and it eats most things that move — even a fox if he can sneak up on one. Those with the dangly legs are big peeps called storks, they eat frogs and toads. That even bigger bird is no peep but a vulture, it eats dead things. The Purple-Bellied Parrot asked why its head was bald.

'So it doesn't get your blood and guts all over any feathers when it sticks its head in your belly to rip out your vitals.'

The Purple-Bellied Parrot was alarmed by all the preds, from tiny male spugghawks to big eagles. A tree close by was loaded with what at first he thought was a crop of huge fruit, and he was on the point of flying over for a snack — until the fruit transformed into shaggy plumage and hooked beaks. The fruit stared out sullenly at the activity around it, yawning and scratching. He asked Millie what they were, but she didn't know and said they were probably from the east somewhere.

'Anyway,' she said, 'you don't need to fret about all these big fellas. They are more worried about getting themselves across this spit of sea, and they can't do that with you in their belly. They are lazy like most hunters and don't like to flap. But they have to get across somehow, so they grab their opportunity when the winds and whirly-ups are right.' She shifted her gaze higher. 'And they seem right this afternoon.'[1]

The Purple-Bellied Parrot followed her gaze. A big column of birds was spiralling higher and higher. When a bird reached the top of the column, it broke away and drifted towards the knobbly land across the blue.

''Will we leave for Efricah before sunset?' piped up Number 3.

The Purple-Bellied Parrot was expecting so, after all, everybirdy else was aloft.

'Nah, no rush. We'll have a good feed up and roost in those bushes tonight,' Millie said. 'And anyway, we need a bit of a chat before we go. There's something you guys need to know before we get to Efricah.'

———

When they had fed and settled into a bush for the night, Millie gathered the Purple-Bellied Parrot and the five chicks together and told them. They hadn't seen Steve since the afternoon, and now he was probably using the day's last whirly-up as a bed for the night.

'Raht,' Millie began, 'I'm going to give it to you straight. No point moggie-footing around, especially after what happened to the turtle dove.' She took a deep breath. 'When you get across you will be attacked. The noras will come after you, as sure eggs-is-eggs.[2]

'What's a nora?' piped up Number 2, beating everyone to the question. The Purple-Bellied Parrot remembered Sar'nt Troggers mentioning 'the noras.'

Millie paused for a moment as she thought. 'Think of a kestrel. Now think of one bigger, darker, bigger muscles, longer wings, and faster — way faster. Able to hang in the air like a kestrel but stoop like a peregrine — the perfect predator.' She sighed. They may as well hear it all. 'And they just love marties, and if they love us they will adore you my bright green fella.' She shot a glance at the Purple-Bellied Parrot. 'And you know the strange thing about noras? It's when they have their kids. They don't have their kids in spring like we do. No, they have them now, in the autumn. Now why do think that might be?' She gazed at all the birds that were coming in to roost, and those already hunkered down in the bush.

The Purple-Bellied Parrot gulped. 'Because in the autumn lots of birds are flying past for them to hunt and feed to their chicks?'

'Preee-cisely. And you know what? You know what they eat the rest of the year? Bugs, beetles and butterflies, that's what. Then come the autumn, we're on the menu.' She looked at each one of them in turn. 'Now, what do you think we should do?'

Number 1 was up for staying put and spending the winter right there and asked why they couldn't. The Purple-Bellied Parrot saw her point.

Millie was resolute. 'Not an option. We have to go to the

south — it's what we do and what we've always done. No, we go on but we stay alert.' She sighed again. 'This is the most dangerous part of the trip, so we need to be brave. We stay sharp and we look out for each other. I'll give you more instructions tomorrow before we leave.'

That night the Purple-Bellied Parrot dreamed about a beaky-hatted hunter shooting his gun at him. But no hot metal balls roared out of the tube. It shot a black blade the shape of the new moon. The blade was huge and he wondered how it ever had fitted in the tube. No matter how hard he flapped and how fast he flew, how much he veered and swerved and twisted and dodged, the blade replicated his every manoeuvre. It closed implacably — and sliced his purple belly in two.

A sudden dazzling dawn and all the birds — from eagles to warblers — were calling. A breeze from the north-west, and already, the dicky-birds were in the air. The non-flappers stayed put, waiting for the sun to wake the whirly-ups.

The littlies flitted about, eager to be off. Millie told them to calm down, while she had a word with the Purple-Bellied Parrot.

'Listen, we need to do something about your plumage. That green is just too conspicuous. They'll spot you a mile off.'

They flew about a bit looking for what she needed. 'There, that'll do,' and they dropped down to a dusty depression.

Dust. Sooner or later dust means spuggies — and there they were. They had already saucered-out little craters where they had been scrooching about. The Purple-Bellied Parrot's heart soared, and he was transported back to those days in the park and their communal dust-bath by the goals and the never-ending conflabs. These spuggies too were in mid conflab, but in no lingo he understood. He knew the topic though: at this time of day it would be where to get the best grub.

Millie said, 'Get in there and get yourself covered, but don't preen it out. It'll slow you down a bit, but you'll be less of a target.'

The Purple-Bellied Parrot picked a big crater and flapped and scrooched, rubbing even his neck and head in the grey, working the dust deep into his plumage. He even lay on his back and wriggled. What joy, but after a few moments Millie called, 'That'll do.'

She looked him up and down and nodded. Even the purple belly had disappeared. 'You look like one of your cousins, them grey fellas who live in the middle of Efricah.'

The little band perched on a rock overlooking the sea. Steve had joined them after a night spent drifting high against the stars, and had chortled at the sight of the now Grey-Bellied Parrot. 'Hey dude, I thought you was a ghost.' Birds were everywhere, darting about feeding or zipping by, already heading south.

Millie issued final instructions: 'Once we are across you can forget about looking where you are going, just follow my chirrups. You need to keep looking up and behind. Best way to look behind is for one of you to loop-the-loop every few moments. The noras ride the wind, high; they select their target; they strike. So look out for each other, and remember, up and behind, up and behind. They won't attack head-on. And listen out for their calls — 'Keek-keek-keek-keek' — but normally they only make this call after a kill.'

The crossing was easy. The wind light on their tails and being part of a big movement of birds all going the same way infused confidence.

The Purple-Bellied Parrot had been expecting instant jungles, but Efricah was pretty much like where they had just been — a bit yellower and bit drier, but the same roads and towns and cars and patchwork fields. They turned in the direction of sunset and hugged the coast. Millie had already told them that it was pointless to go overland as beyond the green coastal strip lurked the biggest, driest desert in the world, and you were sure to die crossing it. Better to take your chance with the noras.

As they flew along, the Purple-Bellied Parrot wondered what drove the marties to make this trip every year. One thing was for sure, when he reach Brazeel he was staying put. No more mammoth expeditions like this. He'd find a mate and raise some chicks and sit on a stump all day eating nuts and getting fat.

They saw no noras the first day, and the Purple-Bellied Parrot thought that Millie had perhaps exaggerated to keep him on his toes. And they were travelling along in a crowd. Lots of eyes to keep look out, and if somebody got clobbered, well, like the graces had said about their murderation, you'd be unlucky if it was you. As they flew along the Purple-Bellied Parrot relaxed.

The day ended early. Millie spotted some mooers below, and where there's mooers there's grub. So they all dropped down to feast on the fat flies buzzing around the bums. The Purple-Bellied Parrot found some strange fruit growing on low trees nearby and gorged himself until a small shouty bin came running waving a stick.

The next morning they flew over a big town with roads like a drain cover and dust like smoke rising from the cars and trucks, but then bin stuff disappeared apart from a few scratchy roads, and the coast turned wild and rocky. Cliffs reared up from the surf.

The Purple-Bellied Parrot looked over to see Millie suddenly tense. They had eased off on the loop-the-loops a while back and she ordered them to start again. Other birds thought they were crazy — and tweeted to tell them so. The Purple-Bellied Parrot looked up and behind and saw nothing but dicky-birds and marties and swallies and the odd non-flapper soaring. So, after a bit, they eased off again. Millie didn't have eyes in the back of her head.

The first one struck at midday.

In the corner of his eye something big and black and solid flashed by. But the Purple-Bellied Parrot never actually saw it — it was way too quick. He looked below and, against the glittering sea, an explosion of feathers. But no bang like with the hunters. The nora had struck a dicky-bird, a nightingale the Purple-Bellied Parrot thought, but the talons had not held, and the victim tumbled towards the water. The black scythe turned and banked and pitched in a trice — like it was nothing — and collected its prey. He had never seen flying like it, and a wave of terror surged through his body.

Ahead another nora struck — this time a redstart. Now the talons held and squeezed, and the nora soared away, nonchalantly bending to begin plucking its victim. Another struck. And another. A screamer — a *screamer* by crikey — struggled in the grip of the talons until the nora, without breaking the rhythm of its flight, bent and nipped its nape.

The Purple-Bellied Parrot realised then it was just pure luck. If the nora cruising overhead against the blinding sun selected you, then that was it. Your number was up and it was time to croak.

'Keep going! And keep 'em peeled,' Millie called over, 'Remember, up and behind, up and behind.' But the Purple-Bellied Parrot couldn't see the point. Even if they missed you on the first strike, you couldn't outfly them, nobody could — not even the screamers. He'd seen it with his own eyes. But Millie, like she'd read his thoughts, called that if they did miss, they never gave chase. They just floated back up on the wind to hide in the sun. There were so many other targets to pick from.

The littlies took on the duty of the loops. The Purple-Bellied Parrot, less agile, was spared, but he rarely looked ahead — his eyes were always held skywards. He wished he could fly along on his back. Sometimes he'd roll over for a glance up and behind, but he'd soon lose height, and if he did it too much he got dizzy. Now every silhouette seemed deadly.

All day they watched as plumage exploded and little bundles were carried away. But they made it through to dusk. They passed the night in a scrubby valley, in a thorn bush crammed with swallies. Usually, what with so many birds packed together, lots of 'oi's and 'watchits's and stabbing bills would have punctuated the night. But they all huddled close, and the bush was silent.

In the glimmer of dawn they chirruped softly to each other, but then a young swallie was taken barely two flaps from the bush. The littlies watched in horror. Yesterday death had been viewed at a distance.

Millie had come up with another tactic. Instead of flying over the sea, she told them to fly over the land, and to keep as low as possible — just skimming the ground like the swallies do on a cold summer's day. That way, the noras would not be able to plunge down from on high because there would be no room for their dive to bottom out and they would have to crash. They would have to strike from behind, and so be slower. With a bit of luck, they'd go for easier targets.

Millie's tactic did little to cheer the Purple-Bellied Parrot, convinced as he was that he was next to be clobbered and clinched and plucked. Wasn't he the biggest and the brightest bird in their group? Even with the dust he renewed every morning, he felt every nora's eye locked upon him. So he began to zig-zag, but Millie told him to stop it or he'd wear himself out before they reached the roost.

'You'll flah twice as far as the rest of us. We get through today, tomorrow will be better. Tomorrow we leave them behind.'

The strikes continued. They flew close to a crag and saw two half-grown nora chicks grinning out from a ledge. The rocks below were strewn with sticky feathers and tiny bones. One of them turned and shot a jet of poo at them.

Afternoon, and a lull in the attacks. The Purple-Bellied Parrot hoped that the noras were all stuffed to bursting and were taking a nap. He wished he could too. The heat was bouncing off the rocks and sand and burning him from below. But by the time the sun settled over the sea the noras had clearly had a good burp and stretch, and it all began again. Numbers 1 to 5 did their jobs and called out the sightings as they looped, Millie chirruping continually. A couple of times they had to take evasive action. But the Purple-Bellied Parrot thought that Millie only did this to give the chicks heart, to make them think they had some kind of a chance.

He ignored Millie's advice and zig-zagged again. Millie opened her bill to scold him, but then turned away to shepherd Number 4 back on course. Soon, because of the extra distance he was flying, he was lagging behind. The marties quickly became specks, and then vanished.

What had he done.

But the urge to zig-zag was overwhelming, and he couldn't force himself to fly straight and catch up. They were watching him, biding their time. He knew it. But now no littlie watched his rear, so every couple of zig-zags he closed his wings and rolled over to glance behind, and then flipped back before he lost too much height and crashed into the dirt. But, so many shapes over-head, it was hopeless.

'Keek-keek-keek-keek!'

He was almost reassured by the call. After all, hadn't Millie said they usually go 'keek-keek-keek-keek' only *after* making a kill? But, like a teazel caught in his belly feathers, 'usually' trou-bled him.

He rolled again and saw a stone plummeting from the sky — like someone had hurled it straight at him. The stone fell vertically, and as it fell the Purple-Bellied Parrot saw it change shape; watched it flatten and extend. And as the shape changed, the trajectory changed, curling from vertical, to horizontal. The stone now had wings, long, dagger wings. They beat the air like a screamer.

The Purple-Bellied Parrot almost crashed into the ground, he'd been so mesmerised. But he rolled and flapped hard and felt himself accelerate. 'Thank you Sar'nt Lofty Troggers! Now I eat lightning and trump thunder.' He dodged round a boulder and wove through a group of low bushes. He glanced back and realised that the nora hadn't gained on him. Was that surprise he saw on its face? 'Yee-haw! Yee-haw!'

But he knew he couldn't keep it up much longer.

His pecs were screaming. He rolled over again. He saw the hooked beak and the dark, yellow-ringed eyes — eyes that were locked onto him. The Purple-Bellied Parrot realised that he was admiring the nora, even as he knew it was about to croakify him. At least he was getting clobbered by a supreme pred, not some galumphing moggie.

It was upon him, and the Purple-Bellied Parrot relaxed as he saw the talons extend, saw the glint of the hind 'killer' talon. Time to croak. Shame.

So rapt had he been on his imminent croakification, the Purple-Bellied Parrot had forgotten that he was still gliding along on his back, getting lower and lower. He crashed into stony ground, a cloud of dust billowing behind him. As he scraped along, the nora shot out of the dust. He closed his eyes. He felt a rush of air like when he'd nearly been hit by a truck during the spugghawk chase.

Something struck him. He expected to be carried aloft, but he was bowled through the hot dust and stones. He cartwheeled into a rock.

'Ooof.'

Beyond the rock he heard a clunk and a rattle.

He lay crumpled and dazed. The world was suddenly silent. Somehow the attack had seemed cacophonous.[3] A dust devil twirled towards him, had a change of mind, and twirled away. He shook himself and struggled up. It dawned on him that the nora might be coming around for another attack. He scanned the sky from horizon to horizon. Nothing. He remembered the clatter and looked from behind his rock to where the clatter had come from. At the foot of an ancient fence post, the nora sat hunched and — apart from one blinking eye like Old Stumpy's — motionless. The Purple-Bellied Parrot dodged back behind the rock, but he realised that the nora hadn't seen him, even though it had been looking right at him.

He peered out again at the nora. Something was definitely amiss. Eyes like Stan's that time he'd drunk the cider, the nora was looking straight through him. It rocked about like it was windy — but there was no wind.

The Purple-Bellied Parrot considered dashing over and giving it a push to see if it would topple over. The nora sagged against the fence, and the Purple-Bellied Parrot realised it must have been blinded by the dust and clobbered into it. He couldn't resist a snigger. Masters of the air indeed.

The Purple-Bellied Parrot sidled over, taking a circumbendibus in case it perked up. Apart from a wobble, the nora remained still. The Purple-Bellied Parrot paused a moment to be sure, and then tweaked a primary and darted away. Milky eyed, the nora gazed fixedly ahead. The Purple-Bellied Parrot stood in front of it and bobbed his head and yelled, 'WHOO-HOO! … HAY-LO-HO!'

Nothing.

He turned and lifted his tail and waved his bum about. He called the nora rude names the spuggies had taught him. Still the nora gazed, although the Purple-Bellied Parrot sensed it now knew what was going on.

Well — what to do? A top predator at his mercy.

He might never get another chance.

He took off, chuckling. Even Sar'nt Lofty Troggers would have allowed himself a chuckle at this. He'd give the tail feather to Number 2 as a present. He glanced back. The nora was reviving and not looking too gruntled, a pile of tail feathers at its feet. Its pimply pink bum gleamed in the sun.

In all the excitement the Purple-Bellied Parrot had forgotten that he had lost Millie and Steve and the littlies. He flew high and scanned the terrain to see if he could spot the little band, but it was hopeless. A wave of panic washed over him. He heard chattering approaching from behind and soon he was overtaken by another group of marties and swallies.

'Excuse me,' he called over. 'Where would a group of birds roost tonight on thees coast?'

They told him there was only one place on this dry stretch, and that they were sure his friends would be there. They spoke in an accent that reminded him of Chickova, and he wondered if she'd made it to the Ganges. They asked him about the huge feather he carried in his beak. 'Nora's,' he said, and he told them how he came by it, and they all chirruped in admiration and looked him over quizzically.

The roost looked like the one they'd slept at the night before, and the Purple-Bellied Parrot cruised over the low bushes calling softly. They'd soon recognise him — nobody had a voice like him. And sure enough after a bit he heard, 'Down here dude!'

He settled beside them and waved his feather about for all to see and told the tale in a right old circumbendibus, ending with, 'You should have seen his bum!' But something was wrong. While they listened quietly and Steve kept saying 'awesome dude,' the sombre atmosphere was like a pile of sodden leaves on a bonfire. He waved the feather about again and, to spice things up, he invented how he'd even nicked a feather from the nora's bum and stuck it in its crown.

They nodded and looked down. Millie could not even meet his gaze.

The Purple-Bellied Parrot was crestfallen. He thought they should be overjoyed to see him and be cheering his story. But perhaps they were all exhausted after another awful day and just wanted to sleep. Yes that'll be it. He'd tell it again in the morning.

The Purple-Bellied Parrot looked again at the solemn group all squashed tight together. A dark thought thudded into his belly and began to swell like a stale white crust after a drink of water. He gulped.

'Where is Number 2?' he asked. 'I have brought thees as a present for him. I wanted to show him they are not invincible.'

He sidled over to Millie who until now had been silent. She turned, and her eye pierced his. She shook her head and buried it under her wing.

<hr />

The Purple-Bellied Parrot never again heard Millie speak of Number 2.

Once, though, after they'd met the albatross and shortly before they parted forever, she talked about the noras and how she didn't hate them. She had said the same by the white tower shortly before they left for Africa. They were only trying to feed their chicks like she and Steve had fed theirs. It was the order of things. If the marties were big enough, they'd have no qualms eating the noras — and probably the Purple-Bellied Parrot too.

The Purple-Bellied Parrot considered this. The marties ate the flies, and the noras ate the marties. There you were, buzzing along all happy, looking forward to your next steaming pile of poo to guzzle, while behind you was this big beak opening up about to turn you into mush. And what about all those baby-fly orphans the marties created, all wondering where mum and dad had gone? A memory of the hole in the tree near the sea blazed through his mind, the day his parents did not return. The bins and the yellow monsters had taken them. Why had they not eaten him? He wondered who ate the noras, but even though he tried hard he couldn't imagine a bird more agile and powerful. Perhaps one of the big non-flappers might filch a chick or two if they got the chance. He decided that he was glad he was, as the spuggies had called him, a 'veggie-hairy 'n.'

As usual, Millie was right. They saw only a couple more nora strikes, and as they left the rocky coastline behind and signs of bins reappeared, the strikes ceased.

———

The Purple-Bellied Parrot glanced about to see if he could spot Steve. Steve was the best flier in their bunch. Everything he did was graceful and effortless, but he could still be as quick as a toad's tongue. He had a habit of going flyabout alone, sometimes for hours, sometimes all night, but now he was drifting lazily along overhead, occasionally swerving to snap up a happy fly. Steve was also easy to talk to. The Purple-Bellied Parrot climbed and dropped in beside him.

'Hey dude,' Steve said without looking at him. 'What's up?' His eyes were half-closed and he appeared to be nearly asleep.

'Hello Steve, will you tell me pleeze about the albatross? When will we find him and where?'

Steve yawned. 'Can't tell you much. Millie knows him better than me — but best though not to be bothering her at the mo'. I'll tell you this though, he's like nobody else you ever met dude. I guarantee it.'

He banked away and returned with a huge multi-coloured butterfly, its legs and antennae waving goodbye as he chomped it down. He gave a final gulp. 'I know where he hangs out. And unless he's been clobbered by something big and nasty, he'll still be there. He ain't got nowhere else to go. Well he has, but he's too scared. Be there in a day or so, maybe two, depending on the wind. Look out for a piece of land like a thorn sticking out into the ocean.'

'But what is he like? We have to make a long journey together.'

'You surely do. You surely do.' Steve turned and looked the Purple-Bellied Parrot over as though for the first time. 'You remember the huge georges we used to see flying over the park on their way to the dump? Massive black wings they had.'

'Yeays.' They were fearsome things the spuggies told him to steer clear of, or they'd chomp you given the chance. Until he came on this trip they were the biggest birds he had ever seen.

'Well, his wings are twice as long as those fellas's. Remember that big shed where the parkies kept the big mowers? Remember the big doorway? Well wider than that. Lie two of those parkies noggin to noggin. Wider than that. Remember … '

The Purple-Bellied Parrot looked at Steve askance. He remembered him telling tall tales about the albatross's wings before. 'He has long wings then,' he interrupted. If they were as big as Steve claimed, he must get awfully tired holding them up all day.

Steve was still talking. 'Those big wings mean that he can ride the wind all day without getting tired. He's the king of the non-flappers. I'll bet he doesn't use any more energy than when he's having a kip. And he's quick. Those last five days we've been on the wing. How far we've come? Over the ocean and with the right wind, he could do that in one day. One day dude. Makes us look like fat old coots.'

The Purple-Bellied Parrot opened his beak to speak but nothing came out. He felt like he was choking. Why had Millie brought him all this way? She'd said that the albatross would show him the way to Brazeel. But how could he ever keep up with a flyer like that — over all that ocean? No land for days on end.

Steve saw the shock on the Purple-Bellied Parrot's face. 'Don't worry dude. Millie'll have cooked-up some plan for you both. You'll be fine,' he lied. 'And by the way, his name is Shug.'

'Shug?'

'Search me, dude,' Steve chuckled, and swept away to grab another butterfly.

The land below became drier; the signs of bins scarcer and more uncertain — like scratches on a rock. The Purple-Bellied Parrot realised that he had seen nothing green for a couple of days; all was rock and sand, the dye of the land reduced to shades of brown and dirty yellows and pinks. Old rivers like writhing snakes poked with a stick coiled through the dirt, but they contained no water, and when they descended to scratch for a drink they found only more dirt. The ground billowed into dust as they landed. Millie told him that they were on the edge of the great desert. The Purple-Bellied Parrot gazed inland: beneath a blinding sun the yellows and pinks and browns stretched to the horizon. The emptiness scared him more than the sea.

The Purple-Bellied Parrot felt his tongue sticking to the roof of his beak. He saw Millie, fretful, searching the desert below. The sun was low when they found their first drink.

From nowhere, a turquoise square, like a jewel the maggies might seize, sparkled out from the dirt. The jewel reminded the Purple-Bellied Parrot of the paddling pool in the park. As they neared, they saw a big house standing before the jewel. The marties swooped down and opened their beaks and scooped the water up as they whizzed across its surface. It was a trick the Purple-Bellied Parrot had always envied. He had seen them do it so often at the duck pond, but with his big hooter he'd crash into the water for sure. Vertical sides to the pool meant he wouldn't be able to clamber down, but there was a shiny ladder in the corner. He tried to climb down but it was slippery and with a 'Way-haeey' he almost fell in. The marties tried to cheer him up by telling him the water 'tasted funny.'

He spotted a table, and his heart soared like a non-flapper. A glass jug filled with water, a bowl filled with fruit — peaches and grapes and melon and those hairy green things the spuggies called 'wee-wees.' The Purple-Bellied Parrot perched on the edge of the jug and shoved his head right inside. He gulped till he was bursting, burped loudly, and then gulped some more. Then he started on the fruit.

He'd chomped about halfway through— swallowing the grapes whole but ignoring the wee-wees — when then the marties started calling. A bin. The Purple-Bellied Parrot looked about, but he couldn't see any bins so he hopped back to the jug for a last drink. Who knows when he'd get his next. He plunged his head in again.

The marties, now frantic.

He took one last gulp — but he overbalanced and, with a 'plunk,' toppled into the jug. Panic surged through his breast as he realised he was stuck like a cork. Upside-down, encased in glass, he couldn't move a barbule.

He could open his eyes though, but soon wished he couldn't. Through the glass he saw a shape appear and grow larger. The glass made it look all weird but he knew it was a bin shape. The Purple-Bellied Parrot would have gone 'uh-oh,' but he couldn't move his beak.

Millie and Steve and the littles were now in a frenzy. The Purple-Bellied Parrot saw a black shape flick past the bin and knew it was Millie trying to bat the bin away. A big yellow square thing came hurtling towards him. It looked solid. He thought it was one of those big blocks they build houses with. But then the block hit the jug and it didn't make the right noise — Whumpff!

The cushion didn't smash the jug, but it knocked it over and sent it spinning towards the edge of the table. There it tottered, turning slowly, the Purple-Bellied Parrot watching the distorted world pass by. The jug wobbled. It wavered. It stopped.

The bin had reloaded and was taking aim, so the Purple-Bellied Parrot moved the only part of him he could. His legs were sticking out, and he flailed them about, trying to get the jug in motion again. It rocked. He felt the balance shift and gave a final kick. The jug tumbled off the table and crashed onto the floor. The Purple-Bellied Parrot sat in the twinkling shards for a moment, head spinning. A rush of air as the second cushion skimmed by. But then Millie was pecking him on the head and he realised he was free and he spread his wings and fled. The bin yelled and waved his arms and chased them, but by then they were aloft.

He feared the marties would be furious at such a near miss, but when they met up on a big rock Steve and the littlies were guffawing, and even Millie was having a chuckle. 'You should have seen yourself stuck in that jug dude,' Steve snorted. 'A jug of parrot!' He laughed so much he could hardly breathe and had to go and fly about a bit to recover.

'Pour you!' Millie said, and winked, and the Purple-Bellied Parrot laughed more than it was funny. She was becoming her old self again.

Onwards they flew and, though it seemed impossible, the land became more parched. Mottled with charcoal-black and ash-white patches, it was like a giant parkie had been along and burned it with one of those flames-on-a-stick they used to kill the weeds. Millie told him that the patches were salt, where there had once been lakes. She told him never to go near them: 'They will burn your feet, and any water you find is poison.'

Amazingly they saw a couple of rivers, but rather than twirling lazily towards the ocean, they made a stick-straight dash, frantic to get to the waves there before being boiled dry. Now, bands of rock broke through the dirt to form low saw-tooth ridges and, towards the sunrise, countless hills of sand rose shaped like new moons. Below, where it met the waves, the land crumbled into the sea as though exhausted.

The Purple-Bellied Parrot saw countless slugs slouched along the coast — and then they got close and the slugs turned into the rusting hulks of ships. Some were stranded, leaning at a crazy angle. Some looked like they had been parked a moment ago, and the sailors had just wandered off. Others were half-buried in the sand, and the Purple-Bellied Parrot wondered how they ever got there, so far from the ocean. The ocean and the salt winds had blasted holes, and their remains stuck up out of the sand like the upturned claws of a monster bird long-croaked. As they flew by, the wind stirred their bones and they clanked and groaned. The Purple-Bellied Parrot glanced back. Bin-sized holes were cut into the hulls; cooking pots steamed and washing flapped.

14

SHUG

They saw the thorn-shaped land mid-morning. But the clear air and the pancake terrain — flat as the ocean — lied about the distance, and it was long after midday when they settled on the thorn's rocky outcrop and felt the spray of the surf. Beyond, the Purple-Bellied Parrot was amazed to see the brown and yellow desert abruptly end, transformed into emerald jungle by the sprawling delta of a fat river.

'No more desert now,' chirruped Millie. 'From now on it is jungle and then savannah and giraffes and elephants, and then we are home.' She sighed and added, 'And this is where we part.'

The Purple-Bellied Parrot had tried to prepare himself for this day, but Millie's words felt like the time he'd slammed into the hoarding when chased by the spugghawk. He turned away and gulped and stared out across the ocean.

Millie scanned the dazzling sky. 'Shug should be around here somewhere. We'll wait with you till he turns up. There's stuff we need to talk about. He'll be out fishing, but he won't be long. He doesn't stray far from the shore these days — after what happened.' She left the last phrase hanging, and for a moment the silence weighed heavy. The Purple-Bellied Parrot stared hard at

Millie, hoping his gaze might prompt a few more words. But none came. She wasn't telling him something — something big.

Steve and the littlies busied themselves preening, while Millie and the Purple-Bellied Parrot stared out over the endless waves, into the direction the Purple-Bellied Parrot might soon be heading. Georges and other birds the Purple-Bellied Parrot didn't recognise played on the wind. A band of screeching terns arrowed past.

More to take his mind off their parting, the Purple-Bellied Parrot asked Millie to tell again why Shug was in the north and not the south where he belonged. But Millie remained taciturn.

'He took a wrong turning. I'll let him tell you.'

———

The sun was the colour of a brambling's breast when he spotted him.

The others were dozing and he wanted to be sure before he woke them. But even from this distance the Purple-Bellied Parrot knew it was something different. It was like a white blade sailing, impossibly, across the face of the wind. Like a sailing boat he'd seen earlier on the trip: a stiff breeze, the sail set across it, and the boat skipping across the waves. But this blade-sail was not bound to the water. One moment its black tip touched the water, and then without any apparent effort it rose high and arced, mimicking the swell, before sweeping back down to the whitecaps. A flying wave.

At first the blade-wave was a pair of wings. But as it closed it twisted and caught the sun and he saw a tubby white body slung between them. Now he saw a head on the end of the body, and on the end of the head an enormous beak. The head was gazing about nonchalantly as though unaware of the acrobatics the wings were performing on its behalf, as if they were two independent creatures and the tubby body had merely hitched a ride on the blade-wave. In all that time and for all that distance, he never once saw the wings flap. All of Steve's tall tales were true.

The Purple-Bellied Parrot nudged Millie. 'Is that Shug?'

She peered sleepily out and nodded, 'Yep, that's him.'

For a moment Shug was lost in the breaking waves until they had another glimpse of him before he scythed down below their rock.

'Quite something isn't he,' Millie said.

The Purple-Bellied Parrot expected Shug to rise up before them on an updraught and deftly drop in beside them, but for a few moments he was lost from sight. Then, from behind, they heard an almighty clatter, and they turned to see Shug chin-down in the dirt, wings akimbo, legs a-spraddle, looking like a wrecked daddy-long-legs.

Millie whispered, 'I forgot to say — Shug's lousy at landing.'

It took a while for him to right himself and concertina the enormous wings, which he did meticulously one at a time, as though stowing away a great treasure. He shook himself and had a preen, all the time paying their band no heed. Nothing cringe-worthy — like an embarrassing crash — had happened.

The Purple-Bellied Parrot noticed that something was hanging around Shug's neck. It was a knobbly orange oval of plastic, attached by a red plastic loop. He must have got tangled up in it by accident while out fishing. Perhaps he wore it for decoration, like a collar. His eye was captivated by Shug's plumage. He'd never seen anything so white as the crown and nape of this bird. Not even the blinding fresh snow that morning in the park a lifetime ago. And the plumage didn't seem to be composed of feathers, but seemed more akin to the fur of a mole. He found he had a sudden urge to touch it and run his beak through it to get a sense of it. But his gaze was now being drawn to Shug's beak. What on earth was going on there? It was like whoever had put this bird together had stepped back to survey their work, rubbing their chin all satisfied, when, with a slapped palm to the forehead, they had shouted 'Beak!' and ran off in search of a tube of quick-drying glue and whatever leftovers they had in the pile marked 'Beaks – XXL.' Nevertheless, the Purple-Bellied Parrot noted the fearsome hook on the end.

Shug had a final shake, clacked his beak twice, stared towards the ocean and, at last, acknowledged them.

'Oorayt?'

'Alraht,' confirmed Mille and Steve, and, after glancing at each other, the rest chimed the same.

'Alraht yourself?' asked Millie, and Shug said, 'Aye.'

'Good fishing trip?' said Steve, and Shug said, 'Aye.'

'Wind good?' said Millie, and Shug said, 'Aye.'

The Purple-Bellied Parrot guessed he was a chap who didn't spray his words around like walter poo. They all stood around for a bit, no one saying anything. Steve coughed. The Purple-Bellied Parrot looked at his toes. Number 4 bit a piece of loose skin from his leg. And then Shug, whose gaze had been drifting along the line of them until it had settled on the Purple-Bellied Parrot, said, 'Now who's this wee fella?'

The Purple-Bellied Parrot opened his beak, but it was Millie who spoke first, 'He's the Purple-Bellied Parrot. He's come south with us, and we have a great idea for the both of you.' She looked over to Steve for support, but Steve had just found a dot high in the sky that needed his attention.

But Shug had apparently reached the end of his attention span, and was waddling over to the Purple-Bellied Parrot, one eye fixed upon him. He looked him over for an age and came close, so close that the Purple-Bellied Parrot could smell his breath, breath like the old prawns the spuggies used to find outside the Dragon's Garden. Shug walked around him so as to inspect every angle, which the Purple-Bellied Parrot thought most rude. Finally he stepped back and spoke slowly, barely audibly.

'I know ydouggghh.'

The Purple-Bellied Parrot was certain they had never met —
how could they? And he surely would remember if he'd seen *him*
flying about the park.

'I know youggh!' Shug growled, and he closed his eyes like his
head was hurting, and was quiet for a bit. He shook his head
violently as if trying to shake something loose from inside. 'I
know yoore kind ... From the old times ... From befoore.'

And Shug lifted his pure white head, curled his neck into an S
against his back, and snapped his head high. His gargantuan beak
opened to the sky and cried out into another world:
'OWWEEEEEKK-EEEEAARKKK-EEEEEAARRKKK-
OOOOOOAAAAWWWWAAW'.

He strode to the edge of the rock and leapt off.

They all watched, slack-beaked, as he disappeared.

'Wow!' said Steve. 'That was a new one. Never seen him freak
out like that.' He turned to the Purple-Bellied Parrot. 'You *really*
spooked him dude.'

The Purple-Bellied Parrot was crestfallen.

'Didn't know he was *so* flaky babe,' Steve said.

'Yis,' said Millie. 'Maybe the decades of solitude have finally
unhinged him.' She stared hard after Shug. 'But now we are sure.
He knows where Brazil is.'

They all went off for a last feed before the light vanished. While
the marties whizzed about, the Purple-Bellied Parrot dropped
into a clump of trees and munched on some tart red berries he
found. While he fed he sensed eyes watching him, but when he
turned, apart from the flick of a leaf or the snap of a twig, he saw
and heard nothing.

When the stars crept out Millie called down and said they
were off to roost in a nearby patch of reeds, but the Purple-
Bellied Parrot said he would join them later and headed back

towards the outcrop. He discovered he wanted to be alone for a bit, like he used to in the poplar.

Shug was there.

He was stood on the highest rock, silhouetted against the dying light like a black statue. The Purple-Bellied Parrot hesitated, then called softly as he approached so as not to startle him. He settled beside him and Shug nodded before returning his gaze to the ocean. They remained silent, both staring out into the black water, until Shug spoke.

'I hoped you'd be here Chief,' he said. 'I wanted to say ... I wanted to say that I was oot of order earlier. I am very oold, and sometimes I am very sad. You made me remember things that I thought I'd forgotten, things that I didnae want to remember.'

For a moment the Purple-Bellied Parrot's thoughts were diverted by Shug calling him 'Chief', but he put it aside for another day and finally said, 'It is alright. It is okay.'

For moments, only the ocean spoke.

Staring out, Shug said, 'I saw you. We came in ... once, close to the shore, and it were forest, and I saw you, and others like you, in the trees.' He sighed. 'I couldnae have been much older than Millie's weans.[1] So many summers ago.'

The Purple-Bellied Parrot's heart soared like an eagle. 'Pleeze, you must tell me,' the words tumbling out. 'What were they like?'

Shug eyes searched the stars. 'Dinnae remember much Chief. I was sat on a rock by the ocean. They were just, you know, going aboot their business, flitting aboot, feeding.' Another long pause. 'They seemed, happy. Ahh ... now this I do remember, you had the sweetest song ... the sweetest song. And two of you were singin' to each other. You know — like a duet. Rayt bonnie so it was.' Shug's head drooped onto his belly, as though exhausted by all the remembering and talking.

The Purple-Bellied Parrot was hopping up and down in excitement. 'We are going back,' he said, 'You and me.'

'Back where?'

'Home. We will see our home again.'

'What? What do you mean?'

'Millie. She has planned it. We go home together. You show me the way.'

Shug snorted. 'You're talking oot your bahookey flaps.'[2] He nodded out to the last glimmer of light on the horizon. 'See that, see all that ocean? Your hame is on the other side of it by the way. Would there be residing in your napper any idea how far that is?'[3] Shug surveyed the Purple-Bellied Parrot from head to toe and snorted again. 'Noo, impossible.'

He was silent again, his head slowly dropping, until he said, 'And anyway, there's another wee problem to take under consideration, the doldrums.'

The Purple-Bellied Parrot noticed that a shiver travelled the length of Shug's body as he said 'doldrums.' His beak now almost touched the ground.

'I cannae cross them,' he croaked. 'I tried, but I just cannae.'

'Then why are you here? Why you not stay in the north, in — in Scotland? You must theenk there is a chance.'

Shug went silent again. The Purple-Bellied Parrot realised that he would have to allot sufficient time for any future conversations.

'One day I'll go. Been waiting my chance that's all. I have nowt to go back north fer. And I do not belong here in all this heat. This is not my ocean, though I have wandered it these winters and summers. No, one day I'll go, and it matters little if I die trying.' He shot the Purple-Bellied Parrot another glance. 'But you!'

'We will try, and we will succeed. I knew somebody once who said that "Most folks can do most things if they've a mind," and thees trip has taught me that. Millie has a plan. Tomorrow she will tell us. Millie is wise.'

'Spare me the inspirational aphorisms will you pal. I've lived a long time, seen things your tiny heed cannae imagine. Coontless seabirds, wrecked in a storm, washed onto a frozen shore like rags. Moontains spootin' fire and smoke. Waves higher than trees smashing icebergs into continents.'

The Purple-Bellied Parrot realised he'd been told off, but couldn't work out how. He assumed the conversation had ended, and made as though to leave for the reeds.

'You can sleep here,' Shug said. The Purple-Bellied Parrot looked around at the bare rock. 'Dinnae you worry. I will be awake. I dinnae sleep. Not here at any rate. I sleep oot there.' He nodded towards the ocean.

The night was long and moonless. Even above the roar of the ocean the Purple-Bellied Parrot was awoken by strange cries and calls. But when he looked up Shug was there, framed by the stars, standing sentry. Once he was jolted awake by a sound that had already disappeared and he only half remembered as shrill and angry. He jerked around, staring into the black. Shug was gone. Behind, he heard scuffling in the rocks, and a shriek. He was about to flee, and then the huge frame of Shug shuffled into view and settled in beside him. The Purple-Bellied Parrot could see black liquid gleaming on the tip of his hooked beak.

'Rat,' Shug explained. 'Big-un.'

Next morning Millie did not return.

The Purple-Bellied Parrot waited with Shug till the sun was hot and the breeze began to blow in off the ocean. Plenty of time for the marties to have a leisurely breakfast.

'I must go and see what has happened,' he told Shug.

He'd spread his wings to leave when they saw a martie beating the air towards them. Number 3 flopped onto the dust, exhausted.

'You must come,' she gasped. 'They've been taken. All of them. I don't know where. Bins. Cages. Please, hurry.'

They left Shug behind — he said he was hopeless flying over land — and sped off. At the reeds they cruised around for a bit but there was no sign. The Purple-Bellied Parrot stretched out his legs to land and look for clues.

'No — don't!' Number 3 shrieked. 'Please don't. This way.'

She led him to a low tree overlooking the reed bed, but she didn't land. She hovered, touching the twigs and branches repeatedly with the points of her claws until she seemed satisfied. Then she settled and called the Purple-Bellied Parrot over. He asked her what all the hovering was about, and when she had her breath back she told him.

She said that her mother had been nervous coming into roost so late with the night almost upon them. Steve had wanted to spiral up into the sky and sleep on the wing like the screamers, but by now the family were used to roosting on something firm. Yet all had seemed normal — if quiet. They circled for a bit. Through the gloom they spotted a fallen tree deep in the reeds, and they tumbled down. As soon as their toes touched the bark they knew something was wrong.

When they tried to shift, they couldn't. The tree clung to them, their feet stuck fast. Only Number 3 who had perched on a higher branch was free. Number 3 thought some kind of sap had seeped out of the branches, but Millie said that, yes it was sap, but not from this dead tree. It had been daubed there by the bins with only one purpose: to catch them. Number 3 said that she had never seen her mother so angry.

They called out to see if others were nearby in the dark, and were answered by a chorus of soft calls. All seemed resigned to their fate. Steve started to peck at the sap, but it gummed up his beak, and he was lucky to scrape enough free to breathe. Number 3 wanted to help, but she had no idea where was safe to land. So they just sat in the dark and waited.

The first glimmer of dawn revealed their plight. Swallies and marties and dicky-birds surrounded them — all stuck fast. Some sang to give themselves courage. Some, exhausted from the night-long struggle to free themselves, had already fallen.

As the sun left the horizon a cloud of dust appeared. A truck bouncing along a potholed track. Stacked in the back were cages woven out of sticks, the size of moggie baskets.

Bins began to work the reed bed. Number 3 stayed as long as possible, trying to blot out the cries as the birds were wrenched away. But then a big shadow engulfed her and she too fled. She perched somewhere and saw her family stuffed into a cage, watched them lugged away. She flew and harried the bin who carried the cage, slapping with her wings and nipping at his ears, just like she had seen her mum do so many times. He batted her away. A good hit, and she somersaulted through the air, but she regained control and attacked again. This time he took his hat off and whacked her hard. She tumbled again and for a moment she was blind, flapping instinctively. Her sight came back, blurred, lights flashing all around her. She forgot where she was and what was happening, and found herself circling aimlessly. Her sight cleared and she looked down: bins tossing cages into the truck, starting the engine, driving away through the billowing dust.

The Purple-Bellied Parrot listened in silence. Then he asked Number 3 to point to where the dead tree was. Unlikely, but they might have missed someone.

The tree looked like any other dead tree, but it was empty of birds. He dropped lower, and managed to hover just enough to put a toe on the branch. The glue grabbed, and for a horrific moment the Purple-Bellied Parrot thought he might not wrench himself free.

As he pulled away he saw that the bins had missed someone. Deep in the wet reeds perched a wet warbler on the end of a twig. It had probably been too tiny to be worth the bother of getting wet feet. Perhaps they had left it there to convince others that this was a good place to roost. The warbler reminded the Purple-Bellied Parrot of Chickova. He wondered if it too was booted. As their eyes met the warbler shrugged and looked at its feet wistfully and let out a call that sounded like, 'Bugger ...'

The Purple-Bellied Parrot pondered for a moment and then called down, 'Is there anywhere safe to land?'

The warbler nodded to a higher twig and said that he thought he'd seen somebody escape from it earlier. The Purple-Bellied Parrot hovered and tested it with his toe. It seemed clean. He landed on one foot then gingerly placed the other down. To his relief, he was able to lift both free. The twig, though, could barely take his weight and it bent alarmingly so that the Purple-Bellied Parrot almost got his toes wet. But at least he now found himself at the same level as the warbler.

They surveyed each other. He had an idea. As ideas go it was not a great one, but it was better than nothing, and he put it to the warbler, and the warbler agreed: it was better than nothing. The warbler said that if he got free then he'd find a quiet nook to work away at the rest.

The twig was old and tougher than he imagined, but he managed to snip the end off with that big old hooter of his. Chalkie and Flo and the rest would have been proud. He worked away at the glue around the warbler's feet. Number 3 was right. You had to be careful or it would glue your beak tight shut. But he had the freedom to shuffle down the twig and wash it in the water and give it a good old scrape before going back to work. He removed as much as he could, and then said, 'That is the best I can do. Ready?'

He severed the twig between the warbler's feet, and then, with another gnaw further down, cut the warbler free. With an, 'I owe you one mate,' it flew, feet dangling like it was wearing clogs.

The Purple-Bellied Parrot flew back to Number 3. He asked if she knew where the bins had taken the cages. She shook her head. She looked numb. The Purple-Bellied Parrot thought hard about why bins would catch swallies and marties and put them in cages. All the reasons he came up with involved nasty consequences for Millie and the family. He needed to be quick — but how to find them?

He flew to the potholed road, to where the tyre tracks cut the dust and followed them. But he reached a crossroads and the tracks mingled with countless other and it was hopeless. He flew high to see if he could spot — what? He would see them, would he, close by, all ready and waiting for him to rescue them?

It was hopeless.

He landed on a telegraph pole and, no matter how hard he tried to block it out, a vision of Millie and Steve and the littlies engulfed his mind: the orca of the skies — trapped in tiny cages awaiting their fate. Millie would be angry but philosophical. 'If we were big enough, we would eat them,' he could hear her saying. Steve would take it hard. He liked to be free, zipping through the air, racing all-comers. Steve didn't deserve an end like this. He should have been clobbered by a nora.

It was hopeless. He sobbed. He tried to sing his little song, but it wouldn't come.

What was he going to tell Number 3? She would have to carry on to the savannah alone. He decided he would go with her, to make sure she was safe. Millie deserved that at least one of them should make it. Shug could wait.

He took off and flew slowly back to the tree where Number 3 waited. She greeted him, wings quivering like a chick. He couldn't look at her. He took a long deep breath and opened his mouth to tell her it was hopeless.

'I know where your friends are.'

The voice came from the foliage behind. The Purple-Bellied Parrot peered into it and saw plumage of yellow and green and grey. The wearer of the plumage clambered down into view, and the Purple-Bellied Parrot was flabbergasted. It was a parrot — like him, but not like him. The grey belonged to his head and the green to his shoulders and breast. The yellow belonged to his belly. The Purple-Bellied Parrot was startled to see he was wearing goggles. Perhaps it was to keep the flies out of those bright yellow eyes as he was flying along.[4]

It took a moment for him to take the spectacle in and then he stammered, 'You … You are a parrot like me.' He gazed again at the mustard yellow that extended all the way down to his tail. 'Are you a Yellow-Bellied Parrot? Because I'm a Purple-Bellied …'

'Nobody has ever called me yellow-bellied and been able to fly without a limp,' interrupted the visitor. 'I am Moussa Caku-caku. You may call me Moussa. The colour of my belly is not the salient point right now. You need to act quickly if you want to save your friends from the cookpot.'

The Purple-Bellied Parrot longed to ask him what it was like to be a parrot, but knew it would have to wait. 'You say you know where they are?'

'Of course I know where they are. You think I live all these summers and not know things. I know many things.' The last phrase was charged with mystery. 'They will be at the market. That is, if they have not already been sold. Then, my friends, you have little chance of finding them. Come.' He clapped his beak together twice, which the Purple-Bellied Parrot took as a sign they should follow.

Moussa led the pair on a winding flight through the forest. They emerged on the banks of the fat river and looked out towards the far bank and a town. They skirted the town and then Moussa cut inside and flew over the roof tops. The streets were crowded. The Purple-Bellied Parrot had never seen so many bins.

'Market day!' Moussa called.

They alighted on a tower on the end of a big building over-looking a square. Stalls, bins selling an array of goods and wares, bins milling about bartering and buying. Moussa surveyed the stalls, his eye roving over the vegetables and the fruits and the pots and pans and the spices and the rolls of cloth and the tools and the mobile phone covers and CDs and brightly coloured trainers hanging like fruit. He caught his breath.

'There!'

Behind one of the stalls, the stick cages were stacked high in a big pile. Between the sticks the Purple-Bellied Parrot could make out living creatures moving about.

'We need to be cunning,' said Moussa, 'As cunning as an empty-bellied hyena in the dry season with six cubs and a buffalo thorn in his foot.' He watched on and then said, 'We will send this little one to fly over and see if she can locate them. She will attract less attention than you and I. We must pray they are not at the bottom the pile.'

Number 3 took off and flew over the cages, pretending to catch flies. They could see her mouth working and the Purple-Bellied Parrot knew she would be chirruping the contact call he so knew well. She made a few passes and sped back.

'It's terrible,' she gasped. 'They are halfway down and in the middle somewhere. I couldn't even see them. What ever shall we do?'

'Hmmm ...,' said Moussa, 'It is truly a challenge. We must be more cunning than a hyena at a lion's funeral trying not to laugh. Let me think.' He ruminated for what seemed like an age, the Purple-Bellied Parrot hopping about, impatient to begin the rescue. Sar'nt Lofty Troggers would have assessed the situation and barked out an order by now. Moussa though was simply staring out over the market, his beak working like he was chewing a nut.

In the shade of an awning beside the pile of cages sat the bird-seller. His elbows leaned on a makeshift counter formed of a couple of planks, and his baseball-capped head bounced up and down to shouty music blasting from a battered beatbox. In front of the pile of cages, a donkey was tethered. The donkey looked grumpy. Earlier, the donkey had stood in the shade of the awning, but now the sun had gone around and he stood baking, head drooping below his knees, a dish of water just beyond the range of his tether. He gazed at the water and huffed. A small boy made the mistake of trying to pat his rump. The donkey bared his teeth and flung his head around and nearly took a chunk out of him.

A female bin stopped by the cages and looked inside. She motioned to bird-seller bin and they talked for a moment. Bird-seller bin waved his arms around. The female waved her arms around. The female handed bird-seller bin some coins. Bird-seller bin hoicked one of the cages off the pile and put it on the ground with the door uppermost. Inside, birds thrashed about, bashing themselves on the woven walls. The Purple-Bellied Parrot couldn't see what happened then. It was hidden by bird-seller bin's legs and the counter. Then bird-seller bin was stuffing something into a small sack and handing it to the woman. He tossed the cage on to a smaller pile behind him, empty. The sack now held little bulges like tennis balls, and like tennis balls, they were still.

The Purple-Bellied Parrot was about to fly off and do something — what that something was he had not yet calculated — when Moussa shouted, 'Ahah! I have it. It is risky but it jaaaahst might work.' He sidled over to the Purple-Bellied Parrot and told him his plan. Moussa turned to Number 3 and said, 'You will wait here.'

The two parrots sped towards the stall and then separated. The Purple-Bellied Parrot wheeled around the front of the stall and swooped down to settle on an upturned bucket — right in front of bird-seller bin and the donkey. He squawked very loudly and jumped about. He turned and stuck his tail up in the air, spread the feathers and bounced his bum up and down. All the nearby bins turned to goggle.

Bird-seller bin's eyes lit up. He rummaged about under the stall and produced a net. He slowly took off his cap and crept towards the Purple-Bellied Parrot, unravelling the net. The crowd, spellbound by the spectacle, parted before him. The Purple-Bellied Parrot continued the rumpus — apparently unconcerned by his imminent capture — still wagging his bum about. Bird-seller bin steadied himself and took aim.

Behind, Moussa had flown down, and landed on the donkey's rump. He clacked his beak together, as though to test its functionality. He sank his magnificent mandibles into the donkey's tenderest parts.

The bray drowned out the beatbox, 'EeeeeEEEEHHH-HAAAAAWWWW', and the donkey kicked out with both feet. Moussa was ejected skywards. The cages went everywhere.

The net hurtled towards him, but the Purple-Bellied Parrot was now airborne. The net grew bigger; he climbed vertically and felt it brush his dangling toes. He swept down and criss-crossed the tumbled cages, yelling, 'Millie!' 'Steve!' Escapees from the broken cages filled the air. He heard Millie respond, and pounced on a cage lying on its side.

Undamaged. Typical.

The bins closed in. He grasped the cage with both feet and flapped with all his might. His mind flashed to the first time he had tried to fly — in the pink-faced man's flat — the spuggies watching. He thought of Sar'nt Lofty Troggers growling 'most folks can do most things ...' He thought of singing a duet.

'HHuuuuuuuuuuuuuuuUUUUUUUUUUUUUUUUUU-UTTTTTTT.'

He was airborne, but only just. The bins were now forming a circle around him, and bird-seller bin had gathered his net and was pushing through them, glowering beneath his replaced cap.

Then the cage was suddenly lighter and he, they, sprang into the air. He looked back and saw Moussa had grabbed the other end, and he too was flapping with all his might. They rose over the mob. Bird-seller bin again hurled his net. It spread, and for an instant it looked like it was going to engulf them. It reached the limit of its trajectory and fell away. Bird-seller bin took off his hat and threw it on the ground and jumped up and down on it and shook his fist. Sticks and stones hurtled towards them.

All missed, and they were away and free.

'Tell again the bit where he bit the ass's bahookey.'

That was the part of the story that most impressed Shug. He thought that was genius, what with all the cages tumbling over and the bins going wild.

'That must have been pure magic Chief,' he said.

The Purple-Bellied Parrot was peeved. After all that had been Moussa's idea. But he'd had plenty of praise from the others about his bravery, even though at the time Steve had moaned about the bumpy landing when they'd dumped the cage in the ditch outside the town.

'Hey dude,' he'd called out, 'Careful with the merchandise!' But the Purple-Bellied Parrot and Moussa were by then exhausted, and just had to let go before they fell out of the sky. Steve had also chuntered when it took the Purple-Bellied Parrot a moment to gnaw through the bindings around the cage door. The reed was all stringy and he couldn't just snip it like a twig, but had to saw his beak back and forth. He was almost knocked flat, as Millie and the family — and sundry swallies and marties he didn't recognise — fled the cage.

Shug asked him how he got to be so strong for a 'wean'. And the Purple-Bellied Parrot told him about Sar'nt Lofty Troggers and the boot camp. Shug nodded approvingly. He'd known troggies in Scotchland. 'They nest on the cliffs in the tiniest of crannies. Survive the worst that the ocean and the winter can hurl at them. Aye, tough wee fellas.'

The marties were away over the delta, feeding-up after their ordeal. Millie said they'd be back well before dusk to go through their plan.

And say goodbye.

15

PLAN AND A SPANNER

The marties lined up on a flat rock, the ocean the backdrop, big waves roiling. Must be a storm out there. The six of them looked chipper considering their ordeal, although the Purple-Bellied Parrot noticed that Steve was missing a toe.

'Left it behind on the branch dude when they yanked us off,' he explained. 'Don't hurt much. Hey, I'm like them pigeons back in the park!' He waved his foot at Number 4, who went, 'Eeeuuww.'

Moussa was there too. After the raid on the market he'd disappeared and the Purple-Bellied parrot was sad to think he'd never see him again, and yet here he was. How he had known about the meeting was a mystery, but then again, Moussa 'knew many things.' He'd bought along a big chunk of pineapple he'd filched from the market to share. How had he known it was the Purple-Bellied Parrot's favourite?

'I returned to the market because I knew it would be chaos,' he said, 'and I just helped myself, cunning as a jackal at a carcass when the hyenas have eaten too much fermented fruit and have wobbled home to nurse hangovers.' Moussa was big on hyenas.

Shug, who had been shuffling about looking edgy, spoke up.

'So what's this plan Chiefy boy has been talkin' aboot? The plan to get us hame.'

Millie hopped up onto a knob of rock and took a deep breath, 'Well, you're going to work as a team. You are going to use each other's strengths.' She looked at Shug whose mouth was dangling open. 'Shug, we all know that you are matchless when it comes to flying at sea. The way you just sail over those waves for days on end like it was nothing, well ...'

Shug puffed out his chest.

'But we all know that when the wind goes away you are like a chick.'

Shug deflated.

'And, for very good reasons we won't mention, you won't settle on the sea and wait for the wind to return.'

Shug began to wave his head about. 'I'm gonna take a heeder off of this rock again. I will, I'll take a heeder.' He unfurled his great wings and flapped them, and let them fall to the ground. 'Thas why a cannae do it lassie. I tried. You know I tried. It's them doldrums — I just cannae get through them.'

Millie leapt on top of Shug's white head and bent over his ear. 'And so, he's going to help you.' She nodded at the Purple-Bellied Parrot. 'You are going to help each other. Calm down. You're embarrassing yourself.' She returned to the knob.

'Dinnae tell me to calmy doony hen,' Shug chuntered.

'Now,' said Millie to the Purple-Bellied Parrot, 'you couldn't give a fig about the wind — in fact you prefer it calm.'

The Purple-Bellied Parrot had to admit she was right. Headwinds were a real pain in the bum, and a couple of times on this trip he'd dropped down to take a rest — only to be scolded by Millie.

'But you can't fly as far as Shug can in one go. And you will have to over this ocean.' She nodded out towards the water in case they had forgotten what the ocean was. 'But you are strong. Goodness, you proved only today how strong you are. So, most of the trip it will be windy — that's just how it is out there.' Shug nodded in agreement, and Millie turned her attention back to him. She took a deep breath. 'So most of the trip the Purple-Bellied Parrot will sit on your shoulders while you do that wave thing of yours. He can hold on to that thing around your neck.'

Shug snorted and opened his big beak, 'What! You saying — I carry him? You've nae got the rumblegumption you was born with.'[1]

Millie ploughed on. 'He's strong but he's light. He must weigh less than a bellyful of squid or whatever slimy thing you guys eat out there. You'll hardly notice him.'

'I fly alone hen.'

'Yes, Shug flahs alone. And how long have you been here, alone, on this rock, waiting for your 'chance'? Waiting for your pairfect wind? Two, three summers? This *is* your chance Shug. Take it. And stop calling me hen.'

Shug's beak creaked closed.

'Now, if you get becalmed — and remember it may never happen — he'll do your flapping for you. He has enough strength to haul you to the top of your wave, and then jump back on board as you glide back down. You glide back up again and, just when you run out of speed, he takes over. He won't have to tow you for miles. He'll probably only ever have to do the last little bit.'

Millie stopped talking. Shug turned to look the Purple-Bellied Parrot over again. The Purple-Bellied Parrot saw a faint shake of the head.

He was thinking hard. This was going to be nothing like when he towed Sar'nt Lofty Troggers on the famous matchbox raid. But now he was so fit and strong. He'd even led that nora on a dance — well, for a bit. And, how about today, when he'd even managed to get a cage stuffed with marties and swallies airborne. He pondered on for a bit, Millie watching him anxiously, and then said, 'I would like to try something pleeeze.' He turned to Shug, 'May I?'

Shug shrugged. 'Knock yersel oot.'

The Purple-Bellied Parrot clambered onto his shoulders. He grasped the plastic ring and a couple of clawfuls of Shug's plumage. He flapped.

He didn't even have to go 'HHuuuuuUUUUUUT'. He had Shug off the ground. He reckoned he weighed about half of that cage he'd lifted that morning. Shug dangled, wings flopping, Steve and the littlies cheering, Moussa joining in.

'He is like a cub being carried to safety in the jaws of a lioness when the hyenas are near.'

Millie shouted up, 'Well you are not going to carry him like he's a bag of spuds are you. Shug, spread your wings!'

'Ahhh Ookay. Come on guys, time to go to work.' He stretched out his wings. They caught the breeze, and the Purple-Bellied Parrot went 'Woo-hoaaaAAWW' as they rocketed skywards. The explosion of lift slapped him sprawling into Shug's back. His mind flashed to when he watched the spiders getting sucked up the spout of the pink-faced man's whiney thing. This must be how they felt. They rocketed high until the marties and Moussa were specks below and he could see the outline of Efricah stretching north and south.

And yet Shug wasn't doing anything. He'd just opened those wings and held them.

Shug called back, 'Hold on Chief — and dinnae do nowt.'

The Purple-Bellied Parrot sensed a movement in Shug's tail, saw a flick of his primaries. And then they were planing down at full tilt, hurtling towards the sea, the Purple-Bellied Parrot clinging on.

'Keep your whallopin heed doon!' Shug yelled back, and the Purple-Bellied Parrot fastened his beak around the red plastic collar.

The waves raced towards them. They were going to plunge in — the Purple-Bellied Parrot was certain. He felt the spray sting his face. Another almost imperceptible movement from the wings, and Shug levelled and banked. A wave, now higher than them, looked about to engulf them. A wing tip dipped the water. The turn tightened and they sailed across the face of the curling wave and then they were rushing upwards. This is what the Purple-Bellied Parrot had watched that first time he'd seen Shug — *they* were becoming a wave. They reached the top of the arc, and the wings held them on the breeze.

Shug called over his shoulder, 'What diyyae reckon to that then Chiefy boy?'

The Purple-Bellied Parrot yelled back, 'Again! Again!'

Shug obliged three more times, the Purple-Bellied Parrot becoming more and more ecstatic, Shug wondering what the fuss was about. The Purple-Bellied Parrot yelled above the roar of the ocean and wind: 'Shug! Thees is amazing! How do you do thees?'

'Search me,' he called back. 'I just open these big fellas up and let them do their stuff. I have nowt to do with it except have a wee chat wi' them noo and then to make sure they're ookay. I'm just along for the ride.'

As they glided back towards the others, the Purple-Bellied Parrot thought it best to jump off before Shug attempted to land. He didn't want to get tangled-up in any wreckage.

Millie said, 'Well?'

But the Purple-Bellied Parrot couldn't say anything. He jumped up and down and bobbed his head for a long time, but when he opened his mouth only a squeak came out and he had to go for a fly about to calm down.

When he returned he cried, 'We can do thees! We can do thees! We are going home! We are going home! Yippee!' and he went for another fly about.

Millie turned to Shug who was reassembling himself. 'No

sense hanging about getting worked up Shug. Best leave tomorrow.'

Millie had a few last words of advice. If the wind even hints at going calm, land on the first thing you see: a boat, rocks sticking up, floating rubbish. Just land and wait it out. She told the Purple-Bellied Parrot to eat whenever he had the opportunity — but not so much that he couldn't take off. She talked of islands that were out there, but Shug interrupted and told her he already knew what islands were out there — and there weren't many of them, and there were no rocks sticking out of the water, by the way.

Millie walked around the Purple-Bellied Parrot and inspected his plumage, stopping to preen a dishevelled tail feather and a secondary. His mind whirled. In amongst the jostling thoughts, a fuzzy one shouldered through, about him sitting on Shug's back while they floated on the ocean and waited out a calm, and why this could never be. But the thought was overwhelmed before it knitted together, because the sad thing was about to happen.

Moussa had already left to feed when they said their good-byes. The Purple-Bellied Parrot said thank you to Millie for everything she had done for him and how he wouldn't be here if it wasn't for her, and Millie said thank you to the Purple-Bellied Parrot and said they wouldn't be here if it wasn't for him.

'And anyway, put those thanks on hold,' she said. 'You might be cursing me in a couple of days when you're out over the ocean riding out a storm.'

Steve and Numbers 1, 3, 4 and 5 said, 'Good luck,' Steve of course adding 'dude'. Number 3 sobbed. They all gave him a peck on the cheek, apart from Steve who gave him a hefty slap on the mantle. And then they were off, just like that, and the Purple-Bellied Parrot was left there with Shug and the Ocean.

The Purple-Bellied Parrot watched them until they were dots in the crimson light. He followed the dots, straining his eyes. The dots bounced around a bit and the Purple-Bellied Parrot was glad because they'd found a last feed for the day. The bouncing stopped and the dots faded, and then disappeared. The Purple-Bellied Parrot stared after them until it was dark and he could see no more.

Neither of them slept. With the darkness and the roaring ocean the Purple-Bellied Parrot's excitement faded. He thought moths were flying about in his belly. Then, as the night creatures began to shriek and howl, his belly felt like a sickly walter had taken up residence and eaten all the moths. No matter how much he told himself that he, like Shug, had nothing to lose, he found himself wishing he was back with the spuggies, snuggled together in a comfy bush with bellies full of chips.

The Purple-Bellied Parrot sensed Shug was awake, but his silence added to the weight of the darkness. Once he risked an 'Alright?' and got back a sighing, 'Aye, oorayt,' but that was all. All, until the very dead of night, when a mist fingered in off the ocean and blotted out the stars, and even the shrieking things stopped shrieking.

Shug coughed. 'You awake Chief?'

'Yeays.'

'I need to tell you something. I need to explain something Chief before … before we set off.' The Purple-Bellied Parrot waited out one of Shug's long pauses. 'It's about why I cannae land on the water and wait out a calm. I mean …' he gave a snort, 'that's what we're supposed to do, we albatrosses. I'm going to tell you why I cannae.'

·   ·   ·

It was maybe our sixth summer oot over the ocean — my wings still more black than white, still seeing what we could do together. I'd seen orca hunting penguins amidst icebergs as big as moontains, flew through storms that lasted for a moon and tore the water off the ocean and threw it in your face, flew through canyon waves where you couldnae see the tops. I was with my older brother Buzon, and we wandered north, just to explore, you know? A little too far north as it turned oot. It got hot and I wanted to go back to the icebergs, but the grub was good so we stayed.

Well Chief, one day we finds the rear end of a whale just flootin in the water. Sperm I think. Perhaps a Blue. It was hard to tell. Just its bum was left, bobbing there in the water, the rest … eaten away, all raggedy. Bits of bone sticking oot. Anyway, we stuffed ourselves, although I dinnae care for whale meat much ma'sel — too oily — but you never know when you'll get a free feast like that again. We was cleaning ourselves up after, just bobbing there preening, and this noddy comes a-paddling over. Gives us a sob story about her colony and how all the chicks are starving on account of the bins hoovering the ocean with their big ships. She points yonder to a rock on the horizon and says, bold as you like, could we take the bum over there to feed her colony. So we ask why they dinnae come get it themselves and she says the chicks had fledged but they couldnae fly properly yet and they were dabbling about at the foot of the cliff getting scrawnier and scrawnier. Okay, it was only a bum but it was still huge so I said how do you propose we get it there? She says that we were big strong young fellas and we could tow it over. She points at some long flaps of skin hanging off and tells us that we can use those. We paddles over and give them a tug, but they pull right off so we tell her to awae and bile her heed.[2] She's offski, but is soon back with some long stalks of kelp like rope that she got the colony to tie together. She says use these. Well Chief, it was summer and we was kids and had no mates to go back to. We had full bellies, and with the bum we'd have full bellies for the foreseeable future. Most important, the wind was picking up and shearing across the route to the island — pairfect for maximum power. So we said aye ookay why not. Better than the sharks and the orca getting it all. So we wrap the kelps around a bit of boon to make two tow ropes and we take off. It was hard to get the bum going at first, but when it was under way it was easy if slow progress, and we felt like real heroes as we sailed along the face of that pairfect wind. Turns out though the noddy had not been one-hundred percent truthful with us, and when we get to the rock it was barer than a bins bahookey, not a chick in sight, nary a scrawny wee helligog, and she points to a rock on the next horizon.[3] She says she never did say it was this rock and starts talking about the poor starving weans again. So we heave-ho and we arrive at the next rock about mid-afternoon, a full-on, raucous, keech-stained rock, scrawny chicks moping about at the bottom of the cliff like she said, some already floating in the water like rags. Well Chief, if we'd had a dinner gong we'd no need of it. They was all over that bum like ants on a jam butty before we lets go of them tow kelps. We watch 'em feed for a while, and we are loathe to leave this free meal, but we notice that the sea is flattening doon from a heavy swell and we can feel the wind fading so we decide to fly. A calm sets in on these seas, it can last for days and we dinnae want to be loafing about on the ocean, legs a-dangling, with all them sharks the bum would draw. So we chomp off a last few chunks and we sets off to chase the wind. Still a stiff breeze, but we could hardly get our bahookeys off the ocean, we was so full of bum. The white island was dipping below the horizon behind us when something happened Chief that I've not experienced before nor since, and never want to again. The wind died. Nae warning. One moment we was planing along, okay, by then it was only a breeze, the next nothing, ekkert, dad, nada — we almost fell right in to the ocean it was so sudden. And I mean Chief it was *deed* calm. We started to flap and Buzon lost a primary and it dropped vertically down. Well Chief, wings like these can only flap for so long before they are knackered. So we know we will be passing the night on the ocean. Which is ookay, we done it before. But I had a terrible feeling about this calm. The sea was still as a plate of bin glass. We was too young to know it then, but it was the doldrums, and they had us by the short and curlies. And with all that bum inside us, we'd be struggling to take off again. So we are about to drop into the sea when we spot a big raft of seabirds ahead, likewise becalmed. It looks like a mixture of albatrosses and mollymawks shearwaters and a few lazy boobies and noddies.[4] So we make for them. Safety in numbers we reckon. The sun is low and red when we slap into the ocean amid that raft. Not much of a greeting by the way. All seem fair nervy.

The last of the sun is dipping below the horizon when the first shark comes toddlin along. That big berg-fin of his slicing the water. What the bins call a Mako. Longer than my wing span. You know how to tell that in the ocean, Chief? You tell by looking from the bergfin to the tail. Add on, another third. Mako's teeth? Two rows of them, curling inwards, like it's beckoning you in. That shark, he does nothing but cruise around. Then he goes away. And it's dark.

Well, the stars are fading, Chief, and the sharks come. First they just cruise. Sometimes their backs break the surface and the low sun glances off them and their sand skin glints and you almost marvel. Sleek. Efficient. Nothing wasted on a shark Chief, and they have but one purpose. Anyhow, we gather ourselves into tight groups. The idea being that the shark comes to the closest bird, we all start a-flappin and a-squarkin and … well, sometimes that shark he go away … sometimes he don't go away. Chief, that shark looks rayt at you. Rayt into your eyes. And you know, a shark, he's got dead eyes. Stone eyes. When he comes for you, he dinnae seem to be a living thing … till those teeth take you, and those black pebbles roll and turn to milk, and then … ah then you hear … Well, the sea turns red, and all your flappin and your squarkin dinnae do no good.

End of that first morning, we'd lost a good shoal of birds, feathers and wee bones floating in the water all over the shop. I dinnae know how many sharks there was, they was like sardine. Everywhere you looked the water was a-boiling and wings a-flapping was being dragged under. They was taking around a dozen an hour. Buzon one of them. Chief, I bumped into a pal of mine, Birdy Robinson from Tierra Acantilada. Barnacle slayer. Buzon's mate. Looked like he was taking a nap, bobbin in the water like a cork. I stretched over to wake him, gave him a peck. He flipped over. Well, he'd been bitten in two, his bottom half filling some shark's belly somewhere.

Morning of the third day, we felt a change, the glass sea lique-fying. A wee riffler stirred our feathers and we knew there was a wind coming. You know, Chief, that was when I was most scared. Waitin for the wind. Waitin to be picked up. I'll never settle on the ocean again.

Anyway, we delivered the bum.'[5]

Shug was quiet for a bit, his head slack, the tip of his beak resting on the ground. The Purple-Bellied Parrot thought hard for some-thing to say. Then Shug started again.

'And this is how I came by this thing here,' he nodded to the oval of orange plastic. 'This is no whigmaleerie. Just as I was about to take off, the boobies and the noddies all grab me. They say there was no sharks till I arrived. So they leap on top of me and hold me doon in the water. I think they mean to drown me, maybe make a meal of me. Then they let go, and they've put this around my neck. It's nearly worn away now, but it's the figure of a bin. They said that as the bins always bring bad luck, you'd better have that round your neck as a warning to others. Never have been able to get it off. My beak's too long to get at it, and I cannae hook it off with these webbed feet. Anyhow, probably meant to be. I have had lots of luck in my life. Trouble is, all been bad. Best to warn folks.

'Anyway, the wind comes. I am confused and heart-broken because of Buzon. My wings pick me off of the ocean and I just sail away. Didnae care which direction. A storm hits and drives me and I let it take me where it will, as long as it is away from the sharks. Didnae see the sun for days. When the storm leaves me, I know something is wrong. Everything back to front. Where I come from was summer. Here it is winter. The sun behind me when it should be ahead. The sea grey. The penguins — flying. No albatrosses. I should know, I searched and cried out many summers.'

Shug's beak touched the ground again. Mist curled in around them. The Purple-Bellied Parrot said nothing. It was a story that needed to be pondered, and as he pondered, even though the mist glowed grey from the coming dawn, he fell asleep.

IV

THE OCEAN

16

OFFSKI

Two things caught the Purple-Bellied Parrot's attention when he woke: Shug waving his head about, and Moussa standing on the knob rock, head cocked, watching.

Shug was uttering a low moan, and as the Purple-Bellied Parrot shook the sleep from his head, he realised it was a phrase, repeated over and over again to the rhythm of his waving head: 'It's an oomen ... It's an oomen ...'

The Purple-Bellied Parrot had no idea what an oomen was, and discombobulation must have been written on his face because Moussa called over:

'He means that it is a portent.' The Purple-Bellied Parrot stared back at Moussa, slack mandibled. Moussa rolled his eyes and said, 'A presage, a sign ...,' he rolled his eyes again, 'a ... a warning ... a warning of things to come. He means the weather. Everybody knows he is scared, scared of landing on the sea.'

It was then the Purple-Bellied Parrot noticed. Flat calm. On the land, no dust devils danced. The mist still clung to the ground like cobwebs on a cold morning in the park. The ocean was still as a plate of bin glass.

'You leave today, yes?'

'Yeays, I theenk we leave today.'

'In this I think you do not!' Moussa cackled.

The Purple-Bellied Parrot's mantle slumped.

'Relax,' said Moussa. 'I make a joke. I live here many summers. We have many days like this. When the sun climbs high, the wind will rise and blow all this mist away, and you will go. He should know this.' He sidled over to Shug, ducking as his head swept towards him. 'Pull yourself together man. You are an embarrassment to the avian race. Did you not hear what I said? Soon you leave.' He took aim and kicked Shug right up the bum, before ambling back to the Purple-Bellied Parrot as though nothing had happened. Shug was oblivious to the kick.

The Purple-Bellied Parrot thought that Moussa had perhaps come to say goodbye, but he mainly wanted to relive yesterday's heroic rescue — which apparently was mostly down to him. The Purple-Bellied Parrot, getting more and more worried, watched Shug as Moussa re-told the tale, with lots of 'I's and great physicality, opening his beak wide and licking its tips as he told the donkey-bite bit.

The Purple-Bellied Parrot tuned out. Shug was surfacing from his head-waving trance. Perhaps the kick up the bum had done the trick after all. His head had stilled, but now he was staring at the ground, at a desiccated, hollowed-out, long-dead beetle.

'Are you okay Shug?' the Purple-Bellied Parrot called. 'Shug?'

Shug, motionless, staring at the beetle husk. He stayed so an age. The Purple-Bellied Parrot looked up at the sun. This was a waste of time, so he flew back to the forest for a last feed. He stuffed himself with nuts and fruit. He even thought about forcing down a few wriggly things seeing as he didn't know when he would eat again, but immediately felt sorry for it. When he managed to take off again, his belly swayed about like a fat bin in a hammock.

The sun was halfway up the sky when he landed back on the knob with a 'crump.' Shug still hadn't moved. Neither had the beetle. Shug staring, immobile. Moussa dozing next to him.

What to do?

'The omen has him under its spell.' Moussa had woken. 'When the omen breaks, so will the spell.'

Shug stared on.

Noon.

The beetle rocked, though you could barely discern it. Shug stared on, and the beetle shifted again, and again. It corkscrewed along the dust, then tumbled away, Shug's eyes following it.

When it had disappeared Shug raised his head and opened his beak wide: 'OWWEEEEEKK-EEEEAARKKK-EEEEEAAR-RKKK-OOAWWWWW-EEEERRRKK'. He turned to the Purple-Bellied Parrot. 'You gonnae get your bahookey into gear or what Chief? We cannae hang aboot here scratchin our goonads all day.'

Moussa, talking into Shug's ear. Shug impatient, flapping his wings, Moussa saying, 'There are islands, a day's flight for you my friend, where the sun sets. Let him stop and feed. There will be little for him from then on. You must let him feed.'

Shug bent and slid his beak between Moussa's legs. He jerked his head upwards, and Moussa was airborne, turning somersaults.

'Dinnae teach your Granny tae suck eggs!' Shug called after him. 'I've been to them islands more times than you've eaten mobola plums.' Moussa twisted and gained control just before he crashed.

'Everybody's full of advice,' Shug was chuntering. 'Everyone knoos best. But I've lived oot there.' He turned to the Purple-Bellied Parrot, 'You Ready Chief?' The Purple-Bellied Parrot said he was. Shug lifted his head high and sniffed the air. 'Rayt. Still isnae much wind. I'm gonnae need to taxi.' He waddled over to a flat sandy area and turned. 'Once I'm airborne, jump aboard — but you'll need to be quick!'

He took three deep breaths. He unfurled his wings and said softly, 'Oorayt fellas? Now dinnae let me doon now.'

He jumped up and down. He strode towards the ocean with an angry look on his face. He turned and strode back, turned again, glared at the ocean, and shouted 'Huh!' twice. He spread his wings and broke into a run.

He ran for a very long time. As he trundled past, Moussa and the Purple-Bellied Parrot heard him wheezing. Moussa shook his head and rolled his eyes. Shug tripped over a pebble and staggered forward, and had to run faster and windmill his wings to prevent his chin ploughing the dirt.

He carried on running, and the Purple-Bellied Parrot thought he was going to run straight into the ocean and flounder. But at the last minute he flapped, and though his dangling pink feet grazed the water, he was airborne. His great wings caught the meagre breeze and he sailed skywards. Suspended between the twin arcs, he called down:

'Are you coming or what you numptie?'

The Purple-Bellied Parrot nodded to Moussa and leapt away.

'Oorayt, jump on. Let's get this show on the rood.'

'You carry on — I will jump on when I get tired.'

'Dinnae be a dobber! You've nae chance of keepin' up! Listen. Oot there, I say what goes. Not you or some wee witchuk.[1] Remember that!'

The Purple-Bellied Parrot jumped aboard.

'Flatten yer'sel!'

The Purple-Bellied Parrot flattened himself; he dug his claws in and gripped the plastic collar with his beak. He could just see over the top of Shug's head.

'And keep your whallopin heed doon.'

Below, Moussa was watching goggle-eyed, beak agape. A

passing fly wandered in and out. 'He will have to be stronger than the spawn of an elephant and rhinoceros,' he said, 'yet as fleet as the spawn of a cheetah and gazelle … and … and … Curses! I cannot get hyena into it. Anyway, they will never make it. If they do make it, I swear I will bite a hyena on the bottom while he feeds on the rotting carcass of another hyena amidst a clan of hyenas. There,' he sighed, 'I did it!'

Above, Shug shouted back to the Purple-Bellied Parrot — or it could have been to his wings — 'All set?'

He didn't wait for a reply. With a flick of his tail, they were offski.

They flew until the sun was halfway down the sky. At first, the Purple-Bellied Parrot was as excited as before to be riding on Shug's back. But by mid-afternoon the excitement faded, and he realised that this means of transportation was going to make for a boring trip. And every time he lifted his head so that he could look where they were going, Shug called back, 'Keep your whallopin heed doon! You're ruin'n my aerodynamics.' The constant rising and falling made him sleepy and he thought about taking a nap, but was scared he might fall off and tumble into the sea.

Shug rose and hung on the breeze. 'I'm hungry. I didnae have nae brekkie like you. Look doon there. See that log in the water?' The Purple-Bellied Parrot peered over his shoulder. The remains of a tree pitched on the swell, roots and a single branch still attached. 'I'm gonnae drop you off and go and do a spot of fishing.'

The Purple-Bellied Parrot hadn't planned for this. He had imagined that anywhere they landed would at least have some steadiness to it. But Shug drifted down and as they got close the Purple-Bellied Parrot leapt off.

'I willnae be long! I'll be back quicker than you can say

Benbeculacollcannamullrumeiggandmuck.[2] Dinnae let the wirri-
cows get you!' As Shug swept away, the Purple-Bellied Parrot
thought he heard him laugh.

The Purple-Bellied Parrot was at least glad to stretch his
wings, and he flew about a good bit to give them a workout. He'd
better keep them in good shape. They might be needed any day
soon if they hit the doldrums. A couple of unfamiliar seabirds
flew past, dagger-winged and hooked-billed, staring. One, its
eyes glued to the alien avian, crashed into the ocean.

The Purple-Bellied Parrot considered following Shug, to see
where he went and what he did, he told himself, but mainly
because now he felt so alone. But Shug was so fast he was already
distant, and soon the Purple-Bellied Parrot lost him against the
heaving ocean.

He got fed up of being buffeted about on the breeze with
nowhere to go, so he decided to land on the log and rest. It had
vanished. Yet it was there a moment ago. He climbed and
scanned the surface of the ocean, but still he saw no sign. He saw
nothing; nothing, except the pitching ocean and blue sky and
strange birds. On the horizon: no land ahead, and Efricah already
a fuzzy line behind. When he'd flown over the sea before, there
had always been land within easy reach. The Badhbh, who had
slept for so long, woke with a vengeance and told him he could
never make it back.

'Shug! Shug!' he cried, expecting no answer. He swooped
down closer to the ocean — he didn't know why. He spotted it:
the log, the outline of its branch against the sky as it crested the
swell. He flew over and landed and had to dig his claws in hard to
hold on as it rose and fell with the waves. The ocean washed over
his feet.

He hunkered down and looked about. All the strange birds
wheeling about knew what they were doing and where they
were. All except him. Some cruised close, inspecting him, and

then moved on as though unimpressed. Terror surged in his breast, urged on by the beast. He forced himself to think what Sar'nt Lofty Troggers would do. Sar'nt Troggers would keep calm, analyse the problem and think of a solution. So the Purple-Bellied Parrot took a deep breath and asked himself why he was scared. He couldn't work out why he was scared. As far as he could see, nothing nasty was about to clobber him. It was something to do with the bigness and the emptiness all around him, and the indifference of that bigness and emptiness to him.

But a more urgent problem now seized his attention.

The log began to roll. The Purple-Bellied Parrot discovered he had to walk its circumference so as not to plunge in. But he found that, as he walked, the log rolled faster and faster — until he was running at top speed just to keep up. Sharks, their big fins slicing the water, flashed through his mind. He leapt off.

He flew about a bit and wondered if the log would stop rolling. It did. But when he landed, the roly-poly thing happened again. It became exhausting. Aloft again, he had an idea, and the more he pondered it the more he thought it was a good idea. When the log stilled he landed again, but this time he stood with his feet astride the log. As soon as he felt the log begin to turn, he shifted his weight in the opposite direction. The log did not roll.

'Yippee!' How proud of him Sar'nt Troggers would be. He'd definitely remember this for future use.

His triumph, though, was brief. The log fell into the trough of a huge swell, and waves towered on both sides. For a moment he thought the tops were going to topple in, but then the log rose and he was sitting on top of the very wave that had just towered above — although he had no idea how. It was a bit like riding Shug's back.

Shug. He wondered how Shug would ever find him again — after all he'd lost sight of the log in a moment. He felt the terror rising again.

He decided to sing his song to himself. He would need to practice for when he got back to Brazil. He tried hard, but then the bigness and emptiness surged in, growing and cresting until it engulfed him and his heart was about to burst out of his breast and he had to leap up and shriek and go for a fly about.

When he landed back on the log he was trembling. Where was Shug? This is too long. What if a big shark had got him? The Badhbh was fighting hard. He tried to sing his song again and searched the sky.

A white blade ripped the air apart. Shug wheeled around.

'Oorayt?'

The Purple-Bellied Parrot leapt off the log and clung onto to Shug's shoulders.

'Hey! Ease off willya. Your claws are like needles!'

'Shug, where have you been?'

'What d'ya mean where have I been? I've been away nae longer that it takes you to peel a monkey nut.' Shug's shoulders were going up and down. 'Miss me, did you?' he chuckled. 'Miss your old Shuggie? Aye, he still has his uses.'

'How on earth did you manage to find me in all this ocean.'

'How do you manage to find those nuts? I'd be useless. You have your forest. Oot here — all this,' he surveyed the ocean around them, 'this is my domain.'

As they resumed their course and Shug became a wave again, the Purple-Bellied Parrot noted that Shug reeked of fish. He didn't, as the spuggies used to say, care tuppence.

Shug sang. Well, not so much sing as emit a string of trumpy noises.

The Purple-Bellied Parrot thought this a good sign. Shug was becoming a different creature now from that statue-on-theverge-of-a-nervous-breakdown back on land. He flew even faster.

Later, he tired of singing and told a story with no beginning.

'Like that sea leopard that felt the business end of my beak doon near what the bins call South Georgia. I showed him. I'd landed on a floe to dismantle a big toothyfish that had been causing me no little difficulty.[3] You should see a sea leopard Chiefy boy.[4] Long as my wingspan. Looks like somebody has poked two holes in its head. Then you see the glint, and you know its eyes is in them holes, watching you. That head, all mouth, and it grins at you and that mouth gapes open — open their mouths wider than a snake they can — and you see them big saw-teeth made for ripping up your flesh. Then it bites you and drags you down. Partial to penguins so they are. But this fella, he fancies a taste of yours truly. So he comes for me, snake-mouth a-gaping, not as slow as you might think notwithstanding being oot of his element. Well, I let him come, I even dangle a bit of that red toothfish gut to bring him on. I stare past those yellow teeth right doon that pink gullet. I step aside. Well, he slithers off that floe and plops into the ocean and as he slides by I help myself to a chunk oot of his bahookey. It tastes like a piece of old keech so I spit it oot after him.'[5]

———

Late afternoon they saw a curtain of rain approaching. 'I should get your brolly ready Chief,' Shug chuckled, 'and your sou'wester.'[6]

The rain turned out to be doubly serendipitous for the Purple-Bellied Parrot. Though they were out at sea, it had been hot all day, with only the odd puffy cloud to provide shade and he was thirsty. When the rain hit he rolled on his back and opened his beak and let the raindrops fall in. Bliss. But on his back it was awkward to hold on and he almost slid off when Shug careened and turned. He thought how to solve this, and he had to do it quickly, as through the curtain he could see the brightening sky. Lying on his belly he couldn't raise his head to collect the drops, or Shug would yell back, 'Keep your whallopin heed doon!'

And then he had it. Still on his back, he swivelled so his head was pointing backwards, and then hooked his feet under the plastic collar. He clamped his wings to his side so they wouldn't get too ruffled by the wind. He opened his beak again and, relaxed. Aaahhhhhh. Why hadn't he thought of it before. It was so comfy, he decided he was going to stay like it for the whole trip. This trip was going to be a piece of cake.

They passed though the rain, and the sun warmed his plumage. It began to steam and he fell asleep.

He woke all groggy. He didn't know how long he had slept for, and after he'd unhooked his feet and swivelled round he blinked and saw land silhouetted against the red sun. These must be the islands Moussa talked of.[7]

He asked Shug, but Shug said nothing. He asked again, this time yelling — but still no response. He inched forward and peered over to look at Shug's face. Already this was strange. There was usually a 'Keep your whallopin heed doon' by now. Shug's eyes were all glassy like the nora's when he'd clobbered into that fence post.

Shug was asleep.

It took a moment for this to sink in. Shug was asleep, and yet here they were sailing along, ascending and descending the big wave, just as before. The Purple-Bellied Parrot let him sleep on until the islands loomed large, and then he thought it best to wake him. He didn't want Shug to go crashing into a cliff or something. He ruffled the feathers on Shug's crown. He woke with a start.

'Wha?! What's happnin?' Shug shook his head and looked

about. 'Ahh, here we are.' He looked back at the Purple-Bellied Parrot. 'And here you are. What did you wake me for? I was having a lovely wee snooze. I was dreaming aboot … Well never you mind.'

'I thought you'd like to know we have arrived at the islands.'

'What?! Of course we've arrived at the islands you numptie!'

The Purple-Bellied Parrot had done something wrong, but for the life of him couldn't think what.

Shug shook his head again. He flapped his wings — for the first time the Purple-Bellied Parrot could remember all day.

'Rayt, we'll find ourselves a nice rock to pairch on for the night and have us a good long kip.'

'I thought you didn't sleep on the land.'

'Not usually, but I'm pure knackered so I am. Who's doing all the work here?'

Shug sailed on past the first island, which looked sandy and rocky — much like where they'd come from — and on towards a bigger, greener island. The Purple-Bellied Parrot saw mountains, the first since he was shot by the hunters. They found a big dry rock close to the shore surrounded by water.

'Pairfec,' said Shug.

The Purple-Bellied Parrot noted that two white birds already occupied the rock. Wispy crests waving in the breeze, the two little egrets were primping their already pristine plumage, exchanging admiring glances.

'Yah, you should really do that. That looks so cool.'

'Do you think? Oh shut up!'

Shug landed between, barging them aside. They hrrumphed. One said, 'Some people,' and tutted. Facing the opposite way, Shug stared out to sea for a moment. Then, lifting one foot after the other, he booted both into a slimy rock pool.

'Eeek!'

'Eeek!'

'My long life on the oceans of this world has taught me that any baird in possession of a crest is a nincompoop.'

The night saw Shug's dark mood return. They stood together on the rock and he told him the Purple-Bellied Parrot they were about to embark on the longest landless stretch of the journey.

'We are aiming for some wee rocks stickin' oot oot in the middle of the ocean. We get there, we are as good as hayme.'

The Purple-Bellied Parrot asked how long it would take.

'With a pairfect wind, and nae doldrums,' he looked at each of his wings as though consulting them, 'we could do it in two, two and a half days, including fishing stops. If we get becalmed? Well Chief, your guess is as good as mine. Maybe we doon't get there at all.'

The Purple-Bellied Parrot gulped.

'If we are to be caught by the doldrums, it'll be on this next bit. You'll need all the strength that wee troggie squeezed into you.'

At dawn the Purple-Bellied Parrot flew off and stuffed himself. He thought nuts and seeds were the best for strength, so wherever he found them he ate them up. Then he found a grove of low trees, leaves splayed out like the park's fountain that had worked just once, and bark like pineapple peel — which he took as a good sign. Suspended below the leaves were big bunches of fruit the size of chicken eggs.[8] Bins had wrapped the bunches in netting. He gnawed through the netting and tried one. Sweetness flooded his mouth — sweeter than the juice in any pineapple tin — and he gorged himself. As usual, a bin appeared and started waving his arms about, so he fled.

Later he peeled a banana. He'd never eaten a banana from a tree before, and he was amazed how big the bunches were and how they grew upside-down. As he munched, he wondered if

Shug and his wings would notice if he loaded provisions onto his back. But how would he stop them tumbling off? Hmmm. What about a flattened-matchbox trailer? But he would need to devise some way of tying everything on.

He found a dented can by the side of a road and levered it open. White sludge oozed out. It didn't look too appetizing, but he tried it, and it tasted like coconut, so he slurped the lot. He heard a huffing noise and turned to see a donkey watching him and wondered why donkeys always looked grumpy. Perhaps it was because they got bit on the bum by birds like Moussa.

He landed on the donkey's back. At first the donkey flung her head back and tried to get him, but he was out of range so she gave up and the Purple-Bellied Parrot went for a walk about. After a bit, the donkey quivered and huffed and the Purple-Bellied Parrot concluded she was enjoying it. He dug his claws in a bit more and trod all the way to her head — he could always jump off if she got frisky again. Behind her ears he found a couple of ticks wedged tight, their swollen red bums glistening in the sun. He wheedled them out and the donkey sighed and made a noise like a moggie's purr.

The wind was yet to stir, so he went and sat in a big-leafed tree and, shaded by its big leaves, let his breakfast go down. He had a good preen to make sure that his feathers were all pukka before they set off, and thought about the long flight ahead — not knowing if they would ever see land again. It might be a good idea to do some of Sar'nt Lofty Troggers's exercises.

To practice taking off with a heavy weight, he found a flat stone and lodged it on his shoulders, and flew repeatedly from a low branch to a high branch, 'Hup-two, hup-two,' till he was out of puff. He spotted a net bag with a couple of yams in it, and so to test his endurance he tried to see how far he could carry it: 'Huu-uuuUUUUUUT!' When he thought his pecs were about to explode he dropped it, 'PAaaaaaaahhh,' and collapsed into the fork of a tree, gasping. Then he did it again, and again.

'You look pure knackered so you do,' said Shug, back at the rock.

He had been out fishing, 'so we dinnae have to stop on the way,' but the Purple-Bellied Parrot thought he didn't look too good. 'I dinnae feel good,' Shug finally confirmed.

The wind was picking up, but Shug made no move to leave. He shook his head and flapped his wings. 'I dinnae feel rayt,' he said. 'I think I knoo what it might be.'

He opened his beak, the Purple-Bellied Parrot thought to yawn, but it gaped wider than he had ever seen it before. Shug bent forward and his body convulsed, breast heaving repeatedly, until he made this noise: 'whhee-ehck … whhee-ehck.' A big dollop of fishy porridge plopped out over the rock. The Purple-Bellied Parrot leapt to a position upwind.

Shug lifted his head and clapped his beak together a couple of times, 'Ahhh, tha's better. Rayt as ninepence noo.' He bent and inspected the dollop. He rummaged about in it. The Purple-Bellied Parrot turned away before he too vomited. After a moment Shug said, 'Aye, just as I thought. Here's the wee fella. Now would you take a swatch at that!'

The Purple-Bellied Parrot turned to see him holding up his prize. It was a model of a yellow animal. The animal squatted on hind legs like a dog's, only much bigger and more powerful. Its front legs, though, were puny, and it had a nose a bit like a dog but ears like a rabbit. It looked like it had been cobbled together out of spare parts from other animals. Most oddly, it had two heads — another, smaller, one was sticking out of its belly of all places. Why would anyone make a model of such a strange creature then chuck it in the ocean?

Shug tossed the figure to the Purple-Bellied Parrot who, beak clacking, pretended to try to catch it. The creature wedged itself in a crevice.

'Never happened when I was a wean. But seems like every

time I go oot fishing now I swallow doon a chunk or two.' Shug clapped his beak together a couple of times. 'Rayt, no good dilly-dallying aboot. You ready Chiefy boy?'

The Purple-Bellied Parrot looked down at the yellow crea-ture, and noticed its extremities — stained red.

17

BONXIE

The sun was half-way between the bottom of the sky and the top of the sky when they set off.

They flew past nearly naked bins toasting themselves on sand. As they headed out into a bay, Shug had to veer violently as a huge sheet of plastic raced towards them. As they climbed away, the Purple-Bellied Parrot saw that the sheet was tied to a bin dressed in rubber clothes standing on a plank on the water.

'They do that for fun,' Shug said.

At the end of the bay the Purple-Bellied Parrot saw the ocean open up. Beyond the headland it changed, from tinkly ripples to a seething white-capped swell. How long would they be out there before he stood on land again — before he sat in a tree? He gulped as he thought he might never again sit in a tree and have a good preen and munch a juicy nut. He reached forward and preened a tatty feather on Shug's neck and hunkered down.

They passed the headland and were out over the broken water when Shug abruptly banked and planed down towards the surface. The Purple-Bellied Parrot would have fallen off were it not for Shug's collar.

'Bonxies!' Shug yelled. 'Begger it. I didnae think they came this far sooth.'[1]

Shug bottomed out and hugged the surface of the water for a good distance — he even flapped so he didn't have to climb and become conspicuous.

'If I can keep ma'sel between them and the sun, hopefully they won't spot us because of the glare booncing off the water.'

The Purple-Bellied Parrot looked up and behind, but all he could see were seagulls flying about. But then again, a couple of them did look unusually brawny, and they were not meandering about like normal georges. These were flying with purpose, like they were on patrol.

Shug was chuntering. 'I dinnae like them bonxie bullies! I've lost many a fine meal to them beasties.' He turned and shouted to the Purple-Bellied Parrot. 'If they spot us they'll hound us and whack us and try to knock you off. They'll make mincemeat of you, Chiefy boy.'

The Purple-Bellied Parrot looked back. One bonxie peeled away and flew across the face of the sun and, though the Purple-Bellied Parrot squinted, he lost it. Shug began to wheeze. He was getting tired with all the flapping. Sure enough, his wings stilled and he banked and planed across the wind and shot aloft. 'I just need a wee breather,' he said.

They were not like the noras. The Purple-Bellied Parrot heard no call. The approach came from below — not above, and suddenly the bonxie was alongside. It was the size of one of the spuggies' 'errin' gulls, but it looked as if it had booked into Sar'nt Lofty Troggers's boot camp and forked out for extra lessons. At the near end of a beefy barrel-breasted body, hooded eyes glared out along a hooked bill — a bill even more vicious looking than Shug's. The Purple-Bellied Parrot noticed that it flapped hard and constantly — but seemingly without effort.

The bonxie, matching perfectly Shug's course and speed, turned to look at them. 'Oi-Oi!' it called.

The Purple-Bellied Parrot looked away, and clung tighter to Shug's shoulders.

'I said, Oi-Oi! Not a very gracious couple are you, ignoring a polite salutation like that.'

Shug veered away, but the bonxie reproduced the movement and was again alongside. The Purple-Bellied Parrot thought back to the graces, and how they flew tight together, replicating each other's every move. He risked a glance across and he saw the bonxie wink at him, but he was even more astonished by what it did next. It came even closer, opened its hooked beak, and tugged Shug's wing.

Shug spun and plunged. For a moment it looked like they were going to stall and somersault, but Shug fought and flapped hard and regained control.

The bonxie, back abeam. 'Well, I thought I'd seen just about everything there was to see out over the ocean,' the bonxie said, 'but I've never seen a couple like you. So what's going on with you guys? What's with the piggy-back?'

'Awae and raffle yersel!' Shug yelled back, and turning to the Purple-Bellied Parrot he said, 'Strap yersel in!'

Shug careened and dived.

The Purple-Bellied Parrot felt a surge of acceleration as Shug found the perfect angle to the breeze, and, despite the impending peril, he had to marvel. For a moment he thought they were away and free, but the bonxie was beating his wings again and was soon hard on Shug's tail.

The Purple-Bellied Parrot had an idea. It was a brilliant idea. He had one all primed and loaded. He gripped the red collar with his beak and stuck his bum in the air. Shug protested, 'Keep doon ya wee …,' but the Purple-Bellied Parrot ignored him and took careful aim.

The bonxie veered. It was great flying. Watching upside-down from between his legs, the Purple-Bellied Parrot had to admit it, and his big poo only caught him on the shoulder. The bonxie barely missed a wingbeat, and was soon back on their tail, the Purple-Bellied Parrot out of ammunition. It reached forward and tweaked Shug's tail. Shug yawed and lurched, and, losing his perfect angle to the wind, decelerated like someone had yanked the handbrake. The bonxie cruised up to his shoulder again.

'Oi-Oi! Oi-Oi! You ... Parrot boy. Not very convivial was that. Good job I've got such an unflappable nature.'

The bonxie mirrored their flight for a bit, eyes locked onto them, and said, 'You know what guys — all this excitement has made me feel a bit, erm, peckish, and ...' he clacked his beak twice, 'and I'm in the mood for ... hmmm ... something exotic.' He gazed across at the Purple-Bellied Parrot again, and this time the Purple-Bellied Parrot glared back. He was about to use a spikey phrase the spuggies had once taught him to tell someone to go away, but the bonxie spoke again.

'I'm going to terminate you. I'm going to terminate you and I'm going to have you for my dinner.' Beneath their hoods his eyes narrowed, and the Purple-Bellied Parrot saw the blank gaze of a spugghawk. The gaze switched to Shug. 'Your parrot — or your life.'

Shug swerved again, but it was like the bonxie was attached by a piece of string — a very short piece of string. Now the bonxie didn't pinch Shug's wing — he grabbed it, and yanked hard. Shug spun and instantly stalled and tumbled towards the ocean. The Purple-Bellied Parrot, feet again now hooked under the collar, tumbled with him, flapping pointlessly.

'Stop your flappin you twally!' Shug yelled as they spiralled down.

The Purple-Bellied Parrot clung on and thought they were going to splat into the ocean, but at the last moment Shug's wings located the wind and they zoomed away, like the first time when Shug was showing off. The bonxie remained in pursuit, beating the air implacably. It seemed impossible, but it was gaining on them.

He must leap off. Shug would surely escape without his weight slowing him down. He began to untangle his feet from the collar.

Shug called back, 'How we doing back there Chiefy?'

The Purple-Bellied Parrot now had his feet free.

'Talk to me Chiefy boy. How close is that bonxie?'

The Purple-Bellied Parrot looked back at the yawning gape of the bonxie about to bite Shug's tail. 'Shug! Say hello to the icebergs for me!'

He cast off Shug's white plumage.

Shug rocketed away. The Purple-Bellied Parrot realised he hadn't planned what to do next, but he knew he was not going to wait around to be clobbered like he'd done with that nora. The bonxie was high above now, so he swept up and opened his big beak for the attack. The bonxie would soon be sorry he'd taken on a graduate of the Sar'nt Lofty Troggers boot camp. If he could only latch onto something with that big old hooter of his.

He didn't even get close. The bonxie regarded him. It called 'Oi-Oi! Parrot boy!' and dangled out a leg. Just as the Purple-Bellied Parrot was about to sink his beak into it, it flicked its wings and climbed away. The Purple-Bellied Parrot was shocked to find himself giving chase, but he soon lost sight of it in the sun.

These seabirds. If ever he could get one of them in a forest he'd show them.

'Oi-Oi!'

WHAAMMPHH!

He knew he was tumbling towards the ocean. He knew he ought to be doing something about it, and he told his wings to flap and his tail to twist. He told them very sternly indeed. But they didn't hear. And he knew the thing he most feared of all was about to happen. The groaning seething thing was about to swallow him.

He tumbled. He saw the ocean and the sky changing places. He must be dreaming, because he glimpsed a huge white star arcing across the sky and for an instant it blotted out the sun. He heard the white star roar something he didn't understand: 'Fill your wings, you son of a fish!' The ocean … the sky …, and in his dream he saw an explosion of mottled brown feathers. The ocean … the sky.

The ocean.

The ocean sighed. The Purple-Bellied Parrot noted curiously that the white star was now below, and that it was rising to meet him. Now he was being carried aloft on a warm white pillow. This can't be the ocean. The ocean is all wet and cold.

Shug swept up with his green and purple cargo and hung on the breeze. 'Phew Chiefy boy, that was touch and goo. I skelped him a good'un — you should've seen it.[2] But I didnae know if I could get to you before you hit the briny.'

The Purple-Bellied Parrot shook his head, and was just regaining his senses when Shug said, 'Look! Look doon there!'

They watched the bonxie tumble the last few feet and flop onto the ocean. It stayed still for a moment, and the Purple-Bellied Parrot thought it had croaked, but it suddenly revived and righted itself and preened as if nothing had happened. It plunged its head into the ocean and casually tossed a fish into the air, caught it and began to tear chunks off it.

'Aye, he's foond an easier meal than you,' Shug said. 'Strap yersel back on and we'll get oot into the ocean. They're persistent beggars, bonxies, but they won't follow us oot there once I get going.'

They were about to leave when the Purple-Bellied Parrot saw something, something that his brain found impossible to comprehend — it happened so fast. Had the ocean really exploded? Had a pair of giant teeth at the end of a huge fish erupted from the water and grabbed the bonxie, performed a twirl in mid-air, and plunged back in? The Purple-Bellied Parrot rubbed his eyes with his alulae and looked again.

'Nae, your eyes didnae deceive you,' Shug said. 'Aye, that's a shark alrayt. Lightning ain't they. You never knoo they are there, and then, wham! You get malkied. Just like I telt you.'

Mesmerised, they watched the water thrash. And then something even more astonishing happened. One wing, then two, beat the water, and from the roiling boiling ocean, the bonxie emerged. They saw gaping, snapping jaws, tortilla chip teeth, a final lunge. They saw the bonxie dodge and then dance on the end of the snout, thrashing the air, feet dangling, bill stabbing, blood running from the torn snout, and then, the bonxie, impossibly, airborne. It shook itself, the droplets cascading into the ocean, and turned and beat the air, back towards the bay.

Shug said, 'Come on, we need to be offski pronto, or it'll be back after us. Tough fellas them bonxies.'

It may have been some freak wind over the ocean, but as they left the Purple-Bellied Parrot was sure he heard, 'Oi-Oi! '

18

HOOLIE

S hug was faster than ever that day. His technique now practiced, he found the perfect angle to the wind every time to soar and dive … soar and dive. The Purple-Bellied Parrot thought bins would feel clumsy in comparison if they hurtled past in one of their hairy planes.

He leaned up and called, 'Shug you are amazing! We go so fast. We will be home soon.'

'Hold your wheesht Chiefy boy.[1] We need to concentrate. We need to exploit this blow and get this bit done quick. Never know — we might be lucky and them doldies might be creating havoc elsewhere. And keep your whallopin heed doon by the way!'

So the Purple-Bellied Parrot swivelled round and hooked his feet under the plastic collar and lay back. He watched the sky changing overhead and, every time Shug banked, the ocean at his side.

In the afternoon the wind strengthened. The Purple-Bellied Parrot hunkered down as best he could but the wind was whipping his plumage hither and thither. The harder it blew, the faster Shug flew. The sea was now more white than blue and was like the hills and valleys where the hunters had shot him;

and often they caroomed between teetering waves on both sides, before Shug rocketed skywards again to begin the next descent.

The faster they went the more the Purple-Bellied Parrot felt Shug relax. Once, after a particularly steep descent and climb out of a deep trough where the waves seemed about to topple in on them, he heard Shug whoop.

'Whoo-hoo! Ain't this something! I've not felt like this since I were a wean. You willnae be getting any of this in your wee forests laddie! It'll pure clean the clooters oot o' your crevice!'

The Purple-Bellied Parrot unhooked his feet and carefully swivelled, making sure that at least claw or beak was clinging on to Shug. He risked lifting his head a little. 'Shug! Shug! Is thees what the bins call a storm?'

'A storm?! A storm laddie? This is nothing but a wee wafty breeze a bin might peg his skiddies oot in.[2] You should see them iceberg oceans doon sooth. The bins call them the roaring forties and the furious fifties. No land there. You can fly towards the sunset on and on until you get back to where you started and not see a scrap of land. I know I've done it. And with nothing to hinder them, the winds just roar roond and aroond like mad things. Not many bins doon there.' Shug clapped his beak. 'That's my world.'

The Purple-Bellied Parrot thought hard but he couldn't imagine flying and flying in the same direction until you got back to where you started from, but he was learning to trust Shug when he spoke of the mysteries of the ocean.

They didn't speak of the Bonxie until late in the day. As the sun was setting Shug soared high and hung on the wind, still as a kestrel. The wind had fallen away a little, so the Purple-Bellied Parrot stood and stretched his wings and gave them a good flap.

'Aye, that's it Chiefy boy. You keep yersel limber. You may be needing them fellas soon.' Shug preened the bits of his wing he could get at. It looked like he was kissing them.

'I want to thank you for saving me from the Bonxie. The way you clobbered it ...,' the Purple-Bellied Parrot began.

'Aw awae and pot,' Shug interrupted. 'You'd do the same for me. I knoo what you were doing — when you abandoned ship like that. Took some gizzard did that by the way. It's like the wee witchuk said, we need each other if we are goin' to make it through this trip. We've still a long way to go and we dinnae know what's ahead.'

Shug looked over to the sun and scanned the horizon. 'We've made good distance today. I bet you are hungry, I knoo I am. But I'm nae losing what we've gained. And anyway, the sea is still too rough for me to drop you off on a log and go fishing.'

Shug banked and shot down towards the sea and once more became a wave.

He flew on towards the red sun. He flew on as the first stars appeared. He flew on as the moon rose behind them, an orange globe you could reach out and peck.

The wind still ripped against them and Shug told more stories: a colony wiped out by a huge wave which hurled an iceberg against it; a mountain with fire shooting out of the top, vomiting molten earth into the ocean and making the water boil; the boobrie he tangled with off Cape Wrath over the beluga's body, the boobrie turning into a giant eagle and bellowing like a bull before making off with the beluga locked in his talons; a ghost ship with nary a bin, creaking on the swell, sails flapping, lines slapping against the masts; the tongie he rode out of a moon-long mist shrouding the waters of the narwhal.[3] The images butted into each other, a jumble of tales from which the Purple-Bellied Parrot could pick out only fragments. Shug was telling the stories to himself.

The Purple-Bellied Parrot was amazed at how many birds

flew about at night. They drifted by, fleeting yellow ghosts illuminated by the moon. He would normally be fast asleep by now,
and he wondered what they might be up to in the dead of night
when everyone else was asleep. It seemed to him much too dark
to find grub or do anything else useful. He surely had the better
deal, tucked in the nook of a tree snoozing — well, usually.
Perhaps they were on a long journey like he and Shug. He leaned
forward to ask Shug, but though he muttered on, he slept. He
caught one last fragment of a story, the end of another dispute:
'See you. You try and drag me doon with your tentacles pal, I'll
bite one off and have it for my supper.' The Purple-Bellied Parrot
leaned up and watched the wings as they went about their work.

A creeping dawn as the sun rose behind a bank of cloud. The
Purple-Bellied Parrot woken by Shug who was saying, 'You need
to shift your bahookey, Chiefy boy.' He was hanging off the side
of Shug's back. Good job his feet were hooked under his collar.

Shug was high and drifting, scanning the surface of the ocean.
The swell had subsided, the mountains and canyons now the hills
and valleys of south Blighty. Shug looked up to the sky. Clouds
like fishes' skeletons glowed red. The Purple-Bellied Parrot felt
Shug's body tense as he said, 'Storm comin. You'll be needin to
hold on tayt today.'

The Purple-Bellied Parrot looked up at the red and turquoise.
It looked friendly to him. He stared hard at the way ahead and
tried to imagine a wind blowing harder than yesterday and
couldn't, but for Shug to describe it as a 'storm' it must be so.
Ahead, all was clear, but he lowered his gaze towards the horizon
and as he peered he could just make out a grey snail-shaped
smudge.

'Anyway, I need t'eat something,' Shug continued. 'Who
knows, I might be eating for two if we get held up. I'll get you
champin' squid yet.' He chuckled and clapped his beak. 'I'll find
you something more solid than that old log to perch on while I
go fishing.'

His eyes raked the ocean. 'Ahah! Looks like a raft of seaweed. You can drop off here and fly doon yersel for the exercise. You'll get your feet wet but you willnae be rollin over.'

The Purple-Bellied Parrot hesitated as he remembered the last time. He felt his claws tightening and his heart beating and the Badhbh stirring in his head as he looked around at the unbroken horizon.

'Goo'on then. Off you go Chiefy boy. I'll be back quicker than you can say Benbeculacollcannamullrumeiggandmuck.'

Flying felt good after all that lying around, and the Purple-Bellied Parrot even took a detour — always keeping one eye glued to the raft. If he lost sight of that he'd be 'right up the swanny' as the spuggies said. He circled and came in to land, and he realised that the raft was not made of seaweed after all, not unless it was some kind of exotic seaweed with gaily coloured foliarge and flowers. Could be, he supposed. He was not an expert on seaweed like Shug.

A 'splosh' and he planted his feet and poked around. There were bits of seaweed mixed in, but this was bin stuff. Bottles and containers, and bits of bottles and containers, children's toys, a couple of footballs like they used to play with in the park, plastic bags and other rubbish, were all woven into a tangle of torn fishing nets and bits of old rope. Still, as the raft rose and fell on the swell he was glad of it — better than that rolling log.

He realised how hungry he was. A big hole had appeared in his stomach and a tit had flown in and started pecking about. He inspected the raft. All was packed pretty tight, but he had a probe and managed to shift a few bits and bobs. He levered up a green figure of a bin with a gun and found some kind of a nut, but it was all soggy and salty and he gagged as he choked it down. It stayed there, but it didn't shift the tit and block up the hole to keep him out. He crept to the edge of the raft and peered over, locking his claws tight. Ribbons of seaweed had attached themselves to the underside of the raft, and amongst them he saw fishes swimming about. He thought about Shug and wondered what they tasted like, but he had no way of going fishing. He watched the fish for a bit, head cocked, and then crept back to the middle of the raft where he felt safer.

Snails. All huddled together at the end of a jagged blue bottle. Back at the park, the thrushes and blackbirds loved snails. He remembered watching a thrush bashing snails on a brick until the shells broke and then chomping the squidgy bits. Even the spuggies, in desperation, would try and winkle out a snail — if no kebabs or chips were about.

He peered down at the little bunch. One of them squoze in tighter to the group as if it knew something bad was about to happen. The Purple-Bellied Parrot thought about what Sar'nt Lofty Troggers would do. He would have them in his gizzard quicker than you can say 'yee-haw.'

'I'm so sorry little snailies,' the Purple-Bellied Parrot said, 'Eez nothing personal. Eez jus that I am so very, very hungry.' He thought of Millie and said, 'Remember thees, you would eat me if you were big enough.'

He took a deep breath and opened that big beak. The shells wouldn't stand a chance. Had he a finger and a thumb, he would have held his nose.

Shug, circling overhead. 'You ready or what Chief. We need to be offski.'

The Purple-Bellied Parrot sprang up, feet dripping with seawater, and flew to his shoulders.

'You manage to find something t'eat doon there?'

'Yeays, I found a nut. I also saw a crab, but it was too nippy for me.'

'That it? One nut?'

The Purple-Bellied Parrot nodded. He thought of the snails

still snug in their bottle, and Sar'nt Lofty Troggers shaking his head, 'Pitiful, truly pitiful.'

'Open wide and I'll wretch doon your throat if you like. I've plenty to spare. It's one big smorgasboord oot here for me!'

'No, thank you Shug.'

'Ookay Chiefy boy. But just say the waird.'

Shug was soon pelting along like yesterday.

'This wind keeps up, we'll be there this time tomorrow. Primaries crossed ay?' Shug, a full belly and a stiff breeze makes for a good mood.

The Purple-Bellied Parrot asked him where 'there' was.

'Those rocks I was telling you aboot you numptie. Only me and a few boobies and noddies know about them. Stickin' oot of the ocean like shark's teeth so they are. Discovered them when I was a-wanderin' in my second year. Even the bins havnae found them yet.'

'Excuse me, but will there be anything there for me to eat?'

'Certainly will Chiefy boy — the contents of my bulging crop once I've done a bit of fishin. Easy pickings for me aroond there. If thas too uncouth for your refined palette, well we might find you morsel washed up on the shore. With no land in the vicinity, if anything is going to wash up, it's going to wash up there.'

Noon, and the wind picks up. The grey smudge had transformed into a big flat-topped mushroom like the ones that grew in the park in the autumn before the dogs tromped all over them. Its cap was fat and dense and fuzzy on top, its stem a thick column of rain. They were heading straight for it.

'Can we not go around it?' the Purple-Bellied Parrot called forward.

'No we cannae. Too big. And keep your whallopin heed doon by the way.'

The Purple-Bellied Parrot may have imagined it, but he was sure Shug altered his course to head directly for the storm's centre.

The wind began to howl. Above it the Purple-Bellied Parrot heard a noise, and it took a moment for him to work out what it was. Shug was singing again. The song was tuneless and the voice trumpy. The Purple-Bellied Parrot could barely make it out above the din and some of the words were snatched away, but he heard something like:

> *Oohh Ah'm back in the roarin' forties*
> *Where the icebergs float so free*
> *Oohh Ah'm back in the roarin' forties*
> *Where the wind still never does be*
> *Where the penguins they're all a-chatter*
> *And there's plenty of squid in the sea*
> *Oohh Ah'm back in the roarin' forties*
> *Where there's nary a bin to be seen*
>
> *Oohh Ah'm back in the roarin' forties...*

The storm slammed into them. Shug sang on. The wind tore at the water, shredding the ocean mountains. Clinging on tight, head 'doon,' the Purple-Bellied Parrot was instantly drenched as the column of rain struck. It was impossible to tell where sea ended and sky began. Shug plunged into the canyon troughs, and sheared across the face of steepling waves, and sang even louder. As they rose out of the troughs the wind struck hard and a couple of times the Purple-Bellied Parrot lost his grip on the white plumage and it was only the red collar which saved him — he'd stuck his head through it. In the sea canyons the Purple-Bellied Parrot longed for the open sky, and in the screaming sky he longed for the shelter of the canyons.

Shug sang on, but broke off long enough to yell, 'This is somethin' ain't it Chiefy boy! What a hoolie! Whoooo-Hooooo!'

The storm raged and the Purple-Bellied Parrot lost all sense of time. The rain stopped, but, impossibly, the wind strengthened, and Shug rose and fell with it. They plunged pell-mell into yet another canyon. The Purple-Bellied Parrot glanced up. The shear walls rippled over them, their tops invisible. Shug dipped his wingtip into the water to tighten his turn, so not to smash into the wall.

The tip bit too deep.

It was like stamping on the brakes, and although Shug still had enough momentum to carry him to the top of his climb, it would not be before the wall crashed in.

The Purple-Bellied Parrot looked up to see the wave curling over them, its crest shredded. 'Shug's leaving it late this time.'

The wave struck, and it was like the collar didn't exist as he was washed out from under it and away from Shug's warm body.

'ShuuuuUUUUUG!

He fell away, somersaulting. He glimpsed Shug vanishing into spray and whirling grey.

The storm hurled rain at him. He realised he was flapping. His wings were still working so he can't be under the ocean. Good. They were wet, but they weren't yet waterlogged. That was good too. The image of the bonxie flashed into his mind and he flapped harder, thrashing the jumble of water and air.

'HHHUUUUUUUUUUUUTTTT!!!'

He didn't know if he was going up or down, and concluded he was going sideways.

He glimpsed the sky. 'HHHHHUUUUUUUUUUUUU-UUTTTTT!!!'

The rain stopped, like somebody had turned off a tap. 'Thank you!' he yelled — he didn't know to what. The constant pounding had been about to dash him into the ocean.

He climbed but the wind struck hard and he was bowled along and he fought to right himself, flapping like the bonxie. Soon his wings felt like they were full of stones, so he tried to plane across the face of the wind like Shug, but it was impossible — he just didn't have Shug's wings. So he gave up and stretched them out and let the storm take him where it willed, and the storm shrieked all around him, a million crows and georges all having a big fight.

Now he was enveloped in whirling wet concrete grey, and he sensed that he was spiralling around and around. The storm now had him by the scruff, and he knew even his outstretched wings were useless and he may as well fold them — so he did. The spiral tightened and the winds quickened, and an image flashed through his mind: the bathroom in the pink-faced man's flat, the basin there, and how he watched the water going down the plug-hole. But he wasn't going down — he was going up — giddy with all the spinning. Another image flashed: the washing machine whirling, the clothes stuck to its walls.

Suddenly the wind shrieked no more, and he found himself turning inside a tube of whirling cloud. He looked down and far below he saw a circle of ocean. He looked up and saw a circle of sky — bluer than a dunnock's egg. Against the tube's grey walls he saw stuff spinning about: gobsmacked fish, gills pumping, trying to swim in air; a couple of upside-down georges beating the air, bamboozled; a sail and bits of a boat and a splintered timber that was probably a mast twirling about; a piece of spouting like the one he used to perch on with Millie and Steve to plan this trip. Around the tube's walls, all were being sucked up skywards — and there was not a thing they could do about it. He thought again about the spiders at the pink-faced man's flat. Oddly, at the centre of the tube, they were drifting down, towards the ocean. He was glad he was not at the centre. High, near the top against the dunnock blue, he saw the outline of a bin spinning around, all flappy arms and legs.

The ocean now a tiny dot. The walls whirled and above, the

blue widened as he ascended. The bin was gone. For a moment he thought he would arrive at the top and simply fly out and go off and find Shug. But the higher he got the more dizzy he felt. He noticed the heaviness of his eyelids and how it took all his strength just to keep them open. He thought for a bit and decided it best to save his energy for when he needed to fly again. So, with a last glance at the twirling fishes and georges, he let his eyelids to fall shut.

Was it another dream? He was getting thoroughly tired of weird dreams. The Purple-Bellied Parrot was careering towards the ocean in thrashing rain. He decided it was a dream and that he would settle back to watch what happened. But if it was a dream then why was he so wet? He watched the ocean hurtling towards him and thought. Last thing he remembered he was floating skywards surrounded by fish and georges flying upside down. Now that was surely a dream. Salty water slashed his face; he woke. Too late.

SPLAT!

The first thing he thought was how hard the ocean was. He had expected something soft and splooshy, but it reminded him of the time he flew into that hoarding during the famous spug-ghawk chase. The ocean fair knocked the wind out of him. And then he was under the water, and he thought about how bonkers it was to say 'under water.' If he was *under* the water wouldn't he be somewhere dry? Now then: breathing. What was it Sar'nt Lofty Troggers had drilled into him about breathing?

'Sir, if you end up under the briny do not breathe, Sir!'

So he didn't breathe, and while he wasn't breathing he looked about. Nothing much to see though; all was blurry, and he wondered how fishes managed to find their way when they were flying about through ocean. His mind was wrenched away from the navigational skills of fishes. Sar'nt Troggers's order to not breathe had its drawbacks. His lungs were about to explode. He would just have to disobey orders. Sorry Sar'nt Troggers.

He broke through the surface into dazzling sunlight.

'PAAAHHHHHHHH!' as he expelled the bottled-up air and, 'HhheeEERRRRPP!' as he sucked in more.

He floated, refilling his lungs. Now what.

'Sir, keep calm and assess the situation, Sir!'

He assessed, and was crestfallen. He was completely water-logged. He looked like one of those chunks of seaweed you see floating about the ocean, and he had as much chance of taking off. His wings floated beside him. He tried to give them a flap, but they were glued to the water.

He thought of another Troggers adage: 'Sir, negativity is the enemy of success, Sir.'

He had to admit, he never liked that one. Sometimes, all things considered, you had no choice but to be negative. And it was hard to take any positives out of this situation, which seemed to him to have a huge croakage potential. He thought hard, though, and eventually did come up with a positive.

In all his adventures, whenever he had seemed about to croak, right from Frank Ramphard to Bonxie, including the hunters and the nora's — from whom everybody had said there was no escape — someone or something had always come along to save him, from the toe-end of a teenager to a rotten old fence post. Now, to the east he saw the ragged mushroom moving away, its stem still sucking the ocean. It must have spewed him out the top of that tubey thing. So that was a positive thing — wasn't it? But then here he was and, he noticed, sinking lower and lower in the water. What he wouldn't give for Shug's waterproof plumage.

Shug! Where was Shug? It was all Shug's fault that he was in this mess. He should have flown around that storm, not straight towards it, the dobber. But no, he had to go on, go on and what? Prove himself the World Champion Flier or something. Big

Shuggie the Storm Conqueror. He felt a tightness in his purple belly, like one of those big non-flappers had him by the claws and was squeezing hard. It was squeezing something up into his breast and throat and he clamped his beak down hard to keep it all in. He found he was grinding his mandibles together. What was this? Some kind of seizure brought on by all the wind and wet? Then his brain presented a name for it. Yes, that was it; the perfect name: rage.

But stop it. That was thinking negatively. Stop it now. But he looked at himself, alone, at his beautiful plumage now like seaweed and, as he reached the top of the swell and saw the infinite horizon, he sobbed.

He tried to flap again, his pecs heaving, hoping for the something that always saved him, but the ocean simply sucked him down a little further. He searched the sky for Shug. Surely he wouldnae just leave him behind?

He wondered what croaking would feel like, and whether it would hurt. Water lapped into his beak and he choked a little, and he decided that it might. Most of his body was now under the water and he could feel the ocean tugging. He concluded that it was only his spread-out wings that were keeping him afloat. He craned his neck to get a lung full of water-free air. He had never realised how great air tasted. Sweeter than pineapple juice. He looked at the receding storm and thought how amazing it was. And weren't clouds amazing with all the different shapes they made. Chalkie used to mention that.

Well, if the thing that usually happened to save him was going to happen, it had better happen soon. Shug would appear; that's it, the white star, like before.

He tried to sing his song to himself but had to give up because he ran out of puff and water was running into his beak and making him burble. He heaved his pecs one last time. But now, even the power of the HUUUUUTTT!!! deserted him.

He slipped under.

He looked up and kept his eyes on the light as it faded. As he sank he wondered what would come along and eat him — for something surely would. The ocean was full of bitey things, Shug had said. And, there it was, right on cue, a bulky blob looming into his sideways vision. Didn't look like a shark though, but he couldn't decide if that was a good or a bad thing. A shark would be quick.

The thing came from below. Typical, sneaky ocean blighter. Although his lungs were bursting again, the Purple-Bellied Parrot noted that the thing didn't look like a fish. It was round and it had five legs. It must have a mouth though — they all have — and full of spikey teeth to boot.

He waited for the bite. None came.

He felt the merest of nudges, and then under his belly something solid held him and halted his descent. He felt himself ascend. Was this the thing that usually happened come along at last to save him? It had cut it fine. Or was it some kind of bitey thing that only chomped you once you were on the surface. Knowing the ocean, probably the latter.

He, and it, broke the surface.

'PAAAHHHHHHHH!'

'HhheeEERRRRPP!'

He breathed hard for a moment, which was the most important consideration, and then assessed. He was sprawled on a hard thing shaped like an up-turned bowl. It reminded him of something else, and he thought hard, but the best he could come up with was the pasty crusts that spuggies used to hunt. The ocean had flowed off the pasty, and it was already dry apart from a few dancing beads. He dragged his head up and tapped at it with his beak, and concluded that this huge pasty was made of the same beaky stuff as his beak.

Meanwhile, no big teeth had materialised to chomp him, which the Purple-Bellied Parrot took as a positive. Something was happening though on the edge of the crust. He levered his seaweed plumage up and flopped over to take a look.

One of the five legs was poking up, but then, it can't be a leg because it has eyes and a mouth — and a beaky mouth like his. Or was it a leg? For all he knew the bonkers world at the bottom of the ocean contained creatures which swam about with heads in their legs. The Purple-Bellied Parrot regarded the beaky leg-head. It seemed familiar, and it dawned on him that it resembled his own head. Well, anyway, his head that time all his feathers fell out. Was this pasty some kind of relative?

The leg-head turned towards him and opened its mouth. It said, 'Boa tarde.'

Without missing a beat, the Purple-Bellied Parrot said, 'Boa tarde.'

Now where had *that* come from!

He was back in the hole in the tree, then in the skin cage. A new memory, a dark lurchy thing where he was sick all the time. The bins said it all the time — 'Boa tarde … Boa tarde.' And there was another similar one. 'Bom dia.' That was it.

The Purple-Bellied Parrot's mind raced, trying to decide if he should be happy or sad. 'Boa tarde' connected with many bad memories. But the pasty was no bin. He must know his home — perhaps he *is* a relative. The Purple-Bellied Parrot's heart soared like an eagle.

'Boa tarde,' the pasty said again.

'Boa tarde! Boa tarde! Boa tarde! Boa tarde!' the Purple-Bellied Parrot cried. If his feathers had still worked he would have gone for a fly about.

The leg-head regarded him, eyes widening, and said 'ahem.' The Purple-Bellied Parrot shut up. 'I saw you in the water. Sinking. I thought, hhhmm, now what is thees? And I was about to eat you when I saw, all theez … all theez feathers, and I thought about the trouble I would have spitting them out and if they come out the other end, well, the tickling is just unspeakable. I ate a bird once ... A pássaro minúsculo that fell out of a tree by the coast — never again.' The pasty lowered its leg-head into the water.

The Purple-Bellied Parrot didn't listen to the words, he was just dumbfounded that the leg-head said 'thees' like him. He didn't notice that they were moving through the water towards the afternoon sun.

'So I blought bl'ahh, burble, he is a parrot with his blurple belly. I wonder what he does blout here, burble, so far from blome. I see you in the trees blen I go to the sands to blay my bleggs, burble. What you bloo here, so far from bland ... burble.'

The Purple-Bellied Parrot wondered why the pasty's voice had changed. He craned forward and saw that the pasty was now swimming along with its head half-submerged, water sloshing in and out of its beak.

He answered the pasty's question. He told how he wanted to go home to the emerald forest and that the only way to get home was for him to ride on the old albatross's back and how he'd been knocked off in the storm because the albatross had been stupid and too proud to change course.

'Yes, they'll do blat,' said the pasty lifting its head out of the water. 'They are reckless. They wander the skies above the restless ocean, solitary souls, alone in all this vastness. Always there is wind, uproar and turmoil. Imagine never seeing anything that is still, that is at rest. Never hearing silence. I think it drives them a little crazy.'

The pasty's head sagged back into the water. 'You travel blar with blis albatross, burble. I too travel blar. But I stay in my blele-ment. Not blike you. You should see me on the bland. It takes me the blole blight to crawl up and down a bleach, burble. I'm like a sack of bloconuts. Have you seen what I've got for blegs? Go on, blake a blook.'

The sun had dried the Purple-Bellied Parrot's plumage a bit and he was able to prise his feathers off the pasty and stand up. He gave himself a good shake which ruffled his feathers and felt good, but he came over all wobbly, and he couldn't dig his claws in because the pasty was so hard. So he lay back down on his tummy and pushed himself along with his feet. He inspected the circumference of the pasty. It was true. The front legs were like wings, and the back ones were like flippers. It must be awkward walking about on those. He noticed that she wore a red ring of plastic around one of the wings and concluded it must be the latest fashion.

'Blee what I blean?'

The Purple-Bellied Parrot admitted that he did. 'The back ones are like blippers, I mean flippers,' he said. He inched forward to the front of the pasty and watched the beaky head nosing through the water. It was on the end of, not a leg, but a wrinkly neck. 'Hwhat are you?' he asked.

'A blurtle,' the pasty replied. 'Your blalbatross wanders *over* the oceans? Well I blander *under* the bloceans, where all is calm. My blame is Luna.'

The Purple-Bellied Parrot said he was pleased to meet her, and Luna asked him what his name was. 'I am the Purple-Bellied Parrot,' he said.

Luna snorted. 'Blat's a thing, blot a name you palhaço. I am a blurtle. There's blots of turtles, but my name is Luna, burble.' Luna lifted her head out of the water. 'You must have a name.'

The Purple-Bellied Parrot thought hard. He remembered the spuggies calling him 'Ooterus Maximus' and 'Schnozzmeister General,' but he sensed that may have been jokes, so he decided to keep 'shtum' on those. He told Chickova his name was Betty, but that was only because he panicked under interrogation. Steve had called him 'Dude', which he liked, but he didn't think that was his name because nobody else called him by it. And he wasn't much for 'Chief' or 'Chiefy

Boy' either. So he said, crestfallen, 'I doan theenk I have a name.'

Luna looked back. 'Oh — that is sad. Then I shall call you … hmmm …' She stopped swimming and thought for a long time, twirling in an unseen current rising from the deep. Finally she said, 'Luiz. Yes, Luiz. That is a good name for you.' She plunged her head back into the water.

The Purple-Bellied Parrot thought it was a good name too.

<hr>

'The theeng you are standing on is my shell Luiz. Peck it. Go on — as hard as you can.'

Luiz. My name, he thought and bobbed his head. He hammered the shell with the point of his beak; he cocked his head and gnawed at it. He stood back to survey the results, and saw not the faintest scratch.

'It's to protect me from all the theengs that want to eat me — and there are a lot of those. And I can do thees — watch!'

Luna's head disappeared. He thought she had simply lowered it out of sight into the water, but when he peered over, it had vanished. He circumnavigated the shell looking for it, but not only the head, the legs too had now disappeared.

'Luna! Luna!' he called, terror rising in his breast. Some bitey thing had swept up from the depths and chomped them off. He scampered around the edge looking for the missing limbs — a little too fast, and he almost fell in.

'Eez okay Luiz, eez okay. Here I am!' The voice came from behind, and Luiz cackled and bobbed his head to see Luna and her legs again.

<hr>

Luna swam on silently as though pondering, Luiz basking on her shell, steaming like a neglected kettle. They passed bin rubbish, bottles, buckets, ropes and floats, rags that looked like bin clothes, a sou'wester, a plastic ring painted orange and white with a bin slumped inside it, head lolling, swollen tongue poking out. A george stood on the ring, waiting.

Luna lifted her head and said, 'You know, I cannot take you far. I spend most of my life under the water. Where were you headed with the old albatross?'

'We were going to some rocks shaped like shark's teeth that poke out of the ocean in the middle of nowhere. We planned to rest there before the next bit of our journey.'

'I know those rocks! That is where I am taking you now. They are close. We blill arrive before the blend of the day ... blurble.'

Luiz lay on his belly and watched Luna's flippers. He noticed the flipper with the red ring did not work as well as the other, and the band was cutting into the flesh.

'Why do you wear the red band?' he asked.

'I do not wear it. It is just there. I found it there two summers ago. I do not know where it came from.'

'Does it hurt?'

'A little, but not so much. I have tried to shake it loose many times but now it is too late. I have grown too big.'

He looked again at the flipper. Beyond the band the flesh was swollen. There was no way it would slip off now. 'Will you grow anymore?'

'A little. Why?'

He cocked his head and thought. Then he said, 'I theenk it is a bad thing. I theenk soon it will do you harm.' He clapped his beak. 'I can cut it off.'

They saw them silhouetted, the red disc of the sun spiked on the tallest rock as if stranded there by the ocean. Luna apologised again that she could not take him further, and Luiz said that he understood. Luna told him that he must feed, anything he can find — 'Anything, I mean it' — and once he'd got his feathers sleek and glossy again he must look for a big ship and fly out to it and find a place to hide. 'They are almost deserted of humanos nowadays,' she said. A woolly memory of a ship jostled into Luiz's mind and churned his stomach, but he said okay. Silently, Luna nudged up to the rocks.

Luiz hopped off. 'Hold you flipper up please,' he said.

The band was so tight and cut so deep it was hard to get his mandible under, and he had to work it from side to side, and then he was at such an odd angle and he had to chew at it. But with a pop it snapped and flipped up and smacked him in the eye and plopped into the water to drift away. Luna's flipper looked like it had a valley running around it.

'Obrigado,' she said. 'That feels good.'

Luiz had not expected to say so many goodbyes on this trip. He felt like he had a big nut stuck in his throat. He gulped it down and said obrigado for saving his life. Then he said adios and hopped higher up the rocks.

She slipped into the deep and, mirrored in her shell, the orange moon went with her.

19

SHARK'S TEETH

R ain woke Luiz. He tried to open his eyes, but all stayed black. He squawked and thrashed his head and stumbled and fell into something wet and lay, breathing hard. Take stock. Assess. The salt from yesterday's dunking — it must be gluing the eyelids together. Almost unconscious from exhaustion, he tilted his head and let the sweet water flow in and sloosh them out.

He was dozily aware that the rain was a very good thing. Although his plumage had dried in a jiffy in yesterday's sun, it was so matted and tangled it probably looked like what was left of Old Stumpy's. At best, it would only be good for short hops. He needed to get it properly clean — Sar'nt Lofty Troggers's 'spick and span,' and this rain was perfect. He opened his wings and stood there like a full-bellied cormorant by a fishpond, the rain finding every nook and cranny. A breeze swept away the clouds and, halfway up the sky, the sun emerged. With a faint 'shhlurrp' his eyelids unlocked and he struggled up.

'Crikey!' he yelled, and almost fell off the rock. At his feet, half-submerged in a puddle of seawater, was the skeleton of a bird. He had been lying in it. It had been a big bird with a huge skull and a big hooked beak. Sparse feathers still clung to the bones, white and grey wisps waving in the water. The flesh had gone.

'No — Shug!' he cried, but then gave himself a stern telling off. Not even the myriad beasties of the ocean could strip a body so quickly — could they? A big hole gaped where an eye used to be. They always eat the eyes first.

But where was Shug? Shug, who had been so stupid in the sea canyon and gone and flown off without him. Had he made it through the storm? He turned his back on the skeleton and pondered. If he had made it, well, Shug was depending on him to get through any doldrums. Despite his bravado in the storm, Luiz was pretty sure that Shug wouldn't be brave enough to tackle the next leg on his own, risking bin-glass seas and sharks. He may even have turned back and be heading for Scotchland. Or, this might be him swishing about behind.

Hunger shouldered all these thoughts aside. He peered into the pools at his feet. A few squirmy crawly things darted and scuttled, but nothing that took his fancy — at least not yet. He clambered to the top of his shark-toothed rock and stood on its guano crust.[1]

Shug had been right — and wrong. These few peaks really were the middle of nowhere; he screwed up his eyes and peered, but saw no land on any horizon.[2] On the largest island though, well if the bins had not been here when Shug came all those decades ago, they were here now. A tin-roofed concrete bunker hunkered in the lee of its rocks. Sprouting around it were aerials and dishes and mushrooms, rooty wires trailing. A wooden platform led to where a small boat bobbed, and atop the tooth behind the bunker, a column painted in red and white hoops poked at the sky. Bins always like to declare they are here. Perhaps it was good that Shug hadn't made it — this spectacle would send him into full head-waving mode.

Food. He looked around at the rock pools of squirmies and shuddered. He gazed back towards the concrete bunker. Where there was bins there was food, and there might even be a can or two he could prise open. But would his wings carry him there? Then he spotted it, there below on his own island, wedged in a vee in the rocks above the waterline. A coconut. Yippee! The storm must have flung it there.

He clambered down and gave it a peck. He hoped the ocean might have softened it a bit — not even his mighty beak could open a coconut shell. But sure enough, like Luna's shell, he pecked and gnawed and made no impression. He cocked his head and regarded the coconut. The thrushes in the park. They smash open snails on a brick ... or a rock. He was surrounded by rocks. Hhmmm.

He clambered below the coconut and braced his legs against the rocks. He put his back against the shell and shoved. It moved. It moved! He stopped shoving and looked around. Above was a particularly precipitous rock which dropped to a flat bit just above the lapping water. A shallow ledge wound up to it. Hhmmm.

The sun had moved a fair way up the sky by the time he had huffed and puffed and scrambled his way up the ledge and had the coconut teetering on the edge of the precipice. He'd had to rest a couple of times, the coconut pressing on his back so hard he thought it might roll over his gasping body and squash him. But now he was there and he peered over. Yep, that should do it. He gave it a kick.

The white was like Shug's plumage. Shug. And through his mind flashed a bad word the spuggies used a lot. He leapt down and chomped up the sweet flesh, knowing that he had to work quickly because there were lots of birdies about who were ready and able to shove him aside. Out of the corner of his eye he saw a charcoal-black bird with a pointy beak land on a nearby rock. It watched him, then sidled towards him in a circumbendibus.

'Sir, make yourself big, Sir!'

He wheeled round, ruffled his feathers, opened his wings and went, 'SquAAAWRRRRK!,'

The pointy-beaked bird's black feet dangled behind as he fled.

Wow! It had worked, just like Sar'nt Lofty Troggers said it would. He returned to his feast. Some coconut milk had survived in a cup-shaped fragment and he lapped it up. Nearly as good as pineapple juice out of a can, but not quite.

When he'd picked the coconut shell clean, he hauled his tennis-ball tummy up to the top of his rock and sat and lifted his face to the sun, the tennis ball resting on the rock between his feet. He nearly nodded off, but just managed to jolt himself awake. He had serious matters to attend to. He jumped up and down and shook himself and said 'Hut!' twice, and embarked on the longest preen of his life. His feathers still tasted of salt but the rain had washed most of it out, and he carefully inspected, oiled and zipped-up every single one. The sun was halfway down the other side of the sky by the time he'd finished.

He had a good flap. The wings felt good, and he decided to fly to the nearest island to test them out. He looked about. On bin island he saw bins moving about doing bin stuff, so he aimed for the one next door.

Piece of cake. Not perfect, and they would need another couple of days work, but he was sure his wings would soon be able to fly him out to a passing boat. He examined each feather again and made a few minor adjustments. Then he found a shady nook and had a snooze. He was pretty sure that there were no moggies knocking about here.

He dreamt about Shug. The dream ended in a jumble of a storm and an albatross flying on through the storm and the albatross turning gradually into skeleton, its bones beating the air until they crashed onto rocks sharp as shark's teeth. An empty eye socket stared up at the sky. Luiz jerked awake sobbing.

He shook himself and clambered to the top of his new rock. The air was clear and he could see all the way to the horizon.

Ships. Two ships! Ships were always aiming for land, and his heart soared like an eagle. One was long and flat with a lump at one end. Luna had told him to choose a big ship like that because he was unlikely to meet any bins. For the first time, his dream of returning home, to Brazeel, which for so long had been like the butterflies the spuggies chased but never caught, became like a great coconut just waiting for him to crack open. Who'd ever have thought he could come so far? Certainly not Big Maggie when she offered him that job, and some of the spuggies had doubted — not to mention Chickova. Then his body sagged as he thought of the white star that had carried him away from the Bonxie, and how they had caroomed over so much ocean together.

Another little fly about — that would be a good idea, and he flew to a keech-crusted rock on the far side of bin island. He alighted on a sheltered ledge just below the peak and settled down to watch the ocean for ships and white stars.

He must have flown right past him. He must have been camouflaged against the guano. But as he gazed out, he heard a trumpy cough coming from below, and a low rumbling moan.

'Ooooaarrraggh .... Ooooaarrraggh'

He peaked over and saw a huge coconut-white bird, neck slack, bill resting on the rocks. A red plastic collar around its neck.

He sprang up, but his joy was snuffed out by a toppling wave of anger. He settled and watched for a bit. Watched his breast heave, watched him clap his beak and wave his head about until it looked like it would twist off, watched the beak clunk back onto the rock.

'Ooooaarrraggh .... Ooooaarrraggh'

So he was alive.

He saw more ships that day, nestled in his nook with a view across the flat sea to where the sun set. One came close, so close he could make out bins moving about in its lumpy end, and he decided that prospects were good. Make sure it was going in the right direction; hop on; hop off when it came near land — Brazeel. What could go wrong? A good bit easier than the trip had been so far, that was for sure. 'Just a couple of days' he told himself, 'until your feathers are teep-top.' But ships meant bins, and barging into his mind came memories of a room ceaselessly, sickeningly swaying, and the stinking black din.

He must eat.

He flew around the rocks a few times — steering clear of the one where the big albatross squatted — and squawked with joy when he saw a coconut washed up like before. But it turned out to be a seaweed-shrouded fishing float.

He settled back on his rock and studied the ocean puddles. Food was everywhere if he could just force it down. He picked at a couple of squirmies. He even managed to hold one writhing in his beak and he lifted his head to let it slither down. But his body convulsed like a moggie coughing up a fur ball. He had to investigate the island where the bins were. Surely a few leftovers must be knocking about, and he was overwhelmed by a sudden longing for kebab and chips.

He chose a drizzly dawn when the bins were sure to be snuggled in their beds, and flew over. A big oblong box with a square lid stood apart from the concrete bunker. It was stuffed to bursting, and the lid wouldn't close, so he snuck in and rummaged about. He gnawed the flesh off a mango stone. He found half a banana and munched that with half a bun. He found saucy stuff spilling out of plastic containers, like he used to chomp with the spuggies at the takeaways — ahh, the spuggies. But soon he got fed up of eating leftovers.

A big window and a little window pierced the bunker's concrete. He landed on a sill and peered through the big window. Mounds of bedclothes with tufts of bin hair poking out heaved up and down. Sounds of snores leaked through the glass. He glanced over to the little window and saw its top was open, just a bit. He flew over and peeked inside. A storeroom, stacked high with boxes. He listened. Snoring. He breathed in tight and squeezed through the gap and tore open a box. Cans, labelled with pictures of fishes. Fishes! Typical! He tore open another box. Beans! He would eat beans at a push, and had dined on many a fine bean with the spuggies, but he tried one more box.

It was a box of sunshine. The golden image of a pineapple shone out and he got to work with his hooter like he did when he worked for the maggies, and soon as the sweetness filled his belly he too shone. When he got to the bottom of the can he eased it aside to get at the next. Too hungry, too eager. The empty can flipped out of the box and tumbled.

CLATTER!

He froze, straining his ears to pick up any sounds from next door. He'd rather plop into the ocean again than get caught by the bins. He heard a trombony trump but the snores remained constant. No squeaky bed springs or coughs or angry voices.

He levered open another can.

He had his head in deep, slurping the last bit, taking care not to get stuck like he'd done in the water jug, when he sensed a change. A draught, maybe? He extracted his head from the can and looked around. The door was open, and framed there was a bin. Its fat face was stubbly and greasy hair stood up on top of its head and its jaw dangled showing crooked teeth and a pink tongue which wagged as its brain debated what to do. It was naked apart from a pair of tiny bulging pants half-hidden by bin-belly overhang. It scratched its bottom and pulled the tiny pants out of its crack and went, 'Uurrgh?'

Pineapple juice dribbled down Luiz's breast as they regarded each other, the bin's half-closed eyes gradually widening, its jaws beginning to work as its brain began to make make sense of what its eyes saw.

It stretched out its arms, made an 'Aiyee!' sound, and lunged.

Luiz squawked and flew, but more pineapple juice had got into his plumage than he thought, and he was slow to the open window and had to flap hard. He looked down at his tennis-ball belly. He looked up at the gap. He said, 'Uh-oh.'

He dived for it, flattening his wings and breathing in, and felt the metal frame scrape his feathers and squeeze his belly.

Thhudoink!

Stuck fast, he twisted his neck around and saw the bin lurching towards him, jaws now tightened into a grin. But the pineapple juice that had so hampered him now changed sides, and the bin slipped and skidded and now Luiz was no longer seeing face and the arms closing in, but whirling legs and a bum.

'Caramba!' the bin yelled, and thunked onto its back. 'OOooaaarghh.'

Luiz, breathing in tight, 'HUUUUUUUUUT,' and with a 'Thwock' he was out into the salty air.

As he flew back to his rock he thought about how he must stop getting into these scrapes, and how the spuggies said the moggies had nine lives — which they had to explain to him — and he wondered how many he had left. After this trip, surely only one or two at the most.

He took a circumbendibus which happened to take him past the rock where the albatross squatted. He was on the same spot, beak resting on the rock. He appeared not to have moved since Luiz last saw him.

Luiz settled in his nook, jutted out his beak and looked out for ships. He felt strong after his feed, and his wings had powered him away after he had exited the window, full belly and all. If a ship came close enough, it might be today.

He stared out, but found he couldn't concentrate, and soon his eyes were watching the seabirds as they drifted by. Not bad fliers he supposed, but not as good as … He stretched up and looked back to the rock where he knew the albatross squatted, and then huffed and settled back to watch the horizon.

A movement on the rock at his side caught his eye. The husk of a long-departed beetle. Now how had that found its way to this desolate place?

A breeze swirled in and the husk rocked.

***

He really hadn't moved, and the groan, 'Ooooaarrraggh …. Ooooaarrraggh,' continued. But now, part of the groan had crystallized into words. After every half dozen or so 'Ooooaarrragghs', the beak would creak open and murmur, 'Oh Chiefy boy … Chiefy boy … Ah'm soo sorry.' As he said it, his whole body rocked.

He'd not looked after himself. Weight had dropped off him, and he looked like he'd not preened since before the storm, his glossy white plumage now flat and grey. A fly landed on the end of his beak, and he did nothing. A tiny crab appeared, scrattled over the rocks and nibbled at his feet.

'Aw, goo awae wee beastie and leave me alone — I just want to pop ma clogs.' He nudged it away — it would normally be in his crop by now — but then said, 'Aw noo, on second thoughts come back wee beastie and eat me slowly. I'm doomed.'

Luiz searched the rocks at his feet and spotted an upturned limpet shell. That would do. He sidled over to the edge of his rock, took aim, and gave it a good kick. He'd not intended to hit Shug, just to startle him, but the result was better than he ever expected.

The shell landed squarely on top of Shug's head and sat there like a helmet.

'Wha!? … What the ….?' Shug looked about bamboozled. The

helmet didn't fit properly and it swivelled about as he turned. He looked up and the shell fell off.

He saw the Purple-Bellied Parrot.

'Nooo! ... How ... Wha ... Ah mean ... Noo ... How ... Chiefy boy! Ez you! Ez you!'

Shug began to clamber up the rocks. It was pitiful to watch him trying to haul that big gangly frame of his up, so Luiz said, 'Eez okay. I come down to you.'

They looked at each other for a long time, Shug goggled-eyed repeating, 'Nooo ... How ... Wha ... Ah mean ... How?' Luiz, silent.

Presently, Luiz leaned forward and said quietly, 'What have you done to yourself you beeg numptie?' He preened Shug's sorry nape and Shug lowered his head and let him. Then Luiz said, 'Shug, will you do me a wee favour?'

'Cairtainly ... Sure thing, Chiefy boy. Anything for you. What? Just say the waird.'

'Turn around please.'

'Nae bother! And, hey, look at you pickin up the lingo — sayin' 'wee' and 'numptie' like that. Pure magic so it is.'

Shug turned.

Luiz considered taking a run-up, but concluded it might be a bit excessive. But he put all the force he could summon into that boot up the bum. Shug nearly toppled off the rock.

'That's for dumping me off in the storm. Not coming back for me. How could you? How could you Shug?'

His beak clunked back onto the rock. 'You're rayt. You're rayt,' he groaned. 'I've been pure cracked up aboot it, so I have. Couldnae eat nae wash ma'sel. I even sat on the ocean ages hoping a sharkie would come along and give me the malkie. Me, sat on the ocean.' He looked up and faced Luiz squarely. 'I couldnae come back for you. I didnae knoo where I was ma'sel for half a day. I was lost. Thought I was gettin blasted up north again. I thought you was deed Chiefy Boy ... deed. D'ya understand that.' He began to sob. 'I was an old twally trying to be young one last time. I never knoo … swear on this ocean … I never knoo it was a hurricane.'

For a long time the only sound was the ocean washing the rocks at their feet, and then Shug sniffed and looked at Luiz side-long and said, 'Come on laddie … Look at us. Look at everything we've been through together. And we're still here, both of us, still a-flappin'. Forgive and forget, ay?'

Luiz was quiet. Then he sighed and said, 'Forgotten? No. Not for a long time Shug.' His mantle sagged. 'But forgiven? Yeays my friend.'

Shug sobbed.

'But on one condition: you must stop calling me Chief, Chiefy, Chiefy Boy or any other offshoot of 'Chief' — and laddie and pal for that matter. My name is Luiz. We decided that, me and Luna.'

'Ookay … Ookay — Luiz.' Shug said 'Luiz' a few more times as though testing it out. 'Aye, Luiz, that's no bad. Fair suits you so it does. I like that.' He clapped his beak. 'And who's this Luna when she's at hame?'

'A blurtle — I mean a turtle. She saved my life.'

And it was Luiz's turn to sob as it all flooded out. Shug disappearing, tumbling about in the storm, sucked up with the fishes and the georges and the boat and the bin, spat out at the top to splat, alone, into the vast ocean, the seaweed plumage, and the sinking and holding his breath and all the blurry shapes coming to eat him. Shug preened his neck as he told it.

'I thought I hated you,' Luiz sobbed. 'And I never hated anything in my life before, not the bins who cut down my home, not the pink-faced man, not the bins who stole Millie away, but I thought I hated you.' He leaned away from Shug and huffed. 'But I was wrong. Let us go to Brazeel.'

CAUGHT

The wind stayed slack for the rest of the day, the ocean lapping the shore with as much force as the water in the duck pond, so they hung around the islands, preening and eating and sleeping. Shug found squidgy stuff around the shore to chomp and, come dusk, Luiz raided the bins' bin.

The wind returned on a morning of sun and scudding clouds shaped like pampered poodles. Shug surveyed the sky, nodded with approval, and said he would go out fishing for a bit before they set off.

'I willnae be long Luiz,' he called as he taxied by. 'You'll be back in your forest with your pals befair you can say Benbecula-collcannamullrumeiggandmuck.'

Luiz watched him go. Watched him climb and become a wave. His gaze slipped, caught by a shape on the horizon. A fishing boat ploughed the waves. He looked back and searched for Shug, but he was lost in the whitecaps.

Luiz was already frantic by the time the booby arrived with the news. He'd even pulled a feather out.

'Er, I … I think you should come. It's your friend. He's in trouble.'

Luiz leapt into the air. 'Why? What? Is he okay?'

'Er, I … I doan no. I expect you'll see when you get there.'

The booby led him towards a whirling cloud of seabirds. As they neared Luiz saw shearwaters and georges and noddies and boobies. Below the cloud, the fishing boat chugged along, belching black diesel. Bins in orange trousers sliced bellies and chucked innards overboard. From its stern, fishing lines stretched off into the ocean, where they vanished in the turmoil.

'There, look!' said the booby. 'Oh Dios mio — looks like there's two of them now.'

Luiz could not make sense of what he saw. The fishing lines were dragging two ragged old towels through the water. What concern of his was this? He stared again, and the sodden towels resolved into waterlogged plumage. Two albatrosses had dived in for the easy lunch of the bait.

'Which one's Shug?' Luiz called over to the booby,

The booby stared at him dumbly.

'My friend. Which one is my friend?'

The booby said, 'I do not know. But, but I think that they are fools.'

Luiz flew over to where the two albatrosses tumbled, but they looked identical. He knew what to do. He dropped down to where the lines cut the water, and hung on the wind, the ocean spraying his face. The lines bobbed wildly, driven by the wash from the boat. The wind buffeted him too, and whenever he was about to fasten his jaws around a line to sever it, it was snatched away from him. The ocean sprayed him again, and he knew he couldn't stay any longer or he would be waterlogged.

He looked towards the boat. Bins, but he had no choice: he had to cut the line closer to the boat. In a moment he had landed on the steel frame from where the lines stretched out. The lines were moving and he realised that they, and the albatrosses, were being hauled in. He glanced over his shoulder. The bins hadn't noticed him, yet, but this would surely annoy them. He flew a little way astern. Then, still flapping hard, he clamped his beak around one of the lines and bit down. The line was tough, tougher than he'd expected. It whipped him up and down but he clung on. Out of the corner of his eye he saw the stern of the boat looming as he was hauled towards it. The line ran over a steel wheel and down to a winch. He didn't want to get caught up in that. He began to saw his jaws like when he'd freed Millie and Steve.

The line snapped and whipped away, and one of the albatrosses drifted, motionless. He flew up and circled. So many lines, it was hard to work out which one dragged the other albatross. He followed a line back from the tumbling rag and dropped down and bit hard and sawed. It snapped and he looked back. But the albatross still tumbled and was now so close to the boat it would soon be hauled aboard. Bins now stood on the stern and were pointing and shaking angry fists, like bins do.

He would get soaked but he would have to do it. He flew closer to the albatross and fixed his eye on the line that hooked it and followed it to a point where he'd certainly be drenched but perhaps not flounder. The boat was almost upon him. No time for it to be the wrong one again. It was now and then never. He clamped his jaws down and sawed. The ocean doused him. The wind tore at his feathers. Something whizzed passed his head and he saw a bottle splash into the ocean. The line reared up as it reached the stern. TWANG! It snapped and, as another bottle spun towards him, he wheeled away.

The boat chugged on leaving the two albatrosses floating on the swell. Luiz dashed to the first one. He landed and gave the plumage a tug, but the bird was lifeless. As he tugged, a current forced open its wings and they floated on the surface. They were edged with black. Shug's were pure white.

He was instantly aloft and searching the swell for the other albatross — for Shug.

There! Outstretched wings, of the purest white, floated. His head, of similar purity, was underwater.

Luiz landed on the sodden back. He jumped up and down, 'Shug! Shug!' He reached into the water and grabbed Shug's neck and tried to drag his head out. But it was too heavy, and just as he got the beak out, it splashed back in. He tried again, but he wasn't strong enough — not strong enough. How could that be? He had to leap off to avoid a breaking wave. He landed again and jumped up and down on Shug's back.

'Shug! Shug! Come back … Come back! Don't croak on me like this, you great whallopin bahookey. We've come all thees way together. Now come on! Shug … pleeze … pleeze … Shuuu-UUUUGGG!'

Luiz tugged at the plumage. The feathers swirled as the ocean washed over. He wished he had something to cover Shug's eyes.

'Sir, keep calm and assess the situation, Sir!'

He looked at Shug's wings, flat on the water. Think! He thought, and Shug's words flew into his mind, 'I just open these big fellas up and let them do their stuff. I have nowt to do with it except have a chat with them noo and then …'

'Okay wings,' Luiz shouted. 'Time to go to work. You are the most amazing wings on thees earth. You know it. I know it. I've seen it. Now, do one more amazing thing. Save Shug! Pleeze save Shug.'

He hovered and grabbed a wing with his claws and lifted it out of the water, 'HuuuUUUUUT!'

It slapped back. Then he darted over and did the same to the other. 'HUUUUUUUTTT!'

They floated, slack in the water.

He landed again on Shug's back and yelled at them, 'Come

ON wings! Remember: most things can do most things if they've a mind. Now, come on! Try. For Shug!' He flew back and heaved at each one. He did it twice more, then flopped on to Shug's back, soaked and exhausted. The wings stayed sodden, and still.

The ocean sucked, and Shug sank a little. It was a feeling Luiz knew well. Soon Shug would be in the blurry world. He clung on to Shug's red collar for the last time and waited with him.

It happened.

As one, both wings slowly rose. Water pearled, and flowed away. The wings hung for a moment, testing the wind. And then, as they determined speed and direction, they tilted and arced. They found the wind, and Luiz felt Shug's body shift. He leapt off and hung on that same wind. Shug's body rose, but the ocean still sucked. Luiz saw a minor adjustment to the secondaries, and the wings began to draw Shug's limp body free. A gust, they found it, and with a 'Sshhllopp', Shug was clear. From his sagging beak, blue fishing line dangled.

They were so close, just a fisherman's cast away, but they had given all they could. Luiz landed on the rocks and turned to see the wings crumple and Shug slap into the ocean. He leapt aloft and flew back. The blue line floated in the water.

He hated to do it, but there was no choice. He grabbed it and heaved. The thought of Shug and the big bum flashed through his mind. Shug seemed to weigh about as much as a whale's bum. He dragged him into the shallows to a flat rock. Then he dropped the line and grabbed hold of his nape and hauled him out. He jumped up and down on his back again. He didn't know why, but this seemed like a good idea. As he landed, water pumped out of Shug's beak.

'Come on Shug … Come on Shug … You can do it.' Jump—jump—jump. 'You will fly the furious fifties, see the icebergs again.' Jump—jump—jump. 'You might find a mate. You're not too old. Theenk of that!' Jump—jump—jump.

He thought Shug's plumage would be waterlogged but was amazed to see the water bead. He carried on jumping and the water kept pumping out, but his thighs burned and he knew he couldn't keep it up much longer.

Shug coughed.

He coughed again.

A mixture of ocean and squidy slime flooded out over the rock. Luiz leapt off and scampered round to inspect. A squid tentacle hung out of the corner of Shug's beak like a soggy cigarette. He yanked it out. The beak opened and gently clapped. After a bit the beak opened again and said softly, 'Is tha ... is tha' you Ch ... ah mean, Luiz? I tell you, you wouldnae believe the dream I just had ... Pure mental.'

Shug lay on the rock, wings splayed, steaming, until the sun was high, Luiz watching him to make sure he didn't croak. At noon he shifted and gathered his wings and folded them and tucked himself into a sitting position. He snoozed. Luiz occasionally preened him, but he didn't seem to notice.

Luiz examined the fishing line. It was clearly hooked to something inside, and he hated to think what. It really had been the last resort to tow him that last bit to the shore, and he tried not to think about what more damage he may have done.

Shug woke, a rattle emanating from his throat. He wobbled for a bit, as if he was being blown about by the wind, but the wind had fallen away. Luiz asked him how he was. He spoke very slowly.

'I am fair diminished so I am. I remember diving in to snaffle a wee bit of squid. The last thing I remember is being dragged along like a clump of old kelp, and then ... all a blank.' He clapped his beak together and, for the first time, noticed the line.

'Whaaa! What's this?? WHAAAAA!!'

Shug stood.

'Get it oot of me … get it OOT of me.' He waved his head about, the line whipping around. 'Whhaaa! I knoo what this is … I knoo what this is!' He thrashed his head until he was exhausted, and then it slumped and his beak clunked onto the rock. He muttered, 'I'm doomed … I'm doomed.'

'Let me look at you,' Luiz said, and he led him, beak scraping, to a tall rock he judged the right height and leaned him up against it. He climbed to the top.

'Shug, look up.' Shug's beak remained on the rock like it was made of lead.

'Shug, look at me. Shug, look up … Look at me.'

Shug heaved his beak off the rock, and slowly raised it. He was muttering, 'I'm_done fer … pure done fer. I'm doomed. Doon't waste your time on me. Save yer'sel. I'm doomed.'

'Shug! Listen to me. Point your beak at the sun. Shug! Stop feeling sorry for yourself and do that for me, pleeeze.'

He pointed his beak towards the sun.

'Now, open your mouth, that's it, well done. Wider … Now straighten you neck so I can see, that's it, nice and straight for me now … leedle beet straighter. Perfect. Now.'

Luiz dreaded what he might find. For an instant that thought was shouldered aside by Shug's old-prawn breath, but he peered down, amazed how wide Shug could open his beak. He could see a long way — so far, he half-expected to see the rocks at the other end.

'Shug, just tilt your head a leedle beet … that's it.'

Shug groaned.

Luiz saw the steel glint as the sun caught it. It was hooked into something pink and pulsing. He gave the line the slightest tug and a tiny jet of blood spurted out. Shug yelped and his beak clamped shut, trapping Luiz's head. Shug jerked his head up and Luiz was hoisted off his feet. Upside-down, staring into the depths of Shug's gullet and beyond, this must be how a fish feels.

'Shug! Let me out! Let me out!' and Luiz wriggled and yelled until the beak yawned open.

When Shug had calmed down, they repeated the process. The hook was too far down for him to get at, and anyway he had the wrong-shaped beak. It needed something long and thin, not his bulbous Ooterus Maximus. He thought back to when he was shot, and to the beach and how Herman had whipped out the metal ball. But this was different, this was a hook, and it was inside Shug and, when you moved it, there was all that blood shooting out. And there were no Hermans about.

The noddy shot him a sidelong glance. He was chewing a fish bone and he spat it out at the Purple-Bellied Parrot's feet. A little too close.[1]

'What's in it for me?' he said. 'Here, I gotta go stick my beak down some albies throat that I ain't never met before — some bird that don't mean nuttin to me, nuttin. I gotta have an angle.' So Luiz assured him that if he saved Shug, Shug would go out and catch him the biggest fish he ever saw. And he asked him if he had any friends.

Later, Luiz clambered down to the shore and started poking about in the pools. Eventually, he found what he was looking for, and he spoke to it for a very long time.

'Just leave me to die … Just leave me to die. I'm doomed.' As Luiz gathered the last of his team together, Shug was in full head-waving mode.

'Hold still or you'll make it worse,' Luis said.

Luiz and the noddy climbed to the top of the tall rock. He showed the noddy the thing he had kept hidden under his wing so as not to frighten Shug, and gave him some final instructions. The noddy nodded.

'Okay. Let's do dis ting.'

Luiz said, 'Shug, leeft your beak again for me please.' Shug lifted his beak. 'Open wide.' He meekly opened wide — he now seemed resigned to his fate.

The noddy said, 'You gat it? I told you — I ain't getting swallowed by this big galloot.'

'I have got it,' Luiz replied. He turned to Shug. ' I am just going to pop thees into your beak.' He waved a thin piece of wood before his eyes. 'It is a beet of driftwood I found to prop your beak open — so you do not swallow thees noddy here.'

Luiz then opened his wing and carefully placed the thing on the rock next to him. The thing was flat and fan-shaped, about the size of a bin's fingernail.

'Everyone ready?'

Luiz wrapped his wings around Shug's outstretched neck. The noddy's buddies pressed up against Shug to hold him against the rock. Luiz nodded to the noddy, who peered down the gaping throat.

'I see it … I see it.' He pushed his head further in.

Shug kept still — but he made a lot of noise.

'OOoooaaAARRRRGGH … OOoooaaAARRRRGGH …'

A voice boomed out from deep inside. 'Tell him to shaddap will ya! I can't hear myself tink down here!' Shug quietened down, apart from a continuous low moan.

It took longer than Luiz had expected. At one point the noddy called up, 'This darn hook gotta barb on it!' Luiz didn't know what a barb was, but he knew the noddy was frustrated. But presently the noddy called out, 'I got it! I got it!! Whooaa!!! Will ya look at all that blood!'

The noddy's head emerged from Shug's throat, its beak clasping the bloody, glistening hook. He spat it out and it landed with a 'tink' onto the rock, the line ribboning out behind it.

'Hand me that clam. I gotta work fast!'

Luiz bent down to the tiny clam and spoke softly to it. Then he passed it to the noddy.

Shug didn't faint like Luiz had expected. But he wobbled. When they all let go he stood there rocking like a chopped tree about to topple. He sagged against the tall rock.

Luiz wanted to let him rest, but he had to tell him something first — hammer something into that brain of his before it was too late.

'Shug! Can you hear me? Shug!'

Shug nodded and groaned, 'I always knoo this trip was a bad idea. Look at me. Just look at me. Pure ruined, so I am.'

Luiz ignored him and shouted in his ear, 'Shug! Listen to me. Can you feel something deep down in your throat?'

Shug clapped his beak. 'Ahh … Ahh — yes. I can,' he said groggily. 'What ez it.'

'It's a wee clam we have put in your throat. It is stopping you from bleeding to croak. Whatever you do, dinnae, I mean, do not cough it up. What are you not to do Shug? Tell me.'

'Dinnae cough the wee clammie up. Aye, got it. There's no need to shoot.'

'And do not eat anything or you might knock him off. Repeat that to me.'

'Aye, dinnae eat anything. Message received and understood. Oover and oot.'

'And in a day or so, when you have stopped bleeding it is going to let go. All you have got to do his breeng it up and put it in a rock pool somewhere. Do you understand Shug? He is doing you a beeg favour.'

Aye! Aye! I've got it. Rock pool. I'm awful tired though,' and he promptly fell asleep.

The noddy tapped Luiz on the shoulder. 'We're leaving. I gotta go clean up.' His beak and crown feathers were stained with Shug's blood. 'But don't forget about the fish. You promised us a fish. A big fish. I earned it. When he's better, we come collect. Capisce?'

After they'd gone, Luiz spent a moment wondering what 'capisce' might mean.

Shug slept on through the afternoon, into the night and on until dawn. Luiz leaned his head on Shug — Shug made a good pillow — but he only slept fitfully. When he woke he pressed his ear up to Shug's breast and listened hard to make sure he hadn't croaked.

Luiz was jolted awake as he fell over and his beak clonked onto the rocks. It was dawn and Shug had woken and shuffled off somewhere. He looked about and saw him standing at the shore, his feet in the water. Shug unfurled his wings and gave them a flap, then clapped his beak and preened his pinions. After a moment he folded his wings away and stretched his neck, high.

'Shug!' Luiz yelled, 'Pleeze be careful!'

'Ez ookay. It feels ookay. I feel as rayt as ninepence.'

A breeze was blowing hard. Shug opened his wings and allowed them to take him aloft where he hung for a few moments.

'This ez ookay,' he called down. 'I feel okay. Are we offski or what?'

'Offski! Are you completely bonkers?' Luiz leapt up and was soon alongside. 'Yesterday you nearly croaked. Do you know that?'

'Aw, awae and pot. I'd have been alrayt with a wee bit of kip,' and he drifted off down the shore.

'Shug, did you not see that beeg hook you had inside you. And now you have the leedle clam inside you, like I told you? We cannot leave.'

'Aye, aye. Wee clammie. I remember. And, hook you say … no, I never did see it.' He was quiet for a moment, 'Now you mention it, I do feel a wee bit queasy.' He dropped and clattered onto the rocks.

Luiz was by his side in a jiffy, Shug struggling to his feet and putting away his wings, wheezing. 'I'll be alrayt … I'll be alrayt. Just need a wee breather. Old Shuggy boy's not the spring chicken he used to be.'

Luiz ticked him off and told him to rest and then said again, 'Do not forget about the clam.'

'No, the wee clammie. I willnae forget. I'm not the eejit you take me fer.'

The sun turned red, and Luiz asked him if he could still feel the clam. He thought it might have let go by then.

Shug hesitated. He lifted his head and gulped a couple of times and clapped his beak. 'Aye, Aye. The wee fella's still there — hangin on — doin his stuff.'

'Shug?'

'What?' and he wandered away.

He was back in a moment, beak scraping along the rock. When he started speaking Luiz could barely hear him.

'I've … I've a confession to make Luiz,' he said. 'I had a wee snackie a bit ago. Thought it couldnae do nae harm. Forgot aboot the wee fella down below, so I did.' He paused. 'Luiz … I cannae feel him nae more.'

'What! How could you! You great bahookey head.'

Luiz had to go for a fly about to calm down and have a think.

When he came back in to land he lowered a foot early and cuffed Shug on the head.

'Shug, how do you feel?'

Shug said he felt 'oorayt.'

Luiz looked him over and then into his eyes. If he was bleeding inside surely there would be some sign, but he did indeed look 'oorayt.'

'Have you coughed up blood?'

'Nae.'

'Have you coughed up anything?'

'Nae.'

He marched him to the tall rock and peered down his throat. The clam had disappeared. It took all the willpower he possessed not to clout Shug on the head again.

'Shug, have you had a poo since the snack?'

'Havnae.'

'What gives you diarrhoea?'

Shug told him.

Luiz found the red seaweed in a pool nearby. He dragged it out and, Shug watching on, jumped up and down on it to mash it. Perhaps mashing it up might get it into his system quicker. He told Shug to eat it up — every last bit of it.

They stood and waited as the turtle-shell sun peeked above the horizon and sank, illuminating the underside of the clouds. Shug shifted from foot to foot, his face apprehensive, Luiz regularly asking if anything was 'moving.'

It was almost completely dark when Shug said, 'Hello, helloo. Here we goo! Battlestations!'

ThhhhhhrrrrrrrRRRRRRAAAAAAAAAAAARSSSSSP

ThhhhhhrrrrrrrRRRRRRAAAAAAAAAAAARSSSSSP

ThhhhhhrrrrrrrRRRRRRAAAAAAAAAAAARSSSSSP

Thrarrrsp …. Clatter.

'Now find it.'

The sound of beak scraping against rock as Shug delved into the poo.

'Aye, here it is … Here's the wee fella. And he's alive. Seems none the wairse.'

'How do you know he is alive?' Luiz couldn't think of a worse fate than travelling through Shug's stomach, intestines and bottom, and then being pooed out.

'Aw, he's all shut up nice n' tayt. If he were deed he'd be open.'

Luiz's heart soared.

'I'll put him a rock pool then ay?'

'No.'

'Noo?'

'No. First you tell him you are very sorry and then you thank him for saving your life.'

Shug bent towards the tiny clam. 'I never conversed with a shellfish befair but, ahem …'

'Rinse him off first!'

'Oh … aye, ookay. Doon't get your knickers in a twist.'

He picked up the tiny clam and carried it to a nearby puddle. Luiz was surprised how tender he was as he rinsed it. After, he saw Shug's head bent low and his beak moving as he spoke.

Shug looked up. 'I'll put him in a wee rock pool then shall I?'

'Aye … I mean, yes, put him in a rock pool. And find a nice one!'

He was gone some moments. When he returned, Luiz asked him if the clam had said anything.

Shug sighed. 'Dinnae be a numptie. Clammies cannae talk.'

LAST LEG

E lephants holding onto each other's tails replaced the pampered poodles. The wind blew hard from the direction of the icebergs and Shug had only to open his wings and he was aloft. Soon he was back with a big fish for the noddies.

They must have been watching because they appeared out of nowhere and devoured the fish in seconds, squabbling like crows. Surgeon noddy flew over.

'Yeah, that that was a nice fish,' he said. 'You held up your end of the deal. I like that. Listen, you guys wanna to stay around, maybe we can do business.'

But Luiz was already clambering onto Shug's back.

'Thank you noddy, but perhaps some other time.'

'That's okay with me too. Badaboom-badabing.'

As they rocketed away, Luiz looked back at the shark's teeth and was glad. Enough time spent there. He hankered for leafy trees and shady pools, a patch of dust to have a bath in, for juicy fruits and oily nuts. He made a vow: from now on he would eat no more scraps from bins' bins.

'If it stays like this,' Shug called over his shoulder as they powered along, 'we'll be there by tomorrow afternoon, and you'll be awae in your forest looking for a wee girlie friend. Now, keep your whallopin heed DOON!'

Shug flew on all day and into the night. Luiz lay there, idly watching the ships they overtook, occasionally taking short flights to stretch his wings while Shug circled.

The only thing that happened was that Shug had one of his mad moments. He plunged down towards the bows of a huge ship. As they approached, Luiz thought for a moment that they would clobber right into the hull or at least it was going to run them down. But Shug found more speed, and as the prow arched over and the curling bow wave sprayed them, with a 'WHHHHOOOOO-HOOOO!' they caroomed past.

'Look doon there!' yelled Shug.

Dolphins rode the bow wave, leaping and twisting. One was even swimming upside down. Shug proceeded to zig-zag in front of the ship for a good way, showing off.

'Pah! Think *they* are masters of the ocean!' He then climbed high — higher than he'd ever climbed — before diving and zooming away at a speed Luiz thought impossible. It blew out one of his purple belly feathers.

Later as he was nodding off, Luiz saw winged fish flying above the ocean — which was clearly impossible because fish can't fly. So he let his eyelids fall closed to continue the dream. He felt Shug's body shift, heard him go 'OooooOAWfff' followed by an enormous gulp, beak clapping together. He heard 'thud' as something landed in his stomach. A bit later Shug went, 'BurrrRRPP.'

Dawn, a cloudless azure streak. As the sky brightened, Luiz noticed Shug was getting twitchy. He thought he might be getting hungry — he was feeling pretty hungry himself — and wanted to go fishing. But as Luiz looked ahead, he saw a grey line clinging to the horizon where Brazeel was.

Shug looked about and muttered, 'I dinnae like it. Ooh, I dinnae like it.'

Luiz too looked about, but he saw nothing to worry about. The wind was still blowing, and they were travelling as fast as ever. Weren't they?

It happened just as Shug had told it in the story about the bum. The wind slackened off. Shug's 'I dinnae like its' got louder. Shug waved his head about. And then the wind was gone. Just like that. Like somebody had flicked a switch.

Shug made it to the top of his arc and then began his glide towards the ocean.

'It's happnin.' It's happnin.' We've been struck by the doldrums. Just like I tolt you we would. I knoo this would happen. Dinnae let me drop into the ocean willya Luiz. Dinnae let the sharkies get me.'

'I willnac ... I mean, I won't. Do not worry. We will make it.'

Luiz looked around for something, anything, to land on, but saw only ocean, suddenly bin-glass flat. For a moment the sight captivated him: the first time he had ever seen the ocean without waves, calmer than the duck pond on a summer's day, like it had ceased breathing.

Well this was it. This was what all the training was for, those long hours with Sar'nt Lofty Troggers. Right. He clamped his claws around the collar, and not a little of Shug's plumage, and watched as Shug approached the glass sea. He waited as Shug skimmed the surface and began his climb. No need to worry about any big waves toppling in on them.

'Dinnae let me drop willya Luiz!'

Luiz waited as Shug's climb slowed, waited until he sensed Shug was about to flap. Then he leapt off and flapped hard and, relieved, felt them lift. 'Shug! Tell me when we are high enough!'

'Ahh wean — you're doing great. Keep flapping. Pure magic is that. Just a wee bit further.'

Shug's 'wee bit' seemed awfully long before he called, 'Ookay! Back aboard.'

Luiz flopped onto Shug's back. He had barely got his breath back by the time Shug bottomed out and began to climb again.

But it was okay. They got into a rhythm, Luiz leaping off at just the right instant — so as to maximise Shug's climb but just before he ran out of speed — before diving back aboard and flattening down so as to exploit Shug's glide and next climb. They worked together wordlessly until the sun reached the top of the sky and began to go down the other side, and then Luiz felt that little metal balls, like the one he'd been shot with, were gradually filling up his wings.

'How long do the doldrums last?' he gasped to Shug.

'Mayt be a few hours. Mayt be many days. Never can tell with the doldies.' Shug jerked his head around. 'Why? You're not feeling tired already are you Luiz?' Panic tinged his words.

'No,' Luiz lied. 'Just wondering.'

Shug started talking. Luiz thought that he was telling stories to himself again, but soon he realised Shug was talking to him.

'I wanted to say something to you Luiz. It willnae mean much to you now because you're still nae more than a wean. But one day you'll think on these words. I just hope it's sooner than I've done. Anyway, it's this. Life flies awae from you so it does. Life flies awae from you and you dinnae realise it. And before you know it, you are knackered old bird, cannae flap off a flat sea or outfly a Bonxie without wheezing your lungs oot like a decrepit donkey on fifty Park Drive a day. What have I lived? Sixty, seventy summer? I dinnae knoo; I cannae coont. I just knoo it flies awae from you. That's all I wanted to say.'[1]

Luiz knew he couldn't make it to the end of the day. He was now uttering a silent 'HhhuuuUUUUTTT' every time he lifted Shug, and it was only the middle of the afternoon. Each time he was back on board he searched the horizon for land. Nothing. He searched the ocean for something — anything — for them both to land on. But all the ships, logs, rafts of plastic, even bits of driftwood had disappeared. He did spot a coconut, but he couldn't imagine them both teetering on that. He would have to stand on Shug's back and Shug would be constantly running.

And then — he wondered if he was seeing things — but what was that he glimpsed in the silver glare? A ship? But he had to leap off and flap again and whatever it was, was lost.

He wondered when to tell him. They were going to have to ditch in the ocean — as sure as eggzizeggs as the spuggies said. His pecs burned —his wings now packed with metal balls. He had only one or two more climbs left in him. Surely Shug was not going to get chomped by a big shark as soon as his bahookey touched the water, but where could *he* land? He couldn't just stand on Shug's back — could he? After they ditch perhaps he should set off towards where Brazeel might be. But he didn't know how far he would have to fly, and with his knackered wings ocean ploppage was almost certain.

He glanced across Shug's back. Was *that* land? Way over there on the horizon? But he was so exhausted he couldn't trust his eyes anymore. He leapt off and towed them up once more. Shug was now so silent, Luiz thought he might have nodded off.

He had.

Anger fuelled his next climb, but he knew he couldn't manage another. He'd better wake Shug and break the news.

'Shug!'

But there it was again. It *was* a ship. A long flat one with a lump at the end. He reckoned it was two, maybe three, good glides away.

'Shug! We need to make for that ship. I cannot go on any further.'

'Wha!?! How!?!" Shug shook the sleep out of his head. 'Oh, aye, ookay Luiz.' He banked. 'You getting tired boy?'

'I do not theenk I can manage another climb,'

Shug looked towards the ship. 'Dinnae you worry Luiz ma boy. I'll get us there, nae bother.' He glided into a climb again and, just when Luiz normally leapt off, he flapped. By the time they reached the top he was wheezing like his lungs were set to explode. 'Phew!' he gasped. 'Like I keep saying ... nae spring chicken nae more.'

The ship was now much closer. And there was no swell in which to lose sight of it. 'Reckon I can do it with one more dive,' Shug hollered back.

'Pleeze, make sure there are no bins where we land,' Luiz called.

'Dinnae you worry your napper. These big beasties are mainly desairted.'

Shug descended, but when he swept up for the climb, the ship was close — too close. The hull towered over them, and the speed and course they were going they were about to smack right into it. Luiz saw them sliding down into the ocean, claws screeching on the metal.

He leapt off. 'Come on Shug — FLAP!'

They both flapped. Luiz climbed, but Shug made no headway. He was flapping hard, but the distance between them widened. 'Luiz!' he cried. 'Dinnae leave me to the sharkies.'

Luiz looked up and saw the rails at the top of the ship, now so close, and looked back at Shug — now dropping towards the ocean.

Luiz careened and plunged and grabbed Shug's collar. 'HHH-HUUUUUUUUUUUUUUUUUUUUUUUUUUUTTTTT!' It was the biggest of his life. He beat the air like a bonxie.

'Flap Shug! Flap!'

The ship lurched and its walls bashed into them, knocking them askew, but they carried on flapping. They reached the rails and sunlight flooded over them.

'HEEEEEEEEEEEEEEEEEE-UUTTT.'

Luiz dragged Shug over the rails and they clattered onto the steel deck.

They lay, tangled together, breasts pumping. After a bit Luiz said to Shug, 'We must stop having theez close shaves. The spuggies say you only have so many lives.'

'Pah! Spuggies. What do they knoo?' Shug wheezed. He heaved himself up and began to concertina his wings, but realised he was too tired and let them slap onto the deck. 'Spend all their lives … wheeze … within a gnat's fart … wheeze … of where they was boorn. Nae, it were never in doot … wheeze … never in doot for a moment.'

A bolt of terror shot through Luiz, and he hopped up onto a big metal box and looked about.

'You willnae see no bins walking aboot, if that's what you're looking for. I telt you — these places are desairted. They're all up there.'

Shug nodded up towards the lumpy bit, an enormous metal box with a long window. Luiz could just make out a couple of bins moving about behind the glass. If he could see them — then couldn't they see him? He leapt back down onto the deck. Images crowded into his mind: darkness, throbbing engines and diesel fumes, a metal room that swayed constantly and sickeningly. The stinking black din. He noticed he was trembling.

'I do not like it here,' he said. 'I have been here before. I know thees place. The bins — they must not see me. They will hunt me down and catch me. They always want to catch me. They will shut me in a cage where I cannot turn around or chain me to a stick I cannot fly away from. It is what they do. I must hide. I must hide now.'

Luiz ran as fast as he could. He looked in vain for a nook to squeeze into. He ran right down to the front of the ship and whirled around, searching. A giant metal rope piled up in coils. Gaps. He squeezed in and made himself as small as he could.

Dusk. Luiz, listening hard and peering out though the gaps. He wished he possessed an owl's eyes to see in the dark and a rabbit's ears to twitch in the direction of danger. He saw only angular steel and heard nothing but the slap of the sea against the hull. When the sun had set, he ventured out and clambered to the top of the great rope.

Below a huge purple sky, tiny orange lights were strung out along the horizon. They twinkled against a smudge of grey. Bin lights. Tierra, so close. Brazeel? He lifted his head high, searching for a breeze, but not a barbule riffled. The doldrums' still held them fast. He wondered if he could fly there alone. But it looked a long way and, as he had learned on this trip, ocean distances were deceptive. But shouldn't he give it a try? He must get away from this ship and the bins before they caught him. Shug would be okay until the wind picked up — wouldn't he? They wouldn't want to catch him.

He heard a cough and swivelled around.

'Soo here y'are,' Shug said, 'I've been wanderin aboot this ship lookin' all over fer you. I was gettin worried.' Shug too looked towards the orange lights. 'Aye, you nearly got us there, so you did. Thas your Brazeel is that. Still, a half-decent breeze tomorrow and you'll be eatin' nuts in the forest by noon.'

Luiz's heart would normally soar. But the hard grey ship ploughing the glass ocean and the closeness of the bins, dragged at his heart like the chains of a trap.

The island was close. It reared out of the ocean, the green of emeralds. And, was he dreaming or were they birds flying about among the trees? Was he dreaming? He looked around in the dawn light and saw Shug, asleep on top of a crane. He gave himself a good shake. He tapped his beak on the metal and chewed off a bit of flaky paint. No, he didn't seem to be dreaming. So the island was real — and close.

He'd be there in a jiffy. As the ship slipped by, the forest parted and the cascade of a waterfall appeared. And beyond the island, that grey line. More land. He hopped about and bobbed his head. He even let out a little squawk.

He looked over at Shug — who was still asleep — and back to the island drifting past. He was so hungry, and right there were oily nuts and juicy fruit waiting for him to pick off the trees. He regarded Shug. No breeze stirred his plumage. He'd be alright though. The wind was bound to pick up soon. On the island there might be parrots — parrots just like him there. There might be a female parrot.

Luiz looked back towards the island, which soon would slip away. He took a deep breath and stretched his wings. He glanced back at Shug. Shug's beak twitched to the rhythm of a dream. He went 'Oooraaagggh' and trumped a fishy trump and clapped his beak.

The metal rope grew hot in the sun — so hot you couldn't stand on it — and even though he was deep in its coils and shaded, Luiz panted. The tit might be pecking again at his belly, but at least he was hidden from the bins. Shug still stood on the crane like a statue, awake now. Luiz knew that he'd be straining every sense for a breath of wind.

Shug jerked his head around. 'Watch it!' and he leapt away and glided out of sight.

Luiz cowered and listened hard, and soon he heard the sound of footsteps and bin voices. Feet and ankles and hairy legs appeared. The conversation slowed, and as he strained his ears he could hear munching. They were eating. And here he was, finally ready to chomp the contents of Shug's crop. The bins lingered, talking and munching. They lit cigarettes and blew smoke which stung his eyes. Then he saw the feet and ankles and legs move away.

Thud.

He craned his neck and peered through the coils. They had dropped half a banana. His heart leapt. He heard a clatter, and he saw two Brazil nuts spinning on the metal deck. Brazil nuts! His heart soared. Bins were so clumsy. He waited but saw no hands reach down to pick them up. Bins were so wasteful of food. The spuggies used to call them 'waste bins' and guffawed at a joke he never did get. Bin waste had so often been good eating, especially when he was in a jam. But he'd made a vow.

He listened as the footsteps receded. They sounded different somehow, but he was so hungry now, his brain couldn't work out why.

He waited.

He waited a long time. And when he thought it must finally be safe, he waited longer. He worried some gull would spot them and they'd be gone. The banana turned brown, and Luiz thought the nuts might be drying up. He wished Shug would come back.

He listened hard, trying to filter out the slap of the ocean and the thrum of the engines. How long could it take? He'd rush out, kick the nuts under the coil, and drag the banana in behind him. What a feast.

He peered out one last time from the coils, and crept into the sunlight.

He had kicked the nuts under and had the banana in his mouth when he heard the whoosh. Later, when he played it back again and again in his mind he thought he'd heard Shug call, 'Luiz! No!' But he couldn't be sure.

Darkness, the din of engines and the stink of diesel.

Luiz tried to understand why everything was dark. He panicked when he thought the bins must have done something to his eyes during the struggle. It was the last thing he could remember. Hands reaching to untangle him from the net; him, fighting, biting. But he sensed he could still see, and he realised he was wrapped in something. He tried to shake it loose but it was too tight and squeezed his body, and he realised they'd left him on perch and put a sock over him — a smelly bin sock.

He got to work with his beak. His ooterus maximus had never failed him — it had saved him from the tawny and the maggies and saved Shug from the fishing boat. It would save him now. He began to gnaw and snip. Snippy shake-shake. Soon he had a hole big enough to squeeze his head through and look out. But he dreaded looking out. What if he saw bars?

'Be brave,' he told himself, and squeezed his head through. No bars.

It was only then, with the relief of not seeing a cage, he noticed a tightness around his leg. He didn't need to look. He knew that tightness from an age ago. He lifted his foot, and heard the clink of the steel chain.

A sound inside his head. It began as a murmur, but soon bloated into a monstrous roar. The Badhbh was laughing.

He sobbed a good while. When he could sob no more, he forced the image of Sar'nt Lofty Troggers into his mind, and asked the Sar'nt what he would do. But even Sar'nt Troggers seemed to be at a loss. He shrugged and looked embarrassed, and all he could offer was, 'Keep calm son, assess ...', and the words faded. And then he remembered something else Sar'nt Troggers used to say, something that he never really understood: 'The darkest hour is always before the dawn.' And he thought what a stupid, obvious, ridiculous saying it was.

He looked around the cabin. It was windowless apart from a glass panel in the door at his shoulder. The glass was filthy, but if he peered hard he could just make out the flat sea, and the lumpy land at its edge, the string of orange lights.

He sang his little song to himself.

The door opened and a fat bin entered. It carried a plate of scraps: an apple core, a mango stone, bits of stale bread. It had a shiny face from which stubby black hairs poked, and he was reminded of the pink-faced man, but this bin's face was brown. It started talking to him, its face right-up close like bins do, so he could see the tiny holes in his skin and the glistening sweat and smell his breath which was like old cheese. The bin tugged at the sock, scowled and wagged a finger. The finger was within range so Luiz fastened his beak onto it and bit hard. The bin yelled and said a bad word and dropped the plate and rubbed his finger which ran with blood and pointed at Luiz and then pointed at the scraps spread out on the floor. It shook his head and wagged its good finger. It turned and opened the door and spat out a few more words. The metal clanged behind it.

Two more bins came, younger and scrawnier, and they stood in front of him smoking cigarettes and joking. Finally, one approached and said loudly, like they always do, like he is an idiot, 'Hola! ... Hola!'

Night fell and he was in darkness apart from a faint light coming from the door glass, and he stared through at the orange lights and wondered where Shug was. The ship began to roll. There must be a swell, and with it would come a wind. They were through the doldrums.

He awoke from a nightmare where all the light had been sucked into the ocean and everywhere was black and he was wrapped in something cold and heavy and couldn't move his wings or his beak. The room swayed and the engine roared and the stink of diesel stung his nostrils. He breathed hard and looked towards the door, desperate for light, and saw a shape outlined against the faint moonlight. The dirty window rendered the shaped fuzzy, so that at first he thought it some kind of ghost bird, pausing to rest during a long journey. But then he saw the ghost clap its beak together and wave his head about, and heard it cry:

'OWWEEEEEKK-EEEEAARKKK-EEEEEAARRKKK-OOAWWWWW'.

Shug stood on the rail for a long time and stared at him. Then Shug spoke, but he could not hear because the wind had risen and was making a whistling noise and waves were washing against the ship. He spread his wings and shrugged. Shug leapt off the rail and landed on the door handle, beak up against the glass. He yelled, but his weight pressed down the door handle and he slithered off and out of view. For a moment the door swung open, and the ocean air filled Luiz's nostrils blotting out the diesel. The door clanged shut.

Luiz thought hard. Shug had opened the door. But had he noticed? Had he realised what he had done? Or did he think that slipping off the handle like that was just a sorry accident. Knowing Shug, it might be the latter. But even if Shug did get the door open again, he was still chained to this stick.

The night deepened but the chain still glinted in light from a hidden source. The engine growled as it fought the gale. Luiz tried to force Lofty Troggers back into his mind. He surely must have some idea what to do. He glimpsed Sar'nt Troggers in his red bandana for a few moments, but Sar'nt Troggers still seemed stumped.

Stumped ... Stumped ... Stumped ...

The word bashed against his brain like a big hammer. But why?

He decided to ask the Sar'nt. But some kind of commotion was going on in there. Something was shoving the Sar'nt aside — something bigger, older and grumpier.

The grumpy bird finally ejected the Sar'nt, and spoke.

'Now bugger off! I'm tekkin over.'

He spent most of the long night thinking about what Old Stumpy had said. He cocked his head and considered it from every angle. It was certainly the grumpiest option, but it seemed his only escape. He thought about the pigeons in the park. Like Old Stumpy said, they did okay. Old Stumpy managed okay, and lived to a ripe, grumpy old age. Whichever way he looked at it, the chain was the problem. But even his beak could not cut steel. He had no choice. It was this or stay with the bins. No emerald forest, no mate.

In the dead of night, Shug reappeared. He stood silently on the rail, staring at him. Luiz's mind worked. Finally he murmured, 'Worth a try,' and shouted and gesticulated for Shug to come closer. He knew Shug couldn't hover, so he would have to land on the door handle. Shug landed on the handle and it duly turned down. The ship was rolling and the door swung wide open, before slamming shut again as the ship rolled back. Luiz made a mental note. It stayed open only for a couple of seconds. The timing would have to be perfect.

He gestured to Shug to land on the handle three more times. Before the door slammed the third time he heard Shug yell, 'Aye, ookay! I gettit! I'm no eejit.'

Luiz tore off the remainder of the sock and yelled, 'You ready?' Shug made no sign of having heard.

He gulped and looked down at his foot. They had been

together a long time. He wondered how much it would hurt. He looked over to Shug who was still staring. He closed his eyes, and opened his beak and placed it around his ankle. He took a deep breath and bit down, hard. He didn't need to saw.

A blur. Perhaps he was giddy from the pain.

When he recalled the events later he remembered flying around the cabin waiting for Shug to grasp what to do. He remembered seeing his foot down there still clinging to the perch, his blood beside it. It looked almost comical. Shug finally leaping onto the door handle. The door not opening because the swell was the wrong way. The eejit! The stink of diesel and the roaring engine. His blood dripping onto the floor. Shug trying again. The door flying open, and then diving towards it just as it begins to swing back, the door clanging as it clouts him out into the howling night. He didn't see him, but Shug must have found him, because he remembers Shug's warm back, shining pure white even in the dark. And then Shug does something strange. He pulls him from his back and carries him, dangling, by his beak. He hovers. Shug — hovers. He hears the 'whoop-whoop' of his wings. He feels heat. Intense heat, and then searing pain from where his foot used to be. His nostrils catch the scent of burning flesh and bone. Shug hurls him up into the night and he tumbles onto Shug's back and he clings to it and to his red collar — tighter than he has ever clung to anything in his life.

THE FOREST

The forest is unusually beautiful tonight. The day creatures are quiet and the night creatures are yet to stir, creating that fragile silence which belongs only to this time, his time. The sun, low under a belly of crimson cloud, waits for the purple hills to rise to meet it. It transforms the foliage into shades of red and green bins could never imagine. The slightest of breezes riffles the leaves, and the colours change once more.

This is their favourite place to sleep. A big bough splays out of the trunk, a hidden platform where they can plump up their plumage and nuzzle together. But he likes to get here first for a quiet moment to look out over the forest canopy, at the view he will never tire of. Through the leaves he can just trace the fat steaming river as it meanders its last to the ocean.

The ocean is close; the breeze carries its salt and, only at this time of day, he can hear it breathe. Strange. Before, he was terrified of the heaving monster and yet now, despite Xylona's pleas, he does not leave it and knows he never will.

Sometimes he spends a night alone by the shore. He has a tree there, like he had the poplar in the park. He listens to the waves and looks to the horizon back towards Blighty. He watches the seabirds play on the wind. He thinks of an albatross, and he sees him in the roaring forties careening amongst the icebergs — eyes horizontal, wings vertical — planing across the face of a toppling wave. He always examines the nook by his perch. Wedged there is a piece of plastic. It is orange and oval and attached is a red plastic loop, like a collar. He prises it out. It was once the figure of a bin, but the bin is now long gone, and the loop is cut. He cut it, not far from this spot, out over the ocean on a sunlit, breezy morning within sight of the waving trees. 'Boa sorte,' was all he could choke out. Shug said nothing. As he flopped into the trees, he turned to see Shug circling a little way out. He circled until dusk. He thought how odd Shug looked without his red collar. At dawn, Shug was gone.

He never knew he could sing like that. The spuggies would be gobsmacked. But alone in that dawn after Shug left, it just bubbled out, like it was the thing he was born to do. Not like his quiet little song at all. At dawn tomorrow he and Xylona will sing a duet.

The crimson cloud is changing. It shifts to purple to match the hills and his belly. He sighs as he knows his quiet time is about to end. Soon all will be here: Chalkie and Flo, Lofty, Steve and Millie, Shug their eldest, and Luna. Xylona will bring him a late snack — like she always does. Usually a piece of pineapple. He hops towards their platform and hopes the littlies don't ask him to tell again of his adventures across the great ocean. He could teach them more new words, he supposed. They like that. They already know 'crikey' and 'conflab' and 'dude' and 'bahookey.'

He finds his spot next to the little knot where he rests his stump and settles. He waits for the sun to reach the gap in the hills and for the amber light to stream over him.

Chattering. Here they come.

His heart soars like an eagle.

EPILOGUE

(PECKILOGUE)

The city is its usual ugly self tonight. All day the sun has been blotted out by a sodden sky the colour of that chip paper blocking the drain. Now, as the cloud absorbs the street-lights, the sky brightens, turning korma yellow. Conflab can barely be heard above the din of the traffic.

Anyway, at least they've suppered well: the remains of kebab and chips hurled into the hedge from a thudding car. And, as they line up along the wire before 'Me-and-Er' to watch telly before kip time, the rain stops and they have a good shake and a good trump. Then they nuzzle together so tight, you could scarcely squeeze a silky spring maple leaf between them.

'I wonder what's on,' chirps Ada.

'Hope its footie,' says Alfie.

Tonight they are disappointed. It's a program about boats. Bins, boats and water — lots of water. The bins are out at sea somewhere doing bin stuff, and the spuggies soon get bored and begin to natter. All except Chalkie. He likes to see the big waves and the big boats crashing about the foamy water. He'd like to see a big ocean before he turns his toes up, fly about over it and shout insults at the georges.

Chalkie's jaw drops open. For a moment he is struck dumb. Then:

'Crikey! Ere, Ere, you lot ... OI! YOU LOT! Put a sock in it and look at this!'

Silent heads swivel to look at the telly. Beaks drop open.

The viewpoint is high — like it's been filmed from the front end of a big ship. A gale rips the ocean apart. The scene undulates to the rhythm of the white-striped swell.

'It's him innit. Tell me it's him. Look, there he goes again!' says Chalkie.

An enormous white george races towards the bow of the boat, way bigger than any of the georges they see commuting to the dump every day. It flies impossibly fast, but, Chalkie notes, without ever flapping. He is astounded — how the ruddy-nora does it do that? But then the big george looks like it is going to crash into the side of the ship. The scene shifts, as the camera is pointing down over the front of the ship. It follows the george, awaiting the inevitable crash.

'Look at that! Do you see what I see?' cries Chalkie.

Something green is riding the kamikaze george's back.

'Blimey O'Reilly, it looks like ...' says Gert.

'Streuth!' says Alfie.

'Lawks!' says Flo.

'Ruddy Nora!' says Betty.

Flo and Madge open a wing each and prepare to watch the crash through bunched feathers. But at the last moment the big george tilts its wings vertically and rockets away above leaping dolphins.

A slow-motion action replay follows, like in the footie. The camera zooms in. The spuggies break out into a clamour bigger than the biggest conflab ever, as they see his forest-green plumage, his ooterus maximus, and just there — look! A flash of purple belly.

'Well, as I live and breathe,' murmurs Chalkie among the

cheering. His mind races back to that dismal morning when he'd flown to the poplar to check on him, like he'd done every morning, and found him gone. 'Old Big Nose 'isself. He's only gone and bloomin done it.'

His words are carried away on the hoorays.

The net curtains twitch, and Me-and-Er bin cups his hands and peers out of the window.

NOTES

PREFACE

1. Corroborative research: poncey for 'proof'.

1. THE POWER OF THE HUUUT

1. Spuggie: House Sparrow (Lat. *Poser Domesticus*). Little brown jobbie (LBJ) of a bird with absolutely no distinguishing features apart from a big beak and a loud voice. Horny-thologists describe them as having a 'primitive vocal repertoire,' and their plumage as 'matted and unkempt.' Pugnacious, cantankerous and quarrelsome, the house sparrow is also gregarious (it likes to hang around Greggs for chuckaways described as 'grub'). House sparrows were once a common sight in our towns, but are now scarce since humans have blocked up all their holes. Eats: kebab, chips, Battenberg, Cornish pasties, nacho chilli-cheese bakes, white bread (never brown), iced doughnuts, deep-fried sausage rolls, cocoa pops, cheesy wotsits, peperoni three-cheese pizza, deep-fried peperoni three-cheese pizza, Frazzles. Call: cheep.
2. 'Robert the Goose' was a Scot of yore who lived in a cave with a spider. He was famous for not giving up. Despite many failed attempts, he eventually managed to stamp on the wily spider.
3. Spuggie corruption of 'confabulate', to chat, to discuss. Specifically to spuggies: to go on and on about something at great length and volume, often around in circles, all talking at the same time, usually without any point or reaching any conclusions.

2. BELLY UP

1. These spuggies don't sound their aitches. Snotty people think if you don't sound your aitches you must be a bit thick. But snotty people think it okay to mangle their words. 'Sex' is what they buy their potatoes in.
2. Mandible: posh word for the toppy and bottomy bits of a bird's beak. The word was coined by the eminent Victorian ornithologist, zoologist, paleo-botanist and sporting woman Lady Amanda Swackthorpe-Erck, author of *Through the Cross-hairs, a Country Diary of a Victorian Lady Naturist.* At the 1901 Olympics a tweed-clad Lady Swackthorpe-Erck bagged bronze in the Skeet Shoot. She was then promoted to Duchess Swackthorpe-Erck and retired to

seclusion in her north Berkshire estate where she raised woodcock for the table.

3. Bert: spuggie for 'mallard.' Habitat: duck ponds. Call: quack. Eats: bread. The bread is chucked to them by humans who say it is bad for them. Bert Millard was a football player of yore who turned up for numerous teams including the Crystal Paris and the Charlton Pathetic. A versatile player, he could slot in at no. 5 as a kicker in the shins, or at no. 9 as a nodder in the box.

3. SPUGNACITY

1. Frankie Ramphard was a famous English footballer of yore. He played mainly for the Roast Ham and the Tottering Hotspurs. After a brief spell in the US with New York club the Boston Corn Doggies, he finished his career with Manchester Stanley as a comer-onner-at-the-end. A lifelong cockney and patriarch, he played proudly for his country on many occasions, turning out mainly as a blaster in the hole. For reasons which remain obscure, Frankie Ramphard was beloved of Chinese commentators.

2. Sundry is a great word. Apart from what you do to tomatoes, it means: various, miscellaneous.

3. Cheeses: feet; derivation unknown, but thought to be related to the associated pong.

4. Maggie: Magpie (Lat: *pica nosa*), toffee-nosed crow in a white tux. Behaviour: struts about thinking itself better than the other crows. Alternative name: 'Mock-a-pie', which is odd as it will chomp one given half a chance. Eats: owt, although especially likes tinned pineapple chunks. Has a reputation as a thief and a hoarder. At the Hoarders Self-Help Conference held at Harrogate in 2009, a hoarding ordered hundreds of hoarders to stop hoarding their hors d'oeuvres. Magpies were the main culprits. In days of yore yokels invented lots of superstitions about magpies as bringers of bad luck. My uncle Alf would turn back from the bookies to lay a pony each-way on a nag in the 3.15 at Fontwell if he saw a magpie on the way — even if it was good to firm going.

   Also the name of a kids program your grandma would have watched in the 1970s presented by Toby Barnstable and Susan Tanks. The theme music went: Do-do-doo do-do-do-do-do-doodle, do-do-do-do-doo.

5. Mincey pies: spuggie for 'eyes.'

6. Alula: part of a bird's wing located midway on the anterior (fronty bit), a bit like your thumb. Named thus because the scientist who discovered it, Albert Knoxious III, was a devout Christian who didn't know the precise biblical expression for 'Praise God' and only had a stab at it when he discovered the as yet unamed thumby bit. The spuggies call the alula the 'bastard wing', because it keeps getting in the way.

7. Bin: spuggie for 'human.' Thought to derive from the fact that humans eat a lot of rubbish, and they throw lots of useful items into bins. With regard to dietary habits, it has been pointed out to the spuggies that people who live in

glass houses should not throw stones. The spuggies rebuttal was: 'Get it up your backside.'

Titfer: spuggie for 'hat.' From: 'tit for tat' (yawn).

4. PARK LIFE

1. Grubbify: spuggie for 'look for grub.'
2. Tawny Owl (Lat. *Strict Aluco*). Standard-sized brown owl. Lives in trees. Eats: goldfish, sparrows, toads earwigs. Call: 'twit-twoo.' Named by the Victorian naturalist Sir Aubrey Pointillist who shot one and found it had torn crucifix knee ligaments.
3. See Appendix I.
4. Phil Loddy was famous for twitching. Phil travelled all over the country to twitch, and his beanpole frame could be seen twitching from the reed-bed beds of Nofolk to the pine forests of Scotchland. There were those who said he was best at twitching in England. He even got a job twitching on the telly.
5. Dandy Murray was a grumpy tennis player and an excellent thwacker. He was also good at tonking and dinking, although his dinking sometimes got him into trouble and he became a problem dinker. He had many epoch battles with his rivals, the loo-brush haired Serbo, Kojak Jockeypants (moderately grumpy), and the bum-scratching Spinster, Waffle Noddle (fairly frowny), who was always pulling his pants down from up his bum crack. Dandy once won Wombledon and climbed up the flagpole and forgot to kiss his mum.

   Big Maggie bears no relationship in any way, shape or farm whatsoever to the former collie-haired British Prime Mini-spinster Maggie Thwacker, no way Hosea.
6. Solving the tin can conundrum would have led to unbounded feastings and the top tier of Maggie pecking order – but the maggie boffins had remained bamboozled. Big Maggie herself had come closest. She had once found a tin in a string bag, and she and three others had struggled up high above the scrapers and dropped it onto a concrete car park. Overjoyed, they saw it dash open and the contents come spilling out. But they were broad beans. So they left them for the seagulls. But the seagulls had a quick shufty and flew past, and the fox trotted by in a wide circle, and a rat sniffed at them and ran off, and so the beans remained on the concrete until the car-park attendant came and swept them up and put them in the bin.
7. Bone in a bird's (and your) foot. Longer in a bird. If you had bird-sized metatarsals you'd be taking a size 57 (UK).
8. This is all before the ring-pull can became ubiscuitus and made things easy, unless it breaks off, which it does sometimes, which endangers the lives of innocent passers-by as the can is hurled out the window.

   Ubiscuitus: crumbs, when you've eaten a biccy in bed.
9. Dun: Posh for browny-grey. Origin is in days of yore when they used to roast

sparrows over the fire for their teas. When they were cooked and had turned the right colour they were 'dun.'

10. Faecal sack: A bag of poo. When chicks poo in the nest it comes out of their bums ready-wrapped in cling film. The parents then carry it away without getting poo all over their beaks and up their noses, so preventing the nest getting full up with poo and the chicks floating on top.

11. Barnet: coiffure, hairdo, in the Purple-Bellied Parrot's case: crown-plumage do. A corruption of Yorkshire dialect: 'bar nowt', meaning lacking nothing, perfect as it is, not requiring a titfer.

5. BRAZIL

1. Grace: spuggie for starling (Lat. *Sternus vulgaris*). Grace Starling was a brave salty sailor of yore who rescued some shipwrecked salty sailors from rocks in a rowing boat in a storm in a bonnet and full corsetry, up north. A toff gave her a teapot as a reward. She became a big celeb in Victorian Blighty and were she alive today she would definitely be on *I'm a Celeb, Strictly* and *Lorraine*.

2. Screamer: spuggie for swift (Lat. *Apus apusaginus*). Call: SCREEEEEEAM. Eats: flies. Flies: crazy, like it's angry at the sky.

3. Martie: House Martin (Lat. *Delichon hurtla*). Bit like a swallow but not as flash. Migrates to Blighty in spring; one of the last visitors to leave in the autumn when it goes off to Africa to follow gnu's bottoms about. When it finds a bottom with lots of flies around it, it rushes off to tell its chums the good gnus. Has a goldfish's tail and a white bum. Other names: Martlet, Window Swallow. Call: chrrrip. Eats: flies. Flies: like the clappers.

4. She means the Congo River, which is often poo-brown where it meets the ocean on account of all the silt it carries.

5. Crownie: Crowned Eagle. Great big eagle that lives in the forest and eats monkeys and such, but wouldn't turn its beak up at a small green parrot as an aperitif. A lazy bird (like most hunters), it hangs about on the canopy waiting for something tasty to bumble along, whereupon it leaps upon it and 'crowns' it with its big feet – whence its name. It then reluctantly uses its wings to carry the prey off to its lair where it dismembers it and chomps some and puts some in the fridge for later.

   Nora: You'll find out later.

   Aperitif: what you grandad chews his food with.

6. George: spuggie for seagull. Derivation unclear, but thought to relate to a Hollywood action hero of the 1960s your grandma would have fancied.

7. He is using his claws like 'crampons' here. Crampons: like what flies use when they walk up the wall, used by climbers in big mountains such as the Andies and the Hima-la-las to walk up slippery snows; pointy things like what your granddad straps on his feet to aerate the lawn. Crampons were invented by a Scot sheep farmer called Murdo McHurghhurgh (pronounced 'Hura-Hura') so that he could

go out and aerate his boggy pastures. He later found that they gave him extra grip when he was seeing to his flock in icy winters. Before Murdo McHurghhurgh's invention, to conquer very steep slopes, climbers used to sharpen their big-toe nails and poke a hole in the end of their boots, but this technique proved useless on ice, where hoards of ice mites (Lat. *Tetraknickers icae*), insect denizens of the snowy peaks) used to crawl into the holes and tickle the climbers' feet. Indeed, many mountaineers plummeted to splattery deaths while roaring with laughter.

8. Barbule: tiny part of a feather; zips together with other barbules to give the feather a feathery look.

9. 'Wake': when folks croak, turn their toes up or snuffit, the party held to celebrate - after they've popped their clogs but before they push up daisies. Usually strong drink is taken and folks eat lots of cakes. They tell embarrassing stories about the wakee and hug each other and tell each other they love each other a lot. Usually a wake lasts for hours and hours to make sure the wakee is really dead. The wake is traditionally concluded by the partyees shouting 'Wakey-Wakey!' at the top of their voices to make absolutely sure. Then the copse is interned.

6. OLD STUMPY

1. Your mum and dad will tell you what a dianthus is. Leave me alone – I'm busy setting up a joke here.

2. Spuggletti: young spuggies; older than 'spuglings' who are fresh out of the nest; a bit like bin teenagers. Of central Italian origin where they still eat dicky birds. A particular delicacy there is to lightly pan-fry the goo-nads of a tender young spuggie, adding turnips, garlic, tomatoes and capers, to produce the dish known as 'Spuggletti Bollocknese.'

3. Before you start ... the misplaced apostrophe was ON THE SIDE OF THE VAN! I'm just QUOTING! What do you want me to do? Put [*sic*]? (*Sic* is Latin meaning, 'this idiot made a stupid error I am not responsible for, it's not my fault and I would never make such a stuped mistake being all educated-like, and you being like me and better than everybody else too know what *sic* means and the plebs don't so NER-NE-NE-NER-NER!')

   'Plebs': the hoi-polloi, the great unwashed, the proletariat, the oiks; what the maggies aren't.

4. Crop: a kind of sack in a bird's throat used to store extra food. Birds are greedy-gutses and shove in food that won't fit into the stomach. In autumn, seed-eating birds will crop a crop and put it in their crop.

5. Escarpment: posh word for 'cliff.' From the Latin: *iscarpmentum*, literally meaning 'unclimbable by fish.'

6. That's the punchline to the 'dianthus' set-up of a couple of pages ago. Oh my aching sides ....

7. Smidgeon: in spuggie lingo, a specific size of grub, in this case, that which can

be comfortably gulped down in one go by a walter. Normally spuggies would break this up into crumbs, or even crumblets.

Like Inuit for snow, spuggie designations for grub size are many and are divided into three broad orders: Crumb, Smidgeon and Chunko. Crumbs can generally be swallowed in one go; Smidgeons are larger and need a bit of pecking at first; Chunkos take more than one spuggie to deal with - think half a Cornish pasty. An upper limit to the Chunko is yet to be discovered. These orders are further subdivided (in ascending order): ORDER CRUMB: crumbletto, crumblet, crumb, crumbo, morsel. ORDER SMIDGEON: tadlet, tad, smidglet, smidgeon, soupçon. ORDER CHUNKO: chunkletto, chunklet, chunko, wedge, half-ender.

8. For 'old-timer in a western' search online for 'Walter Brennan.' For 'western' search 'John Wayne.'

7. DOGHOUSE AND DOLDRUMS

1. Somebody so obnoxious and hard that they are not grateable with a cheese grater.
2. World's smallest insect. Not one to worry about while eating your jam sandwiches in September.
3. Albatross: a kind of big seagull that mainly lives south of a line drawn around the earth called the equator. Eats: fish. Unlike bog-standard seagulls, which live on rubbish tips or follow tractors about, albatrosses find food on the salty wastes of the sea. There are a number of species, including the Soupy Albatross, the Beetle-Browed Albatross and the Shy Albatross. The Shy Albatross (once called the Rufus-Faced Albatross) is endangered because the male becomes beak-tied when it encounters a female, rendering him unable to make the mating cry of 'awooba awooba shraaw shraaw eecky eecky twaaarrwk,' merely going 'eek' instead.

    The largest albatross is the Wondering Albatross, so-called because it patrols the vast southern oceans wondering where its next meal is. Albatrosses are lazy birds who don't like to flap their wings. If forced to flap they get very grumpy and land on an iceberg or float about on the sea, what the boffins call 'loafing about.' Salty seadogs believe that to kill an albatross while sailing about at sea will bring good luck. A chap with a long name called Simon Tayto-Coleridge once wrote a long poem about it called *The Rhyme of the Ancient Moaner*. Fishermen bait their lines with tinned tuna fish – which albatrosses love – and they hook many this way because the albatrosses get their beaks stuck in the bendy tin. Then they reel them in and whack them on the head with a big stick and toss them back into the sea to appease the sea gods and bring good luck.

4. Blighty: affectionate term for Britain used by tommies in yore. May be derived from the Hindustani word for 'home', picked up when brits were tramping

about India in shorts during the Rage potting tigers and playing snooker in a bungalow.

5. Birds of course don't have external balls – Chalkie is being silly. They have internal goo-nads.

8. SAR'NT LOFTY TROGGERS

1. Tsk, Reg means 'reveille' - French for 'wakey-wakey.'

2. Sar'nt: Toffs can't be bothered to say all the word 'sergeant,' so they say this instead. Oddly, they don't do this for higher ranks: Gerl, Cool, Brier, Feall etc. You can only get away with this if you have a posh accent, when non toffs do this, people think they are thick. Other toff words are wehk (work), oarff (off), ears (yes), one (I), pepple (purple).

3. Wren (Lat. *Troglodytes ditto*): Common short-arsed bolshie bird with a tremendously loud voice for its size. If it was the size of you and its voice was scaled-up the same, it would be louder than a big wailing fire engine on its way to a burning orphanage and you'd have to pack your ears with putty (never do this) and wear mufflers. Some people think that the wren is Britain's smallest bird, but they are erroneous. That record is held by the goldcrest and its jazzier cousin the firecrest. But these birds are far more demur, and instead of blasting out their song in the spring woods without a care for the eardrums of all and sundry, they just go 'seep.' But weighing less than a pound coin, wrens are still reet petite (as they say in Yorkshire). Some boffin once worked out that it would take 7,051,006 wrens just to make one ostrich. Wrens being such tiddlers suffer badly from the cold. If they spot a tit box in the winter they all crowd in until the box is absolutely stuffed up to the hole. One boffin once found 7,008 wrens thusly packed into a tit box. A lot of 'after you's go on though, because Wrens are notoriously flatulent birds and you don't want to be the one at the bottom, although it has been observed that some enterprising wrens set up stalls outside the tit box selling snorkels. (Few people know this but this is actually the etymology of the word snorkel: a device that allows you to snore (sleep) in a flatulent area.) Call: TAD-DA-LA-DA-DAT-DAT-TAAR! Usually with a machine-gun flourish at the end just in case you haven't heard it. Eats: anything teensy-weensy and wriggly. Names that folks of yore made up for the wren because there was no telly: bobby, crackadee, crackil, guradnan, jenny, juggy, skiddy, stumpit, skiddy stumpit, stumpy toddy, titmeg, titty todger, tiddly cock-tattler, jiggy tit hen, diddly tackle-whacker, piddly-poddly titty-tit tit, wran (They took a long time to think that last one up ...).

4. So the Hollywood lawyers don't come after me, I have to acknowledge that this is an adaption of a quote from a nasty film you dad might have seen about the tough world of the professional tennis pro: *Full Metal Racket*, directed by Sir Stanley Rubrick's Cube.

5. Sar'nt Troggers has seen the one of your grandad's favourite films, *Rocky,* and got confused.

6. Sgt Troggers has only made a stab at the Latin name here and it shouldn't be taken as gospel.

7. One of the greatest words ever, invented by a Roman chariot-taxi driver named Bertimus who kept getting lost when going the long way round to avoid the trafficus. It means a roundabout way of doing something. We should defo all start using it again. So the next time your mum tells you one of her long-winded stories you could say – 'well mum, that was a right old circumbendibus.'

8. Derek Tankona was a French footballer of yore who played for the Manchest City. He is famous for leaping into the crowd like Bruce Leigh when a Cringing Palace fan shouted that he was a common amphibian unapprised of the identity of his father. Tankona retired from football soon after and became an actor of notable talent, starring in numerous busters before his roles were usurped by Jackie Chan. Tankona was adored by his manager at Man City, the purple-faced, gum-chomping, happy-go-lucky Alec Fergerson. 'Fergy', to his chums, was famous for giving a player the 'hair-dryer treatment' at half-time Jaffas. As the players' expensive barnets inevitably got dishevelled during first-half stooshie, Fergy would whip out his Babyliss and give them a quick once-over. Fergy also coined the phrase 'sticky-bun time' for half-time Jaffas.

   Bruce Leigh, 'Brucie' to his chums, was a Kung-Fu player of yore, famous for going 'Hiii-ya!'

9. See Appendix III.

9. YEE-HAW!

1. What Sar'nt Troggers didn't say was that the spugghawk was a mate of his called Dave. Dave was an escapee from the aviary he'd lived in since a littlie. Which doesn't mean he was Andy Dufresne or anything. A girl cleaning out the cage left the door open while she poked out a text and smoked a fag, and he just sidled away. Anyway, Dave couldn't catch nits from the nit nurse in a knitting factory. So for the odd favour – like this one – Sar'nt Lofty Troggers kept him supplied with worms.

2. Stoop: Boffin word, possibly of Viking origin, for what peregrines do when they are hunting dozy walters from on high. They plunge down at speeds of up to 200 miles-an-hour and clobber the walter who's flying along thinking about crusty bread and doesn't suspect a thing. Not surprisingly, walter fanciers hate peregrines. Peregrine (Lat. *falco peregrinus* [er, durrr]): Beefy falcon that goes like the clappers. The fastest thing on two wings when in stoop mode, although surprisingly it can't outfly a bert in level flight. Eats: walters. Call: 'hi-yack.' Doesn't: grin. You should really look out for a peregrine if you are out near any cliffs, skyscrapers or steeples. They are absolute stonkers.

3. Although Sar'nt Lofty Troggers likes to make out it was his idea, bouncing

conkers were invented by Barn Swallies to stir up flies from waterside vegetation.

4. *Badhbh:* (pronounced: Badub) Mythical Irish bird that defeated its enemies by causing fear and confusion.

5. Wheatear (Lat. *Oenanthe anotheranthe*: dicky-bird with a white bottom that lives up north. Likes to fly about showing off its white bottom to all and sundry, and often perches on a rock and waves it about. So the male (who is a bit more coy than the female) wears a Zorro mask so he can't be identified in a line-up. 'Wheatear' is a poshing-up of 'white arse' which it was called in days of yore (I'm not being rude here – you can read it in proper books and everything). Likes: rocks. Call: heat. Eats: flies. Flies: showing off its white bum.

6. 'Cahncil': A big conflab to discuss a big barney. All spuggies in the gang must attend. It begins with a compulsory period of silence (about two seconds), and then, after saying 'Order … Order,' the elected 'Grand Cahncilor' makes a statement on the predickybirdament to be discussed. Comments are then invited from the bark. At this point the Cahncil usually degenerates into a bog-standard conflab, with the spuggies all shouting at the same time trying to put their ten-penn'th in. A final decision is reached by a show of primaries.

11. CHICKOVA CHICKOVA

1. The elongated eyes are binoculars. Binoculars were invented by a Greek boffin of yore called Euclid. He couldn't make them work though because glass hadn't been invented yet. Because of this failure, he had to endure the ceremonial pulling off of his toga and leave Alexandria in disgrace. At his new town he was known as 'Euclid on the block.'

2. Preds: grace for predator.

3. Mutton chops: Splendid sideboard whiskers shaped like the aforesaid food item; worn by men who don't have girlfriends.

4. Booted Warbler (Lat. *Hiphiphooray caligata*): tiny bird, even more boring-looking than a spuggie but not as scruffy. Looks like a million other small warblers and can only be identified with certainty by mutton-chopped horny-thologists. Eats: flies. Call: 'veery eenteresteeng.'

5. Galoshes: Rubber bootees you wear to walk through a puddly field. They fit over your normal shoes and are absolutely great. Your mum should definitely be pestered to buy you some immediately. They get their name from the sound you make when you walk about in a puddly field: 'galosh-galosh-galosh-galosh.' When a word sounds like what it does it is known as onyor-matapeea, which is also what your cat does if the cat-flap is locked.

12. GUNS 'N AMMO

1. Peep: wader. Martie lingo for those big-billed long-legged efforts you see on muddy seashores anytime but the summer poking around in the mud for something rubbery to eat. (Some have only biggish bills and shortish legs). 'Peeps' because of the noise they make when they take-off or spot a peregrine.

2. This is a Bar-tailed Godwit, so-called because an Afrikaans prospector, digging for gold near what is now the coastal town of Swakopmund in the 1880s, noticed that when it went into the water it 'god wit.' You might notice this particular Godwit is an American who got blown across the Atlantic in a storm when migrating.

3. Feinting: what boxers do.

4. The peep here is a black-winged stilt (*Hermantopus himantopus*). Eats: small fish, molluscs, worms, tadpoles, crushed-asians etc. Call: eep-eep. Its legs are about two-thirds of its total height. Imagine that. This is why black-winged stilts never flies with a budget airline.

   'Yonder': those at a distance, or over there. It's a great word which you should definitely start using. Think of the time it could save you texting. Tweet it to your mates.

13. EFRICAII

1. Whirly-ups: thermals. As well as the vest and pants your grandma wears in the summer, thermals are warm currents of air that flow upwards. Big birds with broad wings they can't be bothered to flap, like buzzards, eagles and vultures, use them to ascend.

2. Noras: Martie speak for what we call Yellow Nora's Falcons. They were discovered in the 1860s by the redoubtable Mrs Nora Fortesque-Blandishment, the first female explorer of the western Sahara, who tramped about the desert carrying a big umbrella and wearing a big hat, a woolly ankle-length skirt and a full complement of corsetry to subdue her blancmange figure. She'd walk about with her native bearers in toe, and when she found a bit of land she hadn't seen before she'd say, 'I'm claiming this for Queen Victoria and England.' When the natives found out what she was doing they chased her waving their assegais about shouting, 'Death to Mrs Nora Fortesque-Blandishment,' and she ran off and hid behind a sand dune and quaked. Which is how she got her nickname. She got lost in the desert and went missing for donkey's ears until an American journalist called Stanley Baldwin found her while out hunting tigers. He spotted a huge-buttocked creature crouched at an oasis lapping water like a cat. He imagined stuffing it and mounting it over his fire mantel, so he raised his fouling piece and took aim. As his journal notes, 'At first I thought it a gargantuan cleft boulder, riven by the fulguration of some dreadful storm, but then it stirred and the air was rent by a sound like that of the toot of a diminutive trumpet, and I thought it a great hammy beast,

in the act of satiating its desert thirst, seized by the vulgar crudities of necessi-ty.' He was about to squeeze the hairy trigger when he realised this wild crea-ture was a human woman. Yellow Nora was all dishevelled and wobbly on her legs and her hair was sticking up. The umbrella had gone as had her corsetry, used, she wrote later, to make two big buckets for water-carrying, a bow and arrows for hunting, a skinning knife, a three-piece fishing rod and reel, a tent, and a gantry for skinning dead carcasses. Stanley's first words to Yellow Nora after years of desert wanderings have gone down in history's anals and are rightly famous, indeed a three-word paragon of pith and wisdom which we would all do well to emulate very greatly indeed. You can read more about Mrs Nora Fortesque-Blandishment in her autobiography: *Ten Years with the Savages of the Sahara: A Woman's Epic Travels in West Africa 1862-70* (Blandish-ment Press, 1875).

3. Nothing to do with cack, although an unrelated word, 'cackophone,' means somebody who loves poo – like Chris Plectrum. Another similar word, 'cakeo-phone,' means somebody who loves cake – like Sue Gherkins. A Francophone is somebody who loves putting postmarks on letters.

14. SHUG

1. Weans: wee'uns, littlies, chicks.
2. Bahookey: Scottish for bum.
3. Napper: heed.
4. This is a Senegal Parrot (Lat. *Poncephalus senegalus*) – the first parrot the Purple-Bellied Parrot has ever clapped eyes on apart from in the mirror. They have dark rings around their eyes that make them look like they are wearing goggles.

15. PLAN AND A SPANNER

1. Rumblegumption: Scottish for common sense.
2. Awae and bile yer heed: leave now and boil your head (go away). In Spuggie: Oppit!
3. Helligog: Shetland for razorbill.
4. Mollymawk: medium-sized albatross. Species include: the Sly Albatross, the Atlantic Belly-nosed Albatross, the Indian Belly-nosed Albatross, the Beetle-browed Albatross. Eats: fish. Beetle-browed albatrosses are thus because they have met a lot of sly albatrosses.
5. So the Hollywood lawyers don't come along with their briefcases and sue me down to my y-fronts, the bit about the sharks is based on a scene from one of your Grandad's favourite films about the salty sea: *Jaws*.
    You should definitely go out and buy the DVD, the soundtrack, the t-shirt, the bumper sticker and the cuddly toy immediately. *Jaws* is a western. A skew-

jawed sheriff gets a posse together to hunt down an outlaw shark who has been terrorising the town and eating their dolly birds. There's a big shoot-out at the end between the sheriff and the shark, but the shark runs out of ammo and throws his gun a way, leaps on his horse and charges the sheriff who shoots at him till he explodes and his bits plop into the sea. The sheriff rides off into the sunset on a pedalo.

'Dolly bird': a phrase of yore that should nowadays definitely only be used ironically by smirkers.

16. OFFSKI

1. Witchuk: Orkney for a martin.
2. Islands in the Scottish Hebrides. Only a few humans can live there because they are mainly inhabited by the 'Scottish Biting Midge' (*Cullincoides epunctureus*). You will note it is not called the 'Scottish Midge' which gives you a clue as to its major habit. After hibernating through the winter in bogs they come out in spring in their hoardings and bite the living daylights out of any mammal they clap their compound eyes on and guzzle their blood leaving hundreds of itchy pimples. They love humans and from April to October humans have to walk about with big sacks on their heads and cover themselves in grapefruit juice which midges purportedly hate but in reality love with a cherry on top. The most effective preventative is whirling a big hoover set on Full Suck around your head. Drawbacks to this method are: you have to empty the bag every thirty seconds; you can't go very far unless you have a very long cable. Especially small midges are called 'midgets,' and very well-behaved small midges are called 'midget gems.' (Midget Gem was also the name of a politically incorrect sweetie from days of yore.)
3. Patagonian Toothfish. Fish that lives in the southern Atlantic, Pacific and Indian oceans. Can grow over 2 metres long. That's way bigger than anything your grandad can fetch out of the canal with his dibbler. Eats: smaller fish. Good with chips, marketing gurners changed its name to the Chilean Seabass, knowing that idiot humans would be more likely to buy it if it had a poncey name. Soon big ships were hoovering them out of the ocean like there was no tomorrow.

    Floe: flattish chunk of ice floating about the ocean.
4. Shug's right; you should – they really are scary. Search: Leopard Seal.
5. Keech: Scottish for poo. Not pronounced 'keech', more like 'keehghghghgh.'
6. Sou'wester: hat salty sailors wear when it chucks it down over the sea. It is bigger at the back than the front so as to make the sailors aerodynamic when they are sailing along. They are usually bright yellow so that if it blows off in a storm they can spot it and jump in the sea and fish it out. You should definitely get one.
7. So you can follow along on a map, these are the Cape Verde Islands, named by a Portuguese explorer of Scottish extraction, Vasco MacGellan who used to

ponce about in a green cloak having sword fights. He was a dab hand with his *cinquedea*.

8. These are dates. Not at all like the sticky things that come with a plastic fork at Chrimbo time. When two dates fix a date to go on a date it's called a 'date date date.' If they store the info on a computer it's called 'date date date data.'

17. BONXIE

1. Bonxie: Great Skua (Lat. *scariarius skua*). Bolshie pirate of the wild coasts. Makes its living by hanging about the cliffs and ambushing birds who have slogged away at sea all day fishing. In the northern seas, puffins returning to their pufflings are a favourite prey. Gets its name because if you don't hand over the loot, you get skewered by its big beak. Call: a coarse 'AAaaarrrrggh', occasionally followed by 'Jim lad.' Eats: fish. Favourite fish: Cutlass fish.

2. Skelp: Scottish for clobber.

18. HOOLIE

1. Scottish for 'please be quiet.'

2. Skiddies: underpants ... think about it.

3. Boobrie: shape-shifting mythical bird of the northern isles. Tongie: shape-shifting sea-spirit of the northern isles, appearing often in the form of a horse.

19. SHARK'S TEETH

1. Guano: posh name for seabird poo, especially where there is a lot of it at a colony and it has mounted up over donkey's ears solidifying into something like rock so that the gannets or whatever are standing on a big pile of poo with a tiny rock at the bottom a bit like a hazelnut whirl. Victorians used to pay the natives a penny to mine a ton of it so they could take it home and put it on their aspidistras.

2. Luiz is on the St Peter and St Paul rocks, a good bit off the north-west coast of Brazil as the booby flies.

   Booby: seabird of the salty seas of the tropics. Like a gannet and just as hungry. Boobies come in six varieties: the Brown Booby, the Peruvian Booby, the Mascaraed Booby, the Blue and Red-booted Boobies and Russ Abbott's Booby. 'Booby' may be delved from the Spanish word 'bobo', meaning 'stupid', as in days of yore when salty sailors used to sail about in gallons, boobies used to land on foc'sles (fo'c'sles) and let themselves get clobbered and chomped as a change from weevils and fruit bread. The famous Cap'n Bligh who got turfed off his ship by Marlon Brando who invented the Pitcairn Islands ate boobies when he got fed up of Bounty Bars. Eats: fish. Does *not* have: boobies.

20. CAUGHT

1. Noddy: seabird of the salty seas of the tropics. This is a Brown Noddy (*anus solidus*), the biggest of the noddies. It is easily mistaken for the Black Noddy, but the Brown Noddy is brown. Has pointy beak; does not have big ears. Eats: fish. Behaviour: nods. Not to be confused with Noddy, the fictional mini-cab driver invented by Enid Blighty who knocked out one a week.

21. LAST LEG

1. Park Drive: brand of cigarette of yore.

APPENDICES

All appendices to *The Purple-Bellied Parrot* are at: www.williamfagus.com/Appendices

APPENDIX I: HOUSE SPARROW [POSER DOMESTICUS] TIMETABLE OF TYPICAL DAY

DAWN: Yawn, stretch; conflab; preen; conflab.

EARLY MORNING: Breakfast grub, conflab.

MID MORNING: Ablutions: puddle bath/dust bath; conflab.

LATE MORNING: Fly about a bit; applied mischief; snack grub; conflab.

MIDDAY: Grub; conflab.

EARLY AFTERNOON: Snooze; conflab.

LATE AFTERNOON: Fly about a bit; applied mischief; bath; snack grub; conflab.

EARLY EVENING: Supper grub; big conflab.

LATE EVENING: Telly; preen; conflab; trump; kip.

APPENDIX III: SAR'NT LOFTY TROGGERS'S TRAINING
REGIMENT

DAY 1 (STRENGTH AND STAMINA): Warm Up (squats, vigorous wing-flapping, jumping up and down, going 'huuut' a lot). Then, Fly Around the Park; Conker Lifting, Curls.

DAY 2 (SPEED AND AGILITY): Warm Up (as day 1); Between the Birches; Catch the Click Beetle.

ACKNOWLEDGMENTS

For their encouragement, praise, criticism, perception and telling me they cried (well, some of them ...), thanks are due to: Zoe Churton, Angela and Tim Laycock, Hefin Meara, Marie Temple, Heather Tracy and, of course, Sonia.

Map of the park by Sonia Ritter.

Cover by Robin Vichnuch

LINKS:

The World Parrot Trust: www.parrots.org

William Fagus: www.williamfagus.com

AUTHOR'S NOTE

William Fagus has already received correspondence regarding supposed factual inaccuracies in this book. All these letters begin, without exception, 'I think you'll find …'. Particularly memorable is a letter from Mr Colin Damp of Tring who cited Professor Otto Schmauser's *The Geo-Morphology of West Africa* (Berlin, 1931; 1001pp + maps and endnotes). The author respectfully asks future correspondents to desist, and to look up the word 'fiction' in any reputable English dictionary. Any future tweet storm is beyond his control.

AUTHOR'S RESPONSE TO PROFESSOR ANAS:
    Do one.

Printed in Great Britain
by Amazon